THE PACT

By

Don E. Finegold

This book is a work of fiction. Places, events, and situations in this story are purely fictional. Any resemblance to actual persons, living or dead, is coincidental.

ISBN: 1-4107-9925-5 (e-book)
ISBN: 1-4107-9926-3 (Paperback)

Library of Congress Control Number: 2003096959

This book is printed on acid free paper.

Printed in the United States of America
Bloomington, IN

1stBooks - rev. 10/07/03

This novel is dedicated to the memory of a very dear friend, Sam Cohen, who left us in his 87th year. Sam was an inspiration to all who knew him and just one hell-of-a-guy. Rest well, Sam. You'll always be in our thoughts.

ACKNOWLEDGMENTS

Assistance and encouragement came from a number of individuals.

Dr. Robert B. Finegold, Dr. Jeffrey B. Finegold, Inspector Lou Edelstein (retired), and my wife Elaine were important contributors, providing valuable information, editing, and concrete suggestions for this novel.

Ellen Winschel and Betty and Barry Berkal, along with other family members, said "Go ahead and do it; you've always wanted to."

Janice and Harold Cohen were very supportive, and I appreciate their good wishes.

Irene Gilberg, Irv. Babner, Jerry Robinov, Lynne Zolot, Neil Zolot, Marie Kowetz, Darlene Cameron, Wendy and Sam Wilder, Arlene Andaloro, Bob Jaffe, and Maxine Effenson Chuck were my avid reader friends who offered good advice.

Author's photograph by Jerry Robinov, Portland, Maine

Thank you all.

DON E. FINEGOLD

“The mind of the bigot is like the pupil of the eye; the more light you pour upon it, the more it will contract.”

Oliver Wendell Holmes

PART I

CHAPTER 1

SEPTEMBER, 1947

The basketball behaved as if controlled by radar, continually finding the hoop and dropping through. It didn't matter which boy was shooting as they were equally skilled, and this one-on-one match-up was a thing of beauty.

I had watched these two boys—I would guess they were 14 or 15 years old—several times before, but they were oblivious to anyone and everything but their game. I didn't know their names, but being the cop on the beat, I remembered faces, and I liked seeing a black kid and a white kid enjoying each other's company. It didn't happen often in this neighborhood, that's for sure.

I moved on, unaware that these two youths would become victims in a series of killings that would haunt me for years.

"Hey, Jerry G., whoever gets the next basket wins," the black boy said. "I got to go home; it's almost four o'clock."

"Okay, but we got to toss to see who brings the ball in."

Harry grinned as he spoke. "You Jew-boys are too smart. You got the last basket, so by the rules of the world, I get to inbound the ball. You know that."

"Screw you and the rules of the world, Black Harry," Jerry fired back. "If you want to quit and make the next basket the winner, then the rules of the universe say we got to toss to see who gets the ball."

Both boys were smiling. They continued to squabble as to whether the coin toss was to be one-out-of-two or two-out-of-three. Once that was settled, they argued over Jerry's insistence that they should play until the first one reached 10 points, as one basket could be just plain luck, while 10 points was true skill, and the winner could rightfully claim to be the top player.

They were about to begin their contest when they were interrupted by a group of three boys and two girls who had come across the clay tennis courts, maliciously leaving deep indentations in the court surfaces. This act of tomfoolery was meant to anger the adult tennis players who came after work to find some fun and exercise.

The boys and girls were all from the same school as Jerry and Harry. Jerry knew two of the group; brothers, Jimmy and Buddy O'Brien. The others he had seen during recess, but didn't remember their names.

Jimmy spoke. "Hey, hotshots, how about a little game of two-on-two? Whoever gets 12 points first wins, and the winners get a buck each from the losers. Okay?"

"No thanks," Harry answered hurriedly. "We're just finishing up, and I've got to go home."

"What's the matter, nigger," Jimmy spat out, "You got no guts or you got no money? Your kike friend will have money. He can lend it to you."

The two girls giggled, and the third boy smiled tentatively as Jerry did a slow burn.

Harry looked uncertain as to what to say.

It was Jerry who answered. "You got two bucks, then we'll play. You put your money up and I'll put up ours."

"What's the matter, don't you trust me?" Jimmy sneered.

Jerry shot back, "Doesn't matter. Put up or shut up."

Jimmy was taken back momentarily by this bit of bravado. He decided he would rather whip their asses first in the two-on-two game, take the money and then flatten the kike.

He turned to his brother. "Buddy, give me two bucks."

"I ain't got two bucks."

"Buddy, you're an ass."

Jimmy turned to the other boy. "Sean, give me two bucks."

Sean pulled two crumpled dollars from his pocket. "It's all I got for the whole week, Jimmy. It's my lunch money. Can I have them back today?"

Jimmy didn't bother to answer. He grabbed the bills and turned to Jerry. "Okay, put your money on the bench, wise-ass." He did so with his own, placing a rock on top to keep the money from blowing away.

Jerry removed two one dollar bills from his wallet. He held them up for all to see, and walked to the bench and placed the money on top of Jimmy's, carefully replacing the rock.

Returning to the group, Jerry pulled a quarter from his pocket. "I'll toss this and let it land on the ground. You call it while it's still in the air."

The O'Brien group nodded their approval.

Jerry flipped the coin skyward, and Jimmy O'Brien called out. "Heads."

Heads it was.

Jerry took Harry by the arm and walked him away from the group as Jimmy, Buddy, and Sean began to warm up.

Jerry spoke softly. "Harry, I've been doing all the talking up until now. How do you feel about this? Are you with me?"

Harry replied skeptically, "If we beat them, there's going be a fight, three against two. How are we going to handle that?"

Jerry grinned his answer. "You Negro guys are all supposed to be like Joe Louis. You take the big mouth and his brother, and I'll take the other one."

Harry's eyes widened. Jerry smiled. "Just kidding, Harry. We'll do the best we can. I won't take that kind of lip from those Irish bastards. What do you say?"

"Okay," came the deliberate reply, and then Harry grinned. "Who knows, maybe you're another Barney Ross."

"Ready?" came the challenge from across the court.

"Yeah," Jerry replied. "Half-court game. First team that reaches 12 points wins. No deliberate fouling, and no foul shots. Agreed?"

"Yeah, agreed," Jimmy barked.

Jimmy O'Brien was a good three inches taller than the other boys, and maybe 20 pounds heavier. His brother Buddy and their friend Sean Boyle were about equal in size, but Buddy was the quicker and more skilled athlete.

It was decided that the two brothers would be the opposing players.

Buddy inbounded the ball to Jimmy and raced to the far side of the court, drawing Harry with him and leaving Jimmy one-on-one with Jerry. Slowly and deliberately Jimmy backed his way toward the basket, using his size to advantage and keeping his methodical dribble low to the ground.

Jimmy made a quick fake to the right, spun left and muscled his way by Jerry, knocking him down. He lay the ball off the backboard and into the basket.

"Two points," he hollered.

On the sideline, Sean and the girls were applauding.

Harry yelled, "That basket doesn't count. That was a charging foul; no question about it!"

"Bullshit!" Buddy shot back. "That was clean all the way."

Jerry got off the ground and motioned to Harry. "Let it go, Harry. Our ball out. Come here for a minute."

They quickly planned their strategy. Harry was to take an outside jump-shot, and Jerry would box out and clear the boards in the event of a miss. There was no miss.

Two all.

Buddy took the next shot, a 15 footer that clanged off the rear of the hoop, bounced high in the air, and was rebounded by an alert, high-vaulting Jimmy O'Brien, who stuffed the ball through the hoop.

Once more there was cheering from the sideline.

It was short lived, however, as a quick drive on Jerry's inbound pass to Harry tied the score.

Four to four.

All four boys were better than average athletes, but there was no hint of mutual admiration. Each time the opposing team scored, animosity increased.

The score was deadlocked at eight when Sean called a time-out from the sidelines.

"You can't call time out," Jerry Gordon yelled, wiping the sweat from his brow, "your not in the game."

"Screw you," came the instant retort, "I'm the manager and…"

Jimmy O'Brien interrupted. "Shut up, Sean. I'm calling time out myself, okay?"

"Yeah, okay," Jerry responded angrily.

Jerry and Harry walked to the water fountain, drank deeply, and moved to the far side of the court to talk things over.

"They're good," Harry said.

"Yeah, but so are we. Problem is, whoever has the ball has been scoring, and unless we break the pattern, they're going to wind up with 12 points first. We've got to figure out how to make them miss. Any ideas?"

Harry thought briefly before answering. "No. How about you?"

Jerry shrugged his shoulders. "Worst that can happen is I'm out 2 bucks. It won't be the end of the world."

"But I owe you one of the bucks, so it's only half as bad," said Harry with a grin, as he wiped the sweat from his brow.

On the other side of the court a similar discussion was taking place. Buddy, wiping his flushed face with his sopping-wet tee-shirt, spouted, "They're good, Jimmy. We'd better start banging them up a little."

"No need, little brother," Jimmy said. "All we have to do is score on our ins and we get there first." He smiled, and added, "Maybe I'll shake-up that wise-ass anyway," glancing at Jerry as he spoke.

Jimmy turned to look at Sally, and gave her a wink. She smiled and blew him a kiss.

Jimmy's mood instantly changed. He turned suddenly to face Buddy, grabbed him by the neck of his sweaty tee-shirt and pulled him in close.

"You protect that ball, Buddy, you understand? No fancy stuff. You get the ball to me the next two baskets, and it's over. No fuck-ups, you hear me?"

Buddy answered, a little shaken, "I hear you. Don't worry, I'll play it safe."

Buddy understood very well. He knew not to mess around because, brother or not, Jimmy meant business.

Buddy had learned that on more than one occasion. Once Jimmy had knocked him out and then sworn him to secrecy, or else.

There was only one person Jimmy feared; Dan O'Brien, his father, who once in one of his frequent rages had broken Jimmy's nose, and grinned afterwards. Jimmy had been 10 years old at the time. He learned never to get in his father's way, especially on a Friday night when his old man stopped for a couple of beers on the way home from work.

Buddy inbounded with a bounce pass to Jimmy. Jimmy dribbled around outside the foul line, moving rapidly and keeping the ball away from Jerry Gordon, who was bent on making a steal.

Suddenly Jimmy flicked a quick pass to Buddy, who immediately lobbed a return pass back to Jimmy. Jimmy streaked with the ball toward the basket, taking at least three steps without dribbling before leaping into the air and dunking the ball.

Jerry cried out, "That's traveling! No basket!"

"Horseshit!" Jimmy retorted. "That was a legal basket, and it's 10 to 8."

Jerry fumed, but knew it was useless to argue.

Harry shrugged his shoulders, as if to say what did you expect.

On their next possession, Harry received the inbound pass as well as an elbow thrown by a tight-guarding Buddy O'Brien. He ignored the blow, moved quickly to the foul line, made a head fake, went high into the air, and made the shot.

The score was now deadlocked—*10 all.*

"Time out," Harry called in a loud excited voice, and beckoned Jerry to join him on the sideline.

"Great shot, Harry," Jerry said as he embraced his friend.

Harry smiled broadly as he accepted the accolade. "Now what, Jerry?"

Jerry spoke softly. "No question who's going take the next shot. We've got to block it."

"How?"

"I think the big mouth will try to move the ball in close and muscle it in. We've got to force him to give up the ball. Leave your man when Jimmy has the ball and has his back to you. I'll keep his attention on me while you go for the steal. It's our only chance."

Harry answered, "It's risky, Jerry. If he manages to pass off to his brother, we've had it. It will be all over."

"I know, but I think it's our best chance."

"Okay. I agree."

"Come on," Buddy yelled from across the court, "stop stalling. Time's in." "We're ready," Jerry said, as he gave Harry an encouraging slap on the backside.

As expected, Buddy inbounded to Jimmy, and headed cross court. Harry followed Buddy, loosely covering him, hoping that Jimmy would move to the center of the court, so when he made his move to steal the ball, he wouldn't have to cover too much ground.

He got his wish. Harry broke toward the ball at full speed just as Jimmy made his spin move away from Jerry to drive to the basket.

The timing couldn't have been better. Harry got all ball as he slapped it away. Jimmy was surprised, and froze long enough for Harry to retrieve the ball and pass to an unguarded Jerry Gordon, who streaked in for an easy lay-up.

The game was over.

Harry animatedly shook Jerry's hand.

Jerry whispered, "Okay, pal, we did it. Let's get the hell out of here before there's trouble." He walked over to the bench where they had placed their wager, discarded the rock and pocketed the money. Rejoining Harry, the two walked off the basketball court, their ears on full alert for any sign of pursuit.

Jerry and Harry proceeded across the playground without incident and headed for home.

Jimmy, Buddy, Sean and the two girls stood in a close group.

No one was talking. Jimmy and Buddy mopped their faces while the others glanced at one another, not knowing what to say.

Then Jimmy blew up. His face reddened, and with deep scorn, he uttered, "I'll kill those sons-of-bitches! They'll wish they were never born, those two bastards! I'll break them in half! I'll break their arms…"

The tirade continued. No one dared interrupt. Buddy had seldom seen Jimmy this angry, and feared his brother might blame him. But it wasn't his fault. He didn't have time to warn him of the double-team. It happened too fast.

Besides, he wasn't the one who lost the ball. He remained silent, as did the others.

Jimmy eventually quieted down. "Wait here," he ordered. He headed off the basketball court and walked through the open gate to the nearest clay tennis court and kicked up a section of the rolled clay surface. It seemed to give him satisfaction, for he grinned evilly as he left the court, as if he could envision the faces of the tennis players who would certainly be miffed when they came to play.

He returned to the group and spoke in a commanding voice. "Sally, you and Dory go home. I'll call you tonight. Maybe we'll go for a walk."

"Okay," Sally replied warily. She was well aware of Jimmy's frequent mood changes, and decided to say nothing more.

"C'mon, Dory," she said, and the girls left, walking arm-in-arm.

Jimmy turned and barked at the two boys, "Tonight! Seven o'clock! In the club house. You both be there!"

Buddy and Sean nodded their acquiescence.

The three boys walked home in silence.

CHAPTER 2

The Boyles and the O'Briens lived next door to each other in the city of Pemberton.

Their street, Clement Avenue, was attractively shaded by many huge elms and chestnut trees, planted decades earlier by a town planner with vision. The effect pleased the neighbors. They were proud of where they lived.

Of more importance to the families, however, was that their neighborhood was predominantly Irish.

When Jimmy and Buddy were kids, they collected hundreds of chestnuts and stored them in boxes under their front stairs.

Some times they would fashion make-believe smoking pipes from these chestnuts by coring them out and adding lollipop sticks as stems.

Other times they made necklaces and bracelets for their mother by drilling holes through the chestnuts and stringing them.

But the main reason for collecting the chestnuts was to use them as missiles. They would choose up sides with other boys in the neighborhood and, using trash barrel covers as shields, wage war. If you were unlucky enough to get hit in the face with a chestnut traveling at high velocity you were in for a lot of pain, and a bruise that would hang around for a while. It was fun.

The O'Brien home was a two-story wooden structure that had been covered with white asbestos shingles the year before. It appeared fresh and neat, and Mary O'Brien was very proud of her home.

The windows were framed with green shutters, and Mary had added wooden flower boxes beneath each window, planting the boxes annually with bright flowers from her garden. It was a touch that pleased her, and she noted with pride that a few other women in the neighborhood liked her idea so much they copied it.

The front of the O'Brien two-family home faced Clement Avenue. The downstairs apartment was fronted with a large roofed-in screen porch, and the porch was furnished with a white metal glider-hammock, a camel-colored caned settee with two flower-patterned blue and white cushions, and a matching cane chair.

Mary O'Brien's mother lived alone in this apartment. Mary and her family occupied the apartment above.

The upstairs apartment was identical in size to the lower, but had access from both the front and rear to staircases that led to two attic bedrooms. Jimmy and Buddy had originally shared a bedroom, but when they became fifteen and fourteen respectively, Mary gave her boys the choice of either continuing to share a room or each taking their own bedroom. The boys opted for separate rooms, welcoming the opportunity to be apart, for deep down they were very different.

Buddy, although only a year younger than Jimmy, was considerably smaller in build. Buddy felt he would never possess the physical attributes of his older brother, and it bothered him.

He feared Jimmy, and sometimes hated him, but he learned to live with it. Having his own room at least gave him some privacy.

Jimmy thought Buddy was okay as a brother but felt there was something odd about him. Something in the way he looked whenever they had one of their frequent arguments.

A crazy stare—*almost evil*—he thought, but he'd crush Buddy, brother or not, if he had to.

Jimmy's reasons for wanting his own bedroom were far different from Buddy's. Jimmy believed he could eventually sneak his girlfriend Sally up to his room when his folks were out, and maybe get laid. He thought he'd come close a couple of times at her house and that she would have gone all the way but feared her folks would come walking in.

He knew Sally liked him as she had flattered him on many occasions, bolstering his already inflated ego. On their last date he prematurely promised her that she could wear his varsity football sweater, which she desperately craved to enhance her standing with her girlfriends. She even delayed removing his hand that evening, which he casually allowed to slide down to cover one breast.

He fantasized everything would work out the way he had planned—and soon.

Jimmy's primary objective at this time, however, was to make first-string on the football team in this, his junior year. Once he did that, he would concentrate on nailing Sally.

Thinking of Sally this way usually gave him a hard-on, causing him to smile. Having his own room allowed him to play with himself when he wanted or had to, and that was certainly becoming a more important part of his life.

##

Sean was the only child of Eileen and Phil Boyle.

Eileen had the misfortune of having had two miscarriages prior to delivering Sean. When she was pregnant with him, the doctor insisted that the final four months of her term be spent in bed. As it turned out, she was in the hospital three weeks prior to birthing Sean, and she had a difficult time with the delivery.

The doctor advised Eileen not to become pregnant again, which nearly broke her heart. She was one of seven children, and wanted a large family of her own. Phil, although disappointed, didn't take the news as badly as she did and ultimately convinced her that it was God's will, and that she had to accept it.

Eileen did, but made Sean her entire life. She pampered him, and kept him close by her, refusing to leave him alone with a sitter or even a relative.

Phil finally laid down the law. "You're making a sissy out of him, Eileen. He's always with women and playing with girls. That's no good. He'll never get by in school or in the outside world the way you coddle him."

She was hurt by the accusation and sulked for days, but Phil remained adamant and she gradually gave in.

On Phil's insistence Eileen began spending more time with Mary O'Brien, and Sean at an early age had the O'Brien boys as friends and playmates. Eileen thought that Mary paid too little attention to her boys, and was afraid that Sean would get hurt playing with, as she put it, "those rough and tough O'Brien brats."

Phil only laughed. "Four and five year old boys are never 'rough and tough.' It's only when they get older you've got to kick them in the ass every once in a while to keep them in line."

Jimmy, Buddy, and Sean did get along well most of the time. They acted pretty much as equals in front of adults. However, when the three were alone, Jimmy asserted himself verbally and physically. Buddy and Sean did as they were told.

The boys remained inseparable as they got older. There were the usual heated moments boys experience growing up, especially between the two brothers, but it became physical only a few times, and that was quickly settled, given Jimmy's superior physical size.

Sean, although comparatively timid, had profited by his close relationship with the two brothers. He was much more self-assured with classmates other than the O'Briens, and felt pretty good about himself. True, he was not as strong or athletic as the O'Briens, but he did well in pick-up football and basketball games.

Phil Boyle was pleased with how his son fit in with his schoolmates, and on several occasions expressed to Eileen how proud he was of Sean, and how it was a damned good thing that he had stepped in when he did and stopped her from babying him. Eileen would nod her head in agreement, but inwardly disliked and feared the close relationship her son had with the O'Briens. She thought that Jimmy was a bully, and that Buddy was strange and untrustworthy. She once had mentioned her fears to Phil, and he had put her down so badly that she never talked about it again. But there was something she didn't like about the brothers, and she promised herself to be watchful.

CHAPTER 3

Dan O'Brien had bought the 1936 red Oldsmobile sedan from Mary's mother a week after her husband Michael had died in 1938. He paid her $75. He told her it was all the car was worth.

The odometer read 14,332 miles and the car was in near-mint condition.

"High mileage, low price," Dan quipped at the time of purchase.

Mary's mother had never driven and wasn't about to learn. If her son-in-law hadn't been such a big mouth and know-it-all, she would have given him the car for nothing. Instead, she smiled sweetly, thanked him for helping her out, and took the money. Someday she would tell him she would have given him the car for nothing. Then he'd kick his own ass.

She thought that if her husband Michael were still alive, he would have told Dan to go fuck himself.

The O'Brien boys had built their clubhouse that same year in the loft of the garage above their father's newly purchased Oldsmobile. Jimmy at the time had been 6 years old and Buddy 5. Dan O'Brien, a strict, over-bearing father who loved his children but seldom expressed it, built the only access to the loft—a wooden ladder—and volunteered to wire their clubhouse so they could have lights and a plug for a radio and an electric heater.

The boys, at their mother's insistence, invited Sean to be a member of their club. With his help they furnished the loft with a card table and wooden orange crates to be used as chairs; all confiscated from the city dump.

The loft had two small windows with screens that could be opened in good weather. Mary made them curtains, which turned out to be a little oversized because the boys had taken the measurements, refusing to allow "girls or women" into their clubhouse. Mary had teased them, saying that she wouldn't supply them with any snacks.

But the boys were adamant. "No girls or mothers allowed," they had said in unison.

She had faked a pout, and turned away so they wouldn't see the smile on her face.

The clubhouse through the years would be their meeting place.

##

Sean arrived at the O'Brien home promptly at 7:00 p.m. the night of the ill-fated basketball game. Jimmy and Buddy were waiting for him, and the trio headed for the garage. They made their way to the crude wooden ladder and ascended to the loft, which Jimmy unlocked and illuminated. The grim faced teenagers silently took their seats, the only sound being the movement of the make-shift furniture.

Jimmy waited until they were seated before speaking.

"What happened this afternoon was the worst thing that could have happened to us. We were beaten by a Jew and a nigger! You think about it! It isn't ever going to go away!" His tone intensified. "They'll be bragging and boasting in school tomorrow how they whipped our asses. By recess everyone's going to be laughing at us, or smirking, or talking about it. We gotta decide **now**—and I mean right now—what we're gonna say."

Silence prevailed. The only movement was in their eyes, as they nervously studied each other.

Finally Sean broke the silence. "You know, Jimmy, that might not happen. It wouldn't surprise me if those guys didn't say anything. They know better than to start anything with us. Maybe you should call Sally, and she can call Doreen, and tell her to say nothing about…"

"That's bullshit!" Buddy interrupted. "I'll bet you that five or ten kids already know what happened. Those shit-heads probably have told every friend they've got that they whipped our asses, and the whole school's gonna know. You're kidding yourself if you think it's gonna be any other way."

Sean shrugged his shoulders. Deep down he feared Buddy was right, although he was afraid to say so. He hadn't even played in the game, so it wasn't his fault that they lost. Secretly, he was happy that he hadn't played.

"Buddy's right," Jimmy said. "What we do is pass it off as they got lucky and end the conversation. The less we say, the quicker it's forgotten. We don't let anyone think that we think it was a big deal. Understand?"

Buddy and Sean nodded.

"Okay," Jimmy continued, "but we're sure-as-hell going to do something about it!"

There was a nodding of heads, and Jimmy, his face brightening as he spoke, added, "We're going to be patient. We're going to wait a couple of months, and then the kike and the nigger are going to have accidents, and we'll do it in a way that no one will ever think that it was anything but an accident. We'll break some bones so we can see casts and slings. Something meaningful. You get my idea?"

His voice had become animated as he revealed his thoughts to the others, and he could see the excitement in their faces as they took in his every word.

"I can see we're in agreement," he continued. "We'll go over the details in a couple of weeks. Remember, we're in no rush. We'll swap ideas and make plans." "Yeah," came the simultaneous replies.

"Sounds great. I love it," Buddy added. "Let's fix them good."

"Okay!" Jimmy replied. "Say nothing to nobody, and I mean nothing at all. And remember, if anyone tries to rib us we say they got lucky. In a week everyone will have forgotten about it. Then it will be our turn. That's it for tonight. I'm going over to Sally's and I'll see you guys in the morning."

They locked up and left the garage. Buddy and Sean went home to do their homework, and Jimmy headed up the street to Sally's house. He rang the doorbell and she answered and invited him in. She had a questioning look on her face, as if to ask what kind of a mood are you in, and what do we talk about?

Jimmy switched on the charming smile that had first attracted her to him two years earlier and made a couple of comments about how pretty and sexy she looked. He seemed fine and not disturbed by the events that had occurred earlier in the day. He apologized for his behavior at the basketball court, and said that it was just one of those things, and asked her to tell Doreen he apologized to her too.

She turned down his offer to take a walk as it was nearly 8:30 and a school night, and she didn't want to push her luck and ask her mother anything. At the moment she and her mother weren't on the best of terms.

Sally glanced down the hall to see if her parents were within eyesight. They weren't, so she turned and gave him a lingering kiss, breaking away when he started putting his body into it. She smiled, made a funny face at him, and waved him out the door.

Jimmy walked home, smiling and relaxed, thinking come Saturday night he might just do it.

The boys met as usual 7:30 the next morning and walked to school, mindful that they would have to be calm and stick to their plan.

The school day passed without the hint of a problem. No one mentioned the incident.

Walking home from school that afternoon they were surprised and elated.

"I can't believe it!" Buddy burst out. "Not one fucking mention of it all day; not by anyone."

"Not to me," Sean chimed in, pulling his Red Sox cap tightly over his crew cut topped head. "It's like it never happened."

"I didn't hear anything either," Jimmy joined in. "I saw Gordon and Robinson during recess and I know they saw me. Apparently they never said anything to anybody."

"Yeah," Buddy added, "they're probably afraid that we'd kick the crap out of them. We ought to wait a couple more days to see what happens, and then kick the crap out of them anyway."

"We'll wait more than the couple of days, Buddy, and if nothing happens, it's over for now, period," Jimmy asserted, glowering at his brother.

The remainder of the school week passed without anyone mentioning the game.

When the boys met at the clubhouse 10:00 Saturday morning, the main topic of discussion *was* the basketball game.

"It's hard for me to believe that no one knows about it," Jimmy said.

"Like I said, Jimmy, they're afraid of us and don't want to make any waves," insisted Buddy. "I purposely sat down at lunch break yesterday next to that Goldberg slob who's in my math class. I talk to him once in a while 'cause he's a whiz in math and helps me a little when I get stuck. I know he hangs around with Gordon 'cause I've seen them together lots of times. Anyway, I kind of pumped him for information—in a careful way. He never mentioned anything."

"I didn't hear a thing either," Sean said. "Buddy's right. It's over."

"Maybe, but it's far from over," Jimmy snarled. "Okay, enough for now. I've got a football game and I don't want to be late. You guys think about what we talked about at the last meeting and come up with some ideas. I'll see you both later, after the game."

CHAPTER 4

Jimmy learned just before game time that first-string end Steve Bowder had come down with the flu. He would be starting in Steve's place.

Coach Wilzinski gave Jimmy a private pep talk on how he and the rest of the team were counting on him.

"Powell High ranked second in the State last year, Jimmy, and they lost only three boys from last year's roster. They'll try to take advantage of a replacement player after the line-ups are announced. You'll have to be on your toes every minute."

Jimmy had watched the game with Powell High from the bench last year and the game had been a hard-fought 12-12 tie.

This was his big chance and he knew it. There was no one more keyed-up than Jimmy O'Brien as the team charged out of the locker room and onto the field.

Pemberton High beat Powell 24-14, and Jimmy, playing both offense and defense, had more than held his own. He made four unassisted sacks, caused and recovered a fumble and scored a touchdown.

Coach Wilzinski was thrilled with his performance. More important to Jimmy was that the Team Captain, and last year's All-State Quarterback pick, Al Gillboy, had slapped Jimmy on the back and yelled loud enough for everyone on the bus to hear, "Great job, Jimmy. You were fantastic!"

On the bus ride home, there was a lot of good-natured horseplay, and Jimmy was in his glory. He felt he had earned his teammates' respect, as well as the Coach's, and that he would get more playing time this year, and maybe even a starting position. He knew for sure he had earned a starting position for next year, and he fantasized about seeing his name listed on next year's High School All-American roster.

A mob of frenzied fans were waiting for the team to arrive at the Pemberton High School parking lot, and when the busses returned, there was a great deal of celebrating, with the band striking up the school song as the team unloaded. It had been a big win for Pemberton.

In the locker-room, the Coach gave the team a brief pep talk, congratulated them once more, announced practice for 3:00 sharp on Monday afternoon, and told them to shower and have a safe weekend.

Buddy and Sean were outside the locker-room when Jimmy emerged and waited until he broke away from some of the team players before approaching him. When he did they embraced him simultaneously, and eagerly spit-out the praises they knew he wanted to hear.

"Great game! You were terrific! Four sacks and a touchdown! Wow!"

Jimmy beamed as he answered them with a modest "thank you," and then led them out of the building. He glanced around looking for Sally before remembering that she had to rush home after the game because her folks had company and wanted her to be there. He'd catch up with her later.

The trio headed for home, Buddy and Sean jabbering incessantly, while Jimmy silently reflected that it was too bad that his old man never came to any of the games. He was hurt that his father would rather hang around Moe's bar-room with his cronies on a Saturday afternoon than come see him play football.

Screw him! he thought.

He was anxious to see Sally. He knew she would be as excited as he was.

He was to meet her at 7:00 that evening and go to the school dance. He looked forward to it, feeling that he would be more popular than ever after having such a good game.

He planned to flirt a little with some of the senior girls and get Sally a little jealous. He knew her moods, and when he saw that he was getting to her he would whisper in her ear that she was the only one, along with all the other bull that girls like to hear. He thought that maybe that would heat her up and make her more responsive to what he planned for later that evening. Maybe she would come to the clubhouse after the dance, or even sneak up to his bedroom. Lots of possibilities.

He arrived at Sally's house exactly at 7:00, and rang the doorbell. Sally's Dad opened the door, and gave him a warm welcome.

"Hey, Jimmy, I heard the game on the radio. You were great. What's that now, four wins and no losses?"

"Yes sir, Mr. Marsh, and thank you," he added, his handsome face beaming.

"Well, that's exciting, Jimmy. You and the rest of the team should be very proud of yourselves. I'll make it a point to get to some of the games. Maybe a State Championship this year. That would really be the icing on the cake, wouldn't it?"

"Yes, sir, it would," Jimmy agreed.

"Hey, Sally!" her father shouted from where he stood at the bottom of the staircase. "Jimmy's here and wants you to shake a leg," he added as he turned to Jimmy and winked. "She's just like her mother, Jimmy, never on time."

Jimmy smiled as he replied, "Yeah, I know what you mean. We have that problem with my mother. She always keeps us waiting."

The two men continued to make small talk, stopping when they heard footsteps racing down the stairs.

"Hi Dad. Hi Jimmy," Sally called out in the same breath. "I'm only a few minutes late, and that's no big deal," she added flippantly.

Sally was dressed in a gray, full-length poodle skirt and a white, finely-woven, tight-fitting sweater which had the effect she intended on Jimmy. She thought that his eyes were going to pop out, and she expected tonight would be an interesting evening.

She knew Jimmy fantasized about having sex with her, and she felt she couldn't say "No—absolutely no" all the time because he might lose interest and stop dating her. She didn't really enjoy stringing him along, but deep within she had no intention of going all the way with him or with anyone else.

An Irish-Catholic upbringing instilled in her a wholesome terror of sex before marriage and she wanted no part of a premarital relationship. She had experienced some feelings when they had engaged in heavy mugging sessions, but never to the extent where she was not in control. She realized Jimmy and boys in general wanted to be more sexually active, but that was their problem.

She had allowed Jimmy to touch her breasts on a few occasions, but not for long and never underneath her clothing. Once she had let him lay against her, fully clothed, which really did nothing for her, but seemed to please him. He had soiled her skirt at the time and she had worried her mother might notice, but was relieved when a dampened wash-cloth removed the stain.

All part of growing up, she said to herself.

Since then, she managed to keep him under control, never promising him anything, but allowing him a casual touch to keep him from thinking her a cold fish. She felt she could manage him for this year and next, and after that he would have graduated and probably gone off to college on a football scholarship. She herself would be looking for someone else, for she had big plans for herself. In the meantime, Jimmy was the best-looking guy in the entire school, and no-doubt would be a football star in the coming year, and therefore a good choice to be squiring her around.

Jimmy's thoughts were as Sally suspected. He would just as well have skipped going to the dance if he could have gotten under her sweater, but he knew he would have to be patient.

He realized he had to move very slowly with her if he were to get anything, so he could rule out skipping the dance. Besides, he was interested in knowing how much recognition he would get after his accomplishments at the game. His ego was looking for an uplift.

They arrived at the high school gym 45 minutes after the dance began. Sally planned the late arrival, knowing they would be better noticed. She especially wanted to be seen by her girlfriend Doreen, who was dating Eddie Cahill, the football team's fullback. Eddie was a senior and very popular, and Doreen had been laying it on quite heavily about her and Eddie all week, to the point that Sally had to walk away before she said anything to mar their friendship.

Eddie might be a great football player, but he was nowhere near as good looking as her Jimmy. Sally, by her late entrance, would make sure that everybody noticed that.

The evening was going nicely for both of them. They were approached by couples other than their close friends, who expressed their praise for Jimmy's performance in the football game.

Sally noticed that she wasn't being overlooked either. She caught several of the senior boys eyeing her and obviously talking about her. These were the same guys that wouldn't have given a sophomore girl a glance the day before, and she felt good about it. It was, as she anticipated, an evening of fun and excitement.

Sally excused herself and headed for the powder room, telling Jimmy that she would rejoin him at the soft-drink bar. She latched on to Doreen as she passed her and the girls headed off together, both jabbering at the same time. Jimmy sauntered over to the bar and ordered a Coke, and as he sipped his drink his gaze wandered from one end of the gym to the other. He wanted to make sure he hadn't missed any of his teammates. He wanted to praise each one of them, expecting to receive plaudits in return.

Buddy and Sean and a few friends had come as stags to the dance.

A group of girls also had come to the dance as singles, and some of the guys drifted over to talk with them.

Buddy wasn't interested in the girls. He was pre-occupied with watching his brother play the big-shot, and the more he watched, the more angry and jealous he became.

A thought entered his mind. He knew how to spoil Jimmy's evening, and he wanted to do just that. Rising from his folding chair, he told Sean he'd be right back; he had to see Jimmy about something. He stopped once to exchange greetings with a friend in his math class, but did not take his gaze off his brother. He ended his conversation and headed for Jimmy, reviewing in his mind what he would say. Satisfied, he tapped Jimmy on the shoulder.

"I want to talk to you. It's important."

Jimmy looked over his shoulder, saw it was Buddy, and turned to face him. "What's up?"

Buddy moved in closer and whispered in his ear. "I was at a table across the gym with some of the guys when I spotted Gordon. He saw me looking at him and he walked over to me. You know what he said?"

Buddy lowered his voice even more. "Your brother played a hell of a good football game today. He's a much better football player than he is a basketball player." Then the son-of-a-bitch smiled a shit-eating grin and walked away.

Jimmy's face turned scarlet. In an instant he had forgotten about the dance and the football game. He showed such rage that Buddy was momentarily frightened, and took a step backward.

"Where is he?" Jimmy barked, much too loudly.

The disc-jockey was playing a noisy jitterbug number, and only a few couples standing nearby heard the outburst. After a quick glance, they turned away.

Jimmy repeated himself, but more softly. "Where is he?"

"I saw him leave the gym with a couple of guys, Jimmy, right after he spoke to me. He must have left the building."

Jimmy hurried from the bar and headed for the exit. Once outside the gym, he ran down the stairs and raced to the front door, shoving the door open so forcefully that it smashed against the brick wall with a resounding thud. He ran down the two short flights of granite steps and on to the sidewalk.

He paused to look in every direction, spotting only two girls walking on the sidewalk across the street heading toward the center of town, and an elderly couple walking their dog.

"Bastard!" he muttered half-aloud. "I'll get that bastard!"

Turning, Jimmy retraced his steps and re-entered the building.

A security cop had witnessed Jimmy racing from the building and stopped him as he returned.

"Hey, kid, I saw you run out of the building. Something wrong?"

"No!" Jimmy answered sharply. "I forgot something in my car."

"Okay, but no running on school property. You walk, understand?"

"Yes, sir," Jimmy answered smartly, wanting to end the conversation.

He returned to the entrance of the gym, showed the attendant the ink stamp on his left wrist, and re-entered.

Sally was standing at the soft-drink bar with Buddy, looking very unhappy.

"Jimmy, you look flushed. What happened? Where have you been? What's wrong?" she blurt out in quick succession.

"Nothing!" he answered too sharply. "Forget it. I don't want to talk about it!"

Sally looked at him strangely. She was hurt by his curt manner. Her hurt turned to anger.

She turned and walked away, and sat on one of the folding-chairs that lined the walls on two sides of the gym. Her anger turned to fury. She would make him pay for spoiling *her* Saturday night. Her mind filled with unpleasant thoughts, and she was having trouble keeping herself under control. Her mother called it "her hot Irish blood bubbling to the surface" and that was as good an explanation as any.

Son-of-a-bitch! she kept repeating to herself.

Jimmy was still at the bar, lost in his own anger. Buddy stood next to him; silent, gloating inwardly at the trouble he caused.

Couldn't have worked out better. Now he doesn't look or feel like such a big shot.

Buddy glanced over to where Sally was sitting. She looked good and angry too. He had scored a doubleheader.

Buddy still had a crush on Sally, and often thought about her. He first met her when they were both freshmen in the same homeroom. He considered dating her, but before he got up the nerve to ask her, Jimmy spotted her and moved in.

Once again his brother had taken something he wanted.

Well, screw her too!

Jimmy spoke to Buddy in an angry tone. "Remind Sean to be at the clubhouse at 10:00 tomorrow morning. It's important!"

He left Buddy and walked over to Sally and sat down next to her. She immediately swiveled her body to face away from him.

"Look, Sally, I'm sorry, but something real serious came up; real important."

She made no reply and he continued.

"Please! Listen to me." He related what Buddy had told him and when he finished, he sat awaiting her response. It was not what he expected.

"Big deal," she exclaimed sarcastically. "You spoiled my evening over a lousy basketball game?"

Turning to face him, she continued, with fire in her eyes. "You always think of yourself and never about me."

Her voice had risen and people were looking in their direction.

Jimmy didn't care about the looks, but was disturbed that she wasn't sympathetic to his situation. There was no point in continuing the discussion.

He rose and said angrily, "Okay! Come on, I'll take you home!"

They left the dance, both maintaining their silence.

When Jimmy tried to speak again, Sally cut him off with a sharply worded, "I don't want to talk about anything right now!"

When they reached Sally's house, she offered a sharp "good night" and, without looking at him, went into the house, slamming the door behind her.

Jimmy glared after her. "Fuck you, you bitch." he said out loud, into the emptiness surrounding him.

CHAPTER 5

OCTOBER, 1947

Jerry Gordon was supposed to be staying overnight in Stanton with his cousin Sonny but his cousin turned out to be a pain in the ass. The boys had argued over how they would spend the evening in the first hour of Jerry's visit. There was no way he was going to spend the night with Sonny.

Jerry left Sonny's home and walked down town to the bus station to head back to Pemberton. On the way he passed the Palace Movie Theater and saw "Tarzan and the Huntress" was playing, starring Johnny Weissmuller, his current favorite hero. He wanted to see it in the worst way, and now was as good a time as any.

He briefly considered that Harry would be teed off for seeing the movie without him but he'd square it with him by seeing it again.

Jerry placed his overnight bag under the theater seat, sat, and slid down until he was comfortable. He soon forgot

Sonny and the unpleasant start to the evening as he got caught up in the excitement of the jungle.

The movie ended, and Jerry had enjoyed it. Especially the scene where Tarzan grappled with the crocodile. That had him on the edge of his seat.

As he filed out of the crowded theater he decided to use the rest room before he went to the depot to wait for a Pemberton bus. Two boys were leaving as he entered, and he was alone as he made his way to the row of urinals.

He set his bag down and relieved himself. Finished, he went to one of the wash basins to wash his hands.

He heard the door squeak as someone entered the room, but he never bothered to look. As he reached for a paper towel, he felt a sharp pain, and then another; and then—nothing.

The body of Jerry Gordon was discovered by an employee at 11:30 Saturday evening in a stall in the men's room of the Palace Theater. In a near panic, the employee called the Stanton police. The police responded quickly, secured the crime scene and notified the Criminal Investigation Division, reaching Inspector Barney Osham, the on-duty officer-in-charge, who in turn called the chief to fill him in.

Stanton, a small coastal city 15 miles north of Boston, had few homicide cases. It was a small, sleepy town recovering from the effects of a lengthy major downtown reconstruction that had put many of its small businesses in serious trouble.

The town's claim to fame was in its past history, when hysteria and ignorance resulted in the public hanging of men and women alike.

Inspector Osham, en-route to the crime scene, ironically remarked to his driver that he hoped this case would be cut and dry, and not wind up being another witch-hunt.

The driver didn't find this comment particularly amusing, and said nothing.

Barney Osham and his Criminal Investigation Division (CID) team arrived at the movie theater 10 minutes after receiving the call.

Satisfied that the area had been properly secured, Barney placed a call to the home of Dr. Berl Rodin, the Medical Examiner (ME), who lived in nearby Beverly, and informed him of the murder.

"Be there in 20 minutes," Berl responded.

Barney turned to his forensic team, a photographer and a finger-print specialist.

The photographer was already at work snapping pictures.

"Doc will be here in 15 minutes. You guys cover the room, but be sure not to step in any blood or touch the body until he gives the okay."

True to his word, the ME arrived in record time. He appeared as if he had just jumped out of bed, which, in truth, he had. He was disheveled and in need of a shave, but his brown eyes were clear and he was ready to go to work. Berl donned a pair of rubber gloves extracted from his battered black medical bag and began to examine the body.

Barney watched in silence.

"Dead maybe an hour or two. Multiple knife wounds, and big ones," the ME reported. "We'll get more into that when I examine him at the morgue. You check his pockets?"

"No," Barney answered, "I waited for you before I searched him. I checked for a pulse, but there wasn't one. If you're done, then I'll look."

"Be my guest," the ME said. "Just don't get yourself all messed up."

One side pant pocket was empty. The other contained 35 cents and a ticket stub. One rear pocket was home to a soiled handkerchief. The other was empty.

The photographer called out, "Barney, looks like a wallet in the waste basket."

The wallet was well-worn, of dark-brown leather, with many scuff marks and discolorations. There were no bills in the money compartment, only a ticket to a laundry in Pemberton. In one of the wallet's pockets was a well-earmarked address book with a dozen-or-so names and addresses, and in the other pocket was a single condom packet, with the tell-tale imprint of long time possession imbedded in its lining.

Barney walked into the hall where two theater employees were waiting impatiently. "You see or pick up any anything in the lavatory before or after you called the police?"

They both shook their heads negatively. One added, "Hell, I didn't see nothing and I didn't touch nothing. I got the hell outta there real quick and called the cops."

"After you made the call, did either of you go back in there? Either of you see or touch a wallet?"

"No," again the simultaneous replies.

"Wait here," Barney instructed and left to return to the men's room. "You all set, Berl?" he asked the ME.

"Yep, all done here. The medics can transport the body to the morgue. I'll make all the other arrangements," indicating that he would notify the District Attorney's (DA's) Office to send a State Trooper, as well as a photographer and a pathologist to attend the autopsy.

"We'll do the autop around 10:00 in the morning, as soon as everybody shows up," Berl added as he headed out the door.

Barney returned to the hallway and joined the two theater employees who were now seated on a bench, drawing heavily on their cigarettes. Their hands trembled nervously as he approached them.

"All right, let's start from the beginning," Barney said. "Tell me exactly what happened."

The older man spoke first. "Last show was over about quarter to eleven. George here, he's my helper, and I pick up the trash in the aisles and under the seats, and then we sweep up. Then he takes the ladies' room and I take the men's and we clean up. We always do it that way. I didn't notice nothing at first, 'cause the room's an L-shape. You know what I mean?"

Barney nodded that he did.

"But when I turned the corner to where the stalls are, I saw legs—well, just feet, really—sticking out from under the door of the end stall. So I said, 'Hey fella, lets get out of there; theater's closed and I gotta clean up.' The guy don't say nothing, so I push open the door part-way and I see this kid covered with blood, eyes open, and staring at me. There was blood all over the place. Scared me near shitless. I ran out of there and into the office and called you guys."

His helper had little to add to the story, saying only that he hadn't gone into the men's room after he was told there was a dead man in there, but went with his boss into the manager's office to await the police and let them into the building.

Barney beckoned to the two police officers who had arrived at the scene first and told them to take the names, addresses, and phone numbers of the two cleaning attendants and send them home. He then called the theater manager at his home, and gave him the details of what had occurred.

The manager listened in disbelief. He told Barney that he left the theater about 9:30 that evening and everything had been fine.

Barney told him he would have to keep the theater closed for a day or two until the police completed their investigation, and he would be notified when he could clean up and reopen.

It was close to 1:00 a.m. when Barney drove up to 360 Holten Drive in Pemberton. The house was dark, except for the single light illuminating the inside front hall. He rang the doorbell and heard a buzzer respond from somewhere within. It took several long depressions before he saw inside lights activated. A male voice called out, "Is that you, Jerry?"

"No, sir. I'm Inspector Osham of the Stanton police. Are you Mr. Gordon?"

"Who is it?"

"The police. I need to come in and talk to you, sir," Barney replied.

The door was unlatched and opened, revealing a short, stout, round-faced nearly bald man in flannel pajamas wearing a wool-plaid bathrobe secured loosely with a belt that hung nearly to the floor.

Barney held his wallet open, displaying his Inspector's shield so that the man would not question his dark, baggy, six-year-old suit rather than the easily-identifiable police uniform.

"I'm Inspector Osham, Stanton Police department. Are you Mr. Gordon?"

"Yes, I'm Mark Gordon," came the nervous reply. "What's wrong?"

Before Barney could reply, they were joined by a petite woman, barely 5 feet tall, similarly attired in bed dress and an identical bathrobe.

"What is it, Mark?" she asked in a high-pitched, accented voice.

"This man here is a policeman, Debbie."

As the couple gazed at each other, Barney attempted to take control of what he knew was going to be an unpleasant task.

"Please, folks, if we could sit down someplace, I'll explain why I'm here."

"Yes, yes, come in," the man said anxiously and led the way down the hall and into the parlor, his wife at his side. He flicked a light switch and illuminated the room. "Please sit down," he added, and pointed to an oversized, overstuffed green cloth-covered chair.

Mark Gordon led his wife to a sofa, where they sat on the edge of the cushions. They clasped hands and stared fixedly at Barney in growing apprehension.

Barney remained standing, looking down at the couple, contemplating exactly what he was going to say.

He spoke in a gentle voice. "I'm sorry. There's no easy way to tell you this. A Jerry Gordon carrying an ID with this address in his wallet was found dead in a movie theater in Stanton about an hour and a half ago…"

The woman let out a shriek that seemed minutes in duration and collapsed backward into the depths of the sofa. Her husband held her tightly as tears streamed down his face. They sat that way for several minutes, she wailing loudly before giving way to non-melodious sobbing.

Barney remained quiet, waiting for the initial shock to pass, giving them time to regain some semblance of composure.

He had been through this a number of times before. Those deaths had been the result of accidents, either vehicular or work related, and not homicides. There was no easy way to bring home this kind of news.

Several minutes passed before Mark Gordon could bring himself to speak. Still gently rocking his sobbing wife, his tear-lined face turned upward to gaze at the Inspector, and in a voice barely above a whisper, he asked, "What happened?"

Barney answered the question with his own question. "You are the young man's parents?"

The man responded with an affirmative nod.

Barney related the known details of the incident without describing the extent of the wounds. "Look, Mr.

Gordon, I know this is a terrible time, but I must ask you a few questions—the rest can wait until later."

Another nod.

"Do you know who your son was with last night, and any of his plans for the evening?"

"He was out with Sonny, and staying overnight at his house," he said, struggling with the words.

"Mr. Gordon, who's Sonny?"

"Sonny's his cousin—my brother's boy—Sonny Lund. They live in Stanton, on Lafayette street. Jerry was going to spend the night…" He lost control and began weeping loudly.

Barney gave him a minute, and then decided to end it. "That's all for now, Mr. Gordon. We'll talk later. Is there anyone you want me to call—to help you with your wife?"

"No," he said. "I'll take care of her."

As Barney turned to leave, Debbie cried out, "Where's Jerry? Take me to him!" and tried to break away from her husband's surrounding arms.

Barney explained that the ambulance had taken their son to Stanton Hospital, and that they could make all the necessary arrangements later that morning after the Medical Examiner completed his required examination.

Barney left, leaving his business card on a nearby table, feeling miserable.

"Enough for now," he said to no-one in particular, "a few hours sleep, and I'll visit Sonny Lund."

Sonny Lund, Barney discovered, never went out with Jerry Gordon. The two cousins had quarreled, said Sonny, and Jerry had stormed out of his house, his black over-night bag slung over his shoulder, saying he was not going to sleep over and was going home. Sonny, whose parents were not at home when the altercation occurred, neglected to leave a note to inform his parents Jerry had gone home and instead called two of his friends. Sonny went with them to the movies at the Lynn Paramount. Sonny's parents, returning home from a dinner date, retired early thinking the boys had gone out together. They were unaware that Jerry wasn't staying the night.

"If I had known Jerry wasn't going to sleep over, I would have called my brother," a tearful Mr. Lund told Inspector Osham.

Sonny's two friends verified his story later that morning. Their movie had ended about 11:00 p.m., and they had stopped for a soda and caught the 11:55 bus back to Stanton.

"Okay," Barney mused. "That rules out Cousin Sonny."

CHAPTER 6

The murder was vividly described Sunday morning on Pemberton and Stanton radio. The stories portrayed the brutal murder the evening before of a popular high school student who had been stabbed several times and left to bleed to death in the men's room of a Stanton movie house. One commentator stated that the motive may have been robbery, as no money was found in the deceased's wallet, and the wallet had been removed from the body.

The news items generally concluded with "the authorities have no leads at this time."

Barney turned off the radio in his office. The reporters knew about as much as he did. He had a headache from repeatedly answering the same questions all morning from concerned citizens and from the media.

He had just returned from another visit with the Gordons and verified that they thought their son was spending Saturday night with the Lunds, and that Jerry had not contacted them to tell them otherwise.

Mark Gordon told Barney that his son always had 3 or 4 dollars on him, and would have had at least that much with him on Saturday evening. He had given Jerry a five dollar bill that very morning.

Barney didn't believe that someone would brutally murder someone in that manner just for money. He felt it had to be a deranged person or a pervert, although he kept his feelings to himself.

The ME had briefed Barney after the autopsy earlier that morning.

"The kid never had a chance. There were three deep knife wounds on the body," the ME stated. "The one to the heart proved fatal. The blows were struck from behind, based on their angle of entry, and probably in rapid succession.

"And something else, Barney," the ME added. "The kids fly was open."

Barney's investigation indicated, based on the trail of blood, that the victim—near death or dead already—was dragged several feet before being deposited in a sitting position on the toilet, facing the door. The stall door was pulled closed from the outside, as there were bloody smudges on the outside door and frame. The killer evidently wore gloves and partially wiped the door, as there were no discernible fingerprints near any of the bloodied areas, while there were a host of prints on the adjoining stalls.

The killer should have been splattered with blood, according to the ME, but as yet no one had answered the pleas the police placed with the radio stations Sunday morning asking for any information from attendees of the Saturday evening movie. Barney was bothered that no male came forward to say he used the wash room at the conclusion of the movie and either discovered the body before the clean-up crew did, saw something suspicious, or witnessed the attack itself.

The theater manager told Barney that 317 paid tickets were sold for that movie showing, and nine free passes issued.

The theater had a seating capacity of 405, so there was a good crowd in attendance.

Barney thought someone should have noticed something.

Sunday afternoon Barney called the Pemberton police station and asked for Captain Doyle.

"Captain Doyle? Barney Osham, Stanton police. How are you?"

"Good, Barney. Haven't seen you in a while. What's up?"

Barney filled him in on the investigation to date. "Captain," Barney continued, "I'd like the names of the police officers who cover the high school and the Gordon neighborhood. It's possible one of them knew the Gordon kid, and who he hung around with."

"I'll check and get back to you in an hour, Barney."

"Thanks, Cap. Much appreciated."

Captain Doyle was back to Barney with the information in less than an hour.

"Officer Brady covers the high school area and didn't know the kid. Officer Coben recognized the photo in the newspaper and told me he had seen him with a Negro kid several times playing basketball at Dempsey Park. He didn't know the Gordon kid by name before the murder, and he doesn't know the name of the Negro boy."

"Thanks, Captain. I'll check with the Gordon kid's parents. They'll probably know who the other kid is. Talk to you later."

Barney returned to the Gordon home and asked for the names of Jerry's friends. Three had Semitic names.

Two did not: Harry Robinson and Terry Donahue.

Barney had no doubt that Donahue was an Irishman, but he wanted clarification on Robinson.

"Robinson a Negro?" he asked.

Mark Gordon looked up abruptly, with a surprised look on his face.

"Yes, Harry is Negro, and is—was—Jerry's best friend. The Robinsons have lived in the area as long as we have, and they're friends of ours and good people."

"Please, Mr. Gordon," Barney said. "I have to ask these questions. Try and understand…"

With a wave of his hand, Mark Gordon interrupted. "I know. I'm sorry. I'm just upset."

Barney wrote down the names and addresses of Jerry's closest friends, thanked Mark Gordon, and left.

Barney returned to the station and was told that two calls were received with regard to the Gordon case. One from a female who wouldn't leave her name but wanted the police to know that "they had better do something damn quick and catch that crazy killer, because if it wasn't safe to go to a movie, it wasn't safe to go anywhere."

The other call, from a male, echoed those sentiments.

CHAPTER 7

Barney was on the phone early Monday morning.

"This is Inspector Osham, Stanton police. Is this Mrs. Robinson?"

"Yes," the surprisingly deep voice replied.

"Mrs. Robinson, I'm checking with friends of the late Jerry Gordon. I would like to talk with your son as soon as possible and was wondering what time he would be home from school. I'd like to see him for just a few minutes."

"He didn't go to school today, sir. He's still all broken up over Jerry's death. He's really taking it hard."

"I'd like to come over and talk to him, Mrs. Robinson. It won't take long and it's important. I'm sure he wants to help us, especially where they were such good friends."

"Yes sir. Harry is a good boy, and I know he'll help in any way he can. You come over anytime you want to. We'll be here."

Barney arrived at the Robinson home 45 minutes later. The house was a small white Cape Cod in need of a coat of paint. Surrounding the home and its unattached garage was a painted white picket fence. The grass had been recently cut, and the plentiful shrubbery neatly trimmed.

Barney pushed open the front gate, walked up the fieldstone pathway to the front door, and rang the doorbell. Almost immediately the door swung open, and he was facing a surprisingly tall woman—he guessed about 5'11"—dressed in a flowered white house-coat and wearing purple mules. Her jet-black hair was pulled back and tied with a thin red ribbon.

The lines etched around her penetrating eyes noticeably aged her.

Her thin face was devoid of makeup. She didn't appear particularly attractive at the moment, but she could have been with a little bit of work.

Martha Robinson introduced herself and led Barney into the parlor, offering him a seat next to a carved wooden figure of a boy holding a large glass ashtray. Remnants of a cigar as well as cigarette ashes and butts filled the interior of the tray. Being a non-smoker, Barney opted for the solid-looking rocking chair on the other side of the room. Pointing in the chair's direction, he said, "Mind if I sit in the rocker? I just love rocking chairs."

She indicated with a hand movement that it was okay, but her face remained impassive. Barney knew she was troubled and he attempted to set her mind at ease.

"Mrs. Robinson, this Gordon murder was a horrible thing. We're trying to see all of the Gordon boy's friends in order to find out if there is anything they know that we can chase down and check out. We don't have a lot to go on, and we can use all the help we can get."

She nodded her approval. "I'll get Harry. He's barely left his room since this thing happened. He's been very upset. Excuse me for a minute."

She returned several minutes later with a nervous young man in tow.

Barney eyed the boy. About 15 years of age, 5 feet 8 or 9 inches, and on the thin side. Good-looking boy.

Martha led Harry to the sofa and sat down next to him.

Barney ended his observation. "Harry, I'm Inspector Osham and I'm in charge of the investigation in the Gordon case. I understand that you were one of Jerry's closest friends, and I need to ask you some questions. Will you help me?"

Harry, who had never taken his eyes off the detective, answered in a subdued voice. "Yes sir."

"When did you last see Jerry?"

"I walked home from school with him on Friday. He wanted to shoot some baskets with me Saturday morning, but I couldn't. I promised my father that I'd help him clean up the cellar, and that's what I did. Jerry told me he was staying over his cousin's Saturday night and he'd call me on Sunday when he got home."

Harry stopped talking. His eyes filled and he began to sob. Martha put her arm around his shoulder and squeezed him reassuringly.

Barney waited several seconds. "Did he have any enemies, Harry? Anyone you can think of that would want to—that wanted to hurt him?"

Harry paused, searching his mind, before replying. "No, sir. Jerry had no enemies. He was a great guy. He'd do anything to help you. Kids who knew him liked him. He was my best friend, and I don't understand how this could have happened..."

"Okay, Harry," Barney interrupted in a kindly tone, "How about in school? Any problems there?"

"No, sir. He was real smart in school. He never seemed to have to study much, but he always knew his stuff. He never showed-off like some of those smart-ass..., uh, other guys did. I think he was the smartest guy in the whole school. He helped me a lot without making me feel stupid, if you know what I mean."

Barney nodded his head indicating he did.

"Anything else you can tell me, Harry? Anything he might have said about any problems he was having with anybody?"

"No, sir. Nothing I know about."

"Okay, Harry, that's enough for now, but I'm counting on your help. If you hear anything, in or out of school, from anybody who may have seen or heard anything, no matter how insignificant or seemingly unimportant, I want you or your mom to call me. I'm leaving my card, and the phone number on it will reach me 24 hours a day."

Barney rose unwillingly from the comfort of the rocking chair, handed Martha Robertson his business card, thanked them, and allowed himself to be shown out. He entered his car, pulled a notebook from his inside jacket pocket, and thumbed through it until he located the list of names Mark Gordon had given him.

He headed for the home of the next listed name. It was sure as hell going to be a long day.

CHAPTER 8

Jerry Gordon's funeral was held at 11:00 on Monday morning. Pemberton High School gave early dismissal privileges to any student in the school who wanted to attend the funeral, and all the students in Jerry's home room class elected to do so.

Jimmy, Buddy, and Sean took the early dismissal but went to their clubhouse.

As they took their seats, Jimmy said, "Looks like someone knocked off the bastard before we did."

"Was it you?" Buddy asked sardonically.

"No, it wasn't me, shithead. Maybe it was you!" Jimmy fired back, glaring at his brother.

"No," Buddy answered somewhat sheepishly. He had backed off quickly, seeing Jimmy was in no mood to play.

"It wasn't me, either," Sean said, sensing that he had better say something. "That must have been a real mess, according to the papers."

"I wouldn't have minded seeing it," Jimmy bragged. "It wouldn't have bothered me at all. One less sheenie, that's all."

"Thing is," Sean said, "the cops will be checking on everybody. What if they hear about us and the basketball game?"

"That won't be a problem," Jimmy assured him. "That game was weeks ago, and we never heard one peep about it from anybody."

"Yeah," Buddy joined in, "and we never hung around with him, so if they check with his friends—even with the nigger—they'll never think of us."

Sean wouldn't let the subject go. "Maybe, but the cops will surely talk with Robinson. If by some remote chance Robinson does mention the game to the cops, do we all have alibis?"

Three sets of eyes shifted from one to the other.

"I was home Saturday night—alone," Buddy offered. "Our folks went out about 7:30. I stayed in and spent the night building my model airplane—damn near finished, too—but I got tired and went to bed. I never heard my folks come home and I never heard you come in either, Jimmy."

Jimmy stared unkindly at his brother before relating his whereabouts on Saturday evening. "The folks let me use the car. I called Sally Saturday afternoon, but she was teed off at me about something I said the day before, so she said she was busy. She told me she had another date that night. I asked her who with and she wouldn't tell me. I hung up on the bitch. Anyway, I took the old man's car, like at 8:00, and I drove to the bowling alley. I didn't know you were in your room, Buddy, or I would have asked you to come along. I bowled a couple of strings by myself and got bored, so I left and drove to Varley's for a glamorburger. I didn't see anybody I knew there, so I left. I drove by Sally's house and there weren't any lights on, so I parked a few houses away. I thought I'd stick around for a while to see who she had gone out with, thinking of how I was going to mess up the son-of-a-bitch. I was there about 15 or 20 minutes when I saw her folks' car coming up the street and turn into their driveway. Sally and her mother got out of the car and went into the house. I started up my car and drove by and I could see her old man closing the garage doors. She had given me a load of crap about having a date. I felt a little better about it and drove home and went to bed. I was home before 11:30."

Buddy smiled at Jimmy. "Did you ever tell Sally?"

"Hell, no," came the sharp reply. "I never said anything about it. She called me the next day after she heard about the murder. We never mentioned anything about her date."

Sean, realizing it was his turn, cleared his throat and began. "My folks went to a party at my uncle's house in Brookline. They wanted me to go and spend the evening with my cousin, but she and I don't get along—she's a snob—and I convinced my folks to let me stay home. I stayed in and read until they came home, which was a little after one o'clock in the morning. They gave me hell for staying up so late, but I told them that if I had gone with them, I would have been up that late anyway."

Buddy stated out loud what they all were thinking. "You realize that none of us has an alibi for Saturday night. Sean and I were home alone, Jimmy, and you were out alone. Seems strange, doesn't it?"

"Knock off the bullshit," Jimmy snarled.

"I don't think it is bullshit," Buddy said.

The boys sat without speaking until Sean broke the silence. "I think we're foolish to worry about it. None of us did anything. They'll find some bum did it, and it'll be over with."

Jimmy didn't respond.

"Maybe," Buddy said, and smiled.

CHAPTER 9

SUMMER, 1948

Nearly a year had passed since the murder and the boys never mentioned Jerry Gordon. The police had not caught the killer. Jimmy, Buddy, and Sean were sure they never would.

The boys continued to meet at the clubhouse often, but were kept busy by their summer jobs and found little time to just hang around. Each of them had their own agendas to pursue.

Jimmy, between his work at the Gulf gas station on Central Street and his football fitness program, had the busiest schedule. His boss, an avid football fan as well as a Pemberton High School alumnus, arranged Jimmy's work schedule to allow him to attend all the fitness programs, and football practice when it started in early August.

Coach Wilzinski was a bug on fitness, and you could forget about playing for him if you didn't attend summer fitness sessions to keep yourself in shape.

Jimmy had high hopes for himself and the team for the coming season. He approached each workout with enthusiasm, arriving early and staying late. He made up his missed time at the gas station on the weekends.

He loved football, and he was a natural. He thrived on the physical contact; body against body, strength against strength. He wasn't the heaviest or tallest member of the squad, but he prided himself that he was the fastest and probably the strongest. He stood 6 feet 2 inches tall, weighed 198 pounds, and considered himself lean and mean. He never let up on any play and was always in the right place at the right time. He wasn't taking any chances that the coaching staff wouldn't notice him.

And he had been noticed. Coach Wilzinski, after the second full week of Fall practice, commented to Ed Lassiter, one of his staff members, "I think we've got ourselves a winner in O'Brien. Keep working him hard."

One afternoon toward the end of August, Jimmy was returning home from football practice and crossed paths with Harry Robinson. Harry was playing another boy one-on-one basketball on the same court where the confrontation with Jerry Gordon had taken place. Harry stared at Jimmy briefly before returning his attention to his game.

Jimmy took the stare to be a dirty look. He thought about going into the court area and breaking a few heads, but common sense over-ruled his initial urge. He wasn't concerned it would be two against one; he felt he could handle that. His concern was that there would be talk in school and it might jeopardize his position with the team if the Coach heard about a fight. Coach Wilzinski had broached the subject of team wholeness before, and all the players knew what he meant.

Pemberton was a town comprised of many ethnic groups, and its football team was a composite of boys from various religions and races. Jimmy had to live and work with the members of the team because he had no other choice if he wanted to play football, and his desire to play was stronger and more important then his bigoted feelings. He was thankful that there were no Jews or Negroes on the team at the present time, because they were the worst. His father had instilled that hatred in Jimmy when he was very young, and continually re-enforced his dislike and distrust of almost everyone not Irish-Catholic, especially "Jews and niggers." It was a subject often mentioned in the O'Brien household.

"Think Irish, Jimmy," Dan O'Brien had preached time and time again. "We stick together, and we're the best."

##

The Irish first settled in the Pemberton area in the mid to late 1800's, several decades before the influx of European and Asian immigrants.

At the turn of the 19th century, Poles, Greeks, Italians, Turks, Russians, Germans and others were immigrating en-masse into the United States, with large numbers arriving at Ellis Island, New York, and in Boston. They were primarily impoverished, hard-working people seeking a better life. They had relatives or friends who had come to the United States earlier and written home relating the many opportunities to be found in the New World. Most of what was written was hyperbolized in order to entice their loved ones to leave their homelands and come to America.

A large number of the new arrivals settled in Pemberton, attracted by the job opportunities offered by the ubiquitous leather tanneries. The area was growing, with older, established tanneries enlarging and new ones emerging.

Shoe factories were springing up near the tanneries and, as both industries were labor intensive, welcomed the supply of greenhorns who were willing to work for low pay at back-breaking jobs under odorous conditions.

The Irish, by their earlier arrival, were usually the upper-level employees and foremen in these industries. They passed on the more difficult and malodorous jobs to the new workers.

The Irish were also the mainstay of both the police and fire departments, and the leaders in city management. The fact that they were there first quite naturally led to their belief they were superior, and not merely just the first group of immigrants to rise up through the system.

Initially, the various languages spoken by the new-comers were a problem, but there were always a few individuals who had been scholars in their homeland, and multi-lingual, and thus able to bridge the language barriers. Classes in English were set up for the adults, and the children were quickly integrated into elementary schools.

The ethnic groups were understandably clannish, and ignorance of one another's religions and customs bred mistrust.

Ecumenicism was a word of the future—not endorsed at any great length in this period. Fist fights between groups of teenagers of different nationalities were common initially, but diminished the more they got to know each other, primarily through school contact.

Eventually, assimilation, although never fully achieved, became a reality in many cases.

It was easier for the young people who were in school together five days a week to reach an accord and, in some cases, form close friendships. Their parents, however, were more apt to stick with their fears, mistrusts, and hatreds, and preferred to keep their distance from groups other than their own.

Dan O'Brien never had anything good to say about a Jew or a Negro. If you were to ask him why, he would come up with a dozen reasons. Some were fantasy, some were what he had been told by his grandfather and his father, and some were lies that he made up but firmly believed.

Mary O'Brien never dared to disagree with her husband when the subject arose. She simply didn't care, and felt it wasn't worth arguing about. She lived in her own happy world and maintained only a few close relationships (all Irish) other than her family.

Jimmy and Buddy were raised in a household where intolerance reigned.

CHAPTER 10

That night in the clubhouse Jimmy told Buddy and Sean about his near episode with Harry Robinson.

"That son-of-a-bitch looked at me as if he were king shit," Jimmy said angrily. "I felt like going in there and beating him to a pulp."

"You were smart to walk away," Sean said. "You don't want to bring any attention to yourself by getting into a fight with him. Only this morning, for the first time in a long time, I heard some guys in school talking about the Gordon murder. One of the guy's brother is a cop and he said they have nothing new on who did it but they don't think it was a robbery—just made to look like one. They think that Gordon may have had a falling out with one of his friends, who suckered him into the toilet and did him in. And you know his best friend was…"

"No kidding," Jimmy interrupted. "Wouldn't that be something if Robinson got nabbed for the murder."

"Yeah," Buddy said, an infrequent smile spreading across his face, "that would make a better ending than just busting him up. I wonder if *he's* got a fool-proof alibi."

Sean was about to say something, but Jimmy took the floor.

"I'll tell you something," Jimmy said. "If nothing happens with the cops and Robinson by Christmas, we're going to mess Robinson up ourselves."

"Yeah!" Buddy said, nodding his approval.

Sean didn't agree. "I think that would be a mistake. If the cops find out who did in Gordon, and it wasn't Robinson, then your taking care of Robinson won't cause any problems. But if they don't arrest anyone, and you mess up Robinson, then the cops might think it could be someone from school or from the neighborhood that had some vendetta against the two of them. Remember, they were best friends. And, on the chance that Gordon or Robinson, or even Sally or Doreen said anything to anyone after your basketball game, I think it would be dangerous..."

"Wait a minute!" Buddy cut in, with an angry look on his face, "What do you mean *'your'* taking care of Robinson and *'your'* basketball game? You were just as much involved as we were, and you better not forget it!"

"That's right," Jimmy barked. "I shouldn't have to remind you that we all swore to stick together on everything. We back-up each other in everything..."

"Right," Buddy interjected!"

"...and," Jimmy continued angrily, "this is just another part of the pact. We swore we would always keep the pact. You signed the agreement, Sean, just like we did, and it's still in the hiding place if you want me to take it out and rub your nose in it."

"I know what we said and I know what we wrote," Sean replied in a tremulous voice. "But we were only 5 or 6 years old then."

Buddy said, speaking in a voice dripping with derision, "You want out, Sean? You know what the penalty is if someone wants out, and it only takes two out of three votes to decide and to enforce, and..."

Sean didn't like the way the conversation was going. Jimmy and Buddy never agreed on anything, and although he had considered years ago that the brothers could team up against him in any vote, he didn't believe it possible. He had never known brothers who were so different, and not just in size and appearance.

In fact, it was usually he and Buddy that were mistaken for brothers, and Jimmy as the friend. He and Buddy were similar in size, coloring, and facial features. The most noticeable difference was in their eyes. Buddy's were aphotic and hypnotic, appearing as if they wanted to burn a hole through you. Sean's eyes, as his mother often told him, were "as blue and clear as the lakes of Erin."

There was no doubt in Sean's mind that if he wanted out now, the two brothers would act together.

"...so you better make up your mind where you stand," Buddy concluded angrily.

"No, of course I don't want out!" Sean lied. "I just feel that we have to be careful. I don't think *we* should mess up Robinson until they nail him or somebody else for Gordon's murder. That's all I meant," he finished feebly.

"You really mean it, Sean?" Jimmy barked. "Don't try to bullshit us. You're either with us or your not."

"I'm really with you, Jimmy. Honest!"

The brothers accepted the explanation, and the danger of a confrontation was over.

Buddy, his voice serene and his facial expression now normal, said, "He may be right, Jimmy. We've got plenty of time to take care of Robinson, and you don't want to take any chance of messing up in your senior year. You could be in line for a football scholarship if you have a good year, and maybe get a chance to go to Boston College or Holy Cross."

Buddy secretly prayed that would happen; not for Jimmy's sake, but his own. He would love to get Jimmy out of the house and far away. In fact he wished his brother would get a scholarship to Nebraska or Southern Cal—the farther away, the better. That would make life easier for him, and give him a crack at Sally.

Jimmy's focus returned to football, forgetting the quarrel with Sean and savoring Buddy's thoughts on a scholarship. "Yeah, maybe your right. A good football year is more important than anything else right now, but the other matter is important too—to all of us, right?"

Buddy and Sean said "Yes."

"Okay, we'll let it go for now," Jimmy consented, "but by Christmas, if nothing turns up in the Gordon affair, we make plans to take care of Robinson. Right?"

"Right!" Buddy and Sean reaffirmed, both suppressing their true feelings.

CHAPTER 11

The Gordon murder was still very much on the mind of Inspector Barney Osham as he reviewed the file while sitting in his office in the Stanton Police Station. He had followed every lead that turned up in the past year, but with no success.

It bothered him that the overnight bag the Gordon boy carried with him from his cousin's home never turned up. According to the Gordon parents Jerry had taken pajamas, a change of clothing, toilet articles, and maybe a book, but certainly nothing of real value.

Maybe it *was* a murder resulting from a robbery, but Barney's instincts told him otherwise. He felt it improbable that a robber would believe that a teenage kid with a canvas bag would be carrying anything worthwhile.

`Barney wondered if the boy was followed into the theater, or was he randomly selected by someone already in the theater? Was it a deviate who accosted him in the men's room and was rebuffed, and in a fit of anger pulled a knife and butchered him? Or was it someone who held a grudge against the kid and spotted him entering the theater and followed him and attacked him when the opportunity presented itself? Would the killer be carrying a knife with a huge blade on his person at all times? Hell, there were too many *ifs* and *woulds*, without any real answers. The radio and newspaper requests for information had produced a big zero. The four replies from highly imaginative people had proven fruitless.

Barney was discouraged, but unwilling to let the case go. The brutality of the murder hinted at a sick killer. He had discussed this with the Chief, but the Chief didn't agree.

"Your wrong, Barney. It was either a simple robbery attempt gone bad, or somebody had it in for the kid."

"Chief, it's the ruthlessness that bothers me. And in all my months of investigation, I've got nothing concrete to chase down. The kid was fully clothed and there was no evidence of sexual activity. His fly was undone but it was probably because he was relieving himself. There was urine on his trousers.

"I can't buy the attempted robbery bit, and he was a popular kid. I questioned everyone—family, friends, teachers—and Gordon was an average guy and a better than average student. All I heard from his teachers and classmates was that he was well liked.

"And what about the overnight bag? Nothing of value in it according to his folks. He left his cousin's house with it, but it has never shown up. Where did he stash it, or why did the killer take it with him? Something about this case smells, Chief."

"All right, Barney. You keep working on it, but not exclusively. There are too many other things on the agenda."

"Thanks, Chief," Barney said as he left the office, more determined than ever to find all the answers.

CHAPTER 12

OCTOBER, 1948

It was 8 weeks into the football season and Pemberton was 8-0; all decisive wins. Jimmy was a standout, both on offense and defense, and he was in a state of euphoria. The Coach was happy, the team was excited, and Buddy grudgingly admitted that his brother had talent.

But inwardly Buddy seethed. Now the bastard was getting more and more of the limelight and reveling in it.

Dan O'Brien was now attending the football games. He had never been to a football game, or any other high school event in his entire adult life. Not that he cared a damn about football, but he enjoyed the roll of father to this year's football hero, and the accolades that went along with it. Dan especially liked the apres-football stops at Moe's bar, where he was the subject of much attention, and the recipient of free beers.

Jimmy was the center of attention at supper every evening, for his father continually pumped him for any inside information on the team and the coaching staff.

Dan wanted to know everything about the team, as he wanted to hold center stage at Moe's bar every day after work. This left Buddy sitting silently at the table, with only an infrequent word from Mary on some meaningless matter.

Buddy would get away from the table as quickly as possible every evening, using homework as an excuse. He couldn't wait to return to the privacy of his bedroom where he could distance himself from football talk and find something more pleasant to think about.

He didn't have a girlfriend, and he wanted one. He had made some advances toward Doreen Kelly after he had given up on Sally, but Doreen let him know that she wasn't particularly interested. He presumed that she had a crush on his brother, but with Sally in the picture, she could only look on. That hurt him.

Buddy, now in his junior year at Pemberton High, wanted desperately to go to college when he graduated. He learned that Northeastern in Boston had a 5-year cooperative program which allowed a student to earn money and obtain on-the-job experience during a segment of each school year. He was told that the freshman year was practically all school work, but the balance of the 5-year program consisted of 10 weeks schooling and 10 weeks of work, followed by 15 weeks schooling and 15 weeks of work, and a 2-week vacation period.

He felt that going to school in Boston would get him out of the house and allow him to earn some money and that's what he wanted. At least the future would be promising.

Screw Jimmy, screw Sally, and screw Doreen!

Sally, meanwhile, was riding a high. She was Jimmy's girl and she made sure that everyone knew it. He was the best looking, most popular guy in school—*and he was going steady with her!*

When they were alone, she consented to a touch, a rub, or a brief feel, with the hint of a promise of more to follow. She kept him under control with constant praise and by catering to his ego. She knew how to handle him.

Jimmy in turn had to settle for relieving himself when he got home. He convinced himself that it was safer, for he had heard too many stories of how a rubber broke and the girl became pregnant. The poor sucker had to get married, take some dumb job to support a family, and live a horrible life, just for one fucked-up screw job. He wanted no part of that—he even feared it.

Jimmy had big plans for himself. He expected to wind up with a full scholarship to a major university, make a name for himself, marry into a rich family, and get set up in any field that might interest him.

Sally was okay for now, but he wasn't planning on any long-term involvement.

He'd drop her when he went off to college.

CHAPTER 13

If Pemberton remained undefeated for four more games they would have the State Championship. Their next game was with Chelsen High, which had a five-win three-loss record, and wasn't considered a threat to break Pemberton's win streak. Coach Wilzinski wasn't taking any chances, however, and warned the team not to be over-confident. He had seen an underdog rise to the occasion more than once during his coaching career, and he had no intention of letting it happen to this team. Pemberton's toughest game was yet to come—with Stanton—who, like Pemberton, had compiled an 8-0 record. The Pemberton-Stanton rivalry was long-standing, and the excitement over the match-up had been building for weeks, inflamed by the local sports reporters of both cities.

"Chelsen first, men; Chelsen first. Then we'll get set for Stanton," the Coach warned.

Midway in the second quarter of the Chelsen game, Jimmy leaped into the air for a ball thrown too high and made a sensational catch. On his way down he was hit ferociously and simultaneously by two Chelsen players, twisting his left leg into an unnatural position. Their full body weight landed on top of him.

The Coach could hear the bone snap from 30 yards away.

Jimmy screamed in pain. The Pemberton fans in the stands stood silent as the trainer and his aides ran on to the field. Members of both teams hovered around, looking on helplessly.

The trainer made a quick examination before beckoning frantically toward the sidelines for a stretcher to be brought out. In a matter of minutes Jimmy, with splint having been applied, was placed on the stretcher and carried off the field to await the arrival of an ambulance from Pemberton Hospital.

The applause from the fans on both sides of the field was spontaneous, but fell on deaf ears as far as Jimmy was concerned. Tears of pain streaked down his cheeks in a steady flow, and he was oblivious to the consoling voices of the people about him.

It took another five minutes before the wail of an approaching siren was heard, but it seemed like hours to Jimmy.

The ambulance screeched to a stop inside the stadium. The medical team jumped out and rushed to where the stricken athlete awaited, and were quickly briefed by the trainer. A shot of morphine was administered to calm Jimmy down and ease his pain, and he was transferred onto a gurney, lifted into the ambulance and rushed, sirens blaring, to Pemberton Hospital.

Pemberton beat Chelsen 21 to 14.

It had been a tougher game than Coach Wilzinski anticipated, and he was worried. He was thinking ahead to the Stanton game, and losing Jimmy was a terrible loss for the team. Jimmy was his star, and irreplaceable.

"Damn it," he told his assistant, "what a time for the kid to get hurt. We'll need a miracle against Stanton."

Jimmy was in surgery for more than 2 hours. His left femur had been broken, as well as his ankle.

The Orthopedic Surgeon expressed his dismay after viewing a number of the x-rays. "This kid will be lucky if he ever walks normally again," he told a nurse. "I wonder if football is really worth it."

Jim awoke several hours later, not knowing where he was or what had happened. Then he saw that his left leg was in a cast and in traction.

He was in a large room and his morphine-dulled mind observed two beds to his right and three beds across the way. Lights were visible over two of the beds, while the others were dark. The irritating sound of someone snoring came from a far corner.

A nurse entered, noted his movement and the half-opened eyes, and approached him.

"Hi, Jimmy. I'm Kathy. I'm your nurse tonight. How are you feeling?"

"Terrible," he responded weakly. "What time is it?"

"About 8:15 p.m. You've been sleeping quite awhile."

"I feel lousy, and I hurt."

"I know, but I can't give you any more pain medication for a while. You hang on a while longer, and

I'll take care of you. You'll feel better real soon, I promise. Are you hungry?"

"No. I feel nauseous."

"That's not unusual, Jimmy. There's a plastic container next to your right hand; use it if you get sick. You probably won't need to—the feeling will pass. I've got to go next door for a few minutes, but I'll be back shortly and give you some medication that will make you fell better."

"Wait!" he said. "Tell me what happened."

"I will when I get back. Try to get some rest." And she was gone.

He closed his eyes and was asleep in seconds.

Jimmy was awakened sometime later by the pressure of a hand on his right shoulder, and a voice calling his name.

"Jimmy. Wake up. I'm Doctor Roberts."

Jimmy opened his eyes, struggling to get his bearings. He was looking into the eyes of a thin faced, middle aged man sporting a neatly trimmed mustache, and wearing a white jacket with a stethoscope protruding from a pocket. Balding, bespectacled, tall, lean, and very tired after a day of an unusually large series of accident cases, Doctor Todd Roberts needed very badly to call it a day.

"I'm the doctor that repaired your leg, Jimmy. How do you feel?"

"Lousy."

"Unfortunately that's the way you will feel for a time, but the worst is over and in a day or two you'll start feeling a lot better."

"What happened to my leg?"

"You got hurt in a football game and…"

"I know that. I mean **what happened to my leg?"** said Jimmy, pointing in that direction.

"Your left femur suffered a fracture, Jimmy, and your ankle was broken in a couple of places. I've set everything back in order and with time and therapy you'll be almost as good as new."

Jimmy missed the *almost* in the doctor's explanation because his mind dwelled on the news that he had several breaks in the leg rather than one.

"Aw shit," he said, realizing he had more of a problem than he first considered. He was rapidly tiring, but there was more he wanted to know.

"How long will I be in a cast?"

"About 9 or 10 weeks, if everything heals right."

The news shocked him. "And then what?"

"We'll eventually have you doing leg exercises with the cast, and after the cast is off you'll be put into an extensive exercise program. I understand you're quite an athlete, which should help considerably. After a while you'll be fine."

Before Jimmy could ask his next question, Doctor Roberts said "that's all the talk for now. You're tired and you need your rest. The nurse is going to give you a shot and that will keep you comfortable. Your family is outside and I'm going to allow them to come in, but just for a few minutes. I'll be back to see you in the morning and we'll talk some more."

He turned to Nurse Kathy, issued some instructions, and left.

Kathy gave Jimmy a shot in his backside.

Moments later Mary, Dan, and Buddy entered the room.

Jimmy faked a weak smile and uttered a quiet "hello."

Mary took his hand and stood silently with tears in her eyes.

Dan and Buddy told him of the outcome of the game, their eyes seldom leaving the encased leg and the traction apparatus.

Mary began pouring out a bevy of questions a concerned mother would ask an ailing son.

Jimmy answered a few of the questions, but was fast becoming too drowsy to continue.

"I'm okay, mom; just hurting a little. I'm tired and don't feel like talking any more."

His eyes closed and he dropped off so quickly that Mary became frightened and called the nurse. Kathy explained that she had given him a shot to make him sleep and that he would be feeling better the next day.

The family left and Jimmy slept soundly.

Buddy wore a smile on his face as he walked down the hospital corridor.

When Jimmy awoke 6 hours later the nausea was gone and he was able to take some nourishment.

The pain was still with him, however, and he was kept medicated with diminishing amounts for several more days.

Each new day Jimmy felt more alert and was soon able to examine the flood of mail awaiting his attention.

Most were get-well cards from people he didn't know. Others were from classmates and teammates, all wishing him a speedy recovery.

The entire football team came to visit, but the hospital staff would only allow the Coach and two others to enter the room, explaining there simply wasn't room for more than three at a time. Everyone was being cheerful, and Jimmy did his best to put on a good front. When he was alone, however, he was terribly depressed.

Mary came to the hospital every day, and Dan came after work, but Jimmy only tolerated their visits. His mother talked too much, mostly on subjects that didn't interest him, and his father upset him when he mentioned that he had bet 10 dollars on the Stanton game 2 weeks before Jimmy got hurt, and now that Jimmy wouldn't be playing, he tried to cancel the bet, but the guy wouldn't allow it. Dan rambled on that he had put up the money, and they had given it to a third party, and so on.

Jimmy couldn't have cared less. He said nothing, but was happy when his parents left.

He enjoyed his visits with Sally, who came after school every day, but soon began to skip days.

Buddy and Sean came every day, keeping him current on daily happenings and especially on the excitement building up in school over the coming Saturday's "game of the year" against Stanton.

According to the sports reporters in both towns, the odds now favored Stanton with O'Brien unable to play.

Coach Wilzinski was quoted in the newspapers as stating "while O'Brien will be sorely missed, one man doesn't make a football team, and with an all-out team effort I expect Pemberton to be victorious."

Jimmy smiled at the Coach's words, for if he were Coach, he would have said the same thing.

He hoped his father read the article, so he wouldn't worry about his 10 bucks.

Screw you and your 10 bucks, he said to himself, and the thought made him feel better.

Buddy said very little when he visited Jimmy in the hospital. He just showed up, as if he were obliged to.

He did have a few things on his mind, however, but he bided his time.

One was to find out what the final prognosis would be on his brother's leg. He had mixed emotions over this. Would Jimmy's leg ever be strong enough to play football again? Were his football scholarship hopes now out of the question, and the likelihood that he would be living far away dashed as well? Would he be so badly hobbled that he would no longer be the big-shot athlete that so many admired?

The choice, to Buddy, was a toss-up. He decided he would prefer to let Jimmy have his fame and glory as long as it was a long way from Pemberton.

Buddy hoped that Pemberton would beat Stanton. It wasn't out of loyalty to his school. It would simply show that the team didn't need Jimmy O'Brien to win, and make him far less important than the superstar the newspapers had made of him. Buddy had one more tidbit of information he wanted to share with Jimmy, but hadn't decided when to spring it.

The Chelsen football players who hit Jimmy were numbers 66 and 68—Charlie White and Harvey Cohen. Looking at the game program and locating the Chelsen

High team picture, Buddy was elated to find that Charlie White was indeed a Negro.

Fantastic! Buddy proclaimed to himself—a Jew and a nigger! Brother Jimmy will just love that.

He planned to lay this information on Jimmy when the right opportunity presented itself, and he decided to enhance the information with a story he had concocted.

He planned to tell Jimmy he heard two men talking in Stanley's Cafeteria. One said that when he made a truck delivery to a bar in Chelsen on the Monday after the game, he heard the two Chelsen players that made the hit were supposed to key on O'Brien and do what they had to do to slow him down.

The other guy commented that they had slowed him down alright, but that he still would have liked to have won the game.

The first guy said that the betting on the game was Pemberton by 14 points, and with only a 7-point differential, the gamblers in Chelsen made some serious money.

Buddy had gone over the story in his mind many times and, when he was ready to spring it, knew it would be a bombshell.

CHAPTER 14

NOVEMBER, 1948

Pemberton High lost to Stanton 14 to 6. Both teams played superb defense, but the Pemberton offense just couldn't get going. Pemberton fans felt the loss of Jimmy O'Brien was the determining factor in the game.

Jimmy had listened to the game on WESK radio, and outwardly expressed his disappointment. Inwardly, however, he was selfishly happy that Pemberton hadn't won. He had the satisfaction of knowing that Pemberton fans would say if Jimmy O'Brien had played, the outcome would have been different.

Three more weeks passed before the traction apparatus was removed from Jimmy's leg. He was given crutches, shown how to properly use them, and he now walked the hallway outside his room without assistance.

He was told he would need to master the use of crutches ascending and descending a flight of three steps before the hospital would allow him to go home. It wasn't purported to be easy in a full leg cast but Jimmy accomplished the task easily on his first attempt.

Jimmy had mixed feelings about leaving the hospital. At home he would be under the constant scrutiny of his parents, and he did not relish the thought.

Not that he didn't love his mother, for he did. It was just that she could drive him crazy with her incessant, meaningless chatter.

His father would be even more of a problem.

Dan O'Brien was a bully and a know-it-all. He demanded complete attention whenever he discussed a subject, and more often than not he was wrong. Whenever he ran out of things to talk about, he reverted to his favorite topic—racism. Nobody but the Irish were trustworthy—and the worst people were the "niggers and the kikes." Over and over and over he preached this line, and although Jimmy believed it, he was tired of hearing it.

He would be coming home to listen to the same stories, with no hope of fleeing until his leg mended. The thought did not thrill him.

One day soon he knew he would have to do something about his father.

CHAPTER 15

In his hospital bed the night before he was to be released, Jimmy thought back to the time when he was 6 years old and he and the boys had formed their club. Their first bit of business was to put into writing the club rules.

Jimmy had talked to old man Dempsey, who was the Pemberton librarian, and asked Mr. Dempsey how to start a club. Dempsey had smiled and explained to him that you had to write a charter spelling out all the rules, and that all of the members had to agree to the rules and sign their names, or they couldn't belong.

Jimmy hadn't understood the meaning of the word charter and Mr. Dempsey explained that a charter was a written agreement—a pact.

Jimmy liked the sound of the word PACT and asked Mr. Dempsey how to spell it.

Dempsey, enjoying himself, obliged and Jimmy, after several more questions, thanked the old man and left very much satisfied.

The next Saturday morning, in the privacy of their clubhouse, the three boys painstakingly printed THE PACT.

JIMMY, BUDDY, AND SEAN WILL DO THE BEST TO MAKE ALL THE BAD PEEPULS LIKE JEUS AND NIGARS SORRY FOR BEIN BAD. WE WILL HURT THEM WEN EVUR WE CAN, FOR EVUR AN EVUR.

JIMMY 6
BUDDY 5
SEAN 5
SATERDAY 1938

The boys amended THE PACT several times in subsequent years when questions arose requiring clarification:

1940 Jimmy is lifetime leader.
1941 no one can ever quit.
1941 no other people can join.
1942 THE PACT can never be broken unless two out of three members agree in front of each other.

The document was rolled up, tied with a string, and stuffed into a cardboard tube for protection. It was hidden in a cache beneath a floorboard in the loft.

All of this was very official in the minds of the youthful trio.

CHAPTER 16

DECEMBER, 1948

It was late Saturday morning, exactly six weeks after the Chelsen game, and Jimmy was about to be released from the hospital.

Dr. Roberts had asked the O'Brien family to meet him in Jimmy's room at 11:00 so that he could brief them on the results of the latest x-rays and answer any questions they might have.

Roberts was pleased with the current x-rays. "It appears the fractures are healing well and we are on schedule," he told the O'Briens. "I estimate that we'll remove the cast in about 4 weeks, and then Jimmy should begin an extensive exercise program to strengthen his leg. You must not get the cast wet, Jimmy, so bathing will present a problem, but not an insurmountable one. When you sign out they will give you a sheet of instructions I want you to adhere to, and a prescription for a mild pain killer in the unlikely event that you will need any. Don't fill the prescription unless you really have to.

"Continue to do the same daily exercises that you have been doing here, in addition to whatever else the therapist tells you to do. Everybody understand? Good. Now for the leg itself. I can't give you any guarantees as to how strong it will be. There was considerable damage, but you're young and we'll hope for the best. Any questions?"

Dan O'Brien asked the question Jimmy was afraid to ask and Buddy had come to hear. "What about football, Doc? I mean in the future, like in college. Will he be able to play?"

Roberts didn't hesitate. He expected the question and was prepared to answer it the only way he could. He had no intention of giving the family, and especially Jimmy, any false hopes.

"The leg should be quite functional. There is cartilage damage around the knee and the ankle damage was severe. I'm afraid that the leg will never have the strength and mobility that it once had. You won't be a cripple, Jimmy, and you should be thankful for that, but football or any other highly strenuous sporting activity is out of the question. Your leg simply won't take it. I'm sorry."

Jimmy's face noticeably paled and his eyes watered. Deep down he had feared this report, but wouldn't and couldn't accept it.

Mary didn't give a damn about football; she just wanted her son home and under her care.

Dan was concerned with the loss of prestige he would suffer. People would soon forget about a has-been football star and search for new heroes to worship.

Buddy said nothing.

The Monday after Jimmy was injured, Dan O'Brien had left work early and gone to see Coach Wilzinski at the High School. He wanted to find out about hospital and doctor care. He was worried because he could not afford the huge expenses that were forthcoming, and he was prepared to raise hell with the school if he had to.

His fears were set aside once the Coach got through explaining that a group of alumni had set up a program which they handsomely endowed for just such contingencies. Jimmy's hospital expenses would be covered 100%.

With a sigh of relief, Dan's belligerent attitude was instantly replaced with his concern for the welfare of his son and his son's future, and the conversation ended on a friendly note.

The Coach told Dan he'd be over to visit Jimmy as soon as he could and discuss his future. It was a promise he never kept.

On his way home, Dan reflected on *his* bad luck. Everything that could go wrong always happened to him, he thought with self-pity. God-damn the boy. He should have been more careful.

CHAPTER 17

Buddy had mixed emotions about the doctor's report as he sat on his bed that evening. Jimmy and his father's hopes had been crushed, and Buddy was pleased. But Jimmy wouldn't be going away, and Buddy was not happy about that.

He couldn't wait to spring his story about the Chelsen players on Jimmy and Sean. That will cheer me up, he thought.

Maybe tomorrow.

It was late Sunday afternoon and Jimmy was tired. Neighbors and other well-wishers had been pouring into the O'Brien household since 10:00 in the morning, bringing food and gifts along with their best wishes. Mary loved the company and Dan was on a high again.

Many of Jimmy's teammates showed up, still unhappy over their loss to Stanton, and let him know that they had done their best, but sorely missed him.

"We would have had the State Championship if you had been able to play," they said.

This helped lift Jimmy's spirits, and made more bearable the frequent twinges of pain he felt whenever he shifted his body position.

Sally had been there for several hours, and was very attentive to him, especially when there were team members in the room. She enjoyed the glances she attracted as she flitted about the room.

She had decided the night before she no longer would go out only with Jimmy—there were a lot of fish in the sea. Now, of course, was not the time to break away, or to tell Jimmy. She didn't want herself to be thought of as a fair-weather girlfriend. She would wait a month or so and let the word out that she was no longer going steady.

She had no intention of saddling herself with a cripple or near cripple, as rumor had it that he might be. She had much loftier plans for herself.

It had been a long day. Most of the company had left and Jimmy felt fatigued but elated.

Buddy decided the time was right. He closed the door to Jimmy's bedroom and pulled a chair over close to the bed, beckoning Sean to do the same. Slowly, and with a great deal of expression, Buddy related his story to the two boys, emphasizing the attack on Jimmy by the two Chelsen football players who, by the way, happened to be a Jew and a nigger, and the gamblers who had set it up. The story had inconsistencies, but was believable to the two naive teenagers.

Sean sat shaking his head in disbelief, but believing.

Jimmy was livid with rage. "Bastards! Dirty bastards! I've got a lot of scores to settle as soon as I get on my feet again. You two get out of here. Tell mom I don't want to eat anything. I'm going to sleep and I want to be left alone. If I need anything I'll call out. Now get out!"

CHAPTER 18

JANUARY, 1949

The Sports Alumni Endowment Fund Committee had kept its promise to provide special help to its injured athletes, and the school had made the arrangements for Jimmy to be tutored during the period that he couldn't attend classes. Over the past few months, between the school work and the therapy sessions, Jimmy had maintained a busy schedule.

And at long last the cast would be coming off.

The cast was removed in Doctor Robert's office on a cold, snowy Tuesday morning.

Jimmy didn't like the look or feel of his leg.

Doctor Roberts gave Jimmy a brief discourse on the atrophy resulting from having been encased in a cast for a long period, and assured him that with exercise and therapy his leg would soon look normal.

Jimmy just shook his head. He was scared.

The following Monday Jimmy returned to classes at Pemberton High School, with his cast removed and on crutches.

In a week, macho as ever, he discarded his crutches and walked with the aid of a cane. He was limping noticeably and didn't like it. His leg and foot hurt but he wouldn't admit it to anyone or even to himself, and he fought his way through the pain and the inconvenience.

He stubbornly refused to believe that he was through with competitive sports. He confidently confided in his teammates that in the fall he would be playing college football.

Jimmy, when alone, was bitter and driven by the desire to right the wrongs that had been inflicted upon him. He promised himself he would get even, and then some. No one was ever going to get the best of him—no one! He'd get those two guys from Chelsen; no matter how long it took, and he hadn't forgotten about Robinson, either. As soon as he became mobile—really mobile—he'd have his revenge.

I've waited too long on Robinson as it is, he thought bitterly. I'll get him first; and then the other two. And anyone else who screws with me.

Buddy brought his brother more disturbing news. One night after supper, in Jimmy's bedroom, he told Jimmy he saw Sally with Alfie Dillon—3 days in a row—walking arm in arm.

Alfie was home from Prep School over the holiday break, and Buddy hadn't told Jimmy before because he wanted the timing to be right.

Alfie Dillon was tall, good-looking and one of the few kids his age that had his own car. His family owned one of the larger tanneries in town, and lived in a huge home on Lowell Street.

Jimmy had noticed a change in Sally, as well as her decreasing number of phone calls and visits. When he had mentioned this to her, she had become testy, and had given him several lame excuses.

Now he understood why.

"You know something, Buddy. I don't give a damn—I really don't. I have a hell of a lot more important things on my mind than that bitch.

"First I'm going to get this leg working right. I'm not going to be a cripple—the hell with what the doctor said. I'll make that leg so strong that I'll make him eat his words. You wait and see.

"I've had a lot of time to do some serious thinking. You and I don't see eye to eye on a lot of things, Buddy. I'm well aware of that. I know when I get angry I tend to throw my weight around, and I've taken it out on you plenty of times."

Buddy started to interrupt, but Jimmy waved him off.

"Let me finish, Buddy. You never had a poker face. I think I could always read your thoughts by the look on your face. But we're of the same blood—we're brothers—and that's the most important factor. If you can believe in anyone—if you can trust anyone—it's family.

"Sean is family too, or the same as family. He's always been a good friend. He's kind of—I don't know how else to put it—a good influence. I trust him. Anyway, what I'm trying to say is that it is absolutely imperative that we always stick together in everything we do—*ONE-HUNDRED-PERCENT* together. Nobody, and I mean nobody, can break us up. We're going to take care of the people that screwed us, like we've talked about, and we'll start as soon as I can really move around."

Jimmy paused and, lowering his voice, added, "We're going to mess-up people, Buddy. People who deserve it. People that have screwed us, or will screw us the first chance they get. We'll go after Jews or niggers or anyone else that did us dirty, or tried to. We'll keep our PACT—we'll do what's right!"

Buddy's eyes glistened as he was caught up in Jimmy's fervor. He had always believed Jimmy was just a lot of talk. Sure, he could beat somebody up, but to hear him say "mess-up people"—that was a surprise.

Buddy always thought only he would have the guts to hurt people if he wanted to. He had wondered for many years what it would be like to kill someone, and Jimmy had been number one on the list. *Could he do it? Would he be afraid? Would he feel guilty? And could he live with it?* He had examined all of these questions in his mind at great length and his conclusion had been *yes, no, no,* and *yes*.

He didn't understand why those thoughts always stimulated him, but whenever they came to mind he felt—good. Better than good!

He knew he would have to be older and smarter in order to get away with it, and he had been willing to wait. Now he wouldn't have to wait much longer.

Jews and niggers *would* be ideal targets, like his old man and Jimmy always said, but they would not be *his* prime consideration.

Anyone who gets in my way would fit the bill.

And to hear Jimmy talking about some serious "messing up" was something that turned him on. It was exciting news.

Jimmy was waiting for his response, but Buddy had no intention of letting him know his feelings.

He replied cautiously. "I never heard you talk like that before, Jimmy. I know that I have not always been your best friend. Sometimes you frighten me and I think you're going to hurt me. You've done so a number of times, you know. But I also feel that family is important. And I agree about Sean; he's okay. But about the rest—that's a little scary. Hurting someone a little is one thing, but really messing someone up—that I've really got to think about.

"And what about Sean? What if you and I say yes and he says no. What happens then?"

"I think he'll go along," Jimmy responded.

"What makes you think so?" Buddy asked, curious.

"He once asked me what I would do if someone I beat up died. I told him I could live with it."

"What did he say?"

"He smiled and said 'guess you'd have to—not much you could do about it.'"

"Interesting coming from Sean," Buddy said. "Sometimes I think he's afraid of his own shadow."

"Yeah, but he's no sissy, Buddy. His mother may have tried to make him into one, but I've seen him get riled up plenty of times. I asked Sean the same question he asked me, and he said he thought he could live with it too. I asked him if he could kill someone he hated. He thought a long time and then said 'no, he didn't think so, but he could watch and he didn't think it would bother him.' Those were pretty-much his words."

"Jesus, if he was serious, he's got more balls than I thought."

"He was serious, Buddy. He wasn't joking around, and neither was I. When he comes over tomorrow I'll put it to him. You'll see for yourself."

Dan O'Brien had been listening to the conversation, his ear pressed against the thinly veneered bedroom door. He quietly left; a look of concern on his lined face.

The next day, after school, Buddy brought Sean home with him.

Jimmy's attic bedroom had become the temporary clubhouse as Jimmy couldn't climb the ladder to the loft.

Behind closed doors, Jimmy told Sean about the discussion he and Buddy had the previous day. Sean listened, showing no emotion. When Jimmy finished, the brothers waited for Sean to speak.

Sean's expression remained impassive—he was deep in thought.

Finally, he spoke. "You guys are my closest friends, and have been for as long as I can remember. I don't have anyone else that cares about me like you guys do. My folks are okay, but my father mostly ignores me and my mother—well, you know my mother. She treats me as if I was still 5 years old. It's always going to be like that with her and I hate it."

He paused several seconds, searching for the right words. "I don't want to kill anyone, but I'll help you anyway you say, and I'll never squeal on either of you. I'd die first."

He had finished his speech and felt drained, but understood what he had committed to. He felt he had no other choice, and maybe—just maybe—he could temper whatever Jimmy had planned.

The room was quiet as the three boys studied each other.

Buddy broke the silence. "I guess there's nothing more to say. We've sworn ourselves to secrecy and the pact still stands. Jimmy can call the action whenever he's ready."

Jimmy was smiling. "I need a few more months. Then I'll be ready."

CHAPTER 19

Jimmy and Sally split up in early February, 1949, after a bitter exchange of words.

They saw each other practically every day in school after their breakup, but he ignored her, purposely playing up to any girl in the vicinity. He could see it irked her.

She told her friends that she dropped him to go steady with Alf Dillon.

Her friends didn't believe her. They felt nobody in their right mind would drop the likes of a Jimmy O'Brien for anybody else.

The next 3 months passed quickly, with Jimmy working out 3 days a week in his rehab program.

He mastered the routine in less than a week, and after he had made significant progress, his therapist, with an okay from Doc Roberts, gave him permission to exercise on his own at the "Y" gym. Since he needed to rest his leg between strengthening exercises, he decided to use the rest time to further develop his upper body. He did this the other 4 days of the week, for a minimum of 2 hours per session.

As time went on he looked and felt in great shape.

It was on this kind of a high that Jimmy called Coach Wilzinski's office in early May and asked for an appointment.

Upon learning of the call the Coach called Doctor Roberts. Roberts was unavailable, but his secretary told the Coach that the doctor would call back as soon as he returned to the office.

The doctor did so several hours later.

"Hi, Coach. Todd Roberts. How are you?"

"Good, Todd. I know you're busy and I don't want to take up much of your time, but I got a couple of quick questions for you."

"Shoot. I'm all ears."

"They're about Jimmy O'Brien, Todd. He made an appointment to see me this afternoon, and I've got a feeling that it has something to do with playing college football. Before I talk with him, I want to know his current status and your opinion on what you think of his future possibilities in sports."

"Coach, the kid's amazing. I've seldom seen such dedication and discipline in a young man. But if you're asking me if he could or should play football or any other contact sport, my answer is a definite **no**. His leg would never hold up and he could wind up a cripple. I told him that, and I emphasized it strongly. And you know what? He just looked at me and smiled and said 'thanks for the advice, Doc. I'll keep it in mind.' Coach, whatever you do, don't encourage him. He should forget about playing any type of contact sport, and limit himself on other types of sporting activities as well."

"Okay, Todd. It's about what I expected you to say. He showed great promise as an athlete—one of the best I've ever coached—and it's a shame it has to end this way. But when it's over it's over, and the sooner he learns to live with it, the better off he'll be. Thanks for the info, and let's get together for lunch soon. You can pay," Coach added whimsically."

"My pleasure, Coach, but I'll do the ordering for both of us," Todd Roberts shot back. "I'll see you at the next club meeting."

Jimmy arrived at the Coach's office later that afternoon, 10 minutes before his scheduled appointment time. Coach Wilzinski arrived 12 minutes late, breezing into the office uttering a brief apology.

Jimmy feigned indifference, but he was tense. He followed the Coach into the inner office and seated himself next to the oversized relic the Coach used for a desk. Coach Wilzinski shuffled through some folders looking for a pad of paper, while making some polite inquiries as to how Jimmy was feeling and how he was getting along in school.

"Never felt better," Jimmy replied. "I caught up on my class work long ago, thanks to the special tutoring. Everything's great, Coach."

Coach Wilzinski slowly settled back in his chair, his full attention now on his visitor.

"What can I do for you, Jimmy?"

"Coach, I'm in the best condition that I've ever been in. You told me when the season started that if I had a good year I would be a shoo-in for a football scholarship to a major school. I was having a great year, Coach—you and I know that. My broken leg may have ended the season for me, but I'm stronger now than I ever was, and I'll be better than new by mid-summer. I know I'd be an asset to any football team. It's important for me to get a scholarship, and you said you…"

Coach Wilzinski interrupted. He spoke in a soft and deliberate voice.

"Jimmy, believe me when I tell you I understand how you feel. Everything you've said is true. You have the size, the strength, the desire, the hands, and the ability that make a good ballplayer, and you did have the speed and agility every coach dreams about. But you're not facing reality. You've had the terrible misfortune of being seriously injured.

"It's true that broken bones heal, Jimmy, but you sustained several serious breaks to the same leg. As hard as it may be for you to understand, you've got to accept the fact that your leg will never be able to take the punishment that a football player is subjected to. You could do yourself serious harm—permanent harm. I can't be a party to that.

"I spoke to your doctor today and he unconditionally stated that you should not play football or any other contact sport. Colleges will not give athletic scholarships to athletes with injuries such as yours, Jimmy, and believe me, they check. They check very carefully. It's tough, but it's the way it is, and you've got to live with it."

The two were staring at each other. The Coach had pulled no punches. He sat, hands folded, intently watching the younger man's face, not knowing what to expect. After a prolonged pause, Jimmy rose, smiled, uttered a quiet "thank you" and walked out.

Coach Wilzinski, surprised at the response and the lack of emotion, remained motionless. I'll be damned, he thought. I didn't expect a non-reaction like that. I figured he'd be swearing or shouting or God knows what. But nothing? How do you figure kids today?

Outside, walking down Central Street into town center, Jimmy fought with himself to contain his fury.

Fuck them all, he thought. That Polish bastard made me work my ass off to make himself Coach of the Year, and now when he could help me, he won't. My old man's right. You can't count on anyone but your own. That's another son-of-a-bitch that I owe, and I'll see that he gets his. That's a promise.

Jimmy told his family about his meeting with the Coach during the supper meal. Dan O'Brien, his face red with anger, went philippic about how all those foreign bastards had it in for the Irish, ending his tirade bitterly with "Polocks are in the same class as the kikes and the niggers. I've told you that a hundred times."

Jimmy was not interested in hearing it again.

He waited for his father to finish and then put the question to him that was uppermost in his mind.

"I know, Dad. You're right as usual. But I'd still like to go to college. It doesn't have to be a big-time school. Maybe UMass or Northeastern. I could work part time to help pay the cost, but I would need you to pay for most of it, and I would pay you back as soon as I graduated and got a full-time job…"

"What the hell, are you crazy?" Dan O'Brien shouted. "You know how much it costs to go to college? Any college? I can barely support us now, and you want me to pay for you to go to some smart-ass college? And what about your brother? Am I supposed to pay for him next year when he graduates? Where the hell do you think money comes from? Well, I'll tell you. It comes from working your ass off. You want to go to college, smart guy, then you work for it first and *you* pay for it. You want to waste your time and your money—go ahead, but don't you ever ask me to throw away my hard-earned money. You understand?"

Dan O'Brien stopped ranting, tired of the subject but still fuming.

Buddy tried to catch his brother's eye, but a red-faced Jimmy kept his gaze on his plate and picked at his food.

The rest of the meal was finished in silence. Jimmy picked up his dishes and brought them into the kitchen, placed them in the sink and went to his room.

It had been a bad day and he was in no mood for conversation with anyone. Nearly in tears, he sat on his bed, feeling completely frustrated. Finally, he put his head down and did something he had never done before.

He cried himself to sleep.

Jimmy graduated High School in June, 1949. He was resigned to the fact that he couldn't go to college—at least not now. He planned to get a job for the short term and when he turned 18 join the Army, with or without his father's permission.

He told no one of his plans. He wanted to get away from his father, and he wanted to get away from Pemberton.

In the meantime he planned to take care of some unfinished business.

CHAPTER 20

SEPTEMBER 3, 1949

Nearly two years had passed since Jerry Gordon's death, and Harry Robinson still had a difficult time dealing with the loss of his best friend. At least the bad dreams that haunted him nightly the first few months were gone.

Jerry had been brutally murdered. And for what? A few lousy dollars? Why would anyone in his right mind commit such a horrible crime?

Harry was working part-time in Ordman's Pharmacy, on the corner of Washington Street and Main. He had started in March, working three hours a day after school and eight hours a day on Saturdays. He earned 55 cents an hour, which his parents allowed him to keep with the understanding that he was to bank five dollars a week. He did so faithfully.

His work schedule hadn't interfered with his studies for he was a good student in all subjects except math. Jerry had been a whiz in *all* subjects, especially math, and had been able to explain it to him better than any teacher.

God, how I miss Jerry. I'll never forget him.

Harry began working a full 40 hour week when the school year ended, with plans to triple the money he was putting into savings.

The coming school year would be his senior year, and his folks wanted him to keep his marks up so that he could get into college. He would only be able to apply to a state college because of its lower tuition, and he didn't mind. He did not want to be a burden to his parents.

Martha and Joe Robinson had planned that Harry would have every opportunity to get ahead and make something of himself. They both worked toward this end; Joe full-time and Martha part-time. They wanted Harry to have everything they did not when they were children. He had the intelligence, and they believed if they provided him the opportunity, perhaps he would become a professional—a doctor or a lawyer—and be successful and earn a substantial living. These were their dreams and prayers.

Harry was their only child. Martha had three miscarriages prior to his birth, and had delivered Harry prematurely and with difficulty. Seeing that the Lord had finally given them one healthy son, Martha and Joe were not going to be greedy and ask for more.

Harry was bright, good, and kind; traits they recognized as of the utmost importance. They were proud of their son. He was their life.

It was 7:00 p.m. on a Saturday when Harry finished his work day. He hopped on his bike, turned on the bike-light and peddled west on Washington Street. At Sutton Street he turned left, and continued past Aborn and Putnam

Streets. There was little traffic in either direction and he was singing loudly and enjoying the ride. He had had a pleasant day and he was in a happy frame of mind.

Harry heard the car approaching from the rear, and rode his bike closer to the curbing. Suddenly, he heard the car gun its engine. Before he could react, the car was upon him and struck the bike a glancing blow. Harry and the bike were flung wildly into the air and he crashed head first into the trunk of a large oak tree. The car continued accelerating and sped off.

The noise of the crash brought residents in two nearby homes rushing out their front doors. Seeing the figure of a boy lying at the foot of the tree, Walter Simpson yelled to his neighbor Gerald Rosen. "Call the police for an ambulance. I'll check the kid."

The light was fading rapidly, but Walter Sampson could see blood over the face and head of the young man.

"Jesus Christ," he said, crossing himself. "I think he's dead."

More people were coming out of nearby homes to see what had happened. Two cars stopped, effectively blocking the street. One of the cars was driven by Pauline Keone, a registered nurse, who had just finished her shift at Pemberton Hospital and was on her way to visit a girlfriend. Pauline had been a nurse for 14 years, and had spent several of those years in the emergency room. She was a no-nonsense person, and quickly plowed her way through the hovering group and announced in a loud, commanding voice, "I'm a nurse. Give me room!"

She proceeded to check Harry's carotid and found no pulse. Her trained ear could discern no heartbeat.

She could hear sirens in the distance, and she shook her head sadly, thinking to herself there was no need to rush—*he's gone.*

A police car arrived prior to the ambulance, and two patrolmen stepped out and rushed to the scene. Pauline announced that she was a nurse and that the boy was dead. One officer moved the crowd back and asked loudly if anyone had seen what happened.

Walter Simpson answered that he hadn't actually seen what had happened as he had been facing away from the street. "I heard a car coming fast and then a crash. When I turned around I saw the car speeding off and a figure and a bike lying next to the tree. I ran over to see if I could help, after yelling to my neighbor Rosen to call the police. When I got there, I saw the kid's face and head were all bloody. I-I was afraid to move him. I tried to talk to him, but I got no answer. I didn't know what else to do.

"Some cars stopped and that lady came along and checked the kid. Then you cops showed up. That's about it."

An ambulance screeched to a stop, followed by a second patrol car. One of the newly arrived officers dispersed the crowd to make room for the ambulance personnel.

The other officer was Sam Coben. He walked over to look at the victim as the medics were checking him, and thought he recognized him, but for the moment couldn't place him.

"Is he alive?" Sam asked.

"No. He's dead. Skull looks crushed. No pulse, no heartbeat," the examining medic answered.

"What about an ID?" Sam asked.

"Yeah, I've got his wallet. Name's Harry Robinson. Address is Carlton Street. Hell, that's only two blocks up the street."

Sam remembered the name. Harry Robinson had been the kid that had been investigated in the Gordon case some two years ago. They were the basketball players he used to watch.

"Anyone see what kind of a car or a license plate?" Sam asked the surrounding group.

The officer who first interviewed Walter Simpson spoke up, and brought Simpson over to Sam.

"I saw the car for a second, and from a distance," Simpson said. "I think it was a Ford, but I was too far away to tell for sure. I can tell you that it looked like someone was sitting in the back seat."

Sam took out a notebook and pen and had Walter Simpson repeat his story, stopping him now and then to pose questions. He then spoke to others in the crowd but no one had actually seen the accident, only the aftermath.

The medics moved Harry Robinson into the ambulance and the police and ambulance sped away, leaving an anxious group of neighbors mulling about on a warm and now nearly dark Saturday evening.

CHAPTER 21

The plan to take care of Harry Robinson had been devised in the clubhouse. It was Buddy who suggested they should "run the bastard down." Jimmy liked the idea, and Sean as usual went along.

They had studied Harry's schedule for 2 weeks before deciding that a Saturday night presented the best opportunity for them, as they needed two cars. Every other Saturday evening the O'Brien car remained in the garage, as the Boyles alternated with the O'Briens in driving to the Knights of Columbus (K.C.) dances.

Jimmy came up with the idea of taking his folks' car on a Saturday night and stealing a second car from the unattended K.C. parking lot. There would be a choice of vehicles to pick from, and breaking a side vent window and hot-wiring the car would be easy. Working with the mechanic, an ex-con, at the gas station had taught him a few things.

The plan called for Buddy to drive the family car and drop Jimmy near the K.C. Hall at 6:30 p.m. Buddy and

Sean were to continue on to the Stanton Hospital parking lot, park, and wait for Jimmy to arrive in the stolen vehicle. Jimmy would locate them in the parking lot, pick them up, and drive the 4 miles back to Pemberton in the stolen car—to the corner of Aborn and Sutton Streets. There they would wait for Robinson to bicycle by.

Now this had been accomplished. The plan had run like clockwork.

The stolen car returned to the Stanton Hospital lot shortly after 7:30 p.m.

The parking area was half-filled with staff and visitor vehicles.

Jimmy pulled into a slot between a Buick and a Ford, shut the lights and cut the engine.

"Don't take off your gloves," he ordered. "Wait until we get into the other car. Let's go, but move slowly and don't draw attention to yourselves."

Buddy opened the front passenger-side door at the same time as Sean popped open the rear door and both boys got out of the stolen car. Jimmy nervously wiped the steering wheel with the cotton gloves he was wearing—not remembering whether or not he had touched the wheel prior to putting on his gloves—before he exited. The three boys walked casually to where they had left the family car. Buddy unlocked it and threw the keys to Jimmy. Once inside they each removed their cotton gloves and threw them into a paper bag that Sean had thought to bring.

It was 7:40 p.m. according to Sean's watch and they were just about on schedule with their timetable.

"Mission accomplished," Buddy boasted.

Jimmy smiled at the remark as he drove the 7 miles to Salem Willows, keeping well within the speed limit. He parked on a side street away from the main parking area so no one would see that they had come by car.

The Willows was a popular summertime resort because of its arcades and amusement rides. There were a variety of food and dessert stands sprinkled in with the rides, and it was a haven for young and old alike. It was especially popular with the high school crowd and a place where you were sure to be seen by someone you knew. The boys felt that if they spent an hour or so making the rounds they would meet a slew of classmates, and be alibied in the event they were ever questioned as to their whereabouts that Saturday evening.

They saw better than a half-dozen of their schoolmates, and made it a point to either stop and talk or at least exchange nods.

By 9:30 p.m. they were back in the car and made the 20 minute drive to Pemberton. Jimmy returned his father's car to the garage, put the bag containing the gloves in the trash barrel, and the three boys entered the O'Brien house. Adrenaline still pumping, they each took a Coke from the refrigerator, sat down at the kitchen table, and gulped thirstily.

A minute later Buddy got up and located the Monopoly game. They began to play in earnest, each waiting for someone else to bring up the night's events.

"Well, what do you think?" Buddy asked, breaking the silence.

"I think it went off perfectly," Jimmy answered. "We make a helluva team."

"How badly do you think he was hurt?" Sean asked nervously.

"Plenty, I would guess," Buddy responded. "I couldn't really see too much because it all happened so fast, but I saw him and the bike go flying through the air like a big bird. He had to have broken something."

"I hope it was his neck," Jimmy answered cruelly.

"I'm sure we'll hear about it tomorrow," Buddy said. "We were smart not to go anywhere near there afterwards."

About 12:15 a.m. they heard a car pull into the driveway, two doors slam, and moments later Mary and Dan O'Brien walked into the kitchen.

"Your folks are waiting for you, Sean," Mary said.

"Thank you, Mrs. O'Brien. How was the dance?"

"Oh, fun as usual, but I can never get Mr. O'Brien to dance with me enough."

The remark brought a scowl to Dan O'Briens face, but he had had too much to drink and didn't feel like getting into an argument. He had other plans in mind when he got her into bed.

He said nothing and headed for the bathroom.

Sunday morning at 11:00 the boys met in the clubhouse. Sean had picked up a Sunday paper and brought it with him, and he was visibly upset. A small inset on the front page carried a news brief about a hit-and-run incident that occurred Saturday evening. Page three detailed the accident, *and related the victim had died.*

Harry Robinson's name, age, address and a recent photo were included in the story. The article concluded by saying "police are investigating the incident…"

The boys looked at one another in disbelief.

Sean exhaled loudly and gasped, “Jesus! What do we do now?”

Jimmy nervously responded. “We do nothing, asshole, but keep our mouths shut!”

“I know, but I didn’t think we’d kill him,” said Sean, tears forming in his eyes. “How could that have happened?”

“Things like this happen all the time,” Buddy answered apprehensively. “We didn’t mean to kill him, but things don’t always go according to plan.”

Jimmy, regaining his courage, brazenly agreed. “He got what was coming to him. Nobody is ever going to know who did it, so relax. Remember, we say nothing, we know nothing and we do nothing. We made no mistakes. Everybody okay with that?”

“Okay,” Buddy answered quickly, and Sean slowly nodded his head in agreement.

“I’m sure we all understand that we’re all equally involved in this,” Jimmy stated assertively. “The fact that I drove the car makes me no more guilty than those who were with me. We do understand that, don’t we?”

“Yeah,” Buddy said, “that’s the way it is.”

“Okay,” Sean answered, but he felt sick to his stomach.

CHAPTER 22

Sam Coben was tense and uncomfortable as he informed Joe and Martha Robinson of their son's death. He did so in as kindly a manner as possible and, although she had immediately gone to tears, Martha Robinson hadn't become hysterical.

Joe Robinson put his arms around his wife and walked her into the parlor and sat her down.

Sam followed and waited for them to speak.

"What happened?" Joe Robinson whispered.

"It was a hit-and run, sir," Sam reported. "We've interrogated some witnesses in hopes they might shed some light on the accident, but no one actually saw what happened, other then to see a car speed away.

"The mishap occurred at approximately 7:20 p.m. on Sutton Street. We're looking for the car and the driver. An ambulance took your son to Pemberton Hospital and, if you'd like, I could drive you there. If there's anyone you'd like me to notify—family or friends—I'd be happy to do that."

Joe Robinson, wet eyed but in control, answered "No thank you, officer. As soon as my wife feels up to it we'll drive to the hospital. I'll call her sister and she'll notify the family. Thank you, we appreciate your concern."

Sam Coben left the Robinson home thinking that he would probably never again meet a couple who took terrible news as well as they did.

He breathed a sigh of relief that it hadn't been worse.

Sam slept poorly that night. He dreamt of two young fiercely competitive boys facing each other on the basketball court. He could see their faces as plain as if he were standing next to them. The dream had been so realistic that he woke up in a cold sweat.

When he got to the station the next morning he placed a call to the Stanton Police Station and asked for Inspector Barney Osham. He was told that Osham was off duty, but if it was important he could be reached.

"It's important, Sergeant, and I think Inspector Osham would want to take my call."

Sam was given a number and placed his call. On the fifth ring, a gruff male voice answered. "Yeah?"

"Inspector Osham?"

"Yeah. Who's this?"

Sam introduced himself, and related the story of the hit-and-run incident. "What bothers me, Inspector, is that the Robinson kid was the best friend of the Gordon boy who was murdered in your movie theater a couple of years ago. It might be a coincidence, but the connection came to mind.

"I remembered you were in charge of the Gordon investigation, and wanted to make you aware of this accident. We haven't found the hit-and-run vehicle yet, but at the scene of the accident we found broken glass from a car headlight, and we've notified the surrounding town police to be on the lookout for a vehicle with a broken passenger-side headlamp. That's about it."

Barney thanked him for the call and said he'd keep in touch. Deep down he doubted if there was a connection, but he tucked the info into the back of his mind.

Monday morning the vehicle was discovered. A call to the Stanton Police Station had come from a security guard at Stanton Hospital who had noticed that a car had been in the parking lot his entire shift on Sunday, which in itself was not uncommon, but it was still there, in the same spot, on Monday. He identified the automobile as a gray Ford with a Massachusetts license plate.

It was soon confirmed as the vehicle that had been reported stolen from the Pemberton K.C. parking lot the prior Saturday evening and, as it had a smashed passenger-side headlamp, it was considered likely the vehicle that killed the Robinson boy.

The Stanton Police notified the Pemberton Police and a Pemberton patrol car was dispatched to the area. In a matter of hours the car was towed to Pemberton, impounded and checked for finger prints and other clues. The ash trays were emptied and the contents examined. Nothing there of importance.

The glove box contained the owner's registration, a screwdriver and pliers, a notebook and several pencils.

No prints were found on the steering wheel.

Sam Coben asked his Chief if he could work on the case, as he felt he knew the kid.

The Chief gave his okay, and assigned him to the CID officer in charge.

Sam called Barney Osham and informed him that the vehicle had been found, but Barney was already aware of it. They made a date to meet that evening, when they both would be off duty.

They met at 7:00 p.m. in Stanley's Cafeteria in Stanton, and after 10 minutes of small talk, liked each other.

"Barney, I could be wrong, but this situation bothers me. When I was a beat cop a couple of years ago I used to see Gordon and Robertson two or three times a week, always together, and usually playing basketball. I didn't know their names, but they always seemed to be having a good time, and usually waved at me. I was upset when I heard about the Gordon murder—the sheer brutality of it—over a few bucks, if that's really what it was all about. But when I saw the Robinson kid dead and it dawned on me who he was, I got a sick feeling in my stomach.

"A hit-and-run victim on a street where there never is much traffic, and by a stolen car; it doesn't smell right to me. I'd like to know if somebody was out to get him for some reason. I remembered that you had the Gordon case and must have talked to a lot of people in your investigation."

"Yeah," Barney said. "I met several times with the Gordon parents as well as friends of the family, and I talked to a number of his school mates and teachers.

"I also talked with Robinson. I remember he was very much broken up over his friend's death. The case is still open, Sam, and I'm still on it, but I've got nothing on who killed Gordon."

“No prints showed up on the steering wheel of the stolen car, Barney. That means the driver took the time to wipe the wheel. They’re still dusting the insides of the car because one of the witnesses was fairly certain that someone was sitting in the back seat. I’m sure that whatever prints do show up will be those of the car owner and his family.

“That’s why this thing stinks. The car is stolen in Pemberton. The owner parked in the K.C. parking lot between 6:05 and 6:15 Saturday evening. The Robinson kid was struck down minutes after he left work—at about 7:14 p.m. That’s the time the station got the call for the ambulance. We found the car abandoned in the Stanton Hospital parking lot. That means the car traveled all of 4 or 5 miles after it was stolen.

“If someone was out just to steal a car, why not a luxury car rather than an old Ford? There were Oldmobiles, Buicks and even a couple of Caddies there—there always are on a Saturday night. I know; I used to patrol that area.

“And why be speeding with a stolen car on a street with a 25 mile an hour speed limit and draw attention to yourself? It doesn’t make sense. And it was pretty clever to dump the car in a hospital parking lot where there’s a lot of traffic over a 24 hour period. The driver and whoever was with him could have grabbed a bus at the hospital bus stop and disappeared…”

“Whoa, Sam,” Barney interrupted. “That’s an awful lot of supposing, but nothing has been substantiated; at least not yet. I agree with you, though. Something does smell. The swiping of the car when it was still light was risky. It would have been a lot smarter to wait another hour until it got dark. And the speeding does sound stupid, yet the driver was smart enough to wipe away any prints.

"Taking all the events in perspective it could be that somebody swiped the car purposely at that time because they needed it then and not after dark. It might be that this accident was deliberate. Somebody out to get the kid. Who's in charge of your CID unit?"

"Dennis Rafferty," Sam replied. "He's good. Do you know him?"

"Yeah, we've talked several times over the years. I'll call him in the morning and offer him any assistance he needs from our side. I'll also check with the hospital security people and see if anyone noticed a car with only one headlight entering the parking lot after 7:30 Saturday evening. You find out if anyone saw a gray Ford leaving the K.C. parking lot between 6:15 and 7:00 that night. There should have been other cars coming in and parking or dropping people off at that time in the evening. Maybe we'll get a break."

"Sounds good, Barney, thanks."

They finished their coffee, shook hands and called it a night.

That same evening another meeting was taking place in a clubhouse loft. Sean had picked up a Boston Globe and Buddy had bought copies of both the Stanton Times and the Pemberton News. The Times article described the accident, showing a picture of the deceased and giving the time of the Mass and the funeral arrangements. The News had the same information, but on the front page. The Globe showed no picture and only offered a brief story.

"Good—nobody saw anything," Jimmy concluded.

The three boys were inwardly tense. They had pictured Robinson as being broken up a little, but not that he would have smashed his head into a tree and died. They were desperately trying to show one another they could handle it.

"The wise-ass deserved it, Jimmy," Buddy said. "We're in the clear. The old man never noticed that we took his car or we would have heard about it."

"What about Sally and Doreen?" Sean asked. "Do you think they'll think that we did it?"

"Why should they. We never talked about doing anything to Robinson in front of them. It was a hit-and-run accident by a stolen car and it had nothing to do with us. Besides, we got alibis. We took a bus to Salem Willows and spent the evening there. Lots of people saw us. That's the story, guys. Be sure to stick to it if anything comes up," Jimmy ordered. "It's over!"

CHAPTER 23

OCTOBER, 1949

Jimmy informed his father that he was going to join the Army. To his surprise, his father thought it was a good idea.

"They'll make a man out of you and keep you out of trouble," Dan O'Brien said, his mind calculating the extra beer money he would have with one less mouth to feed.

The next morning Jimmy went to the recruiting office in Pemberton and signed up.

The evening before Jimmy was to leave for the Army, the boys met in the clubhouse, bringing with them two large pepperoni pizzas and two six-packs of Narrangansett Ale. After devouring the pizzas and guzzling a couple of ales each, Jimmy brought up an old subject that was still on his mind. "I only wish that I could have given that bastard Coach Wilzinski some grief before I left. He really fucked up my life, and I'm not going to forget it."

Buddy, feeling spirited as he opened his third ale, said, "Sean and I can take care of that for you while your away, Jimmy. Don't worry about it. It won't be a problem."

"Hell, no!" Jimmy barked. "No way. That's something I want to do personally. You wait until I get back. Understand?"

Sean joined in. "I think that would be wiser all the way around, Buddy. Let things in the town cool off for awhile. It will be a lot safer."

Buddy shrugged his shoulders with indifference.

With that decision reached, they settled down and swapped jokes. Buddy warned Jimmy to stay away from the girls around the army camps, and not bring back any diseases.

Jimmy smirked knowingly, and Sean grimaced at the thought.

By 10:00 p.m. they had finished their drinking and had talked themselves out. They solemnly renewed their pledge to THE PACT, shook hands with one another, and called it a night.

At 6:00 a.m. on a late October morning, Jimmy boarded a bus outside the Pemberton Court House with seven other men and made the trip to the Boston Army Base building on the corner of Sumner and D streets in South Boston. The cursory exam he was given indicated no problems, and he passed his physical without a hitch, having never revealed to the doctors that he had suffered severe leg injuries. At 11:30 that morning he took his one step forward and was sworn in. An hour later he was on a bus destined for Fort Devens, in Ayer, Massachusetts.

His first few weeks at Fort Devens dragged by. Upon arrival he had been fed, clothed, and assigned to barracks. In the ensuing days he was given shots and a battery of written tests. The rest of the time was spent on meaningless work details and absorbing continued harassment from NCO's.

He was told by some of his neighbors—veterans of World War II—before he left to expect harassment before and during basic training.

They were right. He made up his mind to grin and bear it, although on several occasions he had to struggle with himself not to throw a few punches.

It took three weeks of processing before he got orders to pack his gear and prepare to ship out. His group was to depart the next morning for Augusta, Georgia, where he would receive his basic training at Camp Gordon.

The full flight on the DC-3 from Boston to Augusta was Jimmy's first plane trip. He found it exciting. He thought the flight was smooth and uneventful, but a few of the hicks on the plane became ill and were vomiting into bags. One man was even given oxygen to breathe, although Jimmy couldn't imagine why. He himself could breathe just fine.

The recruits were herded into three buses at the Augusta airport and in 40 minutes reached an entrance to Camp Gordon. The buses made their way through the camp, eventually stopping in front of a barracks area, and the men were told to grab their gear and put it on the sidewalk. They were herded next into a mess hall.

Jimmy was famished. He had eaten breakfast at 0500 and nothing since other than a candy bar. He ignored the clamor of the mess-hall—several NCO's verbally expressing their authority over their new charges—and loaded his tray with everything that was offered. He was a little ticked at the manner in which the servers slopped the food onto the partitioned tray, but said nothing.

Jimmy sat at the first available table and ate quickly, fearful that he would be told to depart before he finished. Once he had eaten his fill, he took the time to glance around at the others at his table and at the tables nearby. It was evident there were a large number of Negroes in this group; maybe as many as 30. It had not occurred to him before that he would be eating with them.

He left the table, dip-rinsed his tray as instructed, stacked it, and lined up outside with the others in his group in the area where they had stowed their gear. They were told to pick up their possessions and led into a barracks and assigned bunks.

The six Negroes on his floor in his barracks stuck together and selected the bunks at the far end, three on each side. Jimmy dropped his gear in front of the second bunk at the front of the barracks. He nodded to the two white men who located on either side of him, but said nothing.

The men were hustled to the Company supply building, issued two blankets and a pillow, and told to move double-time back to their bunks. A Corporal and a Sergeant were screaming at them to get their gear put away and get their beds made.

It was a hot, rotten first day in Camp Gordon, Georgia.

It took 3 days, during which time other inductees arrived, to make up his Basic Training Company. Those 3 days were filled with KP duty and endless police-the-area gambits, all intended to humble the hardiest.

It was during this period that Master Sergeant Isaac Berringer made himself known.

Berringer was a career army man, with more than 13 years service. He was a large man, perhaps 5 feet 11 inches or 6 feet tall, weighed well over 200 pounds, and was probably well-muscled in his younger years, when he was a drill sergeant prior to World War II. He had seen action during that war, and wore a chest full of ribbons on his dress uniform.

He was now 31 years old, more than slightly overweight, and the bearer of a mean temper and a bitter disposition.

What bothered Jimmy was that Berringer was a Negro.

The scuttlebutt was that Berringer had been severely reprimanded a year or so before, and busted because of unwarranted actions against several white soldiers. Only his unblemished war-time record, and a CO from Alabama who didn't want to stir up a race agenda, had allowed him to escape a court martial. Berringer had gotten off with only a temporary loss of rank, but he felt he had been railroaded.

Berringer had been transferred to a new Company and a new CO, but he wasn't a man to forgive or to forget, or for that matter, to change.

He felt he could get along with whites, both Officers and Enlisted Men, as long as he was being treated as an equal.

What he hated most were the white men who by their manner and look implied they were superior. They left him on the verge of losing control.

He had two such individuals in his last basic-training group; an 18-year-old New York Jew and a 20-year-old New Jersey Italian who never kept their mouths shut. They had nearly caused him another run-in with the brass.

Now he was with a new Company and had new fodder to contend with—a big Irish bastard from some hick town near Boston, Massachusetts.

He had noticed Jimmy O'Brien the first week of basic training. Over 6-feet tall, good-looking for a white, and the ever-present look in his eyes that said "I'm superior!" He'd be careful how he handled this one, but handle him he would.

As the days went by, it was evident to Berringer that O'Brien was an athlete. The way he did the ever-increasing calisthenic rituals with surprising ease, and the way he moved in the touch football games when the men were on break, indicated he was in top shape and talented. Nobody was close to his time when the men ran the obstacle course.

These observations would only have been of passing interest to Berringer if it hadn't been for the look and the half-smirk that a goading produced when directed at O'Brien. He knew he had another one of those smart-ass whites who thought he was better than anyone else—including him.

Well, we'll see, he thought. But I'll be real careful and real patient.

Saturday morning inspections were a ritual, and Master Sergeant Isaac Berringer, clipboard in hand—dressed to perfection with brass buttons, brass buckle, and insignias ablaze—and wearing mirror-polished combat boots entered the barracks. He was followed by the Company Commander, Captain Grether, and the First Officer, Lieutenant Johnson.

The barracks' NCO shouted a crisp "Attention!" and the men snapped to a rigidly erect position aside their open footlockers, the top shelves displaying neatly rolled socks and underwear as well as their toilet articles. The Captain and the Lieutenant moved quickly from soldier to soldier, glancing at haircuts, checking for clean-shaven faces, and observing uniforms and accessories. Occasionally one or the other officer would make a comment to Sergeant Berringer, and Berringer would make a notation on his pad.

Berringer would periodically approach a clothes rack behind a bunk and examine the clothes, or look under the bunk for any signs of dirt or lint. Invariably, when the officers were in front of Private O'Brien, Berringer selected him for his own personal inspection, and always found a misplaced hair or lint ball or wrinkle in the blanket, and cited this infraction verbally as he listed it on his notepad.

Jimmy and the other men who had been written up would find themselves on extended KP duty the next day.

As Sunday was the only day the men had to catch up on their rest or leisurely visit the PX, it was the day they all looked forward to.

Jimmy found himself on KP every Sunday from the third week of basic training until the eighth. Peter Boudrois, who occupied the bunk across the aisle from Jimmy, swore he saw Berringer place a fuzz ball under Jimmy's bed. Jimmy told him to forget it; he would only get himself on Berringer's shit list.

Bob Barrie, who bunked next to Jimmy and looked up to him with near hero-worship, asked Jimmy why Berringer was on his ass all the time. Jimmy gave a half-smile and answered, "I guess he just doesn't like the Irish."

But Jimmy knew the reason. On the second Sunday of their basic training period there was a pick-up tag football game in which Jimmy had reluctantly agreed to play. Four of the Negroes in the barracks had challenged Peter Boudrois to a friendly game and Peter had enlisted Bob Barrie and Doug Peterson. They wanted Jimmy to play but he had refused.

The comment made by one of the opposition team members, who said "forget that chicken and get somebody else," caused Jimmy to change his mind.

During the course of the game Jimmy caught two touchdown passes and ran down Bobo Simpson from behind, preventing him from scoring what appeared to be a sure touchdown.

On the next play, a furious Bobo threw a vicious elbow at Jimmy. Jimmy saw it coming and neatly cast the blow aside, and with one short, swift, powerful jab knocked Bobo senseless.

Everyone stopped in his tracks, and Jimmy, controlling the rush of adrenaline, turned to face Bobo's teammates.

"He swung at me first and I protected myself. As far as I'm concerned, that's the end of it, unless any of you saw it differently."

Bobo's three buddies looked at one another, somehow mentally communicating, before one of them spoke for the group. "That's the way it was. No argument from us. Bobo's just got a short fuse."

The three black boys gathered around the slowly awakening Bobo, helped him to his feet and assisted him back to the barracks.

Jimmy's teammates attempted to show their approval, but he silenced them with an outstretched palm as he walked to a nearby bench, picked up his sweatshirt and headed to the PX.

Sergeant Berringer had witnessed the incident from his car parked some distance away and concluded that O'Brien must have initiated the fight by something he did or said.

I'll take care of you, buddy, you can bet on that, Berringer said to himself, as he started his engine and drove away.

CHAPTER 24

PEMBERTON
OCTOBER, 1949

Buddy frequently saw Doreen in one of his study periods and developed a crush on her. She knew how to dress to emphasize her figure, which aroused him, and he felt that she and he would hit it off well if she would give him the opportunity. He had always considered her attractive and decided to make his pitch now as he heard earlier in the morning that she had broken off with Charlie Sheehan.

"Hi Doreen, how you doing?" he said as they both approached the entrance door to the study hall.

"Oh, Hi, Buddy," she said with a smile, "doing just fine," and she entered the room in front of him, exaggerating her hip movement as she made her way to her assigned seat. Buddy thought the movement was for him, but in reality it was for every male in the study hall, including Mr. Rosen, the French teacher.

Buddy took the seat next to her and leaned over to talk. "How about going out Saturday night? Maybe a movie or bowling; whichever you'd like."

She eyed him briefly before answering. "Buddy, to me you're Jimmy's kid brother. Sorry, but that's the way it is. By the way, where is he now?"

Her reply hurt him deeply. He was angry and struggled not to show it. With difficulty, he answered that Jimmy was in Georgia. He added in an obviously agitated tone that he was sorry that she felt that way. Doreen smiled and shrugged her shoulders, indicating that was the way it was. Buddy was no longer hurt—he was furious.

Several days later, at recess, he was eating lunch alone, as Sean was at a Camera Club meeting. He sensed someone approaching, and looked up and into the smiling face of Doreen Kelly.

"Hi Buddy. Mind if I join you?"

"Suit yourself," he answered coolly.

Doreen sat down next to him, and moved close so that no one would hear her. "I want to apologize for the way I acted the last time we talked. I was dreadful and way out of line and really didn't mean what I said. I was just having a bad day, and I took it out on you."

"Forget it, Doreen. I have," he replied, slightly mollified, but obviously touchy.

"No, I won't forget it. I was terribly mean and I'm not really like that. I want to apologize and I would really like to go out with you. Let's go to a movie Saturday night, okay?"

Buddy was surprised at her change of heart, but she appeared sincere. He knew she and Charlie were no longer an item, but she was popular and would have no problem finding male companionship. And here she was, asking him out. He was flattered, and decided that he had nothing to lose.

"Sure, Doreen, I'll call you Friday night and we'll decide on the time and the place."

"Great," Doreen said enthusiastically. "Call me Friday," and as she rose to leave, she reached over and pinched the lobe of his ear. He was both flabbergasted and embarrassed, and as she walked away he turned and glanced around to see if anyone had noticed. Apparently not, he sighed with relief, and then broke out in a rare smile.

Their first date went well; better than either of them anticipated. They found they had a great deal in common; both being overshadowed by their best friends, as Jimmy and Sally had always captured the limelight.

Soon after Doreen and Buddy became a constant two-some and a month later were going steady, although they kept that to themselves.

Sean was initially annoyed with Buddy's new affiliation, but soon realized that it was the best thing that could have happened, for now he was left to do as he wanted rather than accommodate the every whim of a difficult friend.

CHAPTER 25

CAMP GORDON, GEORGIA
DECEMBER, 1949

Jimmy completed his basic training in early December and was transferred across the camp to the 225th Signal Support Company. Before the transfer he left a message to be delivered to Sergeant Isaac Berringer.

Jimmy looked forward to starting his Field Radio Repair Course when the next 13 week cycle would begin the first of the year.

Even better news was he would be going home for 2 weeks over the Christmas-New Year Holidays.

His furlough began on Wednesday afternoon, December 21, and after hours of waiting in seemingly endless lines at the Augusta airport, he was on a plane headed for Boston.

He arrived at Logan Airport in the early hours of the following day, some seven hours later than expected. It took another half-hour before his duffel bag showed up, and he used the time to call home, where Buddy had been waiting for his call. Buddy and Sean had taken the day off from school, and Dan O'Brien had left the car home so Buddy could make the run to the airport.

Buddy picked up Sean and 45 minutes later they were at Logan.

The airport was a zoo. Servicemen and civilians were in various stages of transit, and parking was impossible. The State Police monitoring the drop-off and pick-up areas were short-tempered and unfriendly. Buddy dropped Sean off to locate Jimmy in the baggage area, and told him he would keep circling the airport until he spotted them on the sidewalk outside the baggage area.

It took three cycles before he saw Sean and his brother waving from the sidewalk. Buddy thought Jimmy looked taller and broader than ever, and grudgingly admitted to himself that the bastard was a good-looking son-of-a-bitch.

Buddy triple parked while the boys entered the car. Jimmy threw his duffel bag into the back seat with Sean and made his way into the front-seat passenger side. A loud blast from a whistle broke up their initial greeting, and Buddy shifted the car into gear and pulled away from the fast-approaching angry trooper.

"That's a mean looking giant son-of-a-bitch of a cop," Sean exclaimed, and they all laughed.

The ride back to Pemberton passed quickly, with Jimmy doing most of the talking. He told them about Sergeant Berringer and all the extra duty he had to perform because of that bastard, and how he never let Berringer see his anger, and he knew he was driving Berringer crazy.

He told them Berringer had been transferred to Japan shortly after Jimmy's group had completed basic training. Jimmy explained that Captain Grether, the Company Commander, had heard how the Sergeant had mistreated certain trainees by creating excuses to lay on unwarrantable special duties, such as five successive weekends of KP on a certain private. They laughed again when Jimmy told them it must have been a little Irish birdie that got hold of the Captain's ear.

Mary O'Brien, her face beaming and teary eyed, greeted Jimmy warmly. She had missed her first-born but, as was her wont, never let anyone in on her inner feelings.

Buddy, noting how Jimmy seemed to tower over everybody, thought when the old man comes home from work he's in for a surprise. He'll never lay an unfriendly hand on him again and get away with it; that's for sure.

The problem wouldn't happen, for Dan O'Brien had mellowed. He hadn't been feeling well and had cut down on his drinking after Doc Sullivan warned him of the consequences.

Dan arrived home after 5:30 in the evening and greeted Jimmy with a hug, which was somewhat of a surprise to all of them. He never had been one to show much in the way of affection.

"Of all the days in the week, they had to call a union meeting the day my son comes home," Dan cursed. He explained attendance was a must and he did not want to jeopardize his position with a no-show in front of the executive committee.

Sean was invited to stay for dinner, and as they all sat around the dining room table, Jimmy gave them the account of his first 4 months in the military. He told them of the rigid discipline and physical demands he experienced during basic training, and how his life after completing basic training had improved. He told them he loved what he was doing.

Dan asked Jimmy a question that had been on his mind since Jimmy left.

"What about the niggers, Jimmy. You don't have to live and eat with them, do you?"

"Sure do, Dad, but they usually group together at one end of the barracks and in the mess hall. They keep pretty much together with their own."

"Sons of bitches," Dan O'Brien uttered in a raised voice. "You stay away from them, and watch your back."

Jimmy nodded. He repeated for his father what he had told Buddy and Sean earlier about Sergeant Berringer. Dan cursed loudly and frowned, but when Jimmy told the story about Bobo Simpson and the football game, his father smiled broadly and said, "Good for you."

The gathering broke up after 9:00 p.m., and shortly thereafter they all turned in.

Jimmy awoke refreshed Friday morning and an hour later set out to visit Pemberton High. He saw a few of his old football mates as he walked the halls and they were genuinely happy to see him. He spied Coach Wilzinski gazing at him from a distance, but ignored him by turning away.

Jimmy waited for Sean and Buddy at noontime, and the trio sat together in the lunch room. Jimmy was pleased that many students, including ones he didn't know but who knew him, stopped by the table to say hello and to chat a bit.

At one point, he felt a tap on his shoulder and turned around to see the smiling faces of Sally Marsh and Doreen Kelley.

"Can we join you?" Sally asked brazenly, "or is this just boy talk?"

"Sure, sit down," Jimmy answered with a Hollywood smile.

Sally squeezed into the seat next to Jimmy, intentionally brushing a breast against his arm, an act noticed by Doreen as well as Buddy and Sean. She was dressed in a knee-length red and black pleated wool skirt and an off-white cable turtleneck form-fitting sweater that left nothing to the imagination. She was pretty; she was vivacious; she was well endowed—and she knew it and used it.

"How's the Army?" she asked. "It seems to have done you a lot of good. You look very fit."

"Thanks," he answered politely. "The Army is fine, I'm fine, and I'm enjoying myself. How about you? I hear you're getting married in June, after you graduate. Congratulations."

Sally flushed slightly, taken back by his nonchalance. "Thank you. What about you? Anybody special in your life?"

He answered without hesitation. "They're all special in my life, Sally."

This brought grins to Buddy's and Sean's faces and the touch of a smile to Doreen's.

"To tell the truth, Sally," Jimmy continued, "I haven't had the time or the desire to look for a meaningful relationship. But now that I'm in Radio School, I'll have most of my weekends off, and time to socialize."

He abruptly turned to Doreen, who was sitting next to Buddy and listening silently but attentively to every word being said. "You look great, Doreen. How's everything going with you?"

The sudden attention caught Doreen by surprise, but she managed to utter a weak, "Fine, thank you."

"Great," Jimmy continued. "The way you look, the guys should be breaking down your front door."

Doreen was now completely flustered. She blurted out an embarrassed "thank you" that was barely audible. Jimmy gave her his warmest smile, and Sally burned.

The bell rang, announcing the end of recess, and the group broke up. Before Sally left she touched Jimmy's arm to get his attention and, speaking softly so only he could hear, said, "Call me tonight at 7:00. I want to talk to you. It's important."

Jimmy looked at her without answering, causing her to repeat herself.

"It *is* important. Will you call me?"

"Okay," he said, wondering what could be so important, "I'll call you."

Sally smiled, turned away and with hips swaying, walked to her next class.

Jimmy called at 7:00, and Sally answered on the first ring. After a brief exchange, she got to the point. "I wasn't very kind when we broke up, and I've felt badly for a long time about the way I behaved. We had a lot of good times together and I owe you an explanation. I would feel much better about it if I could speak to you face to face. Will you come over?"

"When?"

"Now."

"Yeah, I guess so. I'd like to say hello to your folks anyway."

"They're not home. They just left to play bingo."

"Oh, I forgot. Things never change around here. Okay, I'll walk over in about 15 minutes."

"Thanks, Jimmy."

"Yeah. Okay." He hung up and went in to wash up and brush his hair. He smiled as he looked in the mirror, thinking his hair looked better than the first time the Army cut it. He told his folks he was going out for a walk and would be back a little later.

Sally opened the door before Jimmy had a chance to ring the doorbell. She escorted him into the parlor, took his coat and threw it over the top of a chair as she passed by, and pointed for him to sit on the couch. There were potato chips and pretzels in plastic bowls displayed on a mahogany-lacquered coffee table in front of the couch.

"You want a beer?" she asked.

"Sure."

She returned moments later with two bottles of Harvard beer and two tall glasses.

"I'll drink mine from the bottle, if you don't mind," he said, and proceeded to do so.

Sally poured her beer into a glass and set the bottle on the table. She took a healthy swallow and sat down next to him.

She had carefully dressed in a tan woolen skirt and a white short-sleeve blouse with one-too-many buttons undone. A touch of perfume and a careful make-up job had been administered 10 minutes earlier, and she was satisfied with the results. She wasn't exactly sure of what she intended to do, but hormonal urges that she hadn't experienced to this degree before she saw him earlier in the day were influencing her.

"Jimmy, what I want to talk to you about is not easy for me to say, but I want you to know the truth. I didn't break up with you because you got hurt and wouldn't be able to get a scholarship and go to college and be the football star you wanted to be. It's that I had decided long ago I want to be somebody special and have nice things. I want a big, beautiful home and an expensive car and I want to be able to travel to far off countries and vacation whenever I want to, without having to worry about where the money is coming from. I can't and won't live the life your mother and my mother live.

"The only way I can do that is by marrying someone with a lot of money, and that's what I'm going to do. Alfie's an only child and his father owns one of the biggest tanneries in the state, and is probably the wealthiest man in the area. Alfie's very nice and I know he loves me and I know we can make each other happy. He's also smart and ambitious and he treats me like a lady. I know this must sound awful to you, but it's the kind of life I really want, and that's why…"

Jimmy raised his hand for her to stop. He had heard enough, and although he had once been angry with her, he didn't really care anymore. He was far from considering marriage, and never had any intention of settling down with her and giving up his own dreams. Yes, he had felt hurt for a few days, but that was long ago and long gone from his mind.

"Sally, thanks for being honest with me. Maybe I was hurt at the time, but so was my body, and I was in too much pain to discuss anything with you. I admire you for doing with your life what you want to do with it, and I don't blame you. In fact, I wish you all the luck in the world."

Sally was thrilled with his answer and threw her arms around him and kissed him; a long, lingering kiss.

They felt the electricity simultaneously. They had kissed many times before, but not like this. This was total abandonment and lips parted and tongues touched. He pulled her closer to him, so now their upper bodies were crushed together. She felt the power in his arms and the hardness of his chest, and he felt the softness of her breasts molding into his body.

Her nipples enlarged and hardened, as did his erection. He carefully unbuttoned her blouse, never taking his mouth from hers, and met no resistance. He nervously but skillfully unsnapped her bra, and tenderly covered each breast with his massive hands. She placed her left hand against his throbbing penis that was straining against trousers that were now uncomfortably tight.

He murmured softly, "I want you, Sally."

"I want you too, Jimmy. Please don't hurt me."

They made love urgently and passionately, each finding their fulfillment more than they had hoped for.

Afterward, they lie together for several minutes, catching their breath and reveling in the feelings they had experienced.

"That was wonderful, Jimmy. Unbelievably wonderful."

"Sally, you were wonderful."

"Thanks. You better let me get up and clean up a bit. I don't want anyone walking in on us looking like this."

Jimmy smirked. "That would be something, wouldn't it. Both of us caught with our pants down."

Sally laughed heartily.

He got up and located his boxer shorts and put them on.

Sally rose, gathered her strewn clothing and headed for the bathroom. "I'll be out in a few minutes and then you can get in here. While your waiting, smooth out the cushions on the couch. They look like hell."

Sally rejoined him almost 10 minutes later, looking fit and proper. "Your turn, lover."

Jimmy kissed her on the cheek and said, "I'll be right out."

She checked the couch carefully for any tell-tale evidence and was pleased to find no stains.

When Jimmy returned she said facetiously, "Assuming you put your underwear back on properly, I guess everything is back the way it was."

Jimmy smiled. "Everything is back where it belongs, I assure you."

She picked up the empty beer bottles and glasses and carried them into the kitchen. "You want another beer, or would you prefer cake and milk?" she called out.

"Cake and milk sounds good to me," he answered, suddenly hungry.

"Come in the kitchen. I don't want to leave crumbs all over the place."

Jimmy did as he was asked and walked into the kitchen and took a seat at the table. She poured two glasses of milk, set them on the table, and returned to the counter to cut one monstrous slice of chocolate cake for him and a sliver for herself. She placed everything on the table and made one last trip to get forks and paper napkins.

"There," she said as she took the seat next to him, "a meal fit for a king." They ate silently, occasionally gazing at one another, waiting for someone to speak.

After a few minutes, Jimmy said, "Sally, that was unbelievably great. I just want to say that I think maybe you and I…"

Sally stopped him by raising a finger and placing it vertically to her lips. "Please don't say anything, Jimmy. What happened was that two people who like each other got emotional and—and fulfilled a need. Believe me when I tell you it was wonderful; better than I ever dreamed it would be, and I'm glad my first time was with you. But it doesn't change my plans. What I told you I wanted I still want. Don't say anything or do anything to spoil it for me."

Jimmy felt relieved. He had supposed that their love-making might have meant that she wanted to start up with him again and he had no intention of making any commitment. She had clarified the situation and he was off the hook.

"I understand, Sally, and I wish you the best. What happened between us was great. It's a time I'll never forget."

"Nor will I," Sally answered. "And don't worry about anything; I was careful with my count."

Jimmy nodded knowingly, but wasn't sure he knew what she was talking about.

"Jimmy, there's something else I want to talk to you about," Sally said hesitantly. "Doreen brought it up at lunch the other day, and I assured her that you guys weren't involved, but I've got to ask. What about those two guys that you had the basketball game with a couple of years ago?"

Jimmy fought with himself to show complete indifference to the question and thought he succeeded.

"I don't understand. What about them?"

"I mean," Sally continued, "I-I think it's crazy, but you don't think that your brother or Sean could have been involved in that hit-and-run with that black kid, do you? Doreen thought it an odd coincidence that both the guys who were killed were the guys that you played basketball against."

"Jesus, Sally, you can't possibly think that any of us would do anything like that. That's crazy," he added convincingly.

"That's what I said. I told her that she was terrible to even think like that. She said she knew it, but the thought had entered her mind. I told her I hoped she never said that to anyone and she told me that she hadn't and wouldn't. Then she admitted it was an addlebrained notion."

"I guess it was. God, she's got a crazy imagination. I thought she liked us."

"Of course she does, Jimmy. You know she's been dating your brother, and she really likes him. She thinks he likes her a lot too."

"No, I didn't know. Buddy and I haven't had a chance to talk much since I've been back."

He thought that was typical of Buddy. Buddy wanted to know everybody else's business but kept his own doings to himself.

Sally changed the subject, and asked Jimmy about his Army experiences. They talked for another half-hour, laughing frequently, as Jimmy related some of the highlights of his 4 months in the military.

They had truly enjoyed the evening; every aspect of it.

Jimmy noticed it was nearly 10:30 and decided it was time to go.

"Sorry I missed your folks, Sally. Please say hello for me. I've got to get up early tomorrow and get in some last minute shopping, so I'd better get going. When does Alfie get home?"

"Tomorrow. His leather convention was over at noon today, but he was staying over to wine and dine some of his customers and is planning to catch an early morning plane. We've got a Christmas party at his Club tomorrow night…"

"Give him my regards and…on second thought, you'd better not."

Sally smiled. Rising from her chair, she went to him and gave him a kiss on the cheek. "Goodnight, Jimmy, and good-bye. I hope this evening will always be our secret."

Jimmy rose easily from his chair. "Of course, Sally; and good luck."

She walked him to the front door and opened it.

He waved goodbye as he left, and walked home with a smile on his face.

##

The boys met in the clubhouse at 10:00 the next morning.

"The place looks the same," Jimmy said. "I've missed being here."

"We've missed you, Jimmy," Sean answered, "haven't we Buddy?"

Buddy nodded apathetically.

Jimmy wasted no time in broaching the subject on his mind, changing only a few of the facts to honor a promise. "I went out for a walk last night and bumped into Sally. I wanted to say hello to her folks, so she invited me in. Her folks were on their way out, and after they left Sally and I got talking, and she mentioned something that disturbed me. She said Doreen asked her if we could have had anything to do with the Robinson accident."

"Jesus!" Sean blurted out.

Buddy leaned forward, a concerned look on his face. "What did Sally say?"

"Sally told her that was a terrible thing to say, and hoped she hadn't said it to anyone else. Doreen said she hadn't, but the thought had crossed her mind. Later she admitted it was a stupid thing to think."

"Sally seem okay, or was she asking for herself?" Buddy wanted to know.

"Sally was okay; I'm sure of it. But I don't know about Doreen," Jimmy answered. "I understand you're dating her pretty steady. What do you think?"

Buddy's face reddened and a slight grin appeared. "Yeah, I haven't had a chance to tell you but Doreen and I have been pretty thick for a while."

Sean looked at him with a quizzical expression. "What do you mean by 'thick?'"

Buddy shrugged his shoulders. "You're so damn busy with your books and your own little world that you never notice anything. Doreen mentioned the basketball game to me last week, and I assured her that the aftermath had nothing to do with us. I told her we were all together at the Willows that night. She felt relieved and later apologized for letting such an idea enter her mind. You don't have to worry about her. By the way, I might just marry her in a year or two."

"You, married?" Sean exclaimed in a cracking voice, which broke the tension and provoked smiles.

"Okay," Jimmy concluded, "you're sure about Doreen and I'm sure about Sally. That ends it."

"One other item before we go," Buddy said. "My last class on Friday was a study period, which Coach Wilzinski monitors. He came over to me just before the end of the period and wanted to know how you were doing. He said he was disappointed that you chose not to stop by and see him."

"The guy expected me to visit him?" Jimmy voiced angrily. "That son-of-a-bitch has got a lot of nerve."

"Sure does," Sean agreed.

"Yeah, I thought so too," Buddy added. "I told him you were your own man, and did what you wanted to do. He looked at me kind of funny, then turned around and walked away without saying anything else. I guess I teed him off. Anyway, he got the message."

"Good for you. I owe him, and I won't forget it," Jimmy said.

"You're home another week," Buddy said. "You want to cause the Coach some grief?"

Before Jimmy could answer, Sean chimed in. "I don't think that's a good idea. If anything happened to the Coach while Jimmy's home on furlough, then Doreen and Sally might get suspicious again. They know that Jimmy's teed-off at the Coach."

"Yeah, you're probably right," Buddy conceded. "Maybe after you go back to Georgia…"

"I told you, 'No!'" Jimmy stated emphatically. "There's no rush; I'll get to him. I appreciate the offer, but we'll wait."

Buddy shrugged. "Okay. As you wish."

Sean let out a sigh of relief.

CHAPTER 26

PEMBERTON
FEBRUARY, 1950

After Jimmy returned to the army, Buddy re-assumed Jimmy's leadership role.

Sean resented it, but with Buddy spending most of his free time with Doreen, there were seldom any confrontations.

Sean was left pretty much to himself, and he began to enjoy his new-found freedom.

Buddy and he didn't have many close friends in school, and neither one cared. Most of their classmates didn't like Buddy as he always wanted to be in charge and wanted things done his way.

Sean didn't fit in well because he was basically an introvert. He would just as soon stay home and read as mix with the guys. He enjoyed his interest in photography and his membership in the school Camera Club, but that was the limit of his participation in school activities.

Sean's only interest outside of school was in his church's ski club.

On Saturday mornings, from mid-December through March, the club would bus to North Conway, New Hampshire to spend a full day on the slopes. Some of the adult skiers would give lessons, and after several weeks of instruction Sean found that he could manage quite nicely. His skiing improved with each trip, and soon he was quite comfortable skiing from the top of both the North and South slopes of Mount Cranmore.

Sean's parents were happy to give him the money to participate in the ski club, but for different reasons. Phil Boyle wanted him away from Eileen's constant pampering and Eileen wanted him away from Buddy O'Brien.

Buddy and Doreen now spent a good part of each weekend together. Doreen remained friendly with Sally in school, but on the weekends they went their own way. They didn't double date because Sally's boyfriend Alfie didn't like Buddy.

Each girl had found her niche, and it worked out well for both.

CHAPTER 27

CAMP GORDON, GEORGIA
APRIL, 1950

Jimmy's radio repair school course was abbreviated as his signal company unit received orders to go to Japan. They were to become part of the U.S. Army Occupation Forces. He arrived in Tokyo on April 21, 1950, never imagining that in less than 3 months all hell would break loose in Korea.

On the night of June 24, 1950 the Democratic People's Republic of Korea covertly moved a large force of personnel and equipment close to the 38th Parallel. On June 25th a force estimated at nearly one hundred thousand men swarmed across the 38th Parallel and overwhelmed the South Korean forces.

The United Nations Security Council quickly passed a resolution calling for all United Nations members to aid in stopping the North Korean invasion, and on June 27th,

President Truman committed U.S. Forces as part of the United Nations "Police Action."

Jimmy's unit was assigned to an infantry group assembled in Japan for a rapid transport to Korea. Most of his unit were armed only with light weaponry. Jimmy carried an M-1 rifle and as much ammo as he could manage in addition to his radio communications equipment.

The troops arrived in Pusan and quickly embarked by train to Taejon, a half-day's trip away. After a brief rest in Taejon they boarded a second train and headed north to an area near Osan, below Suwon. Here they joined another infantry group and set-up camp.

Jimmy had the shock of his life an hour later when he came face to face with a familiar face. Master Sergeant Isaac Berringer.

Berringer had a long memory, and smiled as he recognized his former adversary.

"Dig in now and dig in deep," he instructed Jimmy's group. "There's no time for you men to have a smoke so don't ask. I don't want to hear any kind of bitching over weather, gear or food. And you, O'Brien—don't you open your fucking mouth about nothing."

"I never said anything," Jim shot back automatically.

"See, you asshole, you'll never learn. I told you to keep your mouth shut and 2 seconds later you mouth off. I'll break your ass before this war is over—if you live that long. Now you keep your mouth shut and do what you're told."

Jimmy fought off the desire to deck Berringer.

This is not the time, he told himself, but if the gooks don't get him, I sure as hell will. One way or the other, he's going to be a dead son-of-a-bitch.

Berringer continued to stare at Jimmy with a sneer on his hate-filled face. “You got something else to say, white boy? Say it now or do it now, if you got the guts.” He said this from 6 feet away, with a carbine swinging in his hand, its barrel now on the upswing, aimed at Jimmy’s mid-section.

Jimmy glared back unafraid, anger building in every fiber of his body. Now’s not the time, he told himself, but soon, you bastard, soon.

Jimmy suddenly smiled. “You’re the boss, Sergeant,” and turned and walked away, leaving Berringer talking to himself.

Jimmy worked most of that night and into the early morning hours under a light but steady rain, and was exhausted when he finally turned in. Berringer was never far from his thoughts.

Jimmy was awakened in what seemed minutes. A report had come down that there was enemy movement heading their way, and it was identified as a large tank column.

It didn’t take long before the report was verified. When the enemy tanks were within range, the Americans forces opened up with every weapon at their disposal, but had little effect in halting the mass of armored vehicles bearing down on them. The tanks rumbled through, seeking out the heavy artillery further to the rear, intent on demolishing those weapons and attacking Osan.

More than 50 Americans were killed or wounded in the first half hour.

It got worse. As the Americans regrouped, a large force of enemy infantry was en route, supported by additional tanks. The Americans were ordered to hold fast and delay the enemy as long as possible.

Within an hour, the new battle began, and the American Forces threw a deadly combination of mortar and machine gun fire at the advancing enemy infantry. By mid-afternoon, outnumbered and outgunned, more than one hundred men of Jimmy's unit had been killed or wounded. The rest were near exhaustion, nearly out of ammunition, and hemmed in on three sides by a vastly superior force.

The order came to fall back. There was unrestrained pandemonium. Soldiers were retreating, in many cases discarding cumbersome equipment in their haste to flee to a safer zone.

It was at this time Jimmy spotted Sergeant Berringer ahead of him. Berringer was headed in the same direction as Jimmy was, and running like a college fullback. Instantly Jimmy's mind was made up. He pursued Berringer down a hill and as Berringer sloshed his way through a small rice paddy, Jimmy fired a round from his M-1 rifle through the back of Berringer's neck.

Glancing around, Jimmy saw other retreating soldiers in the distance, but no one who seemed to have witnessed the incident. They were too busy fleeing before the advancing North Koreans.

He approached where Berringer lie, face down, and turned him over. Blood was everywhere, spreading over the sergeant's neck, face, and the surrounding water.

There was no breath—there was no life—there was only finality.

Jimmy turned and jogged away, before the blood had a chance to soil his sopping-wet boots.

"Goodbye, Sergeant Berringer," he mouthed, the trace of a smirk on his embittered face.

He made his way up a small hill and on the other side joined three other fleeing American soldiers. The four were heading up a ridge when a burst of enemy machine gun fire erupted behind them. Jimmy was struck by two rounds, one in his left arm and one in his left shoulder, and knocked to the ground. The soldier in back of him had caught the brunt of the fire and was killed.

The other two soldiers somehow escaped the deadly fire and dropped to the earth uninjured. They crawled over to Jimmy, applied a tourniquet to his profusely bleeding arm, and affixed first-aid packs to both his wounds. With difficulty they guided him several hundred yards beyond the next ridge where they joined up with the main body of the surviving unit.

Jimmy received additional, but cursory, medical attention and a shot of morphine before being loaded into a military vehicle along with other seriously wounded soldiers for evacuation to Pyongtaek. En route, he passed out from loss of blood and exhaustion.

In Pyontaek, the news was not good. North Korean tank forces were still advancing and would be arriving soon. The truck convoy of wounded was ordered farther south, through Songhwan, and on to Chonan.

There they were attended to by doctors. Jimmy was told that both bullets had passed clear through. He required stitches and several units of blood, and was heavily medicated.

There was little time to recuperate at the MASH (Mobile Army Surgical Hospital) facility because of the advancing enemy. The next day the wounded were again loaded onto trucks and driven further south.

Retreat was still the order of the day. Jimmy's truck convoy was headed to Taejon.

He rested on his cot in a daze and in pain, listening to the news and the rumors with total disinterest.

One actual day of war had been an eternity. The cacophony of screaming artillery shells, machine-gun fire and rumbling tanks, coupled with the screeches of wounded and dying soldiers had been a nightmare.

He thought his wounds were not life-threatening, but his pain was real, and the frequent jostling of the lumbering truck caused him to vomit frequently. Between the pain and the stomach discomfort, he was miserable all the way to Taejon.

His stay in Taejon lasted only a few days as the wounded were next evacuated to Pusan. Rumor had it the more seriously wounded were to be flown to Japan, and Jimmy prayed that he would be one of them.

The only positive that had come out of the prior week was the dispatch of one Sergeant Isaac Berringer.

On July 10th the Security Council of the United Nations named General Douglas MacArthur Commander and Chief of United Nations' Forces. It was the same day that Jimmy was shipped to Tokyo for convalescent care.

CHAPTER 28

PEMBERTON
JUNE, 1950

Buddy and Sean graduated Pemberton High School, each looking forward to the future. The boys faithfully remained in touch, although their interests continued to be dissimilar.

Buddy had maintained his good grades without over-extending himself.

Sean had to work much harder, and did, because he planned to go to college. His choice was Northeastern, in the heart of Boston, because it offered a program of school work and practical work. This would allow him to obtain on-the-job training and earn money, which would help defray the cost of the academic portion of the program.

Buddy knew there was no way he could go to college. His father had made that clear when Jimmy had broached the subject, and now Buddy didn't really care. He had excelled in chemistry and physics only half trying, and he thought now how to best make use of his abilities.

Chemistry was his favorite subject, and he was aware that some of the larger tanneries in Pemberton had their own laboratories. He decided that lab work would be interesting, not physically demanding, and probably pay well. With this in mind he had contacted the Personnel Office of B. D. Barker & Co. a month before graduation, and made an appointment to meet with the Personnel Director.

To his surprise, Mr. Clancy had been more receptive than he had expected. Buddy explained that he enjoyed chemistry and mathematics, and that he currently held an "A" average in chemistry and a "B+" average in math. Clancy remarked that he knew Buddy's father from the Bowling League and asked Buddy why he hadn't sought employment where his father worked.

"Mr. Clancy; seeing you is my first choice and my first interview. I don't think it would be a good idea for me to work in the same place as my father. I might wind up with a better job than he has and he sure wouldn't like that."

Bill Clancy broke out in a fit of laughter. "I like that, Buddy boy—that's a great answer." The balance of the interview went along nicely.

"By the way, was that your brother who was the football star last year?" Clancy asked.

"Yes sir."

"I go to most of the games and have for years. Too bad he got hurt; he was a hell of a player. What's he doing now? I understand he got busted up pretty bad. Hell, if he hadn't been hurt we sure as hell would have had another state championship last year."

"He's doing fine, sir. He's in the army and is overseas," Buddy answered politely, wanting desperately to get off the subject of his brother.

"Good for him," Bill Clancy said approvingly. "Anyway, when school's over, I'll give you a job in our lab. You'll have to join the union. Is that a problem?"

"No, sir," Buddy replied excitedly.

"Good. Oh, one more thing. The head of the lab—the man you'll be working for—is a man named Larry Sandberg. He's a Jew. That a problem?"

Buddy felt his face flush, but tried not to show any emotion. "No, sir. I'm sure I can work with anybody."

Bill Clancy smiled. "Okay. You come and see me after you graduate and you'll have a job. We Irish got to stick together. Right?"

"Yes, sir!" Buddy answered, his face beaming.

On the walk home, Buddy congratulated himself on the way he handled the interview. I'll tell my old man I found a good job after I graduate, but I sure as hell won't tell him I'll be working for a Jew. I don't think he could handle that. Come to think of it, I hope I can, he told himself.

At supper that evening, Buddy told his folks about his interview with Clancy and of the promise of a job when school ended.

"Good company," Dan O'Brien mumbled, his mouth half-full of food. "How much are you going to be paid?"

"I don't know. I didn't ask," Buddy answered honestly.

Dan O'Brien glared at him, shook his head in disbelief, and muttered, "You dumb bastard."

Buddy's face reddened, but he said nothing.

CHAPTER 29

PEMBERTON
JULY, 1950

Sally Marsh and Alfie Dillon were married 3 weeks after she graduated from Pemberton High School. Their wedding gift from Alfie's parents was a 2-week honeymoon trip to Mexico.

Doreen and Buddy attended the wedding and Doreen hadn't acted the same since. She wanted to become engaged, and talked about nothing else. Buddy, usually outspoken in all matters, was feeling dominated and wasn't sure he liked it, but she was more than a match for him.

Doreen was envious of Sally and the lifestyle she was living, but there weren't many wealthy people like Alfie Dillon around to latch on to. She wanted Buddy to do well in his job and get ahead fast so they could marry by next summer. She had no intention of finding herself single much longer with the horrible prospect of winding up an old maid.

Doreen knew how to handle Buddy. She told him how much she was looking forward to getting into bed and making love, and how she wanted them to make love every night. But when Buddy suggested to her that they shouldn't wait, she came down on him like a ton of bricks.

"Don't you ever say such a thing to me," she shouted with fire in her eyes and venom in her tongue. "I will never give up my virginity until we're married. Don't you ever suggest that again."

Buddy, intimidated, mumbled weakly, "I'm sorry."

Then Doreen softened and pulled him close to her and placed his hands on her breasts, bewildering him. "It's not that I don't want to. I have feelings too, you know, but I promised myself not until I'm married." She removed his trembling hands from the softness of her bosom, kissed him on the lips, and told him that she loved him.

She was in complete control when she said "I know you'll do well in your work, and I've applied for a secretarial job at the bank and I'm pretty sure I'll get it. With both of us working we'll be able to afford to get married next summer. That's what I want to do. I want us to have at least five children and I want us to have a fun life together. How does that sound to you?"

Buddy could only agree. He loved her and she had faith in him. He would not disappoint her.

CHAPTER 30

TOKYO, JAPAN
JULY, 1950

Jimmy was recuperating satisfactorily as neither bullet had struck bone and his wounds had not become infected. He experienced soreness and stiffness, especially with his shoulder, but injury was not new to him. When he was able to begin therapy, he did so with enthusiasm. He had always been conscious of his strength and physique, and intended to maintain both.

The nurse in charge was a good-looker, with a hell of a figure that made him look twice. The problem was that she was an officer—a Captain—and he was a PFC, and out of her league. At least he could look, and he did plenty of that.

Captain Janice Carter was 26 years old. She loved her work and she enjoyed being in the military.

She had been engaged to be married twice prior to her entering the Army but had broken off both relationships. She admired both of her fiancees and thought she was in love each time, but when the wedding plans were in the final stages, she reneged. Something deep within warned her not to tie any knots. She couldn't explain it, not even to herself, but she knew she shouldn't marry.

Both fiancees were doctors. She met the first in her initial year as a nurse at Portland Hospital, in Maine. Perhaps the romance had proceeded too swiftly, for after 6 months of frequent dates squeezed into their hectic schedules, she had gone to bed with him and later accepted his proposal of marriage.

Three months later she broke it off, telling him that what she felt was infatuation, and she now realized it wasn't love. He took it hard, but respected her for her honesty. They remained on friendly terms, but no longer dated. Four months later he left, accepting a position in a Chicago hospital.

A year later she met Jerry Scott, a surgical resident at the hospital. She was lonely and needed some one to talk to, and he was a good listener. She also needed male companionship to relieve her passions and frustrations.

He proposed to her after 2 months and she accepted. But once again she broke it off when wedding plans were reaching the final stages. It was not the sexual aspect of the relationship that frightened her. She reluctantly admitted to herself that she was happiest when she lived alone.

One month later, on a whim, she joined the Army.

Janice had been in Japan less than a year and she loved it. The Tokyo U.S. Army Hospital was not especially large, but it was well equipped. Although the staff was not the best that she had ever worked with, she felt they were competent.

The large U.S. Occupation Force stationed in Japan required military hospitals to take care of the needs of the American troops and their families. There had been some quiet periods, but that was sure to change, as the recent events in Korea forebode the possibility of a serious conflict. After the attack by North Korea and the news of the bloody battles taking place, she knew the hospital would soon be very busy.

Janice couldn't help but notice PFC O'Brien as he entered her office in late July and handed her his file. She examined the file, noting his name, age and the extent of his wounds, as he sat silently, eyes glued to her face. When she completed her study she looked up at him and in a pleasant but business-like manner introduced herself.

"I'm Captain Carter. We will do our best to return you to tip-top shape, Private O'Brien. Please stand up and remove your robe. We'll weigh in first and then I want to exam your wounds."

Jimmy rose without a word, removed his robe and got on the scale. He weighed in at 191 pounds and measured 6 feet 3 inches tall. She instructed him to sit on the edge of an examination table and proceded to take his vital signs, noting the results on his paper work. He remained absolutely still, looking straight ahead whenever her gaze returned to his face, but devoured her with his eyes whenever she looked away.

She wore just the slightest trace of perfume but it was enough to create a slight stir in his groin. His face reddened and he hoped she didn't notice. She didn't, but she herself felt somewhat uncomfortable. She hadn't seen a physical specimen the likes of PFC O'Brien in all her years of nursing; great looks and a body to match.

Janice removed the bandages covering his wounds and carefully examined him, nodding positively before applying fresh dressings and re-bandaging. When she finished, she walked to where he had left his robe, retrieved it, and brought it to him.

"Put it on and take a seat," she said, pointing to a chair in front of her desk. She made her way to her chair, sat, and wrote for several minutes before addressing him.

"Your wounds are healing nicely," she said mellifluously. "I think we can get you back in the pink in short order if you follow my instructions to the letter."

She handed him some paperwork as she continued. "You will report for therapy twice daily, at 1000 hours and again at 1400 hours. We'll start you off slowly. It shouldn't be long before you're as good as new. You're dismissed."

Janice watched him purposefully as he left her office. She had been strangely affected by their encounter and hoped it hadn't shown.

Jimmy returned to his hospital ward in good spirits. The thought of doing his therapy anywhere near Captain Carter suited him just fine.

Jimmy's therapist turned out to be a regular army Corporal, Harvey Ossoff, from Boynton Beach, Florida. Harvey was a World War II veteran who had made Sergeant twice, only to lose his stripes both times because of booze and women, "in that order," he explained.

Harvey was average in height at 5 foot 7, with dark skin, a full head of black hair, huge black eyes that appeared ready to pop out, a prominent nose, thick Groucho-like eyebrows, and hands with exceptionally long fingers. He was a likable guy, blessed with a great sense of humor and a winning smile. He told Jimmy that he had spent most of his time during World War II as a medic, and had been on Guam and at Guadalcanal and been exposed to "a lot of hell."

Harvey loved his work and he loved Japan. "I never thought I would ever see the day that I could live with Japanese people," he told Jimmy, "but the civilians are polite and warm—especially the women," he added with a twinkle in his eyes and a contagious laugh. "I'm living with a Japanese woman, and there's no better relationship in the entire world. She never raises her voice. She feeds me, bathes me and makes love to me. Hell, she takes care of me like I was a king."

"It sounds good but it's not for me," Jimmy said. "Give me an Irish girl with a sharp tongue and a mind of her own. That's much more of a challenge, and when you get her into bed you know you have your hands full."

Harvey laughed appreciatively, thinking the kid's probably been laid twice in his life and makes it sound as if he's the world's biggest lover. But with his looks he's got a great future.

Jimmy became serious. "What about Captain Carter? She married or living with anybody? God, she's gorgeous."

"Naw, she's not married and she's not living with anyone. But I can tell you this. There's not a man in the hospital, from General on down, that wouldn't give his eye-teeth and navel to spend a night with her. To my knowledge, and of course I know everything, no one has. She's dated a few of the officers but rumor has it that no one has ever come close, and anyone who has claimed to is automatically branded a liar. She's been here about a year, and she's everybody's first choice. You got any thoughts about her you can forget them. You'd have about as much chance as a mouse has to screw an elephant."

The old expression caused Harvey to burst into a fit of laughter, and Jimmy couldn't help but join in.

The therapy proved painful, but the pain diminished over the ensuing weeks. Jimmy took every available opportunity to talk to Captain Carter about any and every subject that would require a response. She was always polite and occasionally smiled, but he never felt comfortable and couldn't think of a way to improve the relationship.

Several weeks later Harvey announced that Jimmy's supervised rehab program was over and recommended that he continue his exercises on his own. "The gym is open seven days a week, Jimmy, and everything you need is there. Captain Carter wants to see you, so shower up and report to her office at 1630 hours."

Jimmy shook Harvey's hand enthusiastically, and thanked him for his help and support. As he turned and headed for the showers, Harvey had the final word. "Your welcome, Jimmy, and good luck. It takes a nice Jewish boy to straighten out you Irishers. Glad to have been of service."

Jimmy nearly froze in his tracks, but managed not to miss a step.

Jimmy entered Captain Carter's office at 1630 hours. She was behind her desk studying papers. He remained standing—silently admiring her.

When she became conscious of his presence she looked up and smiled. "Well, Private O'Brien, Harvey says your as good as new. Do you agree?"

"Yes Ma'am," he replied honestly.

"Any significant pain or discomfort?"

"I feel a little sore after exercising, but it usually passes in an hour or two."

"Good. I'm scheduling you for a complete exam at 1000 hours on Friday. If everything checks out, you can return to your unit. In fact, I see you have been reassigned. You'll get all that information when you're released. How does that sound to you?"

"Fine, Ma'am." He didn't know what else to say.

Jimmy reported at 1000 hours on Friday and was first examined by Major Saul Gilbert, a tall, dark-haired, suave-appearing surgeon who evaluated the latest x-rays and blood work, and didn't stop talking during the entire exam. Jimmy was told to perform a series of body stretches and arm and shoulder movements, which he did without experiencing any serious pain.

Next he was examined by Major Garabedian, a psychiatrist, who asked him questions about his attitude, his likes and dislikes, his fears, the war, and his personal life. Jimmy responded rapidly and without much thought, wanting to get that stupid session over with. When the doctor finished, he spent several minutes writing his report before looking at Jimmy and saying, "Okay, soldier, everything's fine; you're dismissed. Report back to Captain Carter at 1630 hours. Good luck."

Jimmy was 5 minutes early for his 1630 hour appointment. He had made up his mind to try and see her outside of military life, where he would be an equal. The worst that could happen is that she would turn him down, although he sensed he had a chance with her. Maybe he was wrong, but he had to try.

Captain Carter was late. When she finally breezed into the outer office, she beckoned him with an arm wave to follow her into her office. She tossed several manila envelopes onto her desk, removed her cap, and sat down. She was exhausted and she looked it.

Jimmy remained standing while she busied herself scanning several memos next to her telephone. She crumpled the first two and tossed them into a wastebasket, and the third she studied before picking up the phone to place a call. The party she wanted was not available and she left a message.

Looking up she noticed him standing and apologized for ignoring him. "Please sit down. I'm sorry I'm late but it's been one of those days. Give me a minute to check your report."

He sat and said nothing.

Several minutes later she looked up. "Everything is positive and you're being returned to duty. I have your release papers here. Give me another minute to check and sign them and you can be on your way. How does that sound?"

"Fine, sir—I, mean ma'am. How about the weekend off before I have to report back? That sure would be appreciated."

She eyed him admiringly. "Why not. You've been an exemplary patient and speaking medically, you've earned a weekend of R& R." She fumbled through his release papers and changed his reporting date to Monday, September 4, 0600 hours. "Done," she said. "Use your extra couple of days wisely. Don't overdo it," she cautioned.

"Thank you for everything, Captain. I have one more request." He paused. "Will you have dinner with me tonight?"

If he expected to shock her, he succeeded. Her face showed surprise followed by consternation, and it took her several seconds before she was back in command. He was unbelievably handsome, nearly 8 years her junior, and evidently infatuated with her. She didn't want to shoot him down and hurt him.

He was also the sexiest looking man she had ever met. The chemistry was all there, but could she chance it? All those thoughts flashed through her mind before she spoke.

"You know that officers and enlisted men can not mix socially, and it could cause problems for both of us. I really am flattered that you think enough of me to ask me out, but it happens quite often that a patient falls—I mean becomes infatuated with a member of the opposite sex. It's—it's something very human. So thank you, but…"

He interrupted her. "I know all that, but it's not just some spur of the moment thing. Please hear me out. The very first time I saw you I was stunned. I was hurting pretty much from my wounds, but I stopped thinking about them when I looked at you. I felt strange and possessed, and asked myself if this was just a sexual attraction, because I haven't been with a woman in a long while. I could honestly answer no. I just wanted to be with you. I wanted to look at you and I wanted to talk to you. I've never felt as strongly about anything in my entire life as I have about this. I just couldn't walk away and never see you again without letting you know. Please don't think I have a lot of nerve, or that I'm a kook. I just had to get this off my chest or I would have regretted it for the rest of my life."

He stopped talking. They both stared at each other without speaking. Finally, she answered from the heart, not from the head.

"I think we're both crazy, and that we will regret it. Yes, I will have dinner with you tonight."

His face lit up with a smile—a smile that had won her over long before today's events—but before he could say anything, she raised her hand in a gesture indicating she had more to say.

"There have to be some ground rules. You can't tell anyone. We will have to wear civilian clothing, and we'll have to dine in an out-of-the-way restaurant where we are less apt to be seen by anyone in the military. I hope you understand this is the only way I will feel comfortable. I'm sorry that this officer-enlisted personnel discrimination exists, but I don't make the rules. I work with a host of male officers everyday, and I cannot have any kind of gossip ruin my career. I hope you understand."

"Of course, Janice; I understand."

He used her first name as if he had said it a hundred times before.

She felt more excited about this date—this possible involvement—than she did about any others she had had in years. She was very much engrossed in her work and, being with many men all day long, found that she enjoyed her privacy. Only on special events, such as birthdays and holidays, would she accept male companionship. An occasional hug or kiss on the cheek was all that she offered, and only to long-time acquaintances.

Her feelings now were quite different. She was excited; girlishly so.

They arranged to meet in a small, out-of-the-way restaurant she located in the telephone book. She called to make a reservation, and had to wait until someone who spoke English was located and could converse with her. This is good, she thought, because it means the restaurant is not frequented by many Americans.

They made plans to arrive separately at the restaurant at 2100 hours. She pondered the necessity of inventing a story in the unlikely event that she met any familiar faces and decided against it. She would rely on her quick wit if it became necessary.

Jimmy was released from the hospital that Friday shortly before 1730 hours. He was back in uniform and had plenty of cash in his pocket, as there had been little to spend his monthly stipend on during his stay in the hospital. His cab driver spoke passable English and recommended a small hotel nearby, in one of the newer sections of post-World War II Tokyo.

He checked into the hotel, noting that it was nothing lavish but seemed modern and clean. The room was small by US standards but furnished comfortably. He unpacked his meager belongings and returned to the front desk for information as to where he could find a store with American clothes. He was in luck, as he had only to walk two blocks to enter a department store that was stocked with American apparel.

Jimmy bought three pair of bikini briefs—a welcome change from GI boxer shorts—tee-shirts, socks, a western-style shirt, a pair of tight-fitting jeans, penny loafers and a denim wind breaker, and returned to the hotel in a great frame of mind. He took a long, hot bath, a careful shave, and stretched out on the bed for a brief nap. But sleep wouldn't come. He was too excited.

An hour before they were to meet, he dressed in his newly acquired attire and made a mental note to get a haircut as soon as possible. He checked himself in a mirror, gave himself the okay, and left his room. He made his way through the dimly-lit lobby, glancing briefly at the faux art and frumpish figurines scattered about. They all looked like junk to him.

He located a cab and was on his way.

Janice chided herself for acting like a schoolgirl. She cabbed home from her office shortly after Jimmy left. She was tired and in need of an hour's sleep before bathing, but sleep wouldn't come. She told herself that she must be crazy for making this date.

But she had wanted to. At least for now she had no regrets. She had been aroused by him, and owed it to herself to see him. She bathed, washed her hair, dried and brushed it, and applied make-up. She tried on three different outfits, finally selecting the most unpretentious one, realizing that he would certainly be dressed casually. She wondered if he had anything civilian to wear. Whatever he wore would look great on him.

Her favorite perfume was a must, but she applied just a touch. She felt like a high school cheerleader on her way to meet Mr. Touchdown, and the thought caused her to smile.

Janice arrived 10 minutes late and found Jimmy seated in a corner booth in the rear of the restaurant, which was three-quarters full of customers—all Japanese. He arose as she approached, and greeted her warmly.

"Hi. You look terrific."

"Thank you. So do you. Where did you get the civvies?"

They sat down facing each other and he told her about his shopping spree. He talked excitedly and she listened intently, at first not realizing he was still holding her hand across the table. When a waiter approached, he reluctantly released it and asked her what she wanted to drink.

"A martini, please. Very dry, with two olives."

"A beer for me. American beer, and cold."

They looked at each other like two teenagers on a first date. He asked her why she had selected nursing in the Army. She briefly told him she felt it was her patriotic duty. As the evening progressed they became relaxed and in tune, and began telling each other their life stories.

After a second round of drinks they ordered dinner, with Janice doing the ordering with the help of an exasperated waiter, while Jimmy sipped his beer and studied her face.

"Your staring at me again," she said.

"I can't help it. You're beautiful."

"You do know what to say to a girl, don't you. Are you going to ask me to dance?"

He rose, took her hand, and led her onto the small dance floor. The music was coming from an expensive-looking juke box tucked away in the rear corner of the room. Sinatra was singing.

Janice was 5 feet 6 inches tall, but felt miniature next to him. She wished that she had worn high heels, but her casual dress hadn't called for them.

She settled into his arms as if she belonged there, and they danced slowly and intimately. Neither one spoke—they were content to enjoy their closeness, unaware and uncaring about the other diners observing them.

It was many minutes later that Janice broke the silence. "The waiter just brought our dinners to the table."

"Too bad," Jimmy said, "I kinda like what I'm doing right now."

"Well, then we'll eat and do it again. I'm famished."

They dined on lightly-seasoned fish and stir-fried fresh vegetables while conversing easily and freely, as if they had been long-time friends.

Jimmy ordered another round of drinks. Janice mildly admonished him and he agreed that it would be the last round. The food was good, but they didn't pay much attention to it.

They danced again, each anxious to feel the touch of the other. It was a wonderful evening, and Janice decided to spend the night with him, but she wanted him to be the one to ask. She didn't have long to wait.

She tried to pay the bill, but he refused.

"I asked you, remember?" She didn't argue.

He paid the check and they left the restaurant and hailed a cab. He leaned over close to her ear and whispered, "I'm in love with you. Please don't say anything, just listen. Come back to my place and we'll talk. I've got so many things I want to say to you and I don't want the evening to end."

She hesitated briefly before saying yes. He put his arms around her and hugged her, and she hugged back. He tried to kiss her, but she said, "wait; not here."

They were in his room 20 minutes later. He flipped the light-switch and locked the door while she walked over to the multiple windows and closed the blinds. She turned to him and extended her arms. He went to her and gathered her in, and covered her lips with his. Their first kiss was long and sensuous, and they were both aroused. Breathing heavily, she slowly pushed him away.

"I don't even have a toothbrush with me. Give me a couple of minutes to freshen-up," and without awaiting an answer she headed for the bathroom.

"Oh," she added, stopping and turning to face him. "Do you have a tee-shirt I can borrow?"

He moved to the dresser, opened the top drawer, and removed one of his new purchases, still in it's original package.

"How's this?"

"Perfect, thank you. Be out soon," she said, and entered the bathroom and closed the door.

He didn't know what to do with himself. He felt that he had better calm down or he was going to embarrass himself.

She reappeared in less than 5 minutes, wearing nothing but the extra-large tee-shirt he had given her, which covered her but left nothing to the imagination. He rose from the chair he had settled in and started towards her, but she coyly shook her head and pointed toward the bathroom.

"Yes, Ma'am," he saluted and headed into the john. He emerged a few minutes later, wearing a bath towel about his waist. He had intended to wear only his briefs, but the excitement his body was experiencing would have made him look ridiculous. He worried for naught for she had turned off the lights, removed the bedspread, and climbed into bed.

The only light to penetrate the bedroom came from the bathroom, its door left slightly ajar. The light fell across her face, and he could see her eyes were closed. She opened them as she felt him get into bed next to her. Their eyes met, and she smiled. He put his arms around her and pulled her close to him. Then closer. Their lips met, their bodies touched, and they soon spent the most sensuously exciting night of their lives.

She was gone when he awoke in the morning, but left a note on the dresser. "I'm working the 1200 to 2000 hour shift today, but have Sunday off. I should be back here by 2100 hours. Be sure you're waiting for me. I will have eaten and suggest that you do too. You'll need all your strength. Love, J."

They spent Saturday evening and Sunday morning in bed, breakfasted at noon, and went sight-seeing the rest of the day.

They were more than lovers; they were in love.

When he tried to get serious and make plans, however, she put him off. "We have plenty of time for that. Right now we have a war on our hands, and neither one of us is free to make any important decisions. If we feel the same way once this mess is over then we'll make plans. We have to be sensible."

He reluctantly agreed. She gave him two phone numbers where she could be reached or a message could be left. If he left a message, he was to call himself Major James. He was to let her know his situation when he found out what it was.

They enjoyed a light supper Sunday evening and returned to the hotel room ostensibly to pack up and check out. They did so only after satisfying their sexual appetites once more.

Jimmy was euphoric when he was with Janice. It was different from his earlier days with Sally. Janice made him feel more grown up; more of a man. A more mature kind of man.

CHAPTER 31

SEPTEMBER 4, 1950
TOKYO, MONDAY, 0600 HOURS

Jimmy reported to his new assignment area as directed. He entered First Sergeant Henry Winet's office and handed the Sergeant his orders.

Henry Winet was a career Army man who had served in the South Pacific during World War II and received three Purple Hearts. He at first hated the Japanese, but after having lived with a Japanese woman for two years, he had changed his point of view—he now only hated Japanese men.

Since the Japanese surrender and the American occupation, Japanese women, especially in Tokyo, were becoming Americanized and experiencing freedoms that were previously non-existent.

But they still catered to their men. Sergeant Winet was treated as if he were a god by Yuko, who he had met in a bar a month after he began his tour of duty in Japan. He never had as much attention and obedience from a woman in his entire life, and he found the arrangement to his liking.

Yuko, who lost her husband in the war, was the eighth and youngest child of parents who never wanted her, and she had lived a miserable life until her marriage. With the death of her husband she once again had nothing.

She had prayed for such a life as she now lived. She found the American to be gruff and bossy, but she could get him to do nearly anything she wanted, a luxury she had never known before. More than once she thanked her gods that she had found a man who showed her some compassion.

Sergeant Winet examined Jimmy's records carefully. When he finished, he studied Jimmy closely.

"You *look* in good shape, O'Brien. You still have aches or pains, or can you pull your own weight?"

"I'm fit, Sergeant."

"Good, because rumor has it we're going to see some action real soon. There'll be a jeep here in about 10 minutes and Corporal Weissman will give you a lift to your new company. Good luck, O'Brien. I think you'll need it."

On September 15, 1950, Allied troops, under the command of General Douglas MacArthur, made an amphibious landing at Inchon, Korea, some one hundred miles south of the 38th Parallel. This tactic cut the North Korean lines and scattered their forces, resulting in the capture of thousands of North Koreans.

Jimmy was with this group. He had not seen Janice again because his unit had undergone concentrated training and preparation for the rumored return to Korea, and no passes were given. He did manage a call the day before he left, but had to settle for leaving a message from Major James informing her that he would be out of town for a while. She would understand that he had been shipped out.

Jimmy was back in the thick of action, with an Allied Force that was heading north to the 38th Parallel. In the ensuing days the United Nations' Forces fought their way back to the 38th Parallel, and continued northward.

On November 1, 1950, Captain Janice Carter succeeded in being transferred to Korea. She was assigned to a forward medical unit positioned near the 38th Parallel. She had no idea where Jimmy was, other then he was attached to a group reported to be further north. Reports were that things were going well.

Janice was happy. She was working long hours and she was very tired, but Jimmy wasn't far away.

On November 25th, 1950, nearly two hundred thousand Chinese volunteers streaked across the Chinese border into North Korea to aid the embattled North Koreans. By mid-December the Allied Forces had been pushed back to the 38th Parallel. It was during this period that Captain Janice Carter, traveling in a jeep with two other nurses and a driver, was killed when the vehicle took a direct hit from an artillery shell of unknown origin.

The North Koreans and Chinese volunteers began the second invasion of South Korea on December 31, 1950, but were strongly repulsed. Shortly thereafter the 38th Parallel once more became the dividing line.

When the action settled down, Jimmy made sick-call because of a painful rash that had appeared on his inner thigh. While being treated, he gossiped with a nurse, a Lieutenant who had recently arrived from Tokyo. He mentioned that he had an old family friend who was a nurse in Tokyo, and wondered if she knew Captain Janice Carter.

"I didn't know her personally," came the response, "but I heard about her. Too bad; her and the others getting killed that way."

Jimmy bolted upright on the examining table. The color drained from his face as he shouted, **"What?"**

The Lieutenant jumped back, startled. "I'm sorry, soldier. I didn't mean to hit you like a ton of bricks, but Captain Carter, two Lieutenants, and their driver were all killed several weeks ago. They suffered a direct hit from enemy fire. That was the word we got."

Tears welled in Jimmy's eyes. "Oh Jesus," he cried out in anguish, "Not Janice—not Janice!"

"I'm sorry, soldier, truly sorry."

Jimmy dressed hurriedly and left the building. He was grief-stricken. His head was pounding, and he began to run as tears streaked down his face. He ran as fast as he could for more than a mile, his mind churning as fast as his legs, until he could run no more. Breathing heavily, he sat on the side of the road, head bent between his legs, and cried his heart out.

CHAPTER 32

PEMBERTON
JANUARY, 1951

Sean continued to write Jimmy once a week, relaying the news items that he thought would be of interest. He wrote that Buddy and Doreen were a constant two-some and were considering marriage in the not too distant future. He told Jimmy he loved going to school in Boston and that he was dating a couple of classmates—and making out okay with both of them. He reported his latest ski experiences and how he was improving every time he went.

Sean's letters were long and painstakingly written, full of so much information that Jimmy read them over and over, enjoying the feeling of connection with home.

Jimmy had answered him regularly when he was initially convalescing in Tokyo, but had written only once since his return to Korea. It was a long letter, and it related how he had met a nurse at a hospital in Tokyo and fallen in love with her, only to learn that she had followed him to Korea and been killed.

Sean knew that Jimmy had to have been feeling miserable when he wrote the letter. He had written a letter in return expressing his condolences, but as yet there had been no response from Jimmy.

Sean was truly enjoying his first year at Northeastern. Every day he bused from Pemberton to Stanton and took the train to North Station in Boston. From there he took the subway to within a block of the school. The trip took nearly an hour and a half each way, but he didn't mind the commuting time. He either read or studied while traveling, and the time passed quickly.

He knew he wanted no part of the leather, shoe, or allied industries that were preponderant in the Pemberton area, and thought he would be happy in some aspect of the retail business. He still had time to think about it.

He loved being in Boston and frequently on Saturdays made day trips into the heart of the city, ostensibly to spend the day at one of the excellent library facilities and keep on top of his studies. However, he often wound up at the Museum of Fine Arts or took one of the many city tours to historical sites. He visited the U.S.S. Constitution, the Bunker Hill Monument and the Harvard campus facilities several times, finding each to have a special meaning for him. There was so much history crammed into a relatively small area of the country, and it was all at his fingertips.

He decided he wanted to live in Boston full time, where he could find fulfillment in a cultured society of which he wanted to be a part. His only real ties to Pemberton were the two people he loved; his mother and

Jimmy O'Brien. If it weren't for them, he could easily kiss Pemberton good-bye, which he vowed to do soon anyway.

He was freer now than he had ever been.

PART II

CHAPTER 33

CONWALL, NEW HAMPSHIRE
1929

Pete Wilzinski was a standout athlete at Conwall High School. The school was located in a small town tucked away in one of the many beautiful valleys in the White Mountains of New Hampshire.

Pete starred in basketball, baseball, and football and was considered to be the number-one athlete in the area. How good he would have been or how well he would have fared in a big city high school system was often the topic of conversation among the many avid sports fans of Conwall, and the consensus was that he would have been tops wherever he played.

In his senior year of high school, he applied and was accepted to the University of New Hampshire. His tuition was to be paid by a group of local businessmen who were enthusiastic sport fans and believers in Pete Wilzinski.

Pete entered UNH in September of 1929 with high hopes for both a college education and a successful athletic career, but his plans were altered by a series of devastating events. The first was the stock market crash on October 29th and, less than a month later, the fatal accident suffered by his father in a logging mishap. With no one to support his mother and two younger sisters, he reluctantly left college and returned to Conwall.

Pete had many friends, and they helped out by giving him whatever part-time work was available during the hard times of the depression. Fortunately, the Wilzinskis had been frugal people and his father had paid off their home mortgage three years earlier. Their small home was theirs, free and clear. It was all they had left.

In his spare time Pete assisted the Conwall coach in football and basketball, and it was his only real pleasure. As the years passed and the depression waned, he became first the assistant coach, and two years later the head coach. Within two years, under his leadership, both his football and basketball teams were drawing state-wide attention by winning division titles.

His name became synonymous with team excellence. He was a taskmaster and drove his teams mercilessly, and his teams responded with their utmost ability to prove to him and themselves that they were the best. In 4 years his football teams amassed an outstanding record of 40 wins and only 2 losses, and garnered three Division Championships.

In 1934 Pete's mother remarried a long-time family friend who had become a widower the previous year. She sold her home and she and Pete's two younger sisters moved into her new husband's home. Pete was invited to live there but figured they would all be better off if he rented a small apartment in town.

In 1935 Pete received a phone call from Ted Baltar, one of the business men who had sponsored him at UNH. The call would change his life.

Ted had been a friend of Pete's father's and an avid Conwall sports fan.

Ted had moved from Conwall in 1930, when his hardware business had fallen on hard times. He and his wife Rita resettled in Pemberton, Massachusetts, where Rita had been born and raised. The move accomplished two welcome events for Rita's parents. They would have their daughter and grand-daughter back home where they could see them on a more regular basis, and Ted would work for their company and eventually run it.

Rita's dad was 72 years old and wanted to retire from the family-owned leather plant. He liked Ted and felt that his aggressiveness and business acumen would be a valuable asset. He turned out to be right, for in the next 5 years, business had improved considerably and the future looked promising.

Ted became active in Pemberton politics and participated in one way or another in many of the major business and social events that occurred in his fast-growing city. He found one major fault in Pemberton, and that was its lack of a successful sports program. Stanton, Lynn, and Beverly, as well as other nearby cities, had active sports programs and teams that were consistently better than Pembertons'. Ted set out to do something about it.

"What we need," he told some of his cronies at dinner one evening, "is a coach who knows how to win, and I think I can get one." He told them about young Pete Wilzinski and his win-loss record since taking over coaching duties in Conwall. His cronies were enthused. "See if you can get him, Ted," Mayor Doyle said, "and if he'll accept the salary we're paying Coach Lewis, then we won't renew Lewis' contract when it comes up next month. He wants to retire anyway."

Pete Wilzinski came to Pemberton in August of 1936, after fulfilling his contractual obligations in Conwall. The money Pemberton offered was much better than what his home town could afford, and Pete wanted a change of scenery. In his first year in Pemberton, he produced winning teams in both football and basketball, and in 3 years he had his first Divisional Football Championship. The fans were thrilled, the mayor was ecstatic, the Coach was pleased, and Ted Balter was considered a genius.

Pete married a widow, Jane Trask, in June of 1939, and moved into her home on fashionable Lowell Street. He had never been happier. He was well-respected in the city, but his aggressiveness and no-nonsense approach to all things was not the best way to gain or maintain close friendships.

"I could care less," he proclaimed to Jane one evening when she broached the subject.

In 1943, Jane, 8 months pregnant, fell down a flight of stairs in her home, and began hemorrhaging. She managed to crawl to a phone and call for help. At the hospital, complications occurred and they were unable to stem the bleeding. By the time Pete arrived at the hospital, Jane and the baby were dead. The entire town offered its heartfelt sympathy by flooding his home with flowers, food and good wishes.

It took months for Pete to adjust to the tragedy. He consoled himself by losing himself in his coaching duties, and slowly resumed a relatively normal lifestyle. He would dedicate the rest of his life to coaching and producing winners.

CHAPTER 34

KOREA
APRIL 10TH, 1951

Jimmy, on patrol along the 38th Parallel, was struck in the left thigh by sniper fire. The patrol never saw the attacker, who likely fled or went underground. This type of attack was taking place every hour of every day. It was a no-win situation.

A compress was slapped on his wound and, following a dose of morphine, Jimmy was evacuated to a MASH unit. There, a doctor operated and removed the bullet.

The bullet had nicked a branch of the femoral artery, and Jimmy had lost a considerable amount of blood, requiring several transfusions. His femur had also been fractured but not too badly. Ten days later, he was air-lifted to Tokyo for further evaluation, treatment, and rehabilitation.

On his third day back in Tokyo, he was visited by Harvey Ossoff.

"I saw your name on the patient-entry list, and I couldn't believe that you would be stupid enough to get yourself shot again. I know Irishmen are dumb, but I didn't think they were stupid."

"Thanks for the kind words, Harvey. I guess it's the luck of the Irish."

"I looked over your records and talked to a surgeon and a radiologist. You did a pretty good job this time. The Rad noticed that you had broken that same leg before, and pretty badly. He wondered how you ever got into the Infantry."

"I didn't, gooney. I'm in the Signal Corp, and far from the action." They both had a laugh over that.

"Well, me boy," Harvey said in his rendition of an Irish brogue, "you and I will have a lot to do over the next few months. Then, begorrah, you're surely looking at an honorable discharge and a trip home."

"My leg that bad, Harvey?" Jim asked, reflecting concern.

"Not too bad, Jimmy-me-boy, but bad enough to end your soldiering." In a serious tone Harvey added, "you'll be okay; just a little weak on that side."

Jim changed the subject. "You hear about Captain Carter?"

"Yeah, rotten luck. She was a helluva good nurse, and a damn nice person to boot. There's an old saying that 'only the good die young,' and I believe it. A damn shame."

Harvey saw tears in Jimmy's eyes. Thinking he was in physical pain Harvey asked if he should call a nurse for some morphine. Jimmy shook his head and muttered that he was okay.

He couldn't look Harvey in the eye. "I guess I'm just feeling sorry for myself," he finally said.

Jimmy wrote home two days later relating that he had been wounded again. He told them he was okay, that he was back in Tokyo, and that he was recovering well. He also wrote he would be discharged in a few months and he would be coming home.

CHAPTER 35

PEMBERTON
SATURDAY, APRIL 28, 1951

Shortly after 10:00 p.m., a figure moved stealthily to the rear of the Lowell Street home. He used a glass-cutter to cut a hole in the doorpane, reached in with a gloved hand, unlocked the door, and entered the house. Replacing the cutting-tool in his black satchel, he groped about and located a flashlight and made his way through the downstairs area, methodically checking every room and closet on the first floor. The intruder had scrutinized the house several times from the outside. The inside of the home was an unknown to him.

The intruder had studied the Coach's schedule the prior three Saturday evenings and found it to be predictable. The Coach went to the Metro bowling alley, arriving between 8:00 and 8:15, bowled three strings, alone or with a friend, stopped at Raymonds for coffee and a doughnut, stayed half-an-hour or so, and returned home, usually before 11:00 p.m. He left his car in the driveway and entered his house through the front door.

This night the Coach kept to his schedule. Coach opened the front door and turned on the hall light. He turned toward the closet to hang up his championship football jacket. He never heard the attacker approach and was felled by a powerful blow to the back of his head. The intruder turned off the hall light, opened the closet door and put on the closet light. He adjusted the closet door to permit just enough light to enter the hall to allow visibility.

The intruder replaced the heavy axe handle in his satchel. Turning to the unconscious victim, he turned him over onto his back before returning to his satchel to take out a large knife. Holding the knife in his right hand, he paused momentarily. Then the knife flashed through the air and plunged into Coach Wilzinski's heart.

The body shuddered fiercely, then went still. Blood spurted from the wound in five pulsing geysers of diminishing intensity. The killer watched the twitching body briefly before wiping the bloody blade on the victim's trousers and returning it to the satchel. He took one last look around before departing the same way he entered, and disappeared into the quiet of the night.

Coach Wilzinski's body was not discovered until Monday morning. When he had not shown up at his office, his secretary assumed he had a meeting that he had neglected to tell her about. When she hadn't seen or heard from him by 10:30, she called his home, allowed the phone to ring at length, and received no response.

The Coach had always been punctual and it was unusual for him not to notify her of his whereabouts on a school day. She thought perhaps he had contacted Ed Lasserter, his assistant, and Ed had forgotten to relay the message. She checked with Ed but he had not heard from the Coach and was surprised at his no-show.

Ed tried phoning the Coach, without success. Concerned, he went to his car and drove to the Coach's home.

The Coach's car was in the driveway. Ed parked in back of it and went to the front door and rang the doorbell. No response. He knocked loudly, to no avail. What the hell, he thought to himself, and walked around the house to the rear door. His heart quickened when he saw the hole in the glass pane. The door was unlocked and he entered the hall and went into the kitchen.

"Pete," he called in a loud voice. No answer. He walked through the dining room and as he entered the front hall his heart skipped a beat. He saw the Coach on the floor, sprawled lifelessly, shirtfront covered with dried blood. He took a step backwards and momentarily froze, staring at the horrible sight. He recovered his wits and dashed into the kitchen, fumbled with the phone, and called the police.

The Police Station was on the bottom floor of the Pemberton City Hall, and less than 2 miles from the Coach's home. In a very few minutes Ed Lasserter heard screeching sirens building in volume, as they raced to where he now sat in a state of near shock.

Captain Doyle, Lieutenant Rafferty and Inspector Sam Coben were in the second police cruiser that arrived at Coach Wilzinski's home. Neighbors and passersby were gathering, and Sam assigned two patrolmen who had arrived in the first vehicle to traffic and crowd control.

"Don't allow anyone on the grounds or into the house, other than medical or police personnel," he instructed.

Sam entered the house and joined Doyle and Rafferty in the front hall.

The scene was not pleasant. "Holy Jesus," Sam muttered.

"Yeah, quite a mess," Rafferty agreed. "Sam, put a man in the back yard and secure the area. The killer came in through the back entrance and we don't want anyone tramping around back there until we've checked it. I already put a call in for the coroner and he should be on his way. Ed Lassiter's sitting in the kitchen. He's the one who found the body. Get his statement."

Sam moved rapidly. He assigned an officer to the back yard and went to talk to Ed Lasserter.

The ambulance and the Medical Examiner arrived simultaneously. Berl Rodin, the ME, grunted a greeting to Captain Doyle, then knelt, put on gloves, and began his examination. After several minutes he rose.

"Been dead quite a while; probably between 24 and 48 hours. A hell of a chest wound. You have the weapon?"

"No," Captain Doyle answered, "none here. Whoever did it took it with them. What was it, Berl, a knife?"

"Wasn't just any knife, Captain, it was a big one. That wound's enormous. Let's get him out of here and to the morgue, and I'll give you a full report after I make a thorough examination."

Captain Doyle nodded in agreement and the ambulance crew moved in and removed the body.

Sam finished talking with Ed Lasserter and joined Rafferty in the back yard. They made a thorough check of the area before returning to examine the interior of the house.

"Who ever did it must have been covered in blood," Rafferty said, "but didn't walk in it. There's no sign of blood anywhere except in the hallway."

"Yeah," Sam acknowledged. "The rest of the forensic team is here, Lieutenant. Let's hope the bastard slipped up and left prints on the back door. I'd like to nail the son-of-a-bitch fast."

"Sam, it's kind of like the way that kid was murdered in the movie house in Stanton a few years back, isn't it? He was butchered with a large knife."

"That's right, Lieutenant," Sam concurred. "Let's see what the ME comes up with. By the way, is it the same ME?"

"Good point. Check on it. In any event, ask for a comparison."

"Will do, Lieutenant. And I'll call Barney Osham. He might be interested in the similarity."

"They never resolved that case, Sam, did they? What was the name of that kid?"

"Gordon, Lieutenant. No, they never nailed anybody."

Barney Osham was interested.

"A big knife, Sam? Yeah, that does sound like the same MO. And the Gordon kid and the Coach were both associated with Pemberton High School. Did the Coach have any contact with the Gordon kid? I wonder if Gordon was on any of the varsity or intramural teams? Did he…?"

"Whoa, slow down, Barney," Sam said, "we'll check all of that, but it will take a few days. I'll get back to you as soon as I get the ME's report and have had a chance to talk to people. By the way, do you happen to remember who the ME was in the Gordon case?"

"Yeah. Berl Rodin; I'm pretty sure."

"Good. He's doing the autop on this one also. I'll speak to you soon."

"Okay, Sam, I appreciate the call. And incidentally, if you throw in that kid that died in the hit-and-run accident last year you've got three people connected with Pemberton High that fall into the sudden death category. I remember that the two kids were close friends, and I'd be curious to know if the Coach was connected in any way to either one or both."

"I'll be in touch, Barney. Thanks."

That's right, Sam thought, three from Pemberton High.

The autopsy indicated that Coach Wilzinski died from a single stab wound that caused massive hemorrhaging. The ME speculated the weapon was a butcher's knife or something similar.

Sam asked him if he remembered the Gordon case, and he did.

"Same type of wound, Doc?"

"Gordon died of multiple stab wounds, Sam, and it could have been the same or similar type knife. A wide blade, probably 10 or 12 inches in length, which makes me think of the knives used in every tannery in the area. I really can't give you much more than that."

In the next few days Sam's investigation found no ties between the Coach, Gordon, and Robinson. Neither boy had been junior varsity or varsity players in any of the school programs. Ed Lasserter didn't know either of the boys and to his knowledge the Coach didn't either.

Sam notified Barney and promised to keep in touch as the investigation developed.

The forensic team found no prints other than the Coach's and Ed Lasserter's. There were no fresh footprints in the rear of the house or on the side leading from the garage, and the macadamized driveway and footpath to the rear door offered no clues. The house had not been ransacked. The Coach's mother, step-father, and sisters—all frequent visitors to the Wilzinski home and familiar with the household belongings—could not find anything of value that had been taken.

Only the Coach's wallet—devoid of cash—indicated the possible motive of theft. But a glass jar more than half-full of dollar bills and coins remained untouched on the dresser.

CHAPTER 36

TOKYO
MAY, 1951

Jimmy received several letters from his mother after she learned of his being wounded again, but Sean remained his main source of information from the home-front.

As he opened Sean's latest letter, several newspaper clippings fell out, and he glanced at these first. He was shocked, then infuriated, as he read of Coach Wilzinski's murder. He read and reread the clippings from the Pemberton and Stanton newspapers before crumpling them angrily and tossing them into a wastebasket.

The newspaper articles stated the police had no suspects and had found little evidence in their on-going investigation.

As Jimmy studied the carefully worded letter, he understood that Sean implied that he and Buddy had alibis and had nothing to do with the murder.

Bullshit! he thought. Too many coincidences. I'll brain those bastards when I see them.

Jimmy arrived stateside on Monday, August 20th and Mary, Dan, Buddy, Doreen, and Sean were all there to greet him.

Mary was relieved to see that he looked fine and didn't appear to exhibit any ill effects from his most recent hospital confinement.

Dan O'Brien showed genuine warmth rather than his usual dour countenance. Doreen noted silently that he looked taller and more handsome than ever. Buddy shook his hand warmly, and Sean hugged him.

When Jimmy walked, his limp was obvious, but everyone had the good sense not to mention it.

Jimmy was to report for therapy twice weekly to the Veterans Administration Hospital in Boston.

During his first hospital visit he was told not to discard his cane for several more weeks. His doctor at the VA told him he thought he would be unencumbered other than the possibility of having a slight limp.

Jimmy smiled at the doctor, but said nothing. He knew he would never allow himself to limp.

##

Patricia Anna Baltar, the 23 year old daughter of Ted and Rita Baltar, slid onto a seat at the counter in Raymonds drug store in Pemberton Square, where she frequently stopped for lunch. She ordered her usual grilled cheese and tomato sandwich and black coffee and was about to open the Boston Globe when the person sitting to her left interrupted her.

“Hi. I’m Jimmy O’Brien. I know I’ve seen you before but I don’t remember where.”

Patti turned in the direction of the voice, curious, but with the intent of cutting off any casual conversation if he happened to be a stranger. He was not a stranger, but she had never talked to him before, only admired him from a distance.

She was peering into the bluest eyes she had ever seen, and the face of an extremely handsome man, wearing a smile that would warm any woman’s heart. After a momentary loss of words, she introduced herself.

“Hi. I’m Patti Baltar. I don’t think we’ve ever met, but I know who you are. My Dad and I are Pemberton sports fans. Have been for years. I remember my Dad saying that we would have won the football game against Stanton and the state championship if you hadn’t been hurt in the game.”

“I was injured in an earlier game and didn’t play in the Stanton game,” he corrected. “That seems like such a long time ago.”

Patti, unflustered by her error, smiled and continued. “Of course. Anyway, I heard that you were hurt quite badly. What actually happened?”

She wasn’t particularly interested in hearing about his injury. She was more interested in looking at him.

Her sandwich arrived and she began to eat, turning on her stool so she could face him.

Jimmy related some of the story, all the while looking at her. She was attractive, but what drew his immutable attention was that she reminded him of Janice Carter. She was not as tall or shapely but her facial features—her nose, her eyes, the color of her hair, even the shape of her face—were similar to Janice's.

Maybe she's not quite as pretty, he thought, but she's a very attractive package in her own right.

He told her that he had been back in Pemberton only a short time. He related that he had been wounded in Korea but was recuperating nicely. They made small talk for another 10 minutes before Patti glanced at her watch and saw that she had exceeded her lunch break by 20 minutes.

"You'll have to excuse me; I'm late for an appointment. I'd love to hear more. Why don't you call me?" she said impulsively.

"Sure, I'd like to see you again. What's your phone number?"

Patti opened her purse, located her wallet, and removed her business card. She scribbled a phone number on the back of the card and handed it to him.

"Be sure to call me. We'll continue our conversation," she said impetuously. She smiled her good-bye, paid her bill, and left.

The card was neat and precise. It displayed her name and title, the company name, address, two phone numbers, the company logo—a picture of an animal hide with a heart in its center—and the words "Bovine Tanners since 1872."

Very impressive, Jimmy thought, and a Vice-President at that. I wonder how old she is?

At dinner that evening, Patti wouldn't stop talking about Jimmy O'Brien. She told her parents about their chance meeting at Raymonds and about his being in Korea and being wounded.

"Mom, you should see this guy. He should be in the movies. He's beautiful."

Later that evening, Rita and Ted were alone and had a chance to talk.

"Who is this Jimmy O'Brien?" Rita asked. "I have never seen her display an interest in any man the way she has over this one."

"He was a standout athlete that would have taken Coach Wilzinski and Pemberton High to another state championship a couple of years ago," Ted replied. "The Coach told me he was one of the best athletes he had ever seen. The kid broke his leg in the Chelsen game. Without him in the Stanton game we lost the game and the championship. I remember the Coach telling me the kid came to him at the end of the school year and asked for help getting a college football scholarship. Coach couldn't help him because the doctor said the kid had two or three breaks in his leg and would never pass a football physical. I guess O'Brien was disappointed and joined the Army. That was the last I heard of him until dinner tonight."

"That's too bad for the boy," Rita said sympathetically. "It sounds as if he was on top of the world and through no fault of his own got shot down. Couldn't the school have helped him get into college anyway? I thought you told me the school takes care of its own."

"We do, Rita, and I don't remember what happened in his case. I'll look into it."

"Good. If Patti shows that much interest in a man, then he's got to be something special."

A week later Jimmy received a phone call from Ted Baltar.

"Jimmy? My name is Ted Baltar, and I'm on the Pemberton School Board and active in the Pemberton Athletic Club. I recently heard that you were out of the Army and was wondering if you had any particular plans for the future. I and the other Athletic Club members like to follow up on our athletes, both past and present, to see if we can be of any service. I never had a chance to talk to you prior to your joining the Army, so I thought it would be appropriate if we got together now and discussed your future plans. Could you meet with me Saturday morning at 10:00?"

"Mr. Baltar, I have a 10:00 appointment Saturday that would be difficult for me to change," Jimmy said. "Could we meet at 11:00?"

That didn't exactly coincide with Ted's plans, as he had things to do before meeting Rita and Patti at the Club for lunch at noon, and then play a round of golf, but if he kept the meeting time down to under 30 minutes, he thought he'd be okay.

"Eleven would be fine, Jimmy, but please be prompt as I have a 12:00 engagement and I'll be cutting it close. Come to my factory office at 133 Foster Street. I'll leave word with the watchman to let you in. See you at 11:00."

What Ted told Jimmy about the Pemberton Athletic Club was true. The Club had placed many of its varsity players in jobs that paid better wages than they could have found on their own. It was their reward for actively pursuing athletic excellence. But the real reason Ted had made the call to Jimmy O'Brien was that Patti hadn't stopped talking about him all week and was disappointed that he hadn't called her.

"I was stupid, mom," she told Rita. "I gave him my phone number on the back of my business card. He must have thought I was showing off, and it probably turned him off."

"Were you?" Rita asked. She loved her daughter, but recognized Patti could be overly-aggressive in a world and in a business dominated by men.

"Yes, I guess I was. When he asked for my number I elected to write it on my business card. I could just as easily have given it to him on a sheet of memo paper or a napkin. It was plain dumb on my part."

Rita softened. "No, Patti, you have every right to be proud of your accomplishments. Dad and I are very pleased with your success in the business, but it has taken too much time away from your social life. You're too pretty not to think about settling down and raising a family."

"Mom, I have thought about it, but there is no one I've gone out with—especially at the Club—that I am even remotely interested in. I don't want a marriage of convenience. I want a marriage for love. I'm a romantic, mom."

Rita put her arms around her and hugged her. "Honey, I agree with you. Marry for love. But you'll have to search harder for it. Now tell me about this O'Brien fellow that you've been raving about."

Jimmy did have a 10:00 appointment on Saturday morning that he had no intention of breaking. It was his first real opportunity to meet with both Buddy and Sean and talk in privacy.

Buddy's five-days-plus work week coupled with his dating Doreen left him little time to socialize with his brother.

Sean's schedule was not much better. Between commuting and studying, he had little free time. It was only at Jimmy's insistence they had scheduled a time to meet, and Buddy had arranged to leave the plant for an hour in order to be there.

Sean climbed the ladder to the loft precisely at 10:00 and found Jimmy and Buddy seated and waiting.

"It's been a long time since we've all been up here," Jimmy said. "Everything looks the same, but smaller."

"That's because we're all bigger," Buddy answered with a rare grin, and he and Sean laughed.

Jimmy ignored the levity. "I've got some things I want to talk to both of you about, and I don't have a lot of time. Right now I want some answers. What happened to Coach Wilzinski?"

Sean answered quickly. "Nobody knows, Jimmy. He was stabbed to death on a Saturday night after coming home from bowling. I only know what I read in the papers and they didn't give out a lot of information. They never found who did it."

"But do either of *you* know who did it?" Jimmy asked acerbically.

"No," Sean answered, "I didn't do…"

Buddy cut in. "Hell, Jimmy, we didn't do anything to the Coach. You made it clear that we were to do nothing until you got back, remember? Plain and simple, it wasn't us."

"I hope not. You both swear to me that you didn't do it?"

"I swear, Jimmy," Sean uttered instantly.

"Me too," Buddy answered. "I had nothing to do with it."

Jimmy eyed both of them coldly. "Okay," he said, "I had to know. He must have screwed somebody else who got to him first. Anyway, there's one less bastard to have to think about."

Buddy and Sean nodded, still appearing uncomfortable.

"What about the two guys from Chelsen?" Jimmy asked. "You locate them like I told you to?"

"Yeah," Buddy answered. "They're gone."

"What do you mean 'gone,'" Jimmy snapped.

"Just what he said, Jimmy," Sean filled in. "When I got your letter from Japan saying you were coming home, I drove over to the Chelsen library and got a copy of their graduation yearbook and looked up their addresses. I phoned them both, using a phony name. The Cohen guy moved to Israel. He's gone to live there permanently, according to his kid sister. And the nigger you can forget about. He got killed in Korea."

"I'll be damned," Jimmy spoke angrily. "I've been dreaming about breaking the heads of those bastards, and one leaves the country and the other one gets himself killed. Son-of-a-bitch."

"Yeah, they had a hell of a nerve," Sean uttered thoughtlessly.

All talk ceased as the boys eyeballed each other. Then Jimmy and Buddy broke out in loud laughter.

Sean blushed. "You guys know what I mean."

Jimmy cut the meeting short, as he had his appointment to keep, and they made a tentative date to meet in the clubhouse in 2 weeks. There was other business on their agenda to discuss.

He arrived at the R. G. Stewart Leather Company 5 minutes early and was escorted to Ted Baltar's office. Ted was at his desk pouring through paper work when the watchman knocked on his door and announced Jimmy's arrival.

"Come in. Glad you could make it," Ted called out amiably, as he looked up to examine the tall, blond, handsome young man walking with the aid of a cane approach his desk.

Ted rose to shake his hand and at the same time excused the watchman. "Thanks, Harry. I'll show Mr. O'Brien out when we're through."

Ted returned to his seat behind the desk and made himself comfortable.

"Well, Mr. O'Brien—or may I call you Jimmy? It's nice to meet you."

"Thank you. Jimmy is what everybody calls me, sir."

"Then Jimmy it is," Ted said, beckoning to him to sit in one of the chrome-framed chairs upholstered in dark-brown leather situated in front of his desk. Jimmy noticed that Ted's eyes had locked on to the cane he was carrying. He held it aloft and said, "This will be gone in another 2 weeks, Mr. Baltar. The doctor wants me to use it until then. I really don't need it anymore, but I'm doing what he told me to."

"Good idea," Ted answered.

The kid's quick, Ted thought. I didn't realize I was staring.

"Please, Jimmy, call me Ted," he continued. "I understand you had a pretty rough time over in Korea. The talk is that you were wounded several times. How are you feeling now?"

"I'm doing just fine, sir. I'm healing well and my limp will be gone in the next month or so."

"That's great," Ted answered enthusiastically. "I'm glad to hear that. Now, if you don't mind, lets get to the reason I asked you here. Have you decided what you want to do with your life?"

Jimmy paused before answering. "I really would like to go to college and play football, but I know that can never be. I guess I'll have to find work and then see in a year or two whether I can afford to go to college or even if I'll want to by then. I really haven't decided, to be honest with you."

In the short time he had talked with Jimmy O'Brien, Ted had made up his mind. He would not place Jimmy with anyone else. He would hire him himself.

Ted was accustomed to making spur-of-the-moment decisions and was not afraid of being wrong. And he had Patti in the back of his mind. *If this kid and Patti hit it off, all well and good. I could certainly be proud of a son-in-law who makes such a nice appearance. And what a striking couple they would make.*

"Jimmy, I've been looking for a young man that I can bring along in my business. But let me tell you a little about a tannery first. It takes considerable time to learn the ins and outs of the operation. A tannery is labor intensive, involves many machine operations, and uses a number of diverse chemicals during the process. My father-in-law was a third generation tanner, and he insisted that I learn every facet of the business if I wanted to be successful, and he was right. You can't make intelligent decisions unless you know what you're talking about.

"I'm willing to give you the opportunity to start on the bottom floor and learn the business. Once I see you understand what you're doing, and can handle the job, you'll progress rapidly up the ladder. If you find you like the work then the sky's the limit. Are you interested?"

Jimmy was flabbergasted. He thought the Pemberton Athletic Club would offer him some menial job that would satisfy their egos as Good Samaritans. But this sounded like a bona-fide opportunity that could lead to a meaningful future. It was a once-in-a-lifetime offer, and he knew it.

"Mr. Baltar—Ted—I don't know what to say, other than of course I'm interested. Actually I'm excited as all hell."

His response was animated, and Ted liked that the kid was smart enough to hop on a good opportunity without having to think about it.

"Then it's settled. How long will it be before you're released from the VA Hospital?"

"They told me 2 or 3 weeks."

"Okay. You call me when you're free and clear and we'll get you started. You'll start at a $150 a week and we'll go from there. Agreed?"

"Agreed," Jimmy managed to reply.

"Okay! By the way," Ted added on the spur of the moment, "I'm meeting my wife and daughter at my Club for lunch today. Would you like to join us?"

Jimmy hesitated. He was dressed in dungarees and sneakers and felt he would be out of place.

"I would have liked that very much, sir, but I promised my mother that I'd drive her to her sister's, and I'd hate to disappoint her."

"That's okay. We'll do it another time. So I'll hear from you in a couple of weeks?"

"You certainly will, sir. And thank you very much. I really appreciate the job offer."

Ted told Rita and Patti during lunch about his interview with Jimmy O'Brien and of his decision to offer him a job. Smiling at Patti, he said, "I can see how he would attract attention wherever he goes. He's very good looking and with a physique to envy. I invited him to join us for lunch, but he was busy. I think he really wanted to come. Said he'd love to another time."

"You invited him to lunch, Dad, after meeting him for only the first time? That would have been very awkward, especially since he's never called me. I appreciate your attempt at matchmaking, but it's really up to him and me. Please don't interfere," she added emotionally.

"Of course not, dear," Rita said gently, glaring at Ted with an expression that ordered him to back-off. "We certainly understand how you feel, Patti. Dad and I want you to do things at your own pace. He does sound interesting, though, and if your father moved that fast then he must have been impressed. I'm looking forward to meeting this young man."

Patti softened as she looked at her father. "Did he happen to mention that he met me?"

"We only talked business, Patti, and I couldn't give him much time, so the answer is no; he didn't mention you.

But if he is as smart as he is good-looking, and his big blue eyes really work, then once he saw you he'd never forget you. I'm sure he'll call you."

"If he does call, Dad, I hope he's half as charming as you."

Jimmy was in an exuberant frame of mind when he left Ted Baltar. In little more than half-an-hour he had gone from the undecided and the unemployed to the soon-to-be fully employed, with the promise of an exciting and rewarding future. Unbelievable, he said to himself. A job at $150 a week to start. My old man doesn't make that. Jesus, will he be surprised.

He decided to tell the family his good news that evening, but would not let them know what his starting pay was to be. No sense in causing resentment in the old man, or with Buddy.

Jimmy told his story later that evening and, as he anticipated, his father asked what he would get paid.

"I'll be making a hundred a week, with a promise of fast advancement."

Dan O'Brien grunted his approval, for it was better than fair starting pay, and 20 dollars a week less than he himself was making.

Buddy was non-committal, but was satisfied that Jimmy wouldn't be making more than he was.

Buddy was annoyed, however, that Jimmy had found a job so easily. Son-of-a-bitch always falls into it, he thought.

Jimmy congratulated himself on his tact. He had handled everything well.

He reminded himself to call Patti Baltar, and the sooner the better.

CHAPTER 37

Buddy had been working for B.D. Barker & Co. for over a year, and liked what he was doing. But the year hadn't been easy. He had not realized how complicated and chemically dependent the tanning industry was.

His immediate boss, Larry Sandberg, spent as little time as possible with his unwanted apprentice. Sandberg didn't like the idea that management forced someone on him, and a smart-aleck young Irishman at that.

When Bill Clancy had told Sandberg the prior year he was working too hard and he was going to give him a helper who could perform the easier tasks, Sandberg had been suspicious. "Anything I'm doing wrong, Mr. Clancy, you just have to tell me."

"There's nothing wrong, Larry. Your work is one-hundred per cent accurate, as always. But we all get older and we all have to have somebody that can step in and cover our work in case of illness.

"It's important for the company to have backup in every area, especially in the technical end. We couldn't operate successfully without your expertise, Larry," he added in a placatory manner. "I'm assigning you a young man who was born and raised in the area, as we like hiring people who are apt to stay where they are most familiar. His school grades are excellent, especially in the sciences, and he made a good impression on me when I interviewed him. I made sure he understood you're the boss and you call the shots. I'm certain he'll work out well under your guidance, Larry, so show him around the lab and then allow him to spend a few days in each of the wet departments and get to meet the department foremen. I want him to have an idea of all the wet processing steps before he gets buried in laboratory work. You let him do all the running around, and I'm sure you'll find it will make things a lot easier for you."

Buddy had started his apprenticeship in the hide house. The adjacent railroad siding had room for the placement of four freight cars of hides, and nearby there was a dock set-up for receiving trucks of hides and chemicals.

B. D. Barker & Co. processed only cattle hides. The cow and steer hides arrived from packing houses after being cured and bundled. The hides, when ready to process, were trimmed of undesirable appendages, weighed into packs, and loaded into wooden drums. Cool running-water was used to wash out excess salt, manure, and other dirt clinging to the animal hair. The hides were removed from the drums and put through fleshing machines, which removed undesired excess adipose matter (flesh) from the underside of the hide.

After fleshing, each pack was loaded into a wooden paddle. Under power, a slow-moving paddle wheel agitated the hide-water mixture in the paddle, much like a paddle boat on the Mississippi River churns the water when underway.

Measured amounts of depilatory materials (customarily sodium sulfide, sodium sulfhydrate and high-calcium lime to raise pH) were used to loosen and eventually pulp the hair. Each paddle wheel was run for longer periods in the initial stages of this operation and then intermittently as the chemical plumping action took effect. A running wash period, followed by an additional lime application, was used in the final stage of the hair-destroying operation to bring about a desired degree of hide plumping. The de-hairing operation was generally carried out over a 2-day time period, and included a final cool wash to rid lingering pulped hair and other impurities. The hairless hide packs were then re-weighed to obtain a limed pack weight.

Buddy was especially interested in the next operations, which were the bate, pickle, and tan procedures. The three steps took place in the same vessel; a large wooden drum. A predetermined weight of the de-haired stock was loaded into the drum. An enzyme material (bate) was used to loosen any remaining fine hair and undesirable protein matter. The amount and strength of bate material used, and the length of time and temperature employed, was a choice made by the tanner, and was governed by the results he wished to obtain.

Pickling prepared the hides for subsequent tannage. It was accomplished following the bating operation and wash by the introduction of a brine solution to inhibit swelling, followed by the addition of a predetermined amount of sulfuric acid solution or a sulfuric acid-formic acid mixture. The brine-acid combination, after a period of drum rotation intermingled with lay-time, penetrated the hide substance and dramatically lowered the pH to a level in which the chrome tanning material, the third operational stage, would most readily combine with the hide substance. The tanning material was drummed into the stock over a period of hours, within an optimum temperature range, and was fixed (locked in) by a series of feeds of alkali, often sodium bicarbonate.

"The chemistry of the linkages and bondings that takes place is far beyond the comprehension of a high school chemistry student," Buddy was told snippily when he asked Larry Sandberg several intelligent questions.

Buddy stewed over the put-down, but said nothing. He was overwhelmed with the complexity of leather-making. He acknowledged he had a lot to learn, and he was fortunate he made friends with someone who could help him.

Arthur Zoltek was the company tanner. He would not talk much of his background, other than to say that he came from a long line of tanners. His father, his grandfather, and his great grandfather had all been tanners in Europe.

Zoltek did tell Buddy he had been educated in Germany but was reluctant to say more. He was a man in his early sixties, 6 feet 2 inches tall, with a full head of black hair (graying slightly) parted down the middle, a rather pointed but not ugly nose, a mouth with almost no upper lip, and a near-perfect set of white teeth.

His most striking facial feature, however, were his eyes. Jet-black, piercing orbs that could hold you in their grasp without blinking or flinching. His body hinted that in earlier years he was athletic, and time had not treated him badly. He seldom smiled.

His appearance belied his character, as he was in fact a gentle man; kind, thoughtful and considerate. He did not flaunt his superior knowledge in his chosen field. His tannery process procedures often differed from the tried-and-true systems that Larry Sandberg considered proper.

Zoltek handled such confrontations with calmness and skill, but maintained his authority over all leather-making procedures. He would occasionally praise and accept a methodology suggested by Larry Sandberg, but Larry would sulk, feeling that he was being mollified rather than recognized for his contributions.

Sandberg despised Zoltek because Zoltek was too good and too German. His appearance, his manner, his ability and his authority rankled Sandberg. Because of these feelings and the friendly relationship he observed forming between his Irisher assistant and the big-shot tanner, Sandberg further withdrew inside the shell he had created for himself. His instructions to Buddy were curtly issued, and he never praised Buddy for any work he accurately and painstakingly performed.

One morning during coffee-break Buddy approached Arthur Zoltek, who was sitting alone in the rear of the room.

"You know, Mr. Zoltek, I'm really trying to do my best and I think I'm doing a good job, but Mr. Sandberg barely talks to me and for some reason he doesn't like me. Sometime I see him out of the corner of my eye, and he's…well, I'd have to describe it as glaring at me. I don't know whether or not to say anything to him. I find it really uncomfortable."

"Hmm—I can understand why," Zoltek said. "He is somewhat of a problem sometimes. If it makes you feel any better, he's like that with me too. My suggestion is to ignore him, or rather, ignore his sullen disposition. Continue to do your work efficiently, answer him civilly, and let him be damned. If it gets real bad, you be sure to let me know, and I'll take him down a peg. I've had to do that before."

"Thanks, Mr. Zoltek. If he's like that with others and not just me I'll live with it. I like my work and I'm learning more every day. I'd like to work myself into a position where I'll be noticed and could advance in the company. I'm planning to get married next summer, and I need a job with a future."

"You're doing just fine, Buddy, and I'll help you and teach you all I can. That's a promise. Keep your nose clean and continue to work hard, and I'll see that you move along within the company."

They parted company and Buddy couldn't have been more pleased with himself. He had laid it on heavy and Zoltek had responded favorably. Still, that bastard Sandberg was going to be a problem.

He decided he would bring it up with Jimmy and Sean at the club house.

The meeting took place the following Sunday. It was a beautiful fall morning, nearly cloudless but for an occasional white, billowy intruder. The temperature was above average for early October, and it was a great day for outdoor activity.

Sean walked into the O'Brien kitchen shortly before 10:00. Mary insisted he sit down and have a cup of coffee with the boys, who were finishing their customary huge Sunday breakfast.

Dan O'Brien was outside washing his car, taking advantage of the beautiful weather. This was one of the few activities he enjoyed doing alone, and he would not accept help from his sons because they weren't thorough enough for him.

Ten minutes later, when the three boys emerged through the back door and made their way toward the open garage, Dan O'Brien paused from his work long enough to greet Sean and to comment on the weather.

"You guys still meeting in your clubhouse?" Dan said. "I can't believe it. I would have thought by now you would have grown out of that kid stuff. You're all old enough to put a wet bar up there and invite me up for a couple of beers."

The boys laughed, agreeing that it was a good idea, but they weren't taking on any new members, and they never had guests.

Jimmy opened the two small windows in the club house as the others took their customary seats. The fresh air felt good and rapidly cleansed the mustiness of the room. They hadn't had a meeting in a month, as they were all busy and going in different directions.

Sean was still commuting to Boston and spending more time there, including weekends. He kept in touch with the boys by phone. They had previously agreed to have one meeting a month on a Sunday morning, as that was the most convenient time for all of them.

"I've got a problem," Buddy began, "and I want to discuss it with both of you." He proceeded to tell them in detail about Larry Sandberg. He didn't mention his talk with Arthur Zoltek, as he felt that they might agree with Zoltek that the problem, in time, would find a solution. He wanted something done now.

Jimmy spoke as soon as Buddy had finished. "He's a Jew, isn't he?"

Buddy nodded in the affirmative.

"What if he were to have an accident," Jimmy said. "Something that would keep him out of work for a couple of months. Could you handle your job and his? If you could, that would make you look real good."

Buddy considered the thought before answering. "Damn right I could do it—or at least enough to get by, as long as Zoltek's around. That's not a bad idea, Jimmy."

Sean was apprehensive. "The last time we talked accident it turned out to be a lot worse than we had planned. I was sick for weeks after that, and frightened for a lot longer. We've got to be sure that what breaks will mend, if you know what I mean."

"Don't be such a worry-wart, for Christ's sake," Buddy said. "We're older and wiser now, and it's about time we renewed our pledge to THE PACT."

Sean took a deep breath before answering. "Okay, but we've still got to be careful."

Buddy had second-thoughts. "The problem is that when the son-of-a-bitch recovers he could be meaner than ever. Then I would have to go through the whole thing again. I think it would be better if we fixed it so he couldn't come back to work for a much longer time—or maybe ever."

There was a period of silence before Jimmy answered. "Yeah, maybe it would be better at that. That's going to take some careful planning, Buddy, and it would have to be done in a way that you wouldn't be implicated. Where you are working with the guy and would benefit by his departure, you could be suspect. We don't want to open a can of worms."

Buddy shrugged his shoulders, and before he could reply, Sean spoke. He was worried and looked it. "Jesus, I don't think we should jeopardize our futures over this guy. We've all got plans and they're just beginning to be realized. Why can't we just arrange it so he won't be able to work for a while. Maybe he'll quit on his own, or the company will retire him once they see Buddy can replace him. You said he's an old man, so it might not take too much to get him to retire. I don't think we should overreact..."

"Bullshit!", Buddy thundered, having decided that he had to be rid of Sandberg—period. "I can't afford the possibility of his return. He's got to go!"

"Okay-okay; both of you calm down." It was Jimmy taking charge. "We've got some differences of opinion, and both of you have valid reasons. Let's take the coming week to think about the problem and how to handle it. I'm calling a special meeting for next Sunday morning, same time, and we'll each present a solution. Then we can decide on what course to take."

The others agreed; Buddy reluctantly.

CHAPTER 38

Jimmy called Patti Baltar the Monday evening following his meeting with Ted Baltar.

Rita answered the phone and introduced herself after Jimmy gave his name.

"Just a minute, Mr. O'Brien. I'll see if she's still in the house. I can never keep up with her the way she flies around."

Rita put the phone on the table and snapped her fingers to get Ted's attention. When he looked up, she mouthed the name "Jimmy O'Brien," and pointed upstairs, indicating the call was for Patti.

Ted mouthed back, "You call her."

Rita impishly stuck out her tongue, and left the room to get her daughter.

"Hi. This is Patti."

"Hi yourself. It's Jimmy O'Brien. How are you?"

"Jimmy O'Brien? Oh, yes, I remember. We met at the lunch counter at Raymonds a couple of weeks ago," she answered with feigned indifference, peeved it had taken him so long to call.

Jimmy accepted her cool response, aware he had been remiss in not calling earlier.

"You didn't answer me. How are you?"

"I'm fine, thank you. And how are you, Mr. James O'Brien?" she answered pertly, not letting him off the hook.

"Equally fine, now that I've almost finished my therapy. Going into Boston by train twice a week is a pain in the butt, but I'll soon be done and have a clean bill of health. I plan to start work a week from today, and I'm looking forward to it."

"Well, that's good news," she answered, beginning to warm to him as she recalled their first encounter and how much he had impressed her. "I'm happy for you."

"Thanks. The reason I called is that I'd like to see you again, and was wondering if you were free next Saturday evening. I thought we could catch a movie and a bite to eat afterwards."

Patti paused. There was a dance scheduled at the Club Saturday night. She was on the dance committee and she had committed to be there to help decorate. She made her decision.

"Jimmy, I've promised to help out…" and went on to explain the situation. "You would be doing me a favor if you would accompany me to the dance. I was going alone—by choice," she continued, allowing him to sort out the implication, "but it would be nice to have an escort."

Jimmy hesitated. He had no misgivings about accompanying her to the dance, but he didn't know if he had the right clothes to wear. He sure as hell didn't want to have to spring for a tux, and yet this was an opportunity to mix with the upper-crust of the community, which is exactly what he wanted to do.

Patti sensed his dilemma. “It’s not a fancy affair, Jimmy. A jacket, shirt, and slacks are what most of the men will wear, and it’s a fun night. There’s a buffet dinner, a great dance band, and an open bar. I think some of the members are ex-football players, so I don’t think you’ll be uncomfortable.”

“Sure, if you want me to go, I’ll be happy to,” said Jimmy, relieved at the dress disclosure.

“Great. I really appreciate it. Now, one more favor.”

“I’m afraid to ask,” Jimmy said in an amused tone.

“The dance is called for 7:00, but I’ve got to be there 5:30 to finish decorating. I could use help from a strong, tall assistant. How about it?”

“I am at your command,” he answered playfully.

They were enjoying the banter and now felt relaxed with the conversation. Patti next solved a problem for Jimmy when she insisted on driving.

“I’ll have a station wagon full of party decorations to bring to the clubhouse, so can I pick you up?”

“Sure.”

He gave her his address and she confirmed she would pick him up at 5:10 Saturday afternoon.

Patti hung up and ran downstairs. She couldn’t suppress her excitement as she told her parents that he called to ask her out, and she had invited him to escort her to the dance, and he had accepted.

"I hope you don't mind, but I wanted to see him again, and I promised to help with the decorations, so I couldn't renege on that."

"Of course we don't mind, dear," Rita replied warmly. "I'm happy that you invited him. Both you and your father seem much impressed with this young man and, frankly, I'm dying to meet him. Will you sit at our table?"

"No way," Patti answered quickly. "I couldn't stand the competition, and I want him all to myself."

Rita laughed. "Then he's got to be someone real special. You be sure to let me meet him, however briefly. Promise?"

"Promise, mom," Patti shouted as she ran out of the room and up the stairs to her bedroom.

Rita turned to Ted, whose head was buried in his newspaper. "I haven't seen her this excited over a date since her junior prom."

Ted merely grunted.

Patti parked in front of Jimmy's home at 5:15 p.m. on Saturday.

Neat and tidy, she noted, eyeing the unpretentious Clement Avenue home with moderate interest. I hope I won't have to go to the door and ring the bell.

As if in answer, the front door opened and Jimmy emerged, crossed the screened front porch, descended the flight of stairs to the walk and approached her station wagon. He was wearing a navy sport jacket, charcoal-gray slacks, polished black loafers, and a pale-blue dress shirt open at the neck. His blond hair was neatly brushed and looked free of the greasy stuff men were using.

All Patti could think of was *he's gorgeous*.

She had painstakingly dressed in a navy-blue taffeta off-the-shoulder outfit with a tight-fitting Empire waist and full skirt. She had spent nearly 2 hours that afternoon in Kay's Beauty Salon with Kay doing her hair and Margaret her nails.

She was satisfied with the results. She hoped he would be.

"Hi," she said, "would you mind driving?" Although she would have preferred driving, she thought most men considered it a put-down if the female was in the driver's seat.

"Hi, yourself," he answered, flashing his dazzling smile. His gaze scanned her with evident satisfaction. "You look terrific. Sure; I'll drive if you want me to."

"Thanks." She slid over to the passenger side as he opened the driver's-side door and got in.

Patti, in heels, was about 5 feet 6 inches, but Jim needed more room. "Do you mind if…"

"You better push the seat back," she said knowingly.

The drive to the Country Club took 20 minutes. Jimmy knew the way, as years ago he had worked there as a caddie. He had only seen the locker room area back then, but he remembered the well-equipped pro-shop stocked with expensive golf bags and clubs, and the men's and women's apparel at outrageous prices.

He had heard that the upstairs walls and floors were fabricated with imported woods, and that fancy wall hangings adorned every wall. It was a domicile for the wealthy, and not a place for a poor Irish kid whose father worked in a leather factory.

That's about to change, he silently acknowledged as he drove the station wagon through the iron and brick-arched Country Club entrance and traveled the sinuous crushed-stone driveway that led to clubhouse.

"Park over there, Jimmy," Patti instructed, pointing to a double-door on the side of the clubhouse. "It will be easier to unload all the stuff."

The rear of the wagon contained half-a-dozen cardboard boxes filled with party decorations.

Patti swung herself out of the car and headed for the clubhouse delivery doors. They were locked. She banged several times before being greeted by a voice inside.

"Wait a minute. I'm coming."

A lock was thrown and both doors swung open, revealing a tall young woman with long red hair. She was a pretty woman in her mid-to-late twenties, with a figure that would make a normal man look twice, especially in the clinging, low-cut green silk dress she was wearing.

The two women embraced briefly, and Patti turned to introduce Jimmy, who was approaching them.

"Jimmy, this is my friend Marilyn Shea. Marilyn, this is Jimmy O'Brien."

Marilyn smiled sweetly. She extended her arm and shook his hand, which was twice the size of hers. His grip was firm but not crushing.

Marilyn scrutinized his face with obvious interest. What registered in her brain was his beautiful blue eyes, handsome features, and winning smile.

"Nice to meet you, Jimmy," she said coquettishly. "Any friend of Patti's is a friend of mine."

"Thank you," he answered politely, still smiling, "It's nice to meet you."

Jimmy had a way with women. He knew he had good looks, and didn't think of himself as being conceited. If women liked the way he looked, all the better. To him it was more important to know how to act. He knew that women expected to be complimented, wanted to be treated with respect and as equals, and liked to be at the center of your attention.

Jimmy had learned a lot about women when he was with Janice Carter in Japan. Not just how to please a woman sexually, but how to make a woman feel very special.

"A woman doesn't want to be a plaything, Jimmy," Janice had said one evening during one of their serious conversations. "A woman wants to be loved in many ways. She wants to feel that she is the only one, not one of many. Love-making is important, but it's only a small part of a serious relationship."

He had loved Janice and would never forget her.

He had learned much from his all-to-brief relationship with her, and he remembered it well.

Patti introduced Jimmy to the other members of the decorating committee; all women. On her first opportunity she whispered to him, "there are some men on the committee too, Jimmy; they should be along soon."

Jimmy faked a pout. "Oh, that's too bad."

She smiled and wagged a finger at him.

"Do you want me to bring the boxes in from the car?" he asked.

"No, the staff will do that. I see them coming now."

Two men in green work uniforms, wheeling a hand truck, had entered the hall.

"Jimmy, if you would unlock the rear door of my wagon they can bring the boxes into the ballroom. I'll tell them where to set-up the tables and hang the crepe paper."

He had wondered how the women, dressed to party—some in high heels—were going to do the physical work of decorating a hall. Now he knew. The decorating committee members were all managers who gave orders and didn't lift a finger other than to point. He smiled and made a mental note that that was the way he wanted to live.

Jimmy had nothing to do, so he caught Patti's eye and mouthed that he was going to take a walk around.

She waved her approval.

While Jimmy was touring, the women were talking.

"Wow, Patti, that's all man," Marilyn began. "He's stunning. Where did you find him?"

The other ladies agreed, adding comments as to his size and physique.

Patti didn't like the way the conversation was going, and did her best to be pleasant without encouraging any further discussion. She merely said that they were friends, and changed the subject.

Marilyn, however, had the last word. "I'd like to make him my friend too, and I'd like to name the place."

The ladies laughed knowingly, and an embarrassed Patti Baltar ended the conversation with, "please, ladies!" and walked red-faced to the far side of the room to decorate a table.

The dance was going well. Patti and Jimmy were at the bar attempting to make meaningful conversation, which was difficult because of the frequent interruptions. Couples from all age groups dropped by to greet her, and Jimmy was constantly being introduced.

"I hope I'm not going to be quizzed later as to who's who," he quipped. "God, you've got a lot of friends."

"Don't worry," she answered, "I'll bail you out if need be."

She kept to herself that *she* wasn't attracting the attention; he was. She was popular, but his was the new face on the scene, and with his looks people, especially the women, wanted to know who he was.

The mention of his name awakened more than a few memories among some of the men, and word got around that he was the football player that would have brought Pemberton another state championship a few years back if he hadn't been hurt.

With the knowledge public, Jimmy was both welcomed and accepted by the members of the Pemberton Golf and Tennis Country Club.

"Come on, Jimmy," Patti said. "About the only one you haven't met is my mother, and you know how mothers are."

"Fine, I'd love to meet her. Is she as pretty as you are?"

"You'll see for yourself, and don't give me any blarney," Patti admonished good-naturedly.

"So you know about 'blarney,' do you," he shot back in his best Irish brogue. "I'll be having to be careful then."

Patti was smiling as she caught Rita's eye. Rita and Ted were talking with the Petersons.

"Oh, here's Patti now. I wondered when you'd be coming over," Rita chided.

"Sorry, Mom. You've met my dad, Jimmy, and this is my mother, and this is Mr. and Mrs. Peterson."

The group made polite talk and Jimmy handled himself comfortably and cleverly, under the watchful eye of Rita Balter and the approving eye of husband Ted.

"Jimmy's only been back from Korea a short time," Ted informed the group. "He was wounded several times. I'm happy to say that he's coming to work for me, starting Monday, and I'm looking forward to having him with us."

Patti wanted to choke her father. She knew that he meant no harm, and never considered that others might interpret his daughter's showing up at a Club dance with a new date, who just happened to be a new employee, as a business arrangement. Rita saw the look and was about to intervene when Jimmy spoke.

"I'm looking forward to Monday, Ted, but right now I'm more interested in dancing with Patti. It's been enjoyable meeting and talking with all of you. If you folks will excuse us, we'll hit the dance floor."

He shook hands, saving Rita and Ted for last. He asked Ted if they might meet in an hour or so and have a drink together, which was fine with Ted. Looking into Rita's eyes, he asked if she would save a dance for him.

Rita smiled, momentarily captivated, and said, "Of course."

As the young couple moved toward the dance floor, Ted looked at Rita and asked, "What do you think?"

"I think you just embarrassed the hell out of your daughter," Rita scolded.

Ted had no idea what she was talking about, and decided not to ask for an explanation.

On the dance floor, Patti began to relax. "You handled yourself well. My father has a knack for telling everyone's life story, and I apologize for…"

"There's nothing to apologize for, Patti. He meant no harm, and everything he said was true. I meant what I said too. I'm excited about going to work for your dad, but I'm more excited about being with you and getting to know you. You're very pretty, you know, and much more charming than I could have hoped for; and that is not blarney."

She didn't care if it was. She was happy being in his arms. He led well, danced smoothly, and she was content. She didn't want the music to stop, and they danced to the end of the set.

Patti and Jimmy sat at a table for eight, with Marilyn Shea and her husband Richard, a doctor at Boston's Mass. General Hospital; Betty and John Caufield—he was in the insurance business—and Marie and Dick Farnsworth. Dick was in the construction business, which his father had started some 40 years earlier.

The men, Jimmy guessed, were in their early to mid-thirties and the ladies in their late twenties and early thirties.

They were interesting people—educated people—both pleasant and friendly. They didn't appear to mind that Jimmy and Patti were considerably younger, and the conversation flowed comfortably.

Marilyn Shea hoped Jimmy would ask her to dance, but he didn't. She tried several times to corner him into one-on-one conversations and he answered her each time by deftly deferring to Patti for her opinion. Marilyn finally gave up.

Patti and Jimmy stayed at the table only long enough not to appear rude.

She thought there was a great deal of chemistry flowing for a first date, and hoped he felt it. He's very nice, she told herself, almost too good to be true.

Jimmy had similar thoughts. She's pretty, smart, clever and fun to be with, and I like the kind of life she leads. I guess the old saying is true: Rich or poor, it's good to have money.

Later in the evening Patti and Jimmy sought out Rita and Ted and exchanged partners for one dance. Jimmy was careful not to come on too strongly, keeping the conversation light and non-specific. Rita, looking for flaws, couldn't find any.

She found him charming. She had watched Patti and him on the dance floor earlier in the evening, and liked what she saw. She could see Patti was happy, and they did make a striking couple. Maybe Ted was right. No harm in giving the young man a little help, and if things worked out, all well and good.

"What do you think?" Ted asked as soon as he and Rita were alone.

Rita was always amazed at her husband's impatience, for in the business world he had the reputation of one who was calm and methodical.

"He's very nice, and I'm happy you're giving him an opportunity. But that's as far as I'll commit myself right now, and I'm insisting that you allow the two of them to develop their own relationship. If it leads to something, all well and good. But it's their lives and their decisions, and don't you dare interfere in any way. You understand?"

Ted was grinning from ear to ear. He was accustomed to putting good deals together, and he was usually right in the way he handled things.

"Of course, dear," he answered smugly.

The dance ended at midnight, and after the obligatory round of farewells, Patti and Jimmy made their way to her station wagon.

"I'll drive if you don't mind," Patti said. "The road out of here is terribly tricky at night, but I've done it a thousand times."

"Sure, I don't mind," he answered casually, undecided as to whether he did or didn't.

"Lordy," she uttered, as she sat in the driver's seat, "I can't reach the pedals," and she broke out in laughter. She adjusted the seat and drove slowly out of the confines of the Country Club.

"I had a great time, Patti," Jimmy said. "Thanks for inviting me. Your friends all seem very nice, and your mother is quite the elegant lady."

"You certainly impressed her. I could tell by the look on her face when you danced with her. You held her kind of close, didn't you?"

Jimmy's face reddened until he caught the grin on her face.

"I kept thinking it was you," he replied impishly.

It was Patti's turn to blush.

They reached Jimmy's home minutes later. The house was dark, except for the porch light and a light in a third floor window.

"Someone's still up. I hope I'm not getting you home too late, especially on our first date," she teased.

"That's my room. I guess I forgot to shut the light. Patti, I really enjoyed myself tonight, and most of all I enjoyed being with you. Can I call during the week and we could make some plans for next weekend? I mean if you're not busy, of course. I'd like to see you again—soon."

Patti was ecstatic. "I'll be in New York until Wednesday, but I should be back by early evening. Call me after 8:00. I had a wonderful time; thank you for taking me and for being such a good sport. I know it wasn't easy to mingle with a group of complete strangers."

She leaned over to kiss him on the cheek, but he redirected her face with a gentle touch of his fingertips and kissed her mouth briefly but firmly. She found herself willingly kissing back.

Without another word, he opened the car door and climbed out. He closed the door, peeked in at her through the window, blew her a kiss, and walked up the stairs and into his house.

Patti started the engine and drove away, pondering a mixture of feelings.

"WOW," she shouted out loud, and wasn't sure why she said it.

CHAPTER 39

Sunday morning was sunny, cool, and clear, and as Sean walked into the O'Brien driveway he was not surprised to see Dan O'Brien busily at work washing his car.

"Mr. O'Brien, you're going to remove all the paint if you keep washing it so often. Don't you ever get tired of working your butt off on that old tin lizzie?" Sean joked, showing a big smile.

Dan O'Brien liked Sean, primarily because Sean was always polite and respectful, both as a youngster and now as an adult. Sean never caused anyone any trouble or gave his parents any grief; something that Jimmy and Buddy were never clever enough to emulate. His own two bimbos were unpredictable from day one, and had always required a strong hand. More than once he had to lay it on them severely to keep them under control.

"Tin lizzie my ass," Dan shot back. "This car will run circles around any of those junks built after the war. And it makes more sense doing some honest work on a Sunday morning than three grown men going into a kid's clubhouse to shoot the breeze. You gotta admit that, don't you?"

"You win, Mr. O'Brien. You're right on all counts," Sean laughingly agreed.

Jimmy and Buddy emerged from the back door of their house, greeted Sean, and wisecracked loudly that they just heard the weather report calling for rain by mid-afternoon. Dan O'Brien was about to tell them where to go, but decided it was Sunday and he would simply ignore them.

Upstairs in the clubhouse, Jimmy opened the meeting. "We've had a week to think about Buddy's problem and how we're going to handle it. You first, Buddy."

"Sandberg's been on my ass all week," Buddy stated. "Some of the foremen told me it's because he doesn't like my close relationship with Zoltek. He's making it difficult for me to get my work done, and finding ways to disrupt me.

"The bastard's clever; he does it in little ways that aren't obvious. Last Friday took the cake. He *accidentally* knocked over a whole tray of samples I had collected and was about to test, and I had to redo all the sampling. The foremen in the tan and color departments were really teed off because they had to wait until I got them the results. It set them back half-an-hour, and being Friday, they weren't happy. I want him out, and I'll tell you how we can do it."

"We're listening," Jimmy said.

"On Sunday mornings, after breakfast, Sandberg hikes up to the Lynn Reservoir, drinks a couple of bottles of beer with his lunch, and hikes back. I heard him mention it in the lunch room more than once. It's a couple of miles each way through the woods and, unless the weather is bad, he goes *every* Sunday—*and he goes alone*."

"You talking about the old reservoir where we used to have the rock fights in the tower?" Sean asked.

"Yeah, and I think it's safe to say that there aren't too many people who head up that way anymore," Buddy replied.

"What do you want to do to him up there?" Jimmy asked. "Break his legs, his arms, or his whole body?"

"As far as I'm concerned, all those things," Buddy answered cruelly. "He's making my life miserable."

Buddy's face showed pure hatred. He paused, awaiting a response.

"Okay, Buddy, I'm in." Jimmy said. "What about you, Sean?"

Sean would have liked to have been anywhere but in the clubhouse. He had thought about the problem all week without arriving at a satisfactory conclusion. He knew that Buddy would not be dissuaded from harming Larry Sandberg, but he had hoped a minor accident would have appeased him. Now he knew differently, *and Jimmy had agreed to go along.*

If he didn't agree, if he didn't keep The PACT, he would find himself in serious trouble with the O'Briens. He had to avoid that. He feared what they might do to him, and he didn't want to lose their friendship.

Other than his parents, he had no one who cared a damn about him. He needed people; he craved companionship, and it had never been easy.

No!, he decided, I won't lose them. They're all I've got.

"I'll help," he said in as strong a voice as he could muster. "Whatever you guys decide is okay with me. I think if we could keep the guy out of work for a couple of months the problem would be solved."

"I don't think so," Buddy said calmly. "And I'm happy to know that we're all together in this."

"Okay," Jimmy said. "Buddy, it's your ball game. You make up the rules, decide on the time and the date, and we'll meet next Sunday at Moe's for lunch at one o'clock and finalize the plan."

ONE WEEK LATER

Larry Sandberg arose at 6:00 a.m. on the Sunday the boys were to meet for lunch and finalize their plans. He made his bed, dressed, and was in his kitchen by 6:30.

Sandberg's Sunday morning ritual began. He made three well-done scrambled eggs, three slices of burnt toast which he heavily buttered, and a cup of strong coffee, which he drank black. He had cut out the half-dozen or so slices of bacon months ago. He blamed them for the weight he was putting on.

Sandberg was 63 years old. He looked older. He was 5 feet 7 inches tall and weighed 226 pounds. His face was round, pockmarked, and unsmiling. His triple chins and thick mustache contributed to his disagreeable appearance, as did the unruly way he mismanaged his full head of auburn hair.

He was twice widowed, the first time in the "old country," when he was in his mid-twenties, and again 9 years later in America.

His misfortunes augmented his sour disposition toward people and toward life. He considered suicide at one time, but lacked the courage. Instead he lost himself in his work during the day and by reading classics in the evenings.

His only exercise was his Sunday morning walk to the Lynn Reservoir with his beer, his two sandwiches, a jar of dill pickles and his container of potato salad, all packed carefully in a haversack. It was one of the few pleasures he enjoyed in his otherwise austere existence.

Sandberg left his Cottage Street home shortly after 8:oo a.m. With his haversack over his left shoulder and his walking stick gripped tightly in his right hand, he made his way to Marlboro Road and continued in his slow but steady pace to Swenson's Lane. From here the path became more difficult but much prettier, as he was entering woods, and the trees were still sporting bright colors.

Swenson's Lane was a weed-covered, potholed dirt road that led to the remnants of a small farm house. The house had gone up in flames years ago and old man Swenson with it. All that remained were some charred timbers, a blackened foundation, and a nearby well that had been covered over with planks long ago and now served as the abode for many of nature's small creatures.

The trail soon narrowed to a footpath and headed steeply uphill. This section was heavily wooded and Sandberg's favorite part of the trip. The tree-shaded path reminded him of his youth in the mountains and forests of his Norwegian homeland, and it was during this portion of his walk that he briefly knew happiness once again.

Lost in thought, he never detected the figure who emerged from behind the huge partially moss-covered boulder flanking the footpath.

Sandberg felt a shock rip through his body as an 11 inch blade penetrated his back below his left shoulder blade and entered his heart. The killer had struck with such force that the blade buried itself nearly to the hilt, and the hapless victim pitched face-forward to the ground, choking and gasping and spitting up blood.

In seconds it was over—Larry Sandberg was dead.

The killer, breathing heavily, checked in every direction for signs of life—human life. There were no witnesses.

He rested a moment longer before stepping forward to wrench the knife from Sandberg's body and wipe the blade on the dead man's pants. He dropped the knife to the ground. Clutching the body by the ankles, he dragged Sandberg behind the boulder and left him hidden in some nearby brush. He returned to the attack site, picked up Sandberg's haversack, opened it, examined its contents, and removed one bottle of beer. He unwrapped a sandwich, smelled it, grimaced and threw it back into the haversack.

The killer, calmer now, opened and drank the beer rapidly, as he had much to do.

He retrieved his knife, put it in the case he wore beneath his shirt, and returned behind the rock. He picked up the surplus army entrenching tool he had brought with him and continued to dig the trench he had started earlier.

The work was difficult and time consuming. He paused frequently, as much to listen as to rest. He did not want to be surprised by any chance hikers coming from either direction.

The earth was hard, rocky, and interspersed with tree roots, but in another 20 minutes he had completed a trench roughly 2 feet deep, 3 feet wide, and 6 feet long. Pausing to listen once again, and satisfied that he was alone, he dragged the body from its hiding place and rolled it into the excavation. He threw in the haversack, walking stick and Sandberg's wallet (after he removed the bills) and quickly covered the skimpy grave-site. He didn't want the money, but why let it rot. He scattered the excess soil and camouflaged the grave site and drag path with a plentiful supply of fallen leaves and a few dead branches. He scrutinized the area carefully, eventually nodding with satisfaction.

He returned to the attack site and dug up the blood-soaked top soil and leaves and discarded them in a swampy area some 30 feet off the path. It took several trips, and on each return trip he brought back a shovel full of virgin soil to replace what he had removed. He finished by scattering leaves and twigs over the attack site, and once more stepped back to examine his handiwork. He decided the rain predicted for the evening, as well as normal leaf-fall, would complete his work.

He was sweating profusely after his nearly hour-long exertion, but his body tingled with the exhilaration he felt over this murder. He ran the episode through his mind to make sure he had covered every detail, and was satisfied that everything was in order.

The killer went behind the boulder, retrieved his knapsack, and put the entrenching tool inside. He was now totally calm, but he was again thirsty and cursed himself for not taking the second bottle of beer. His hands were moist and sticky, but he dared not remove his cotton work gloves until everything had been completed.

After one final look around, he headed downhill at a rapid pace. If he heard or saw anyone in the distance, he planned to leave the path and make his way back through the denser woods.

It wasn't necessary.

He reached Swenson's and went to the abandoned well, where he raised one rotten plank from the well-cover and dropped a rock down the musty shaft. He listened intently and smiled seconds later when he heard the splash. He removed the entrenching tool from his backpack and dropped it into the well, knowing that he would be the last one to ever see it.

He removed his gloves and put them into his backpack, re-strapped the cover, and hoisted the backpack back into position. His long-confined sweaty hands welcomed the cool air.

He smiled, pleased with himself, for all had gone well.

He proceeded home by a different route than he had come and decided to relax a bit before attending to his remaining plans for the day.

He glanced at his watch. It was 11:25 a.m. He had plenty of time to clean up and get ready.

CHAPTER 40

THE SAME DAY

Moe's Restaurant had long been a favorite of the three boys. Large portions of old-style Italian food, fresh garden salad served with spicy Italian dressing, and warm crusty loaves of bread coated in garlic butter were popular menu items, as were a choice of several draft beers served in frosted mugs; all at a reasonable price.

Buddy arrived at the restaurant at 1:15 p.m. Jimmy and Sean were seated in a corner booth when he arrived, and waved off his apology for being late. They ordered beer and asked the waitress to bring them a basket of bread. They told her they would order their meals a little later. The waitress returned with the drinks and bread, set them down, and told Jimmy to whistle for her when they were ready to order.

Once she departed, Buddy spoke.

"Next Sunday's out; I've got to go to a wedding in Connecticut with Doreen and her family. But 2 weeks from today we'll meet at Brown's Pond at 8:00 a.m. We'll bring fishing rods so that's where we'll appear to be going. We'll hike to the reservoir from the Lynn side; past the pumping station and up the dirt road. We'll leave our fishing gear hidden in the woods and swing around just below the reservoir until we reach the approach path from Swenson's. We'll hide off the path at 50 foot intervals. You'll be below, Jimmy, and let him pass by. I'll be in the middle and Sean will be 50-or-so feet above me. You two will do the listening and watching, and if I don't hear either of you whistle, I'll jump him when he goes by me and knock the bastard out. He'll never know what hit him."

"And then what?" Jimmy asked.

Buddy didn't hesitate. "Then I'm going to break both his ankles for starters and, depending on how I feel, go on from there. All you guys have to do is keep your eyes and ears open; I'll do the rest. If you want to get your licks in, you're more than welcome," he added dispassionately.

"You'll have to cover your face, Buddy, in case he hears you coming and turns around," Sean asserted thoughtfully.

"I thought of that," Buddy answered.

"What if there are other hikers already at the reservoir, or on the path?" Sean asked.

"Then we move further down the path, away from the reservoir, asshole," Buddy replied, eyes glaring. "You know, sometimes…"

"Calm down, Buddy," Jimmy interrupted, in a tone that demanded compliance. "The question is legitimate and has to be considered. We could set up farther down, as you said, and if for any reason it looks risky, we abort and re-plan. So let's all cool down and order; I'm hungry."

Without waiting for an answer, Jimmy whistled to get the waitress' attention. She turned to give the whistler a dirty look but, seeing who it was, approached the table with swinging hips and a big smile.

"Well, good looking, I assume you were whistling at me, so what can I do for you, and no wise-ass answers."

It was Jimmy's turn to play. They had known each other since he was a kid coming into the restaurant with his father, and she was egging him on even then. "Irene, my love, and keeper of such a bountiful bosom which continually reminds me that I'm hungry; we would like to order."

Irene pulled back her hand as if to slap him, and then turned on a big smile and leaned over the table, exposing more of herself.

"If I was 10 years younger and you was 10 years older, it would be a match made in heaven itself," she quipped in her Italian rendition of an Irish brogue, "although I don't think you'd make it out alive after the wedding night."

They laughed and continued laughing when Jimmy answered, "but what a way to die."

They placed their order and spent the next hour eating and finalizing their plans.

"In 2 weeks, Buddy, your problems will be over," Jimmy affirmed.

Buddy grinned, checked his watch, cursed, and said, "I'm late again; Doreen will be furious. I'll be in touch; talk to you both during the week."

Jimmy and Sean stayed on, ordering another beer.

"How are things going for you?" Sean asked.

“Great; better than I expected” Jimmy answered. “I’m finding the leather business interesting, and they’re all being helpful. I’m not too crazy about the odors, but they’re only bad in the beamhouse, and I won’t be working there long. They want me to spend a couple of months in the finishing and shipping areas, and there’s a pleasant leather smell there and I won’t mind that.”

“What will you eventually be doing, or don’t you know yet?’

“Mr. Baltar wants me to know about the different types of leathers that are made there, how they are made, and the purpose intended. He eventually wants me to meet with the different customers and get to know their needs and be able to talk their language so I’ll be able to service them better. I’ll be getting a company car and an expense account; and he said he’ll put me on salary plus commission. He plans to personally take me to his major customers—he called them ‘house accounts’—and introduce me, and turn those accounts over to me. He’s going to tell them that I am his main man and they can deal with me as if they were dealing directly with him.”

“Jesus,” Sean uttered, impressed, “it sounds great. How the hell did you ever fall into a deal like that?”

Jimmy grinned. “The guy’s a football nut and told me that he was impressed with the way I played at Pemberton. He said he felt bad when I got hurt, and wanted to do something to help me out. Can you imagine that? He’s a big man in local sports and heads up the Pemberton Athletic Club.

“He’s also the guy responsible for bringing Coach Wilzinski to Pemberton, and he’s plenty miffed that they never caught the guy who did him in. Have you heard anything new on that?" Jimmy asked.

"No, haven't heard a thing or seen anything in the papers. Apparently they're not getting anywhere in the investigation."

"Fuck him anyway," Jimmy remarked with bitterness. "I never let on to Mr. Baltas what I thought of the son-of-a-bitch. Anyway, that's in the past," Jimmy added.

"As far as my job is concerned, Sean; it's great. And Ted Baltar is great. I've got the feeling that he wants me to spend time with his daughter because he's always bringing her name up in our conversations. And that's okay, because I plan to anyway. Patti's nice, but I can tell she resents her old man interfering with her social life. He's very outspoken, and on a couple of occasions he's made it a little uncomfortable for both of us. You should see the looks she gives him. I don't want it to appear as if I'm seeing Patti so I can suck up to her father, especially where I'm the new guy on the scene, but I guess that's the way it's gonna be and there's no way around it."

"So what, Jimmy," Sean said. "Why should you care how it looks to anyone. You know that no one would ever dare say anything to your face, and there's no way you can control what they think; so the hell with them. If you like her, then you see her, and screw them all."

Jimmy smiled. He had known Sean his whole life and Sean had always been a loyal friend. He's more like a brother to me than Buddy, and a hell of a lot more trustworthy, Jimmy admitted to himself.

"Enough about me, Sean. How's school going?"

"Love it," Sean beamed his answer. "School is great and the work program is interesting. I've met a lot of people who have been helpful, and I love living in Boston. I'm in a one room apartment and sharing a bath, but it's working out well. The commute used to knock the hell out of me.

"My mother's still not happy I moved out of the house. You know, she keeps my room at home exactly the way it was and insists that I come and stay with them as often as I can. She just won't let go."

Jimmy laughed, for Eileen Boyle had always been like that.

"How about your dad; how's he doing?" Jimmy asked.

"Unfortunately, not great. He has trouble moving around and finds it difficult to breathe. He's still sneaking a cigar now and then and mom doesn't want to take away all his pleasures, but she makes sure he doesn't smoke more than one-a-day. He coughs a lot, but never complains. The doctor said there's nothing that can be done for him. He reads all the time, and that keeps him happy."

"Tough, Sean. How about your love-life? You seeing anybody steady in Boston, or still playing the field? I don't understand why you don't latch on to some Pemberton gal; there are plenty around."

"You and Buddy always seemed to have had the local girls locked up. I couldn't get any of them to look at me," he answered, half-serious. "I do have a couple of friends in Boston, but no one I'm particularly heavy with right now. There are always parties in the area, so I can socialize just about any time I feel the need. Like I said, Boston's great."

Jimmy checked his watch. “I’m picking up Patti at 4:30 and we’re going to an early movie. How about joining us?”

“I’d like to, Jimmy, but my aunts are coming over at 4:00, and I promised my mother I’d spend a couple of hours with the family before I head back to Boston. Thanks for asking.”

They shook hands and parted, each reflecting on the events of the day.

CHAPTER 41

THE NEXT DAY

Buddy arrived at work 6:45 Monday morning, changed into his work clothes, and headed for the lab.

The lab was a 30 by 20 foot area located between the tan and color departments. Two equally-spaced 3 by 10 foot work benches, each with its own small stainless steel sink, divided the room. The benches were laden with a variety of testing equipment, including pH machines, titration apparatuses, test tube racks, hydrometers and thermometers, many types of flasks and other glassware, and several small physical testing machines.

Two desks, a series of file cabinets, a ceiling to floor bookcase, and several chairs were squeezed into one far end of the room. Directly opposite the desks an area had been blocked-off floor to ceiling to allow for a room that was temperature and humidity controlled. This room contained a muffle oven, two desiccators, an analytical balance and a gram scale. An adjacent room, also temperature and humidity controlled, housed a Scott tester.

As Buddy was about to start his day, Arthur Zoltek hurriedly entered the lab. "Good morning, Buddy," he uttered tersely, as if his thoughts were elsewhere. "Mr. Sandberg's not in, and I've been trying to reach him. I want to try calling him again. Excuse me a minute."

Zoltek picked up the phone and made the call. After a minute or so he hung up.

"I don't understand," he said, concerned. "There's no answer at his house. In the 5 years I've been here he's never been out and seldom been late."

"Maybe he overslept and is on his way in," Buddy offered.

"Not Sandberg, Buddy; but I suppose there always could be a first time. Page me in half-an-hour if he hasn't shown up, and I'll call again. I assume you can handle everything in the meantime. If you need any help, or have any questions, call me."

"Yes sir. I'll take care of everything," Buddy assured him.

Thirty minutes later Buddy paged Zoltek and told him that Mr. Sandberg had not shown up.

Zoltek again phoned Sandberg's home without success.

Something's wrong, Zoltek thought. He headed for the front office, donned his jacket, and told the switch-board operator that he was going to the Sandberg home and would be back shortly.

"Anything wrong, Mr. Zoltek?" she asked.

"I don't know, Nancy, that's what I want to find out. Either he's not in or he's not answering the phone. And that's not like him."

"No, sir, it isn't. I hope everything is okay," she added with sincerity.

Zoltek had been to the Sandberg home twice before, both times on cold days when Sandberg's car wouldn't start. Sandberg had walked to work on those mornings and apologized to Zoltek for being late. Zoltek had insisted on driving him home at night, over Sandberg's objection that it wasn't necessary; he could walk.

Zoltek approached the front door, located the doorbell, and pressed several times. He heard the ring from somewhere within, waited a minute, and pressed again. There was no response.

He banged forcefully on the door, paused to listen, and again was met with silence. He walked to the nearest window, peered inside and saw no activity. He was now seriously concerned. He returned to his car and drove to the Pemberton Police Station.

Sergeant Mallory was at the front desk. Zoltek introduced himself and explained the situation. Mallory suggested that perhaps Mr. Sandberg had been called away on some family emergency and hadn't had a chance to notify anyone. Zoltek explained that there *was* no family, and in any event Sandberg would never go away without notifying someone of authority at the tannery.

"I'll send someone over to check the house and the neighbors, Mr. Zoltek," Mallory said. "Where can I reach you?"

Zoltek gave him three phone numbers to the company switchboard.

"I'll be in touch as soon as I know something," Mallory assured him.

Zoltek returned to the tannery and checked with the switch board operator once again, but there had been no call. He left word in the office that he had notified the police, and when they called to put the call through to him.

He called Buddy and told him he couldn't locate Mr. Sandberg. Buddy made no comment other than saying everything was under control and going well.

When Buddy hung up he was smiling.

An hour later a police cruiser arrived at the Sandberg home. Officers Brady and Coffin got out of the car and approached the front door. Brady punched the doorbell and banged on the door, waited briefly, and repeated his effort.

No response.

Coffin shrugged his shoulders. "I'll take a look out back and try the back door. Be right back."

"Check the garage while you're at it," Brady said, as he banged on the front door again.

Coffin found the back door locked and the shade drawn. The window levels in the rear of the house were too high off the ground to access without a step-ladder, and he was in no mood to gamble on standing on a trash barrel.

He found the side door to the garage unlocked and went in. A car was in residence. He flicked on his flashlight and aimed the beam through the side windows of the vehicle. It was empty. He tried the driver-side door and it was unlocked.

He scanned the area and saw nothing but the usual clutter that can gather in a garage.

Coffin returned to the front of the house where Brady was checking to see if any of the windows had been left unlocked, apparently with no success based on the stream of profanity issuing from Brady's mouth.

"Back door is locked and the shade drawn," Coffin reported. "There's a car in the garage, unlocked, with no key in the ignition, and the hood is cold. There's a cellar bulkhead door back there that would be a cinch to jimmy."

"Yeah, let's go in. The guy might have had a heart attack," Brady said. Coffin returned to the cruiser and removed a small pry-bar from the trunk. He rejoined Brady and the pair headed to the bulkhead. Within seconds Coffin had popped the hook out of the eye and with flashlights in hand, they made their way into the cellar. They located the stairway that led up to the first floor and the unlocked door opened into the kitchen.

The house was cold, as if the heat had gone out.

Brady called out in a loud voice, "Mr. Sandberg."

No answer.

There was a bedroom off the kitchen which connected to a hallway that led to a second room furnished as a den. A bathroom was situated between the two rooms. Sandberg was nowhere in sight.

A staircase off the front hall led upstairs. There were two rooms upstairs; one a bedroom and the other was devoid of furnishings other than three metal filing cabinets and several cardboard boxes stuffed with papers and swatches of leather. "There's nobody in the house," Brady stated the obvious. "Let's check the neighbors."

The owner of the abutting house to Sandberg's did not answer the doorbell. They tried the house on the other side. The name plate on the second house was Katz.

The Katzs were at home and looked uncomfortable when they saw two police officers standing in their doorway.

"Yes—yes, what is it you want," the elderly man asked nervously after opening the door.

"You Mr. Katz?" Brady asked.

"Yes."

"I'm Officer Brady and this is Officer Coffin. We're trying to locate Mr. Sandberg. He's not home and we would like to know if you saw him recently."

"We saw him yesterday, didn't we Sonya?" Mr. Katz answered as he glanced at his wife who had come up to stand behind him.

She nodded in the affirmative.

"Like every Sunday morning, he goes to walk," Mr. Katz said.

"You know where he walks to?" Brady asked.

"Ya, he goes into the woods somewhere and spends most of the day there. Comes back 3:00 or 4:00. A real meshuggener."

"Did you see him come back yesterday?" Brady continued.

"No; we went to visit yesterday afternoon, didn't we Sonya?"

Sonya nodded again.

"We're not such good friends with him," Mr. Katz added. "He's a dummkopf—like you say, ah—oddball."

"Okay, thanks very much. If you should see him come home in the next few hours, call the police station and let us know. Will you do that?"

They Katzs nodded that they would.

"What the hell did he call him?" Coffin asked when they were back in the cruiser and headed for the Station.

Brady laughed. "A meshuggener. It's a Jew swear word. I've heard it before and I think it means that he's an asshole, or something like that."

"There was no sign of him, Sarge," Brady said as he and Coffin filled in Sergeant Mallory.

Mallory called Captain Doyle and told him what was going on.

Doyle called Sam Coben and told him to look into it, and then placed a call to Arthur Zoltek.

"Mr. Zoltek, this is Captain Doyle, Pemberton police. We've checked the Sandberg house and there's nobody there. There's a car in the garage and one of his neighbors told us he saw him set out for a walk sometime around 8:00 a.m. yesterday and hasn't seen him since. We'll keep making inquiries, and if you should hear from him be sure to let us know. I'll send someone over to see you in an hour or so. We'll need a description and whatever other information you can give us."

Sam Coben showed up at Doyle's office 20 minutes later. "Fill me in on this Sandberg guy, Captain. I gotta know where to start looking."

"I talked to his boss just a half hour ago, Sam. He said Sandberg never missed a day of work and supposedly never went anywhere to visit anyone. He has no family and apparently very few friends. His only interests seem to be reading and a weekly walk in the woods. A next door neighbor, name of Katz, said he saw him leave yesterday morning toting a walking stick and some sort of shoulder bag. So far, nobody has seen him since."

"Anybody know where he walks to?' Sam asked.

"The neighbor wasn't sure, but go see Zoltek at the tannery after you read Brady's report. Zoltek's the tanner at B. D. Barker's, and I told him you'd be coming around."

Sam arrived at the B. D. Barker plant at 11:40 a.m. The reserved parking places in front of the main office were nearly full. One open space was fronted with a sign RESERVED VIP

Must be for me, Sam thought facetiously, and parked. He entered the door marked Personnel Office and walked across the well-worn carpet to the receptionist's window.

"Arthur Zoltek, please. Tell him it's Inspector Coben, Pemberton Police." Nancy studied the medium height, medium weight, policeman with the smiling face and flat-topped crewcut while putting the call-pin into the paging box. He had a small nose, thin-lipped mouth, dancing brown eyes, and looked to be in his mid to late twenties.

Not bad looking overall, she decided. I wonder if he's married? She flashed him a smile.

Sam listened to the pager toll three rings—pause—two rings while his eyes scanned everything in sight, including the dark-haired, big-bosomed receptionist.

Not bad, he thought; certainly worth a quickie.

The bell system continued to repeat, as did the buzzing of the page box sitting on her desk. The switchboard was busy and it took several minutes before she plugged into Arthur Zoltek's call.

"Mr. Zoltek, someone here from the police to see you…yes, sir, I'll tell him." She raised her eyes toward Sam, smiled, and said, "he's on the other side of the plant, Inspector, and he'll be up in about 5 minutes. Please take a seat. Would you like a cup of coffee?"

Sam returned the smile, said "no," issued a thank you and took a seat.

Arthur Zoltek breezed into the waiting room 10 minutes later and made his way to its only occupant.

"I'm sorry it took me so long, Inspector. Please, follow me to my office and we can talk where it's quiet."

Zoltek led Sam down a mahogany wood-paneled hall, past three executive offices whose doors bore brass name plates, to a fourth door whose brass plate indicated it was his office.

"Please, sit down," Zoltek said, and pointed to a Tuscany-brown stuffed leather-upholstered chair fronting an immense mahogany desk covered with loose papers, mail, file folders and leather samples. The room was carpeted, and furnished with a matching brown leather couch, a mahogany coffee table sporting a large ash tray with two half-smoked, half-chewed cigar stubs and copious ash.

Two folding chairs and a small refrigerator were positioned along one wall next to six four-drawer metal filing cabinets. A door, partly ajar, indicated that he had a private lavatory, and the door next to it, Sam assumed, was a closet. Several pictures adorned the wall and displayed scenes of the factory.

Arthur Zoltek took his seat behind the desk and spoke as he leaned over to accept the card Sam Coben was offering.

"Is there any news, Inspector?"

"No, Mr. Zoltek, so far we have no information as to Mr. Sandberg's whereabouts. We know from a neighbor that he was last seen approximately 8:00 Sunday morning with a walking stick and some sort of shoulder bag. We understand a hike in the woods was a regular procedure for him on a Sunday; is that correct?"

"Yes, I've heard that," Zoltek responded.

"Did he ever talk to you about these walks? Where he goes and whether he meets up with anybody?"

"No, Inspector. Our conversations were almost always related to company matters. He's a difficult person to get to know, and our relationship was strictly business. I actually know very little about him, other then his wife died a number of years ago and he lives alone. He's been with the company longer than I have and is a capable and faithful employee. He's not prone to making friends, Inspector; he's very much a loner."

"How about within the plant itself, Mr. Zoltek. Is there anybody that he's friendly with, or works with, that I can talk to?"

Zoltek pondered the question. "Friendly with, I doubt; it's not his nature. However, he's frequently in contact with the wet-end foremen because he and his assistant track all chemical process controls. They do the testing that's necessary on a daily basis."

"I'd like to talk to each of them; Mr. Zoltek. Would that be possible?"

"You mean today—right now?"

"Yes sir. I could come back later this afternoon if they're on their lunch break or if it's inconvenient during their regular work hours, but it's important that I get whatever information I can as soon as possible."

Zoltek looked at his watch and confirmed that the men were on their lunch break.

"It would be better if you came back at 3:00. That will allow me time to contact each of the people you want to talk to. I'll have them waiting in the reception room, and you can interview them here in my office where it will be private. If you want me for anything, or if you hear anything, just pick up my phone and tell the operator to get me."

"Thank you, that should work out just fine. Could I have the names of the people I'll be seeing? It will save me some time."

Sam withdrew a notebook and pen from an inner pocket and scrawled as Arthur Zoltek dictated:

Robert Conners—beamhouse foreman
Chick Boufiant—tan department foreman
Peter Vallis—color department foreman
Buddy O'Brien—lab technician

"That's fine, Mr. Zoltek; I appreciate your help. I'll be back at 3:00."

Sam pocketed his notepad and pen, rose from his seat, and shook hands across the desk.

"I hope Mr. Sandberg didn't have a heart attack or a stroke in some god-forsaken place in the woods, Inspector," Zoltek said. "I fear it has to be something like that. He's not the type to just pick up and take off."

"That could be a possibility, Mr. Zoltek. We simply don't know, and it's too early to speculate."

Sam departed, leaving Zoltek to make the necessary arrangements for the 3:00 p.m. interviews.

CHAPTER 42

Sam Coben re-entered the office of the B. D. Barker Co. at 3:00. Three men were seated in the waiting room, and they stopped conversing to study him.

Sam nodded a greeting to those seated as he walked to the receptionist's window and smiled at Nancy.

"Hi Inspector," she said, flashing a smile, "I'll be with you in one second, as soon as I get someone to take over the board."

Several moments later, she joined Sam in the waiting room.

"Please follow me, Inspector," she said, and led him to Arthur Zoltek's office. "Mr. Zoltek said you are to make yourself comfortable and to use his desk," which Sam noted had been partially cleared to give him working space. "There's Coca-Cola in the refrigerator and you can help yourself," she added pleasantly. "Who do you want me to send in first?"

Sam handed her a copy of the names on his list. "Let's start with Mr. Conners, and when he leaves, just follow the list. And thanks for your help."

She smiled a bigger smile and took her leave.

Sam settled into Arthur Zoltek's seat behind the desk and found the swivel chair too low and too soft. He moved it aside and replaced it with a straight, high-backed chair which he found more comfortable.

Bob Conners appeared nervous as he entered the office.

Sam introduced himself and pointed to a bridge chair he had positioned directly in front of the desk.

"Sit down, Mr. Conners; this will only take a few minutes."

Conners was a tall, lean yet muscular man in his late fifties. He had a full head of gray hair that needed to be cut. His eyes were hazel, his nose pointed but not obscenely so, and a lined face indicating a preference for the outdoors. All things considered; he was a good-looking man.

His voice was deep but not guttural.

"Thank you," he answered as he sat down.

Sam reported that Mr. Sandberg was missing and had not been seen since early Sunday morning. He explained that ordinarily there wouldn't be any concern over someone missing for such a short period of time, but where Mr. Sandberg had been so predictable in the past, there was some anxiety over his whereabouts.

Mr. Conners nodded in comprehension.

"How long have you worked with Mr. Sandberg?" Sam began.

"Eleven, maybe 12 years."

"Were you friendly with Mr. Sandberg outside of work, Mr. Conners? Did you ever have dinner or a beer together, or do anything together?"

"No," Conners stated emphatically, "we weren't friends. He's not a friendly person. Smart, very smart, but not friendly."

"Did he ever talk to you about his Sunday walks or what he does in his spare time?"

"No, don't know nothing about that."

"Thank you, Mr. Conners. I appreciate your time. You can go now."

"We're all done?" Conners asked in surprise.

"Yes sir; thank you," Sam replied.

For the first time, Bob Conners grinned, showing a number of pure-white, perfectly aligned teeth. He rose from his chair, said good-bye, and left.

Sam made a one-word notation in his notebook next to Conners name.

ZERO.

Chick Boufiant, the Tan Department foreman, was quite the opposite from his coworker in both appearance and manner. He was a short man in his middle thirties, bald, moonfaced, and wearing a pleasant smile on his freckled face. His file indicated he began working for the company at the age of 17.

His father died when Chick was in his junior year of high school, and it was necessary for Chick to leave school and support his mother and younger brother. He had always been a good student, interested and alert, but recognized his responsibilities and reluctantly but unselfishly ended his formal education.

In the 18 years he had been with B.D. Barker & Company, he had attacked every job challenge with determination. His abilities were soon recognized, and after his first 2 years of employment he was moved into the tan department as an apprentice to Charlie Martin, the department head.

Charlie was a regular guy; smart and unpretentious. He took a liking to this kid who was the bread-winner for his family. He encouraged him to attend night school, and Chick obtained his high school degree in 2 years.

Charlie later convinced the young man to attend Stanton College evenings, and Chick audited first inorganic chemistry, then organic chemistry, and did well in both subjects.

He had been nurtured, instructed, lectured, and tutored for 7 years by Charlie Martin, up until the time Charlie succumbed to a massive coronary.

At the age of 26, Chick Boufiant succeeded Charlie Martin as Department Head.

"Hi, Inspector, I'm Chick Boufiant. You wanted to see me?"

Sam introduced himself and handed him his card. He explained the disappearance of Larry Sandberg.

"He's been missing about 36 hours, Mr. Boufiant, which ordinarily would not arouse deep concern, but based on his life-style and habits, Mr. Zoltek fears that only an accident or sudden illness would have caused his absence without notification."

"I agree. How can I help, Inspector?"

"We've learned that Mr. Sandberg takes walks on Sundays. Apparently he did so yesterday and failed to return. At least no one saw him return, and we've checked with his neighbors. Did he ever talk to you about his walks and where he goes?"

"He wasn't much of a talker about his outside activities, Inspector, but I vaguely remember something he once said that struck me as typically Sandberg. It had to do with buying a dog to take on his Sunday excursions because dogs were not like people; dogs you could trust. He's an odd-ball, but I get along with him okay."

"Did he mention where he took these excursions to?" Sam pressured.

"I really can't be positive because it was a long time ago, but in the back of my mind the reservoir in the Lynn woods pops up. I think it was him, but I'm not absolutely sure."

"How would *you* describe Mr. Sandberg in general, Mr. Boufiant," Sam asked.

Chick chuckled. "That's easy, Inspector. Strange—a misanthrope if there ever was one. He…"

"A what?" Sam interrupted.

"A loner, Inspector, a real loner. I must admit I'm an overly friendly guy who talks a lot and who is not easily put off, but Sandberg's probably the most introverted person I've ever met. It took me nearly a year before I could get more than a single sentence at a time out of him, and that was business related. Every once in a while he took the time to answer my questions on chemistry-related matters, about which he's a crackerjack, so I considered that a positive. Very seldom would he let me carry on a discussion for the sake of just talking."

"You ever spend any time with him outside of work, Mr. Boufiant? Stop off for a beer or visit him at home?"

"Hell no. We live in two different worlds, Inspector, and he's the closest thing to a hermit I've ever met. I don't think anybody can socialize with him."

"Thank you very much, Mr. Boufiant, you've been helpful. If you should think of anything else that might help, I'd appreciate hearing from you. Please send in Mr. Vallis on your way out."

"Will do, Inspector. I hope the old coot shows up okay. And the more I think about it, I do think it was he who told me he hikes up to the old reservoir."

As Boufiant left, Sam noted in his book next to Boufiant's name—

LYNN RESERVOIR.

Pete Vallis was in his late fifties. He was about 6-feet tall, displayed somewhat of a potbelly, was nearly bald, and wore small circular-framed, metal-rimmed glasses with thick lenses. He walked slightly bent over and with a shuffle more than a stride. He had a large unpleasant looking mole on the left side of his face an inch from his earlobe—which he constantly rubbed—and sported a thin gray mustache. A freshly-lit cigarette hung from his lower lip.

"Please sit down, Mr. Vallis. I'm Inspector Coben and I would appreciate your answering a few questions."

"Mind if I smoke?" Vallis asked in a barely audible voice.

"Suit yourself." Sam went on to explain the reason for his being there, and then asked, "Were you friendly with Mr. Sandberg?"

"No, sir. He wasn't interested in having friends."

"Have you ever been to his home or he to yours, or have you ever been out to lunch or dinner with him?"

"No sir to all them questions. I've had coffee with him a number of times here in the plant, but never outside."

"In the plant, then, when you were having coffee with him, did he ever discuss anything about his personal life, like hobbies or interests or any type of activity?"

"I can say with certainty that he did not. We only made company talk, and not much of that. I really have very little to do with him on a day to day basis. It's only when a drum operator makes a mistake and the lab picks up on it that we have any real discussion, and he's always trying to tell me how to correct the problem when he knows damn well I know what to do."

"I'm sure you do," Sam remarked kindly. "Did he ever mention hikes in the woods or where he goes on Sundays?"

"No sir, not that I can remember."

"Thanks for your time, Mr. Vallis. That's all I need now. On your way out please ask Mr.—Sam paused to check the final name on his list—O'Brien to come in. If anything else comes to mind, please call me." He passed him his business card."

Pete Vallis forcefully ground out the remains of his cigarette in Zoltek's ashtray, smiled feebly, and pocketed the card as he left the room.

Sam entered another ZERO in his notebook.

A few minutes later there was a soft knock on the office door. Sam looked up and noticed that Mr. Vallis must have swung it closed on his way out.

"Come in Mr. O'Brien."

A young man no more than nineteen or twenty entered the room.

Sam, in his systematic way, sized him up. Five feet ten or eleven, lean and firm without being exceptionally muscular, neatly combed black hair, thin face and piercing black eyes that seem to look right through you. Small nose, small mouth and unusually clear facial skin; what many women would call good-looking, if you liked the type.

Sam had seen this face before but he couldn't place where.

"I'm Bud O'Brien. You asked to see me." The voice was calm and his statement to the point.

"Yes I did, Mr. O'Brien. You're Mr. Sandberg's assistant?"

"Yes. May I sit down?" he asked, in the same stoic tone.

"Of course; please do," Sam replied, realizing he had not offered the young man a seat, having been too busy concentrating on his newest entrant.

Buddy lowered himself into the chair in front of Inspector Coben, leaned back, and sat expressionless.

"Have we met before, Mr. O'Brien?" Sam asked.

"Not to my recollection," Buddy answered, having no intention of jogging the cop's memory.

Sam dropped the subject. It would come to him, sooner or later. It always did. "Mr. O'Brien, you are aware that Mr. Sandberg is missing?"

"Yes."

Sam paused momentarily, expecting more than a one-word answer, but when it was not forthcoming, he smiled. Okay, Mr. Cool Guy; we'll just pull it out of you, he thought.

"How long have you been working for the Company?"

"Sixteen months."

"And during that time period you've worked directly for Mr. Sandberg?"

"Other than the first few weeks of my orientation period, I've worked directly for Mr. Sandberg."

Well, I finally got a sentence, Sam thought, mentally congratulating himself. "And how would you describe your relationship with Mr. Sandberg?"

"What do you mean?" Buddy asked pointedly.

"I mean do you get along well with him? Is he friendly? Do you work well together? That sort of relationship."

"I would say that we work well together. He is extremely meticulous to details and insists that I be the same. I prefer to work that way, so we have no problem. I can not say that he is friendly to me or anyone else he works with. That's the way he is, which is okay with me. He does not tolerate sloppy work or work habits, and is always all business. I think my work methods and adherence to his high standards satisfy him, although he has never told me so."

"Did he ever get angry with you for mistakes you made, and give you a call-down?" Sam asked, warming to the subject.

"No. I haven't made any mistakes. We haven't had words, if that's what you mean," Buddy added. "My work is always up to snuff."

Sam was back within himself. This guy's damn sure of himself. Where in hell have I seen him? The answer wouldn't come.

"Mr. O'Brien, did Mr. Sandberg ever discuss any of his outside activities with you?"

"No."

"Did he ever talk to you about his family, or any of his interests?"

"No."

"Is there anything that he ever said that indicated he might be having trouble with anyone inside or outside the plant?"

"No."

Sam paused. Damn it, back to one word answers. I'm getting nowhere with this guy.

He decided to end it. "Thank you, Mr. O'Brien; here's my card. If you should recall anything that might be helpful please contact me."

"Okay," came the laconic reply, and without another word Buddy O'Brien rose and left the office.

In the hallway, a devilish grin momentarily appeared on Buddy O'Brien's face.

Sam made an entry next to the O'Brien name.

HOW DO I KNOW HIM?

Sam remained at Arthur Zoltek's desk for another 5 minutes, reviewing his notes.

The only thing I've got here is a vague recollection by Mr. Boufiant that Sandberg possibly hikes to the Lynn Reservoir. It's a starting point, Sam thought.

He slid his notebook into his inner-jacket pocket, returned the ashtray to its earlier position, replaced the chairs, and left the office. Pausing briefly at the receptionist's window to talk to Nancy, Sam left her with words of thanks for Mr. Zoltek's cooperation and the message that he would contact him as soon as he had anything to report.

He glanced at his watch; it was 3:57 p.m.

Once in his car, Sam radioed the station for messages but drew a blank. He retrieved his notebook and thumbed through it until he found the name of the neighbor that Officer Coffin had talked to.

"Okay, Mr. Katz, let's see if we can get any more out of you," Sam said out loud, backed his Ford from its VIP parking slot, and headed for the Katz home.

CHAPTER 43

Phil Katz heard the doorbell ring, but was in no rush to answer it. Sonya will get it, he thought. The second time it rang he remembered that Sonya was visiting her sister, and he was home alone. "Shmuck," he said, admonishing himself, and rose to see who was there.

"Mr. Kates?" the youthful-appearing Sam Coben asked.

"No, I'm Mr. Katz," Phil corrected. "Like the animal," he added with a smile.

"Sorry. I'm Inspector Coben, Pemberton police. Patrolman Coffin talked with you earlier today about your neighbor Mr. Sandberg. He said you saw Mr. Sandberg leave his home Sunday morning. In which direction was he headed?"

"He always goes in same direction on Sunday. Somewhere into woods."

"Which direction is that?"

Phil stepped out the front door and beckoned Sam to follow. Once on the sidewalk, Phil pointed west on Cottage Street. "He goes that way to Marlboro Street and goes left.

Somewhere up there he goes to woods and walks from Stanton woods to Lynn woods. I never been, so I don't know the way. He told me this years ago, on one of the times he felt like talking, which wasn't much. You still not found him?"

"No, sir; we haven't. Thank you, you've been helpful."

"Okay; if I see him I tell him call you right away. That's what I should do, no?"

"Yes, Mr. Katz, that's what you should do. Thanks again."

"Okay, Mr. policeman," Phil said proudly and turned and walked back into his house.

Sam returned to the station, located Captain Doyle and Lieutenant Rafferty, and brought them up to date.

"I think we should make arrangements in the morning for a police dog and bring him to the Sandberg home," Sam suggested. "Sandberg might have gone up to the Lynn Reservoir according to one of the people I interviewed, but there are a dozen ways to get there, and the dog would be the quickest way to track him."

"Okay," Captain Doyle agreed, "you take care of it."

It was a dreary Tuesday morning, damp and cool, when Sam phoned Barry Dunbar, the Pemberton Police Dog Officer.

"Barry? Sam Coben. How are you?"

"Fine, Sam, just fine. Don't see much of you since you went with CID and made Inspector."

"Sad, but true," Sam answered. "I work crazy hours and don't often get into the station on your shift. Barry, I have need of you and your dog."

He explained about the missing Larry Sandberg and arranged to meet Barry and friend at the Sandberg home in an hour.

By 10:00 a.m. Barry and his German Shepherd Duke were in the Sandberg home. Duke was given some of Sandberg's dirty laundry to sniff.

By 10:40 a.m., the pair reached the entrance to Swenson's Lane. Barry removed some of Sandberg's unlaundered clothing from a plastic bag and held it for Duke to renew the scent. The two searchers were off again.

The sky was beginning to show signs of clearing, with the sun occasionally peeking through. The ground, with its burnt patches of grass lining the infrequently used road, was wet, with a few puddles remaining in the deeper recesses of the pathway. Barry was thankful for the yellow slicker he had donned prior to leaving his police vehicle, for every time there was a gust of wind, large droplets of moisture and wet leaves, some still brilliant in color, fell on him from the ambient tree branches.

Duke picked up his pace once the path narrowed and they had passed the remnants of Swenson's home. Barry was forced to slow Duke down because the trail was becoming steeper and he was no match for the quickness of the eager dog.

"Looks like you're on to something, old boy," he said aloud, sensing from experience the mood of the dog.

Twenty minutes later a puffing Barry Dunbar was standing still, catching his breath, while a very active police dog was sniffing an area on the footpath in front of a large boulder. Duke approached the boulder and began to circle around to the rear. He moved back and forth over a patch of land and began to bark as he pawed the ground.

"What have you got, old boy, a dead animal?" Barry swept away the covering of leaves and twigs with his hands and felt the earth below. It was loose; not hard packed.

Barry had no tools with him and began to scoop out the soft earth with his bare hands.

About midway between his elbow and shoulder he touched, then uncovered, the toe of a boot. He was sweating profusely, and paused to catch his breath.

Duke was sitting nearby, watching his every move. Barry looked lovingly at the dog, but couldn't help feel that while Duke was resting, he was working his ass off.

He resumed his work after a minute's rest and seconds later discovered what he feared. The boot wasn't empty.

The return trip downhill was made at a trot. Barry reached his car and radioed headquarters. He contacted his superior officer first and then spoke with Sam Coben. Sam told Barry to stay there until he and the CID team arrived.

Sam nailed Captain Doyle and Lieutenant Rafferty with the news of the discovery just as they were heading for lunch.

"I'll call the ME and have him meet me at Swenson's, captain," Sam said on the fly. "I'll take Lou Edelton with me. And I'd like to take Brady. I want someone up there with Barry Dunbar to secure the area. You want to come along?"

"Can't," Captain Doyle replied. "We've got a hot meeting with the mayor at the Colonial in 20 minutes and I won't be able to reach him to break it. You take whoever you need, and for the love of mercy come back with enough evidence to nail the bastard who did it. I don't want another case 'still pending' on the books. I've got enough problems as it is."

"Okay, Captain. I don't know what we're dealing with, but I'll let you know as soon as I know."

Sam's call to the medical examiner's office landed Berl Rodin as he was leaving for lunch. Berl cursed himself for not leaving 5 minutes earlier. He had been planning all morning how he was going to pig out at the China Sails Restaurant and now would have to change his plans.

Berl made notes as Sam gave him directions to Swenson's Lane and told Sam he'd be there in 30 minutes. That would give him time to grab a quick hamburger and appease his neglected stomach.

Sam sent Officer Brady ahead to join up with Barry Dunbar. He told Brady to take plenty of crime-scene tape and two shovels, cordon off a large section of the area where the body was found, and wait for him and the ME.

"I don't want anyone near the crime scene until I show up, you understand?"

"Got ya," Brady mouthed.

Sam swallowed a semi-stale doughnut and washed it down with what was supposedly freshly brewed, but definitely suspect, coffee. He briefed Lou Edelton as he ate, and Lou disappeared and returned in 10 minutes with his forensic gear.

Sam and Lou parked next to Barry Dunbar's car at the entrance to Swenson's Lane, and sat impatiently for 15 minutes before Berl Rodin showed.

Berl emerged from his Buick wearing red and black plaid pants, hiking boots, a heavy-weight gray flannel shirt, and a gray wide-brimmed canvas rain hat. He squawked his apology for being late, explaining he had taken a few extra minutes to change his clothing rather than take the chance of ruining a 50 dollar suit and having to listen to a raging wife give him a call down. He explained further that he had to mix fishing and hunting outfits because that's all he had at the office.

Lou Edelton snickered. "You look beautiful, Doc. You could make the cover of every sports magazine in the country."

Lou grinned at the ensuing expletive.

Sam and Lou reached the crime scene 30 minutes later, followed shortly thereafter by a red-faced, weary ME carrying a small black bag as if it weighed two hundred pounds.

Officers Brady and Dunbar had cordoned off the area encompassing the trail, boulder, and grave site and were waiting for the go-ahead to fully uncover the body. Duke sat at a comfortable distance silently observing.

"Anybody been up or down the path since you've been here?" Sam asked.

"Nope; nobody been around. Quiet as a graveyard up here," Barry Dunbar said.

Berl grimaced. "Let's dig it up, boys, but do it carefully. I don't want the shovels to bruise the body."

It took Brady and Dunbar less than 10 minutes to uncover the fully clothed body of a middle-aged man, a backpack, a walking stick, an empty beer bottle, and a wallet devoid of money but with papers identifying its owner as Larry Sandberg.

Berl Rodin, on his knees, proceeded to make his examination. After several minutes he struggled to get to his feet, and glared at Sam Coben.

"There's a massive knife wound, from behind, into his heart."

Berl brushed off his trousers, which had wet through to his knees. "Get a team up here and let them bring the body to the morgue. There's nothing else I need to do here, Sam."

Lou Edelton took pictures and carefully collected and marked the items found in the grave alongside the body, while Sam, Brady, Dunbar, and Duke scoured the area for clues. Sam found what appeared to be several drops of blood on a leaf in the pathway, bagged it and gave it to Lou Edelton. He sent Brady back to the car to radio for an ambulance and additional help to bring the body out.

The autopsy the next day confirmed the cause of death as the knife wound, and the ME confided to Sam that it appeared to be the same type of knife wound he had observed with Coach Wilzinski and Jerry Gordon.

"Could be the same weapon, Sam," he added grimly.

CHAPTER 44

Sam was troubled the day after the gruesome discovery of Larry Sandberg's body, and poured out his frustrations to Barney Osham over breakfast in Stanley's Cafeteria.

"We've got a serial killer, Barney; I'm sure of it. There doesn't seem to be any specific time period for his actions, and we sure as hell don't know what turns him on. It's not sex and I doubt if it's money. It's got to be someone local who shows all the signs of normalcy and then goes off his rocker for some reason. I could be next to this guy everyday; drink coffee with him in the same restaurant, even talk to him, and I have no inkling who the crazy bastard is."

Barney was sympathetic. He had also experienced cases that haunted him. Any good cop couldn't help but take his disappointments home with him. It didn't happen any other way.

"You'll get him, Sam. He'll make a mistake—slip up in some way—and you'll bury the bastard. Obviously he's smart; but his luck will run out."

"It better happen soon," was all Sam could say.

Sam and Barney had reviewed the Pemberton murder case histories together on more than one occasion. They acknowledged that someone strong enough to move dead or dying bodies of full grown men was on the prowl. The victims appeared to have no specific ties to one another, although one had been a teacher and coach in Pemberton High School and another a pupil, but with no known links to each other according to the investigative reports.

The third victim was an unfriendly, introverted tannery chemist—almost a recluse—who most likely did not know either of the others. The only suggestion of a connection was that the chemist worked with a kid who had been a classmate of Jerry Gordon, the murdered high school student.

The three murders had been committed with a still undiscovered blunt-point butcher's knife, a type used by every tannery in the area.

"There has to be a link, Sam. We just haven't found it," Barney said.

"Yeah, but what," Sam despaired as he banged his open hand against the top of the table. "And don't forget the Gordon kid's best friend, Harry Robinson. He was from the same high school. He wasn't knifed, but he was killed in a suspicious hit-and-run incident that may not have been an accident. Maybe they're all tied in together somehow."

"May be, Sam, but there's not much we can do until the killer makes a slip or we get a tip. We'll just have to get lucky."

CHAPTER 45

Buddy took charge of running the tannery laboratory the day after the discovery of Larry Sandberg's body and, during his first month as head man, suggested changes that were welcomed by the beamhouse, tan department, and color-room foremen. These changes simplified *their* responsibilities.

Buddy assumed these responsibilities, serving the dual purpose of making him popular with his peers and a more important cog in the overall wet-end operation.

He next proposed a number of changes to simplify process controls, and Zoltek discussed each of these suggestions with him and the foremen. Most of these suggestions were adopted. He also inaugurated a daily written report to Arthur Zoltek with pertinent data recorded in a clear-cut manner. This kept Zoltek abreast of daily operations at a glance. Zoltek voiced his appreciation and approval.

He worked well with Zoltek, never attempting to be anything but a faithful aide, and in no way upstaging Zoltek's authority. Buddy knew how to play the game.

Zoltek was by reputation and fact an excellent tanner but tanners had the reputation of being uncommunicative, unwilling to give anyone information they themselves had gleaned empirically or via nepotism.

Buddy was aware of this but wanted to know everything about tanning, and intended to stay on the good side of Arthur Zoltek. Zoltek would be the key that opened the door for him. He intended to have Zoltek's job, and the prestige and money that went with it. Jimmy was climbing the ladder to success the easy way, but he wasn't Jimmy, and he would have to earn respect and any title on his own.

Screw you, big brother, Buddy mused. I'll do it the hard way, and it will be more rewarding.

Buddy assured Doreen after his first month in charge that things were going well for him in the tannery, and she was thrilled.

"Good!" she said. "Then we don't have to wait any longer. I want to get married the Sunday before Christmas."

Buddy, in an excellent frame of mind, agreed.

Buddy and Doreen were married on Sunday, December 23, 1951. It was a traditional church wedding, as Doreen insisted it had to be.

Jimmy was Best Man, Doreen's cousin Kathy was Maid of Honor, Sally was a bridesmaid, and Sean was an usher.

Later that evening Doreen wrote in her diary, "It was a beautiful wedding. Buddy looked so handsome, and was smiling all the time. I'm very happy."

It wouldn't always be that way.

CHAPTER 46

MARCH, 1952

Jimmy had been working for 6 months, and for the first 2 months had to force himself to stay with the job. He had trouble stomaching both the animal and chemical odors permeating the initial tannery stages, and was thankful after 8 weeks to move to the less objectionable dry-end operations.

In the ensuing 4 months he had put his nose to the ground and paid strict attention to the finishing, sorting, and grading of the various types of leathers, and to the customers who would be purchasing these leathers. It was all coming together for him and he now liked what he was doing.

Patti worked 2 days a week in the plant and this allowed them to lunch together. She spent the balance of the week either in the company office on Lincoln Street in Boston or traveling to meet with New York stylists and customers.

It was her responsibility to put together the sample lines for each season and to stay on top of what was going on fashion-wise in the industry. She gathered her expertise by attending the important showings of the European stylists and designers, as well as those of their domestic counterparts. She was young and pretty and fit in nicely with the designer crowd, and she had naturally acquired the instinct for what would sell and what wouldn't. Patti, more than anyone else in the company, was responsible for obtaining the merchandising advantage over the local competition.

Patti and Jimmy were a steady twosome. They enjoyed doing things together and he was amenable to her every wish. He never exhibited a show of temper or was unkind. He had made up his mind what he wanted in life and intended to gain it. He acted the perfect suitor, and she was already deeply in love with him.

They kissed warmly and passionately on their dates, but he never tried to have sex with her. It amazed her he could restrain himself so well, for on more than one occasion she felt herself losing control and would have gladly given herself to him.

She knew that he liked her and yet he never came out with the words she wanted desperately to hear.

Jimmy, all you have to say is I love you and I'll be the happiest girl in the world.

She wanted it to be his decision and she was not going to push him in any way. She knew he wasn't seeing anybody else, or she would have heard. Besides, she hadn't made any extended trips in 2 months, and they were together regularly.

Rita behaved and did not ask questions about her daughter and Jimmy's relationship. She was content that it was only a matter of time.

Ted brought the matter up several times and Patti managed with difficulty to assure her father that he would be the first to know. On the last such inquiry she had abruptly risen and left the table. Rita proceeded to give Ted hell for being brash and inconsiderate of Patti's feelings.

Ted was mystified that his innocuous questions had created such a stir.

It was Saturday, April 12, 1952; Patti's twenty-fourth birthday. Ted wanted Patti and Jimmy to join Rita and him at the Club to celebrate the occasion, but Patti declined, saying that Jimmy had made reservations for two at Cafe Budapest in Boston. She suggested that the four of them meet for lunch at the Club on Sunday, and they would celebrate then.

Rita agreed, nudging Ted to be silent.

It was after the entree and before the peach melba desserts were delivered that Jimmy raised his wine glass for his third toast of the evening.

"I've toasted your health and I've toasted your birthday, and I have just one more thing to say. To my beautiful and lovely best friend—whom I love very much—will you marry me? I'll only accept yes for an answer."

His proposal caught her by surprise. Jimmy lowered his wine glass and reached across the table searching for and locating her hands, which she had inadvertently brought up from her lap to grip the edge of the table. She was happy but lost control, and tears streamed down her cheeks. For the moment she was speechless, and she just looked at him. Finally, gathering herself, she pulled her hands from his and reached into her handbag for a hankie to dab away the tears.

Composed once more, she smiled, her face glowing radiantly.

"Yes. I love you. That was the most beautiful proposal a girl could ever imagine."

The wedding took place on Sunday, June 22, 1952. The weather cooperated by being comfortable and sunny, true to the forecaster's prediction.

Son-of-a-bitch, Buddy thought, as he stood looking out the window in the bedroom of his apartment. Snowed like hell the day I got married, but it looks like Jimmy is going to get a perfect day. It's always been that way.

He continued cursing as he fumbled with the top button of his tuxedo shirt, which should have been half a neck size larger. Finally, managing to secure the button, he ran his index finger inside the front of the shirt collar to find and smooth out an annoying wrinkle.

He turned from the full-length bedroom mirror and aimed his voice in the direction of the bathroom, where Doreen had been ensconced for more than 20 minutes.

"For Christ's sake, Dory, when are you coming out of there? I need help with this stupid bow tie. I can't tie the fucking thing."

"Be right out, honey; and I don't like that kind of language," came the muffled reply.

True to her word, Doreen emerged a minute later, her face made up and perfumed hair still intact from her earlier 2 hour stint at the beauty shop. She was in her slip, intending to wait until the last minute before donning her dress, fearing the predictable wrinkles.

"Give me the tie and sit down," she ordered.

Buddy noted her body and felt a stirring. He pulled over a chair as if to comply with her command, and as he got close to her, he let go of the chair and pulled her into his arms.

"You look and smell great, Dory. It's early yet; we've got time to…"

Doreen had neither the intention nor the inclination to undo her past hours' preparations.

"Forget it, lover boy; definitely not now. If you behave yourself today, and dance with me whenever I tell you to, and don't get drunk, then tonight, I promise you."

"You promise?"

"That's what I said. Now please let me go; I don't want to smudge my makeup."

He did so, and obediently sat in the chair.

Men are such little boys, Doreen thought, as a smile spread across her face. Promise them something they want and they'll do anything to get it.

She deftly knotted his bow tie, adjusted the corners, stepped back to examine her work, made one minor touch-up, and pronounced it okay with a nod of her head and a flick of her wrist.

"There," she said with satisfaction, "you look absolutely handsome."

Buddy grinned his thanks and gave her an appreciative wink.

"What time do we have to be there?" he asked.

"The wedding party is supposed to be there for pictures by noon. Then there's the dress rehearsal. The ceremony is called for 2:00."

The phone rang, and Buddy walked over and answered it.

"Hello. Oh, hi. What's up? You're what? Oh, for Christ's sake. All right, I'll take care of it. You take care of yourself," he said and hung up.

"What's the matter?" a concerned Doreen asked.

"That was Sean. He's got the flu or something—103 temperature—and is sick as a dog. He won't make the wedding. He's been trying to reach Jimmy but can't get the line. He wants me to let Jimmy know."

"Oh, that's terrible," Doreen said. "Jimmy will be very upset."

"Hey, if you're sick, you're sick. I'll see if I can reach Jimmy or Patti and let them know. You finish getting dressed."

He phoned each number three times in the space of 20 minutes and each time received the mind-nettling busy signal.

Doreen joined him, now fully dressed and looking radiant.

"Were you able to reach anyone?"

"No, we'll just have to let them know when we get there. You look beautiful, Dory; you'll be the prettiest girl there."

Doreen beamed. "That's an excellent start to winning that promise for tonight. Keep it up; I love it."

Doreen and Buddy arrived at the Pemberton Country Club shortly before noon. Jimmy was sitting at the bar, sipping a Coke. He greeted them warmly, carefully bussing Doreen before extending his arm for a solid handshake with his brother. He invited them to have a drink, but Doreen declined and excused herself to find the women to see if she could be of any help.

Buddy ordered a beer.

"Sean's sick; got the flu. He tried to call you but couldn't get through."

"Oh hell, that's too bad," Jimmy answered, concerned. "How bad is he?"

"Sounded terrible. Said he was nauseous and feverish and felt lousy. Sends you his best."

"Tough. I'll tell the accommodator there will be one less usher so he can re-arrange the line up. I'll miss Sean."

They were interrupted by a nervous Ted Baltar, informing them that the photographer was ready and wanted the wedding party in the "Green Room" right away.

The wedding ceremony took place at 2:00 p.m. as scheduled. Father Murphy made it short and sweet, per Jimmy's insistence.

Patti came down the aisle on Ted's arm, looking beautiful in a traditional satin and alecon lace gown with a scoop neck, cap sleeves, and a 4 foot trailing train. She wore long gloves and carried a bouquet of white roses. Her headpiece was an elegant tiara and her face was beaming behind a sheer lace tulle veil.

Ted walked tall and steady, fortified with a double malt scotch slipped to him by an understanding bartender just minutes before. They stopped as they neared Father

Murphy, and Ted lifted Patti's veil and kissed her on the cheek. He moved aside as a smiling Jimmy O'Brien, who was being eyed with mixed feelings by every female in the room, took his place.

"My God, he's something," Marilyn Shea whispered too loud to Betty Caufield.

"Shush," Betty responded, prodding her with an elbow while nodding her agreement.

After the ceremony, Marilyn, Betty, and Marie Farnsworth made their way to the powder room, all talking at the same time.

"Beautiful wedding ceremony," Marie remarked.

"Beautiful couple," Betty added.

"Beautiful hunk of man," Marilyn chimed in, and they all laughed.

"What did you think of the Best Man?" Marie asked.

"He's cute, but you'd never take them for brothers," Betty answered. "I think he's good-looking too, but in a different way. He's darker skinned and shorter but well put together, and did you notice that he never seemed to smile? I loved his eyes, though—mysterious and sensuous. His wife is quite attractive..."

Marilyn laughed. "You've been reading too many romantic novels, Betty. Really! 'Mysterious and sensuous.' That's a little much."

"Actually, Betty's right," Marie said. "They certainly don't look like brothers. The usher that got sick and didn't show up—you know, their best friend—looks more like Jimmy's brother than Jimmy does. I saw him with Jimmy several times and mistook him for the brother. I guess Jimmy's the oddball..."

"I'll take that oddball anytime they want to throw him out," Marilyn interrupted in a tone that indicated that she meant it.

The other girls chuckled, and Marie said, "I think you've got the hots for the guy, Marilyn. At least wait until he comes back from his honeymoon before you steal him away."

Marilyn flushed momentarily but immediately recovered. She struck a sexy pose—hands on hips, chest thrust out—and responded, "stranger things have happened you know," and her face broke out in a broad smile.

After the guests passed through the reception line and entered the dining room, Ted Baltar happily embraced his daughter and new son-in-law and pulled them aside. "I don't know where mom has disappeared to, but I'll tell you without her. First, I'm very pleased with both of you. You make a good team in the factory, and I know you'll make a great team in marriage. Both institutions will require a lot of work, especially the latter, but I'm convinced you're perfectly matched."

Ted paused to grab a glass of champagne from a passing waiter, downed it in two gulps, and continued.

"I haven't told you what we're giving you as a wedding gift. I wanted it to be a surprise, but I'll tell you now. Your mother will shoot me for jumping the gun and telling you when she's not here, but I'm too happy—and maybe a little bit too drunk—to wait any longer. Jimmy, effective today I'm making you a vice-president of the company, with a salary commensurate with the position, and I'll discuss that with you when you return from your honeymoon."

Jimmy started to speak, but was silenced by a raised hand.

"I haven't finished yet," Ted said. "Our gift to both of you will require some legal paper work, which I'll take care of while you're away. Mom and I are giving you the Sebago Lake property; the main house and the guest houses—the whole thing. We've always loved it there, and I know Patti has too. Now it's all yours."

With a satisfied smile on his face, Ted added, "I'm a happy man."

Patti threw her arms around him, hugging him tightly, and whispered in his ear, "I love you, Daddy, and thank you for everything."

As she left his embrace, Jimmy stepped forward and clutched Ted's hand in a powerful grip. "Ted, I—we can't thank you enough for your generosity. Patti and I will work our butts off for the company; I promise you that. As for the Sebago Lake property; well, we're absolutely thrilled. We both love the area and it will be a great place to take the kids when we have them. Thank you Ted; thank you very much."

Jimmy congratulated himself. The fruits of the relationship were already paying huge dividends.

CHAPTER 47

The property on Sebago Lake was extensive. Nearly 4 acres of land with 330 feet of prime lake frontage was nothing to scoff at, and Jimmy knew it was an extremely valuable asset the first time he had been invited there, never realizing that it would be his (well, theirs) so soon.

The main house was close to the water. It was a two-story structure of stone and cement on the first level, and all wood on the second; over 40 feet in width and 90 feet in length. The bottom floor housed one large master bedroom with a private bath and fireplace located off of a trophy room. The trophy room featured a floor-to-ceiling stone fireplace, a pool table, a well-stocked bar, leather sofas and chairs, and two walls of shelves filled with a variety of books collected over a 40 year period by various members of the Stewart family, Rita's side of the family.

The dining room was immense, and nearly all wood. The floor, the walls, and the 18 foot dining room table were constructed of oak and highly-polished cedar. Sixteen high-backed, leather-upholstered chairs surrounded the table, and gave the appearance of a portrait from a Gothic Period.

Only the floor-to-ceiling array of windows, which allowed a view of the lake as well as the outside light to pour in, kept the room from being medieval.

There was a large kitchen which had been upgraded several times over the years, and now had all the modern conveniences. A large refrigerator, an over-sized freezer, an electric stove, an additional built-in oven, a dishwasher, a table and many cabinets and drawers were in evidence; all signs of the modernization. Two more full bathrooms and a storage pantry completed the downstairs layout.

Upstairs there were four good-size bedrooms, two baths, and several linen and storage closets. The bedrooms were furnished simply but in good taste.

The property was meant to be a get-a-way; a place to relax and enjoy the good life. Rita's grandfather had made the original land purchase and built the house, intending it for a summer escape. Rita's father had winterized it and brought in the medieval theme. He also had constructed the two, two bedroom, single-bath guest houses to accommodate what he had hoped would be a host of grandchildren shortly before he died 11 years ago.

Ted had added a tennis court and a boat house to store his 21 foot speed boat, and for a number of years used the property often and enjoyably. For the last several years, however, his fancy had turned to golf and bridge, and he and Rita found themselves devoting far less time to the Sebago Lake property. He hoped Patti would find the time to utilize it.

The wedding reception was in full swing. Patti and Jimmy were introduced and called upon to dance the opening number. All eyes were admiring the happy couple.

One pair in particular carefully scrutinized the newlyweds, concentrating on Jimmy and liking what she saw.

Well, Jimmy, she considered silently, it looks as if we both made it. We'll be traveling in the same circles now, and somewhere down the line we'll have to renew an old friendship.

With a smile on her face, Sally Marsh Dillon turned to her husband and commented, "they make a nice couple, dear. When they get settled, perhaps in the fall, we'll have them over for dinner. I don't know Patti very well—she must be quite a bit older than I am—but she seems nice and I'd like to get to know her."

"Sure, honey, we'll do that. Her dad and my dad are quite fond of each other, and have known one another for years. I've known Patti for a long time, but we hung around with different groups and were never really close," Alfie explained. "I've only met her husband a couple of times, and that was at Tanners' Club monthly meetings. He seemed very friendly and was certainly very popular. The talk was that he was quite a football player."

"Yes he was," Sally confirmed. "He was a year ahead of me at Pemberton High, and his brother Buddy and I graduated together."

Alfie had attended private school in Exeter and was unaware that Jimmy and Sally had been a twosome.

Sally saw no reason to mention it. If it ever came up, she would gloss it over as a brief and inconsequential event in her early teenage years. She loved Alfie, and she loved the life she was leading, but she remembered her night with Jimmy as an experience that had never been equaled. Her mind said forget it, but her body wouldn't let her. She pushed these thoughts from her mind and told Alfie that she wanted to dance.

CHAPTER 48

Patti and Jimmy made love every day of their Hawaiian honeymoon. Patti had wanted to abstain during the dangerous days, but found that she was unwilling to give up the experience. She hoped that she wouldn't become pregnant, but succumbed readily to his seemingly insatiable appetite.

Jimmy hoped that she *would* become pregnant. What better way to cement a relationship. Not that he was worried, but he preferred icing on his cake.

They swam, sunbathed, shopped, dined and danced every evening, enjoying an ideal honeymoon.

Patti was well aware of the attention they aroused wherever they went. She noted that women of all ages unashamedly ogled her mate, but he appeared completely oblivious to their glances and uninterested in anyone but her.

I'll have to make sure that it stays that way by giving him anything and everything he wants, without smothering him, she thought.

The honeymoon lasted 2 weeks, and upon returning to Pemberton, Patti and Jimmy settled in a newly-renovated five room apartment.

On Patti's first day back in the office, Ted, over lunch, suggested that she retire and leave the business decisions to the men.

That didn't sat well with her.

"I'll think about it later, Dad," she said, unhappy with the suggestion. The "men are superior" thing always bothered her.

"Okay, honey, you think about it," Ted answered without noticing Patti's offended demeanor.

Ted wanted them to build a home on land he owned near the Country Club, and Patti nixed that.

She wanted to work for a while before starting a family but she wasn't sure she would be able to. It all depended on how fast she became pregnant. That was all Jimmy talked about.

Well, she thought, we'll just see what happens.

CHAPTER 49

JULY, 1952

Sean Boyle was now 2 years into his co-op program at Northeastern University. He enjoyed all his classes, and loved living in Boston.

He was a different person when he was away from the O'Brien brothers. With them, he put on an act to prove that he was a regular guy. He smoked, swore, and drank beer because they did. More than once he had thrown up his guts from too much drinking, and from episodes of savagery Jimmy and Buddy carried out during their pre-teen and teenage years.

In grammar school and high school Sean feared that without tough friends he would fall prey to the antics of the ever-present bullies and wise-guys in each ethnic group. He had frequently seen schoolmates picked on and subjected to shoves, punches, and ruthless name-calling, which made their lives quite miserable. He wanted none of that.

It happened to him once, when he was in the sixth grade. He was in the school yard during recess. Buddy was home sick and Jimmy had stayed inside to copy some homework he had neglected to do the night before.

Skippy Kronis, an over-weight, over-sized bully decided to show off in front of several of his friends. He approached Sean innocently enough, pushed his index finger into the middle of Sean's chest, and asked in a loud voice, "What's that you spilled on you?" When Sean looked down, Skippy folded his hand into a fist and brought it rapidly upward, smashing Sean's nose. Blood began to flow, and Sean, hurt and stunned, began to cry in front of a laughing group of boys.

Skippy, laughing loudest of all, shouted, "You fell for that old trick, you dumb mick…"

Skippy never finished the sentence. He was spun around and he felt the power of a vicious right hand delivered to his solar plexus. All the air went out of him and he fell to the ground, gasping. His friends had backed away from the icy glare of a furious Jimmy O'Brien, who had come into the yard just in time to witness Sean's plight.

"Anybody else want to mess with me or my friend?" Jimmy challenged. He had no takers.

Turning to Skippy Kronis, who was grasping his stomach in pain, Jimmy stated calmly, "You ever mess with my friend again and you'll answer to me, fat boy. You understand?"

Jimmy didn't wait for an answer. He pulled out his handkerchief, held it to Sean's nose, and led him back inside the school building and into the wash room to help him clean up.

Nobody ever picked on Sean again.

It was that way all through grade school and high school. The boys were constantly together and Jimmy was the protector. Buddy could take care of himself with kids his own size, but there were always a few bigger guys who wanted to rule the roost and would have loved to take Buddy on, but his older brother's reputation prevented that.

Sean, with his mild nature and somewhat effeminate manner, was ripe for targeting, but his close association with the O'Brien brothers assured his safety.

##

Sean realized that life would be different for him with both Jimmy and Buddy married. He welcomed the change.

Too many years had been spent living the life they wanted, and not the way he wanted.

The memories of Gordon and Robinson still haunted him.

The murders of Coach Wilzinski and Larry Sandberg were events that he couldn't push from his mind.

The past was the past and couldn't be erased, but the present and the future could be his and his alone.

He wanted to experience and enjoy the finer things in life—music, dance, the theater—events he had always desired but deferred because of the O'Briens.

Now he intended to lead the lifestyle he secretly desired, and seek the type of companionship *he* craved. He wanted to mix with people who enjoyed what he enjoyed.

So much to see and to do, he announced to himself, and now I'm going to do it all.

Sean moved to a studio apartment on Beacon Hill. The rent was outrageous, but it's where the people he wanted to associate with dwelled, and where he wanted to live.

His father had died six months earlier.

There was no mortgage on the Boyle homestead. His mother had their personal savings, the monthly money from the upstairs apartment they rented out, and the insurance money windfall. It would more than keep her comfortable.

She wanted Sean to come home to Pemberton and live with her, but he convinced her that it would be wrong for him. She reluctantly accepted his explanation, extracting his promise for a daily phone call and frequent visits. She insisted that she had more money than she needed, and forced him to accept a monthly check to help with his expenses. He agreed because that would make his move to Beacon Hill a reality rather than a dream.

With the monthly stipend from his mother and the savings from his own carefully managed earnings, he was able to make ends meet.

Much of the entertainment Sean craved was free or inexpensive, and he was able to enjoy himself without exceeding his financial capability. He spent many Saturdays in the Boston Public Library: reading, studying, or simply browsing. He felt this would be the right place to meet people who would have the same intellectual interests as he did. He never approached anyone unless he had seen them at the library several times frequenting the Art or Music departments.

In this manner, over a period of months, he became friendly with three females, all of whom appeared to have similar interests.

Two of the ladies were more than twice his age. They were friendly and he found them interesting to talk with. Both were college graduates—lifelong friends—who spent much of their free time together. They encouraged him to pursue his interests in the Arts, and suggested literature for him to read that would open his eyes to the greatness of the Masters. Being an avid reader, he spent many a happy hour devouring Hemingway, James, Joyce, and Lawrence.

The third female was a self-acknowledged bookworm by the name of Florence Sloan. She was aloof at first and difficult to engage in conversation, but after three successive Saturdays of nodded hellos, she began to talk to him.

The following Saturday they shared lunch together. She made ham and cheese sandwiches and brought fruit and a thermos of iced tea, all packed in a small cooler. She hadn't told Sean in advance, and simply announced, "I brought us lunch—we'll picnic outside later. I prefer you call me Flossy."

Flossy Sloan was 24 years old and had lived her first 21 years in San Francisco. Her father left for parts unknown when she was 10 years old. He had come home from work early one afternoon and announced that he had quit his job and was leaving, offering no explanation.

She remembered her mother had just glared at him, speechless.

Flossy remembered she herself had become hysterical, but he ignored her, went upstairs to pack, and 45 minutes later was gone.

They never saw or heard from him again.

Flossy tried to get her mother to explain why he had done this to them, and the answer she got was always the same. "Because he's crazy and he's no good."

She stopped asking.

Flossy was pretty, bright, popular with her female friends, and did well in high school. Her only male friends were the studious, serious-minded boys and she openly abhorred the beach boy, muscle boy types. She didn't trust them and wanted no contact with them.

Flossy was raped when she was 15. She was on her way home from art class one Thursday evening when two boys on bikes rode by and gave her the wolf-whistle. She recognized them—two seniors from her school—as a couple of muscle-bound loudmouths who she had ignored before, and now ignored again. Some 5 minutes later, as she was about to emerge from the park and head up the hill to her apartment, a powerful arm encircled her waist and a hand covered her mouth, nearly choking her. It happened so fast she was unable to cry out. She struggled to no avail as she was carried to a dark hedge in a tree-lined area. Her arms were pinned to the ground by one boy while the other sat on her legs, his left hand covering her mouth as his right hand undid her blouse and skirt. She struggled with all her strength, but was unable to protect herself. First one boy had his way; then the other. Before they left they threatened if she ever told anyone they would break both her mother's arms, and that she herself would be considered a whore by every kid in school.

They left her lying on the grass, sobbing and bewildered, and remounted their bikes and rode away.

Flossy, tears streaming down her face, gathered herself and brushed herself off. Her arms were aching from being unnaturally pinned, her buttocks hurt from bearing the weight of her attackers, and she was sore from being forcefully entered. She made her way home, the fear and panic slowly abating and being replaced with unadulterated hatred.

I'll get those bastards, she promised herself. I swear it!

When she reached home she found the apartment unlocked, and a note on the kitchen table. "Over Helen's; be back before midnight."

She was thankful her mother was out as she knew it would be impossible to hide anything from her. She douched, carefully following the instructions, and made a mental note to replace what she used the following day so her mother wouldn't notice anything missing.

She filled the bathtub with hot water and soaked and scrubbed herself, as if to wash the incident away.

Her fury over her rape heightened, and she wanted to settle the score.

Damn it, they're not going to get away with it, she repeated over and over, as tears flowed once more.

She remembered their warning, but was too angry to fear them. She decided she would become the aggressor, threaten them with arrest, and convince them that she meant it.

Once she saw how they reacted, she would know what to do.

The next day Flossy searched them out and found them as they were entering a class room.

She brazenly approached them and stated forcefully, "If you know what's good for you, you'll meet me on the library stairs at 2:30 this afternoon. If you're not there, I'm going to the police and I'm going to tell them you both raped me, and you'll both be going away for a long time. And that's a promise."

She turned and walked away, leaving the two boys speechless.

The boys were sitting on the concrete stairs of the library when Flossy arrived. They had decided to threaten her again and be done with her, but she surprised them by smiling and loudly telling them to shut up.

"You both better understand the situation," she uttered coldly. "I don't give a good damn for your threats, and neither does my mother. You bastards raped me, and unless you do exactly what I tell you to do, my mother and I are going to the cops and you're both going to jail for a long time."

She spoke with venom in her voice and no hint of fear, and she could tell by the looks on their faces she had them.

She wasn't about to let up.

"You understand what I said, assholes? You're both going to jail and the real cons will make mincemeat of your pretty faces and treat you like you treated me." She could tell her bluff worked. They were frightened, shifting glances between her and one another.

"What do you want?" the blond one asked.

"I want two hundred cash from each of you. By noon-time tomorrow. Meet me in front of Stucci's Soda Shop with the money, or I go to the cops."

"Two hundred bucks?" they gasped in unison.

"Each. By noon tomorrow. No later and no less. Where you get the money is your god-damned business," she added icily, and turned and walked away.

"What are we going to do?" Eric asked, turning to Blondy.

"We're going to pay the bitch. You heard her and saw her face. She wasn't kidding and she sure as hell wasn't afraid of us. I'm not taking the chance of going to jail and getting my ass reamed. Besides, my old man would kill me if he ever found out. I'll swipe two hundred clams from my mother—she'll never miss it."

"I guess I can borrow the dough from my brother," Eric conceded, "but next time you get any brilliant ideas about grabbing a broad, count me out."

"Hey, there are plenty that are willing. I just picked a nutcake. Anybody can make a mistake."

The next day, precisely at noon, the boys each handed a stern faced Flossy Sloan an envelope. She examined each envelope, satisfying herself that the amounts were correct, before stating unequivocally, "the incident is closed, unless I hear one rumor, one peep from anybody, that it ever occurred. If I do, I go to the cops. You understand?"

The two intimidated young men nodded.

Flossy had lost her virginity, but gained some valuable knowledge. If you were smart and stuck to your guns, you could handle any situation. And she intended to exact a measure of revenge, as well as money, from every man she would have contact with from that day on.

By the time Flossy was 18, she had a clientele of a half-dozen men calling on her. She was not discriminate by age, but very particular of their status. They had to be educated and they had to be wealthy.

Her mother found out what she was doing and was unable to cope with it, so Flossy moved out and rented an apartment in a posh neighborhood.

She set regulations and rigidly enforced them. If anyone violated her rules, he was no longer welcome and was told so in no uncertain terms. Her clients had to adhere to strict time periods and could not, on a whim, unexpectedly call or drop in. She would accept phone calls only during a 2 hour time period on any given day, and would not return calls.

The men paid in cash—one hundred dollars an hour—and one of her customers always booked 2 hour visits.

She allowed herself the company of no more than six men, scheduled as often as they liked, 3 weeks a month.

Four of her customers visited twice weekly; the other two usually once a week, depending on their schedules.

Her customers not only enjoyed her sexually, but could talk to her on all matters. She was a good listener, and when she wasn't "entertaining" she was in the library boning up on their topics of interest so that she could converse intelligently with them. As their interests were diverse, she soon became knowledgeable in art, music, banking, and the stock market.

Flossy began to invest in the market. Her stockbroker friend, a man separated from his wife and not seeking another permanent relationship, helped her at first, then watched admiringly as she herself determined what to buy and sell.

"You're a whiz, Flossy," he said. "You've learned more in the last year than I did in my first 5 years in the business."

At the age of 21, Flossy decided to call it quits. She liked and admired her male friends and the security they brought her, but she needed a change. She had been frugal with her money and wise in her investments, and had amassed a comfortable nest egg.

Over the next 6 months, she decreased and then stopped her trysts with her faithful six, at first with their pleas to reconsider, but eventually with their best wishes.

She promised to keep in touch, by mail and phone, with her stockbroker friend Jerry Robinow, for their relationship had become special. On their last evening together, he had given her diamond earrings as a gift, which she did not want to accept, but he insisted.

"You've been much more than a lover to me, Flossy; you've given me my life back in ways that I can't explain to you. Please, accept my gift, and when you wear them, think of me."

Flossy, who for the past 5 years used men for her own gain, was moved by his sincerity and whispered an emotional thank you.

A month later she moved to Boston.

Sean and Flossy began spending more time together. It didn't matter to her that she was 3 years older than he, for she found him more mature then men considerably older. What did matter was they shared many of the same interests and they enjoyed each other's companionship. He told her about himself and Jimmy and Buddy, omitting any mention of the PACT.

"Jimmy's a great guy," he asserted with enthusiasm. "Buddy's okay too, but sometimes he can be strange. They're both married now so I don't see them every day like I use to, but I phone them frequently."

"Do you find yourself left out and lonely without that everyday relationship?" Flossy asked.

"To tell the truth, I thought I would, but I really don't. I do miss Jimmy and when you meet him you'll know why. He's a wonderful guy. I've always been a little afraid of Buddy and I guess I'm more relaxed when I'm not with him."

"What about girlfriends?" Flossy asked coyly.

Sean blushed noticeably before responding. "I'm not seeing anybody right now. I've been too busy with schoolwork and—and other things—to get involved with anyone."

"Oh; and what about me?"

Sean's expression showed momentary bewilderment. "I—I didn't mean you," he stammered. "I meant that I wasn't seeing anyone special. I—I mean…"

Flossy smiled. He obviously was uncomfortable with this sort of banter, and lacked the skill to counter.

"I'm sorry, Sean," she interrupted, "I didn't mean to pry. I'm just a person who says whatever I think, and sometimes I get too personal."

"No—no, you didn't say anything that you have to be sorry for. It's just me. I get a little flustered sometimes. I—I've never been too smooth a talker on a one-to-one basis, especially male to female. I—I kinda freeze up."

Flossy knew that this admission had not been easy for him, and she knew what to say.

"Sean, I just want you to know I like you—as a friend and as a man—and I want you to be comfortable with me. You can feel free to discuss any subject you want with me, in any manner you want and at any time. And I'll do the same. If we're perfectly open with one another, then we can fully enjoy each other's company. Do you agree?"

Sean, now more at ease, smiled. "Sounds great to me."

"Good. Then let's shake on it," and they did, grinning at each other.

That Saturday evening, Flossy invited Sean to her apartment for dinner. She knew she had to be the aggressor in every phase of their relationship, and welcomed the challenge. The fact he hadn't made a pass at her was interesting, and she decided he was afraid of being turned down. His lack of assurance, she thought, probably stemmed from an overbearing mother-single-child relationship, which had disastrous results on his libido.

She thought of the task ahead, and smiled.

Flossy broiled two good-sized tenderloin steaks and served them with Idaho baked potatoes topped with sour cream and garnished with chive bits. A fresh garden salad with an oil-vinegar-garlic dressing and hot pecan rolls complemented the entree. Sean contributed a quart bottle of Sauterne, which she graciously accepted but chose not to open, and instead uncorked a French Merlot which she favored, and which Sean sipped and pronounced "great."

They dined by candlelight on fine china, with sterling silverware and crystal goblets, while a Sinatra record provided the background music. Flossy had meticulously attended to every detail using the experience garnered from an old lifestyle. Only now it wasn't for business. She could do as she damned pleased if and when she wanted to, and she enjoyed the feeling.

And she wanted to with Sean. It excited her because she felt certain that she would be his first, and that she could enlighten him and teach and train him to be a perfect lover. And with their sexual appetites satisfied whenever she chose, they could better share the social and artistic events they mutually enjoyed. It could work out to be an excellent relationship for both of them; and she would be in control.

They finished dining, and Flossy announced that she didn't believe in serving dessert or coffee, as they detracted from the meal and deadened the glow of the wine. Sean agreed, and accepted another refill from the nearly empty bottle.

The meal had been excellent, their discussions had covered a multitude of interesting topics, and the wine had done its job. They were relaxed and happy.

"I feel like dancing," she said, "and I love that song."

"I don't dance very well, Flossy."

"I'll teach you," she said, as she rose from the table and held out her hand for him to take.

Sean stood up feeling a little wobbly, steadied himself, and approached her, reaching for her extended hand. She led him into the adjoining room, with its record player and uncarpeted hardwood floor begging for dancers.

She put her arms around him and moved in close, and then closer, and he swayed with her, imitating her movements.

"Hold me tighter," she said, almost in a whisper, and he did as he was told. Their feet barely moved, but their bodies were in sync, and she felt him harden against her. She peered at his face and saw that his eyes were closed and his mouth formed a pleasurable semi-smile.

Sinatra finished singing a lovely ballard and was now crooning another romantic song in his incomparable style. They continued to cling together, vibrating slowly to the tempo of the music.

She raised her left arm until she reached the back of his head, and gently forced his head forward and down until she could touch his lips with hers, lightly at first, and then with more pressure.

They remained that way for a long time, savoring their kiss.

Finally, she gently moved away, took his hand, and led him into her bedroom. Without speaking, she indicated that he was to sit on the edge of her rose-colored bedspread and when he had done so, she artistically began to undress in front of him. He watched her every movement—transfixed.

Soon she was naked, wearing only the hint of a smile. She approached him and began to undo the buttons on his shirt. He remained motionless; only the sound of his exaggerated breathing indicating that he was affected by what was taking place. She took both his hands in hers and pulled him to a standing position, and removed his shirt.

She then helped him remove the remainder of his clothing.

Flossy embraced him, and once again they swayed to the music that filtered in mellifluously from another room, their naked bodies experiencing the pleasure of each other's closeness. When the song ended, she whispered, "take the spread off the bed; I'll be back in a couple of minutes."

Without waiting for an answer, she made her way across the room and entered her bathroom, quietly closing the door.

When she emerged several minutes later, he had removed the bedspread, folded it neatly, and placed it on a chair. Her clothing, as well as his, had been collected, folded, and placed side by side on top of the bedspread. He had pulled down the shades on all the windows, not knowing if that is what she would have wanted him to do, but he had to do something while he waited.

He was now standing in the middle of the room, obviously uncomfortable with his nudity, awaiting her next set of instructions.

She went to him and led him to the bed. Her teaching was about to begin in earnest.

Sean could see the clock on the dresser quite clearly, but couldn't believe it could be correct.

Eight past eight in the morning, he said to himself; it can't be!

He reclaimed his watch from the night table and confirmed the time. He was exhausted, and knew why.

She had done things to him that he had never thought about, and from the soft cries and odd sounds that she made, had obviously enjoyed herself.

She had done nearly all of the work, and instructed him on every move.

It had taken him a long time to reach a climax, and he found it pleasant, but not earth shaking.

It was a first time for him, and he supposed it would take time to get used to sleeping with a woman.

Sean slipped out of bed and made his way to the bathroom. He freshened up but didn't shower for fear of waking her. He would shower later, he promised himself, and for a long time. Not knowing what else to do, he slid back into bed and was fast asleep within minutes.

Flossy awoke at 9:45, and turned to find Sean sleeping quietly beside her. She remained in bed without moving for several more minutes, allowing her mind and memory to clear, and recalling the events of the prior evening.

That was a hell of a session, she thought. Much more enjoyable to be in total command than to be with some guy who thinks he's God's gift to women. But I'll be damned if I can figure him out. I think he enjoyed himself, but I'm not really sure. I've never been with anyone like him before.

Her thoughts were interrupted by his voice.

"Hi. I hope I didn't wake you up," he said in an apologetic tone.

"Hi yourself," she answered. "No; you didn't. How do you feel?"

"Got a little headache, but other than that, fine."

"Great," she replied. "I've got some sore spots, but I guess that's to be expected."

He didn't catch her meaning at first, but when he did he became flustered and began apologizing. She shushed him by putting her finger on his lips and told him she was only kidding.

"How about breakfast? I'm famished," she said.

"Yeah, I'm kinda hungry too. I don't want much, though; juice, toast, coffee is all I need."

"I wasn't going to offer you much more than that anyway," she assured him. "Can you hold off 'til I shower and dress?"

"Sure. You want me to do anything while I'm waiting? Set the table, or something?"

"No. You relax. The paper should be outside the door if you want to see what's going on in town today. You can shower after I'm finished, and I'll have breakfast ready by the time you're through. I'm sorry I don't have a man's razor here for you to use, but the next time you come over I want you to bring a set of toilet articles as well as a change of clothing."

CHAPTER 50

SEPTEMBER, 1952

Flossy insisted on inviting the two O'Brien couples to her apartment for dinner. Sean tried to dissuade her but couldn't give her a justifiable reason and, under her constant urging, reluctantly gave in.

It would be the first time they would all be together. Sean wasn't concerned with the impression Flossy would make—she would fit in anywhere as she was bright, witty, attractive, and a good mixer. He was concerned about how *he* would fit in.

Flossy had her reasons for wanting to meet his friends. She wanted to see for herself what Jimmy and Buddy were like, and attempt to understand their hold over Sean.

Sean had discussed with her much of their boyhood activities, but seemed unhappy and secretive when she asked for specific details. On those occasions he would avoid her eyes and attempt to change the subject, as if it hurt to renew those memories. She sensed there was something wrong in the relationship, and she intended to find out what it was.

Flossy prepared an elegant menu, hired a cook to do the kitchen work, and a waitress to serve and attend the needs of her guests. She wanted to be free of the work entailed by a dinner party—free to be involved in all the evening's conversations.

She dressed casually but expensively in order to impress her female guests, and was ready for what she expected to be an interesting evening.

Doreen and Buddy arrived promptly at 7:30. Patti and Jimmy arrived 15 minutes later, having experienced heavy traffic on their long ride from Sebago Lake.

Flossy greeted each couple as they entered with a kiss on the cheek. The waitress stood nearby with a smile and a welcoming glass of chilled champagne.

After an hour of spontaneous conversation, two bottles of champagne, and a delicious assortment of both hot and cold hors d'oeuvres, the three relaxed, happy couples moved into the dining room to enjoy a "man's" meal of shrimp cocktail, prime rib, Idaho russet potatoes, candied carrots, and Caesar salad.

The French Merlot won ready acceptance from all but Patti, who felt too much of a glow from her earlier two glasses of champagne.

Flossy studied the two brothers with interest and had a pretty good feel for the relationship.

Jimmy was one of the most handsome men she had ever seen. His muscular frame was evident, readily discernible beneath his Louie's tailored shirt and slacks. His quick wit and frequently appearing broad smile added significantly to his appeal.

Buddy looked nothing like him. He had black hair, dark skin, and an apparent unwillingness to smile. Although nearly 6 feet tall and well-built, Buddy's contrast was more evident the closer he stood to his brother. His eyes were his most provocative feature—unusual to say the least. Watchful, scary, penetrating, disturbing—she didn't know how to define them.

I'd never take them as brothers, she concluded silently.

Flossy allowed the others to carry the conversation during the meal, inserting comments a few times when the discussion showed signs of stalling.

Over dessert, however she took over.

"You know, this is our first evening together and yet I feel as if I've known you all for a long time. Sean and I are great talkers, and he's told me all about you boys. I think it's wonderful you've been such good friends all these years. He told me how you were his protectors throughout grammar school and high school, and how you always did everything together. He said you were always there for him when he needed you. I think that's great. I guess you both know he looks up to you men with a great deal of admiration."

Sean seemed embarrassed. "You guys have always been my best friends," he mumbled awkwardly.

Jimmy, in harmony with the conversation, added, "We've spent a lot of time together through the years.

Sean's like a brother to us. We've done a lot of things and had plenty of good times. Right?"

Sean smiled and quietly voiced his "yes."

Buddy merely nodded.

Flossy had watched the brothers carefully. She wanted to see if her reference to her and Sean's frequent talks about the early days caused a reaction.

Jimmy gave no hint of anything bothersome, but Buddy did.

Buddy's mouth tightened and his eyes glared unnaturally. He said nothing, but she felt she had touched a chord.

How do I find out? Enough probing for now, she thought, and turned her attention toward the ladies.

"Patti and Doreen, it's been all boy talk up to now; let's have some girl talk."

The girls laughed, and Doreen added, "it's about time."

The conversation and the drinking continued comfortably for another hour before they called it a night.

Comfortable, that is, for all but Buddy.

Buddy called Jimmy the next evening, expressing his concern that Sean was spending a lot of time with this broad and probably shacking up with her, and he didn't like the idea he was confiding in her.

"The dumb bastard's liable to let slip some of the events we don't want talked about."

"Don't worry about it, Buddy. I had the same thought, and I've already spoken to him. He assured me that he never mentioned anything about Robinson or any of the other goings-on. He's only discussed non-related subjects, if you get my meaning."

"Then you also got the impression she was nosing around?"

"Yeah, but she's just a curious broad, apparently with plenty of money. That's quite an apartment, and Patti told me all the stuff in it is top quality and plenty expensive. I think Flossy's the type that wants to know everything about you so she can decide if you're good enough to be in her company. I said that to Patti and she laughed and said if that were the case she thinks we all passed the test.

"Flossie told the girls that she really enjoyed the evening and wants us all to get together again soon. She's a controller, Buddy; just what Sean needs. Someone to lead him by his nose, or his dick; whichever the case may be. I told Sean an hour ago we all had a great time and we'd have many more, but he was not to say anything about any past incidents. He got the message."

"Okay—I'm glad you covered it with him. I'll talk to you later in the week." Buddy hung up; still in doubt.

CHAPTER 51

Sally Marsh Dillon had just about everything she ever wanted. A large beautiful home, expensive car, exquisite clothes, and plenty of money to spend in any way she chose.

Alfie saw to it she lacked nothing. He adored her and loved showing her off.

Sally was beautiful, knew it, and played the role with elan. It was only recently she had become troubled, and she didn't like the feeling. And all because of Jimmy O'Brien.

She couldn't get him out of her mind. Every time she saw Patti and him she felt jealous. She chided herself, but was unable to control her feelings. She sized-up Patti with a woman's eye and decided that Patti was not as pretty nor had the figure she had. She discounted all the positives about Patti because it served her purpose to do so.

She thought Jimmy was better looking than ever. He exuded confidence, charm, and so much sexuality that she became more obsessed each time she saw him. He was always pleasant and charming in her company, but clearly aloof and seemingly uninterested in her. She had flirted and been openly suggestive on the few occasions they had met by chance and were alone, but he ignored her advances with diplomacy. This angered her all the more.

She decided two people talking on the phone would have each other's undivided attention without being seen together, and it was the safest way to conduct the business she had in mind.

She placed the call to his office on a day she knew Patti was out of town.

"Jimmy? Sally," she announced, after her call was put through.

"Hi, Sally, how are you?" he replied in a questioning voice.

"Fine, thank you. I thought we could…"

"How's Alfie?" he asked, stretching the time to fathom the reason for the call, but fearing he knew.

"He's fine. He left for Mexico yesterday, and will be gone 5 days."

Jimmy didn't accept the bait. "Oh, I wish I had known. I've got tentative plans to fly to Mexico City myself next week. Too bad we couldn't have coordinated our trips and kept each other company."

Sally ignored the comment and got to the heart of the subject. "You know we spent some good times together, especially one night I'm sure you still remember. I told you that night the kind of life I wanted to have, and you understood. I've achieved what I wanted, and you—well, you've pleasantly surprised me—deep down you apparently wanted the same thing. We've both done very well, haven't we?"

"Yes, Sally, we've both done very well. And you're thinking that now that we're both on the same level, socially and financially, there would be nothing wrong if we were to get back together again; secretly, of course."

"I don't think you have to be so flippant about it, Jimmy. I'm sure you must have had some thoughts of your own in that direction, or did I read you wrong?"

Jimmy had considered this sort of scenario long ago, and had decided on the course of action he would follow if and when it came up.

This was the second time to act it out. The first occurred months earlier, with Marilyn Shea.

"Sally, you didn't read the signs wrong. You're one of the most beautiful and desirable women I've ever known, and no man who looked at you could help but want you. But I won't jeopardize your marriage or mine with an affair, even though I'm strongly tempted. No matter how careful we'd be, there's bound to be a slip-up, and it's not a risk I want either of us to take."

He sounded sincere, and his explanation made sense, but something in the delivery made it sound rehearsed. She didn't buy it.

"Don't be ridiculous, Jimmy. We could meet in Boston, or New Hampshire, and no one would ever know a damn thing about it. So don't make excuses. If you don't want to, just tell me so," she added in an angry voice.

Jimmy began to lose a little of his cool. His explanation had worked successfully before, and he and Marilyn Shea could wink at each other and remain on friendly terms.

But Sally was being difficult. "Look, Sally, I meant what I said. I have no intention of lousing up a happy marriage over you or any other woman. I happen to love Patti, and don't have to look anywhere else for any kind of excitement; I get all I want at home. So thanks, but no thanks. I'm not interested, and I'm sure if you'll think about it, you'll…" The dial tone told him she didn't agree.

She was furious. Who does that arrogant bastard think he is, she bristled. She was deeply insulted and felt humiliated, and tears of hurt and anger streamed down her face.

It took her several minutes to recover, and when she did it was a different Sally Marsh Dillon looking at herself in the mirror.

The image was of a vengeful woman who thought only of retribution, and she thought she knew how to get it.

CHAPTER 52

OCTOBER, 1952

Pemberton Chief of Police Don Doyle carefully read the letter. He put it down, picked up the envelope and noted it bore a Boston postmark. He picked up his phone and buzzed the front desk.

"Where's Sam Coben?"

"Probably home in bed, Captain," the desk sergeant answered. "He's on night detail this week."

"Ring him. Tell him I want to see him as soon as possible."

Sam arrived 40 minutes later. His unshaven face and bloodshot eyes suited his disheveled appearance, and he didn't give a damn. To be awakened from a sound sleep of less than 2 hours and told to report to Chief Doyle immediately didn't sit well with him. He was certain whatever Doyle wanted could have waited until later in the day, but Doyle was a bundle of nerves and kept everybody jumping through hoops for no sane reason.

Doyle was a stickler for appearance, and the way Sam looked was at least some form of retaliation.

The Chief eyed him with a look of displeasure, but was smart enough not to provoke his sullen subordinate. He knew Sam had worked all night, but this letter was important, and he wanted Sam on it right away.

"There's coffee in the corner. Then sit down; I want you to read something."

Sam answered inaudibly and headed for the coffee-maker. He filled a large mug, passing on the additives, and took a seat in front of Doyle's desk.

"Read what?" Sam asked.

Doyle handed him a sheet of untitled paper. Sam began to read the double-spaced, typewritten letter, and his manner did a complete turn-a-round after the first few lines.

He was now alert. He finished, and began to read again.

TO WHOM IT MAY CONCERN: MY CONSCIENCE BOTHERS ME. I DON'T KNOW FOR SURE IF THE EVENTS ARE RELATED, BUT I'VE ALWAYS HAD MY SUSPICIONS. TWO BOYS DIED, ONE MURDERED IN A MOVIE HOUSE AND ONE IN A TRAFFIC ACCIDENT. THEY WERE FRIENDS WHO PLAYED IN AN UNFRIENDLY BASKETBALL GAME WITH TWO OTHER BOYS, AND BEAT THEM. THERE WERE BAD FEELINGS ON THE PART OF THE LOSERS; JIMMY AND BUDDY O'BRIEN.

IF THEY LEARNED ABOUT THIS LETTER, MY LIFE WOULD BE IN DANGER BECAUSE THEY WOULD KNOW WHO SENT IT. I RELY ON YOUR DISCRETION, AND ASSURE YOU THAT IF I AM

EVER FOUND OUT, I WILL NEVER ADMIT TO BEING THE AUTHOR.

I MUST REMAIN ANONYMOUS!!!!

Sam tossed the letter back to Chief Doyle. "You check the letter and envelope for prints, Chief?"

"Yes; the paper you're reading is a copy. The original letter had one set of prints on it, and I'm sure they'll call me back and tell me they're mine. The lab's checking the envelope, but I don't hold any hope for it. Any O'Briens come up in your investigations, Sam?"

"I think so, chief. I'll get the files and my notes and I'll be back to you in half-an-hour."

An hour later Sam felt it was coming together. He had reviewed the Jerry Gordon murder in October, 1947 and the Robinson hit-and-run death in July of 1949.

Buddy O'Brien had been in the same grade as the two victims and the older brother, Jimmy, had been in the grade ahead.

Coach Wilzinski's death in April of 1951, similar in manner to Gordon's demise, also had school ties. The older O'Brien had played football for the coach, and maybe there was bad blood. He'd check that out.

And the Sandberg murder in October of 1951, again similar because of the murder weapon—*and the younger O'Brien worked for Sandberg.*

It was all coming back to him now, and he remembered his questioning Buddy O'Brien regarding the Sandberg case. A cool customer!

Sam Coben was excited. For now, the author of the anonymous letter wasn't important, especially after the admission that he or she was only suspicious of the events. But the naming of the O'Briens as possibly being involved narrowed the field and gave him something that he could sink his teeth into. He had names, and maybe he could come up with the answers to resolve and end the brutal, sadistic slayings.

He got back to the Chief and filled him in, and then got in touch with Barney Osham.

"Barney? Sam Coben. How are you?"

"Fine, Sam. What's for the cat?"

Sam laughed at the expression. He had never heard anyone but Barney use it, and wondered where it came from. Some day he would ask, but right now he had more important things on his mind.

"Can you meet me for lunch today? I've got some interesting news and want to throw a few things at you."

"I'm booked for lunch, Sam. How about dinner tonight?"

"Great. Where?"

"How about Strombergs at 7:00 o'clock. I could go for some fish."

"Okay, see you at 7:00."

Strombergs was a popular restaurant specializing in seafood, located on the south side of Beverly bridge. When Barney arrived, he found Sam seated in a booth on the water-side of the restaurant.

"Hi Sam. I didn't see your car in the parking lot."

"I'm on nights this week, Barney. I drove my own vehicle here."

They shook hands, ordered drinks and scanned their menus. Sam ordered a cup of clam chowder, lobster salad, and a black coffee to be served with the meal. Barney opted for the large fried clam plate and french fries, ignoring his self-imposed diet for the second time in as many days.

Sam unfolded a copy of the anonymous letter and handed it to Barney. Barney read it several times before he looked up and made comment.

"Quite interesting, Sam. What have you dug up on the O'Briens?"

Sam filled him in, including the fact that Jimmy O'Brien was in Korea when Wilzinski was murdered.

"You might want to check your files on who you interviewed after the Gordon murder, Barney. I'd be curious to know if the O'Brien name is there. I'm going to revisit everyone I talked to and see if the name crops up. I think it will."

"I'll get on it in the morning, Sam. Let's hope we can tie it in."

A week passed. Sam had put in long hours researching each murder case, and came up with some interesting information. He discovered that Sean Boyle was an inseparable friend of the O'Brien brothers. He wondered if Sean Boyle wrote the anonymous letter.

Two teachers at Pemberton High recalled that the three boys were often in the company of two female classmates.

Sam pursued this, and with the use of a 1950 year book, the teachers identified Sally Marsh and Doreen Kelly.

Sam followed up on the three names, and learned that Sean Boyle was currently a third-year student at Northeastern University and still frequently seen with the O'Briens.

Doreen Kelly was now the wife of Buddy O'Brien, and from what Sam could ascertain, the marriage was a good one.

Sally Marsh was now Sally Dillon, so she certainly had done well for herself. The Dillons were one of the city's more prominent families.

And Jimmy O'Brien had married into money and was also doing well.

A cozy group from all outward appearances, he thought, but maybe there's jealously or dissension under the surface.

Sam was determined to find out, and got a break when he met an old neighbor, Dick Shea, in the post office. He had known Dick for years and knew that Dick and his wife Marilyn were Country Club members.

Dick asked Sam if he had time for a cup of coffee, and saved Sam from trying to think of an excuse to do the same. The two men walked the short distance to Raymonds and sat on adjacent stools.

"How's your golf game coming?" Sam asked, opening the conversation.

"About the same. Some days good and some days bad. Or as Marilyn puts it, just like my disposition," Dick answered with a smile.

"And how is Marilyn? Pretty as ever, I bet."

"Oh, she's fine. She's happy at the Club. Gives her a chance to ogle everyone in pants," he added, with a touch of acrimony. "Right now she's got the hots for one of our new members, but she'd run like hell if he ever showed her any attention. That's the way she is."

Sam was surprised at the comment. He was at best now a casual acquaintance, and to hear Dick Shea make a statement that personal was a little unusual, but the conversation was heading the way he wanted it to, and he pressed on.

"Must be the ex-football star you're talking about, Dick—what's his name; oh yeah,—O'Brien. I've seen him a few times recently. Nice looking guy."

"He's the one, but she'll get nowhere with him. The talk around the Club is that more than one woman has made a pitch for him, but he's either the most devoted husband at the Club or he hasn't been married long enough to want to test the waters elsewhere," he said, smiling at his phrasing. "At least that's the locker-room scuttlebutt."

"No kidding. I would have guessed that he would be quite the ladies' man. He does stand out in a crowd," Sam said.

"Yeah, I guess he does. His old girlfriend didn't seem to make an impression on him either, and that relationship renewal was expected to stir up some excitement. They were supposedly hot and heavy in high school, but it seems he only has eyes for Patti."

"Patti?"

"Yeah; his wife, Patti Baltar; Ted Baltar's daughter," Dick explained.

"Oh, I know Ted," Sam replied, "I didn't remember his daughter's name. Who's O'Brien's old girlfriend?"

"Sally Dillon—her maiden name was Marsh—and she's still a knockout. Marilyn thinks something happened recently between the two of them."

"Oh, why does she think that?"

"I asked the same thing, and she said women have a way of knowing those things. Hey, I gotta go. I have an appointment at the bank, and I'm running late." Dick paid the tab, shook hands, and hastily made his way out the door.

Sam sat on his stool, deep in thought. Maybe she came on to him, got the cold shoulder, got teed off and wrote an anonymous letter. A woman scorned is capable of anything.

It was worth looking into.

CHAPTER 53

DECEMBER, 1952

Jimmy and Buddy felt that Alpine skiing was the "in" thing, and decided to take advantage of their proximity to ski country.

They invited Flossy and Sean to join them during Christmas week. Sean agreed to go—at Flossy's insistence—although he wasn't happy about the prospects of spending an entire week in the company of Buddy O'Brien.

Once committed, Sean suggested North Conway, as it was familiar territory to him and only 3 hours from Boston. He thought the O'Briens would enjoy the quaint scenic town, and Cranmore Mountain would be ideal for the group, as most of the terrain was ideal for beginner and intermediate skiers.

Flossy had insisted that Sean and she join the O'Briens for several reasons.

She loved the outdoors and enjoyed many athletic activities, although she had never tried skiing, and she wanted to know more about Jimmy and Buddy.

Over the past few months she had attempted to pry more information from Sean about his childhood and teen years relating to his friendship with Jimmy and Buddy, but with little success. Sean became nervous and tense whenever she broached the topic. He would try to change the subject, and when she told him that he kept doing so he would deny it.

"There's nothing to tell, Flossy. "We played games and sports like all the kids did. I was never as good as Jimmy and Buddy, but they always insisted I play right along with them, and I did."

"Did they ever do anything you were ashamed of that caused you…"

"No! Why do you keep bringing up such things?"

She didn't know why. She sensed something. In the O'Briens company he often behaved differently—sometimes uncomfortable and wary.

Sean was always warm and pleasant when he was with her. She knew he cared about people. With Jimmy and Buddy he was not the same person.

She felt it would be interesting to go with the group for the holiday week and perhaps satisfy her curiosity about the O'Brien men.

Doreen didn't liked the idea of a week's ski vacation. She would have preferred a trip to Florida where she could sit on the beach in the warm sun, tan her body to a beautiful shade, and be the envy of her lady friends upon her return.

It wouldn't have been that much more expensive, and much more to her liking.

Buddy finally won her approval after promising he would take her to Florida the following year. She realized deep down they probably couldn't afford a Florida trip right now, but with Buddy's recent promotion to be Arthur Zoltek's assistant, and the likelihood of his being trained to succeed Zoltek upon Zoltek's retirement in a few years, or sooner, their future looked promising.

She conceded it would make sense to wait another year, so she let Buddy have his way.

Doreen was pleased with the degree of success Buddy had achieved, and he had done it on his own.

Now that *she* had more, she was less resentful of Jimmy and Patti. She decided that she and Buddy would be able to join the Country Club set in a few more years, and having Patti O'Brien as a friend and ally would be helpful.

Doreen doubted she could count on her old friend Sally for any kind of support, for Sally had changed, and they seldom saw one another. She had left messages a number of times for Sally to call her, and only once had she done so. That was a week ago.

They met for lunch, but it wasn't the same Sally. She talked negatively about Jimmy without offering specific reasons as to why, and Doreen got the impression that Jimmy must have put Sally down in some way.

Doreen recalled how Sally dumped Jimmy to marry money, and now that Jimmy was in the chips, he probably let her know it.

I'll bet that's what happened, she surmised.

The Graypeak Inn in North Conway was a delight. It was a converted one hundred year old farm house, newly renovated and refurbished with all the modern conveniences.

There were eight bedrooms and four bathrooms in the inn; four bedrooms and two baths on each floor. The upstairs rooms all had spectacular views of the valley and Mount Washington.

The O'Brien group arrived mid-morning Friday before any other weekend guests, and got first choice of rooms, with the exception of one upstairs bedroom that was already spoken for. The O'Brien couples selected rooms on the second floor with fireplaces and double beds, while Flossy and Bobby opted for the only bedroom with twin beds, which was on the first floor.

"We single folk use twin beds, in case our mothers show up," Flossy joked, which brought the expected chuckles.

"Right, but don't forget to mess up the other bed in the morning," Jimmy quipped.

Jimmy set out to charm the owner/hostess, and succeeded admirably. Mildred Graham, divorced and in her mid-fifties, had lived in the Conway area her entire life. Her home had been in the family for four generations. She had two adult sons who spent a month with her in North Conway in the summer, and lived 11 months of the year with their father in Philadelphia,

"The boys prefer living in a big city, rather then waste away in the boonies," she explained, "and I let them make the choice. They know they're welcome here if they ever want to come back."

Her older sister and her sister's husband and three daughters lived in a guest house on the property. They all pitched in and helped Mildred Graham run the inn.

"Breakfast is from 7:00 to 9:00 a.m., and dinner from 7:00 to 9:00 p.m.," Mrs. Graham explained, "and if you need or want anything that you don't see or have, just see any of us and we'll take care of it. And I'd appreciate it if you'd kinda keep the noise down after 9:00 at night; some of our guests turn in early. I hope you all have a wonderful time."

"Mrs. Graham," Jimmy said, "just two questions. Who are the other couples who'll be staying in the other upstairs bedrooms, and are there any kids staying here?"

"Young couple from New York staying in one. Very nice people. They were honeymooners first time they came here 3 years ago and liked the area so much they keep coming back. They reserve the same room a year in advance. Three other couples booked last month; from Boston. Don't know them. As far as kids are concerned, you won't have any problem. Only one couple coming with kids, and they're teenagers. They'll be in a guest house. They've been here before, and they're quiet and polite."

"Everything sounds great, Mrs. Graham," Patti said. "I'm sure we'll all have a fabulous time."

Flossy, Doreen, and Patti wanted to unpack and freshen up. The plan was to meet in the lobby in an hour and go for a quick lunch, followed by a walking tour of the town.

Sean suggested they should get over to The Local Ski Shop to see Stan or Dan after lunch and get outfitted with skis, poles, and boots. "That way we won't waste any time in the morning and can get right out on the mountain," he urged.

However, he was voted down by Doreen. "I have no intention of being the first one on the mountain, and the later we get there, the warmer it will be."

The others agreed. The fewer hours skied the first day the fewer sore muscles to contend with. Such was the consensus.

They met the other house guests, with the exception of the couple driving in from New York, at dinner that evening. Mrs. Graham explained that the New York couple had called from Connecticut to say they were delayed by snow squalls. She estimated they wouldn't arrive until after 9:00 p.m.

The next morning brought ideal weather. The sun was out, the temperature was in the upper 20's, and the weatherman predicted it would be a "fifty-center," the local jargon for a perfect day.

The three couples met for breakfast at 8:30, and were the last guests to arrive. Mrs. Graham was there to greet them, poured their juice, and announced their breakfast choices. As they ate, she filled them in with the essentials.

"The mountain don't open 'til 9:00. Some of the folks got up early and went to church, and they go skiing right from there. The New Yorkers didn't get in until 12:30 this morning. They said the ride up Route 16 was treacherous and several cars went off the road. I waited up for them; figured they'd be famished. They gobbled up some roast beef sandwiches and coffee in no time at all, and headed for bed, exhausted. I'm sure they'll skip breakfast this morning; you'll meet them tonight." She had uttered all this seemingly without taking a breath, and now paused to ponder whether or not she had forgotten anything. Deciding that she hadn't, she excused herself and checked with the other guests.

The group arrived at the mountain just before 10:00 a.m. and spent the first half-hour donning and adjusting their boots. They were too late for ski school classes, but a couple of private instructors were available.

Doreen and Flossy had never skied, so one instructor took them, while the others headed for the Skimobile with the second instructor. The plan was to meet for lunch at 1:00.

"I only fell a million times," Doreen said, laughing good-naturedly, "and Flossy fell another million. Poor John, our ski instructor. Probably has a hernia from picking us up all morning. But we both managed to sidestep up the hill a little and ski down a few times. Flossy picked it up a lot quicker than I did. She did great."

"I wouldn't exactly call it great," Flossy said. "I never realized it would be so much work. I'm exhausted. But I did get the hang of it a little bit toward the end of the lesson, and I did have fun. Dory made the longest run of the day without falling and I'm very jealous.

"I hope we can get John as our instructor again tomorrow," Flossy continued, "if he's not in a mental institution by then."

They all laughed and, although in various degrees of fatigue, all agreed they had enjoyed the day.

"You should have seen Sean," Patti chipped in, "he was by far the best in the class."

Sean smiled, pleased. "It was a great lesson; I'm looking forward to tomorrow."

"Me too," Jimmy said, "I didn't really get the hang of it until near the end of the lesson. It's a lot different feel than it was when we used to ski down Ward 2 hill, and the equipment is a lot different. But I think we made progress for the first day, don't you, Buddy?"

"We'll kill them or ourselves tomorrow," Buddy answered with mocking assurance, which got them all laughing again.

At dinner that evening Mrs. Graham introduced the New Yorkers. "Everybody; this is Betty and Barry Berke. They had a terrible time getting here last night, but they made it."

The couple walked around the dining room shaking hands and swapping introductions. When they reached Jimmy's table, Jimmy invited the Berkes to join them. "We just sat down 10 minutes ago, so we're only as far as the first glass of wine."

The Berkes were a handsome, athletic-looking couple. Barry was over 6 feet tall and well-muscled. He was dark complected, with neatly styled black hair in a pompadour, a thin face, Grecian nose, small mouth, and smiling brown eyes. Betty was a knockout. She was tall at about 5 feet 10 inches, shapely, and sported a stylish bobbed hairdo. She had nice features and a pretty face, but what really struck you was her hair—it was fiery red. You couldn't help but look twice.

"Understand you're from New York," Jimmy said, as the Berkes sat down and Mrs. Graham set two more place settings at the table. "That's a long drive, especially in a storm."

"The drive is no problem when the weather cooperates," Barry answered. "We thought we'd beat the storm driving up. It was supposed to go out to sea south of Boston, but it didn't let up until we got a little past Rochester, New Hampshire. If it wasn't for the heavy traffic and a few sections of blinding snow, we wouldn't have had any trouble."

"I thought all New Yorkers opted for the Vermont ski areas," Sean said. "Closer in proximity, and bigger mountains."

"That's probably true," Barry agreed, "but North Conway is special for us. This is where we first met. Betty and I look forward to coming back every year over the Christmas holidays."

"Very romantic place," Flossy chimed in. "I can understand why you'd want to keep coming back."

They ordered a round of drinks and, when they were served, ordered dinner. By the time their entrees came, the men were discussing the stock market, after learning that Barry was a broker, and the women were attacking the current clothing fashions being shown in New York, which was Betty's field.

By 9:30, most of the group were physically and mentally exhausted, and decided to turn in.

"I can't believe it's only 9:30 and I'm ready for bed," Jimmy admitted.

"Me too," Flossy added, "and I for one have no intention of doing anything but sleeping when I get there."

"Amen," echoed Patti and Doreen simultaneously, and the table erupted in laughter.

"Join us tomorrow for apres-ski," Jimmy called out to the Berkes as they headed out of the dining room.

"Thank you. See you then," Barry answered.

The week flew by. Flossy and Doreen took Wednesday off to rest, but the others skied every day.

The weather held up, sunny but cold, and it was a fun-filled vacation.

One event occurred to mar the vacation. That happened on the day prior to their departure.

Buddy made an unflattering remark about Jews. Jimmy laughed, and Barry took offense and let Buddy and Jimmy know it.

"Betty and I are Jewish. We don't appreciate or tolerate that kind of talk. You'll excuse us," and they left the table.

The girls were embarrassed and angry with Buddy, but only Flossy spoke up.

"That was an ass-hole thing to say. They're real nice people, and you should have had the class to apologize," she added bitterly.

"What for?" Buddy snarled. "I didn't know they were Jews. Besides, no Jew will ever get an apology from any of us. We don't take kindly to them."

"Well, that's too damn bad," Flossy said, continuing her blistering attack. "They didn't do a damn thing to you, and you've got a hell of a nerve coming down on them."

She was fuming, and was about to continue when Sean intervened.

"Please, Flossy. *Stop*!" he uttered in a voice unfamiliar to her. "You'll never get anywhere with this topic of conversation. This is what they believe and the way they were brought up, so please, please…" His voice tailed off.

Patti came over to Flossy and put her arm around her. "Flossy, I'm sorry it happened, but they truly don't know any better. I've been trying to get Jimmy to be more tolerant, and I've had some success. He really has been much less outspoken about his views. He has to be if he wants to be successful in the leather business, and he understands that. Buddy's another matter. Doreen has tried, but he's impossible. He just won't listen to reason, and he'll suffer for it in the end. Please; let's not spoil a beautiful week. I'll apologize to Betty and Barry. I don't think it will do any good, but I intend to try anyway."

Flossy took a tissue from her handbag and wiped her eyes. She had regained her composure, and slowly shook her head. "I can't understand why people have to be so mean to each other, Patti. Just because they're of a different religion, or have a different color, doesn't make them good or bad. People should build relationships on the individuals themselves, not on their religious beliefs or skin color."

"I agree, Flossy, but bigotry and hatreds have been going on for thousands of years and, unfortunately, will continue to do so. We'll just have to hope that it can be kept under control, or we'll all be in trouble."

Patti walked Flossy away from the others during this exchange, and they moved into the enclosed, heated front porch and sat down.

Doreen joined them.

"I'm sorry, Flossy," Doreen said with sincerity. "Buddy makes me so mad sometimes that I could kill him, but I can't do anything to change him. He's a pig-headed Irishman who thinks he knows it all."

Flossy reached out and took Doreen's hand. "It's not your fault, Dory. I'm not mad at you. I'm all right now. Where's Sean?"

"He's with the men. He wasn't happy with Buddy's remarks and I guess he's letting him know about it. I'm sure he'll be right along."

Sean wasn't happy having the vacation come to an unhappy ending, but he knew better than to mouth any serious objections.

"Shit, guys, let's cool it, okay? We don't want to get the girls any more teed off than they are now. We've had a great week. It's not worth spoiling over something that's not really important."

Much to his surprise, Jimmy agreed. "He's right, Buddy, it's not important. They'll never understand how we feel. We've got to appear more tolerant when the girls are around. That will keep them happy and off our backs. We can still stick to our beliefs; we'll play the game and keep our feelings under cover. It will serve us better to do it that way."

Buddy's pensiveness was apparent, but he finally agreed. "Yeah, you're right, Jimmy; better off keeping it to ourselves. But first chance we get, let's kick in some Jew or nigger faces, just for the fun of it."

Jimmy smiled, put his arm around his brother's shoulder, and walked him out of the dining room to find the girls and make amends.

Sean wasn't smiling as he followed them.

CHAPTER 54

JUNE, 1953

A second anonymous letter addressed to Chief Doyle arrived at the Pemberton Police Station. He read it, shook his head, and put a call out for Sam Coben.

"Sam; got another letter from our mystery writer. I'll have a copy on your desk when you come in. I sent the original and the envelope over to the lab. You check with them later to see if they get anything."

"I'll be in within the hour, Chief," Sam replied.

The letter was sitting in Sam's "IN" file when he arrived. It was again typed on paper with no letterhead.

"I CAN'T UNDERSTAND WHY YOU CONTINUE TO ALLOW THE O'BRIEN BROTHERS TO GO UNPUNISHED AND MIX WITH THE GOOD PEOPLE OF THIS COMMUNITY. DO YOU HAVE TO WAIT UNTIL THEY MURDER SOMEONE ELSE BEFORE YOU DO SOMETHING?"

Jesus, Sam thought, who are you and what the hell do you really know?

Sally had seen Jimmy and Patti at the Club dance the evening before, and their apparent affection for one another re-triggered her hatred.

It had been Sally's first visit to the Club in months. She had spent a month in Europe and 3 months in Palm Beach. She had been alone a good part of the time, as Alfie could only stay 2 weeks in Europe, and could join her only on weekends in Palm Beach.

She didn't mind being alone because she had male friends who were very attentive toward her. Except for one brief affair in Paris, however, she kept the men at bay. She had no intention of giving Alfie any excuse to destroy her marriage. With Jimmy, however, she would have chanced it.

Seeing him again, obviously happy and very popular, in surroundings that she considered *her* territory reminded her that she wanted that smug bastard and his brother socially ruined. Maybe they *were* guilty; she didn't know, and she didn't care.

She knew she would be in trouble if the O'Briens found out she had tipped the police. But in her frame of mind it was worth the risk.

She had written the second letter in a fit of anger. Jimmy had to be put in his place.

CHAPTER 55

Dan Grady had been with the Pemberton Police Department for 26 years. He was 4 years away from mandatory retirement and looking forward to it.

He was now relegated to desk work, which he wasn't happy about. He would have preferred to walk a beat, but he knew enough to keep his mouth shut.

Grady joined the department at the age of 30 after tiring of the physically-demanding and foul-smelling tannery work which had taken, he figured, years off his life. The fact that his two uncles worked in tanneries all their lives and had both died in their late eighties was not a consideration.

Grady graduated from Pemberton High in 1916, a below average student who thrived on beer and cigarettes from the age of 12. His father was in the Merchant Marines and seldom came around, and his mother was an alcoholic who spent half of each day in bed until the day she died. A product of separated parents, Grady and his two sisters were left to fend for themselves.

Grady went to work for the Kay Leather Company at the age of 17, and for 12 years horsed-up leather from tan wheels. He eventually contacted a severe case of dermatitis, and the company doctor recommended he find other work. This was fine with him, except management put him in the Finishing Department, and the smell of the lacquers were not to his liking.

A cut in pay was the final straw.

His mother had been buddy-buddy with the Chief of Police since high school, and at the age of 30 Grady became a cop. It wasn't long before he gained the reputation of being the meanest and toughest cop to walk a beat. He loved the reputation.

Now, 56 years old and stuck in the station house all day, Grady felt he was nothing more than an errand boy.

"Grady!" Chief Doyle barked, "put this letter on Coben's desk."

Grady took the letter from the Chief and headed for Inspector Coben's office. As was his habit he read the letter and, as he kept tabs on all department correspondence, became instantly alert and curious when he saw reference to the O'Brien brothers.

What the hell is this all about he wondered. He put the letter in Coben's mail file, determined to find out if the reference was to the O'Briens he knew.

Later in the week, he learned this was the second letter the Chief had received accusing the O'Briens—his O'Briens—of being killers. The first letter had apparently been kept quiet, and Grady got his information at the crime lab, where he figured the original letters must have been sent for study. He located the first letter, read it, and returned it to the file.

Some nutty son-of-bitch trying to settle a score, I'll betcha, he thought. The O'Briens are a good, honest, hardworking family that I've known for years. Those letters are all bullshit.

Dan Grady and Dan O'Brien had gone to work for Kay Leather the same year, and although they knew each other as kids they hadn't become close friends until they worked at the leather factory. They sat together during coffee and lunch breaks, and usually got together on Friday afternoons after they cashed their pay checks. They'd spend a couple of hours at Violet's Bar sucking in several glasses of draft beer, and commiserating with each other how hard they worked for lousy pay while their foremen did nothing and got the big money.

Their friendship had lasted for years, and Dan Grady had been invited for dinner Thursday nights on many occasions when Mary O'Brien cooked her tangy boiled-dinner specialty.

It was at these meals Grady got to know and love the O'Brien boys.

Jimmy reminded him of himself when he was a kid. Big for his age and strong as a bull.

I got to admit that he's got a better look than I ever had, Grady had mused. He'll be in the pants of many a colleen soon enough, he had predicted.

Buddy he thought was a different sort. Quiet, even sullen, when his older brother was at the table. When Jimmy wasn't there, however, he was a different person.

Friendly and willing to participate in whatever discussion was taking place.

Grady considered Buddy very bright, and knowledgeable beyond his years.

A good kid, he thought, but he'll always be in his brother's shadow.

He knew the boys feared their father, who had exploded several times over trivial remarks, but he kept his mouth shut, although he sometimes had the urge to throttle Dan O'Brien. Grady didn't agree with Dan O'Brien's comment of "those boys can be real wise bastards, and I intend to keep them in line even if I have to break a few asses."

The relationship faltered after Grady left the tannery and joined the police force.

Grady now only dropped into Violet's bar on infrequent Fridays when he had the day off, and only then did he join Dan O'Brien and other tannery employees for a few brews and some idle gossip.

The Thursday night dinner invitations had stopped because he was usually on duty. He found that he missed the company more than he missed the meals.

Now some asshole was accusing his friends of being killers, and he felt instinctively that it was the work of a crackpot. He knew where he could find Dan O'Brien, and on the next Friday afternoon he took time off to search him out.

Dan O'Brien was seated alone in a corner booth at Violets when Grady joined him. After two brews and 20 minutes of small talk, Grady asked, "Your boys have a run-in with anyone who would try to make trouble for them?"

Dan O'Brien grew attentive. "I don't know. Why?"

"Think for a minute," Grady continued, choosing to ignore the question for the time being. "Have the boys been involved in anything that would make someone really angry?"

"Jesus, Grady, they're grown men and have lived their own private lives for years. Jimmy's a big shot now, and I seldom see him. Buddy's got a big job, and I only see him a couple of times a month. What the hell is going on?"

Grady paused to order two more brews. He removed a cigarette from his shirt pocket and lit it with his Zippo, inhaled deeply and slowly blew the smoke away. He had to decide how much he could tell Dan O'Brien without getting his own ass in a sling. He waited until the empty glasses had been removed and two fresh ones were in place.

"All right, Dan, I'm going to tell you what's going on, but before I do, you've got to promise me that you'll use your head and never—and I mean never—let anyone, including your boys, know where this came from. I'm real serious about this, because I could lose my job and my pension if it were ever traced back to me. Believe me, if we weren't such long time friends, and I didn't admire your boys so much, I'd never take the chance of you fucking me up. I want your word!"

Dan O'Brien hadn't missed a word, and knew this was serious business. "Grady, you know god-damned well I wouldn't do anything to fuck you up. You got my word."

Grady told him about the two anonymous letters. When he finished, there was silence at the table.

Dan O'Brien leaned backward, his face ashen and grim.

Grady sat back and picked up his glass and took a healthy swig.

"Jesus Christ," Dan O'Brien hissed, "That's a lot of horseshit. What son-of-a-bitch would do something like that. If I get my hands…"

Grady interrupted. "Calm down, Dan, 'cause what you're gonna say ain't gonna do no good. I only told you this 'cause you and I go back a long way. I'm sure there's no truth to it, but some screwed-up nut who knew that your kids were in school at the same time as those dead kids is trying to cause trouble. It may even be the killer himself, showing off that he's got away with it. Or it could be somebody that works for either one of your kids and don't like them. Or someone who worked for them and got canned. It don't take too much to set some people off. What I think you should do is get together with your boys on the quiet, and let them know they should watch their backs. Somebody is trying to stir something up, and if they can't, they might get violent. So you warn them to be careful. And remember, nobody is to know where this information came from."

Dan O'Brien nodded slowly. "Thanks, Grady; I appreciate your telling me. I owe you, and I'll get back to you after I talk to the boys."

Dan O'Brien phoned Buddy that evening. "It's important that I see you and Jimmy as soon as possible; either tomorrow or Sunday. I tried to reach Jimmy, but I got no answer. He away?"

"I don't know, but I don't think so. What's so damn important?" Buddy asked derisively.

Dan ignored the question. "See if you can reach him, and arrange for the three of us to meet somewhere, and the sooner the better. I don't need more than a half-hour."

Buddy realized something was seriously wrong, and changed his tune. "I'll get back to you as soon as I locate Jimmy."

Buddy reached Jimmy an hour later at the Country Club grille room.

"The old man called. Said it's important that we meet him as soon as possible. He sounded nervous."

"What's that all about?" Jimmy asked, vaguely curious. "He need some money?"

"I don't think so. Whenever he needs dough he comes right out and asks for it. He sounded up-tight, and wants us to meet him somewhere to talk about it. That means he doesn't want the old lady to know. What should I tell him?"

"How about breakfast tomorrow morning at Stanley's; say at 8:00. I've got something on at 9:00, but that should give us enough time."

"Okay, Jimmy, I'll call him. I'll see you at 8:00."

Buddy arrived at the restaurant a few minutes after 8:00 a.m. Saturday and found his father sitting alone at an out-of-the-way table. Two cigarette butts, along with dead ash, were already in the ashtray, and Dan was on his third cigarette and second cup of coffee. He nodded a silent greeting as Buddy approached.

“What do you want for breakfast, Pop—I’ll order it,” Buddy said.

“Get me a couple of plain doughnuts and another black coffee.”

“Don’t you want any eggs?” Buddy asked politely.

“I don’t want any fucking eggs. Just get me what I told you. Where’s your brother?”

Buddy hunched his shoulders. “He said he’d be here,” he said and headed to the counter to order.

Jimmy arrived minutes later and headed for his father. As he approached, the greeting he got was “go get your breakfast—you’re late—and remind Buddy I said black coffee.”

Jimmy smiled, thinking his old man would never change, and headed to place his order.

The three O’Briens ate in silence. After a while, Jimmy attempted to get the conversation underway.

“What’s so important, Pop?”

“Finish eating, then we’ll talk,” came the gruff reply.

Jimmy eyeballed Buddy, who reacted with a smile and an I-don’t-know look.

They finished breakfast, and Dan lit another cigarette. He had their attention as he leaned over the table and indicated that he wanted them to do the same. He spoke just loud enough for them to hear.

“Somebody sent a couple of letters to the police chief saying the two of you had something to do with two people getting killed—that you did it.” He stopped talking in order to take a couple of deep puffs while his words sunk in. His eyes shifted from one to the other, but other than the ever-present smile disappearing from Jimmy's face, there was no immediate reaction.

"That's bullshit," Jimmy finally spit out. "What son-of-a-bitch told you that?" He had spoken a little too loud, and Dan admonished him with a hand signal.

"It may be bullshit, but someone is trying to cause trouble for both of you. You better watch your backs real good. You got something to hide? Then cover your asses."

Jimmy was fuming, his thoughts flitting among several possible perpetrators. Buddy was quiet, but his eyes took on the disquieting look that was characteristic of him.

"Where'd you hear this?" Buddy asked.

"I swore I wouldn't tell, because he could get in real trouble if anyone found out. But we got a cop friend, and you know who it is."

They both liked Dan Grady, and if it came from him, they knew it was on the level.

Jimmy was over the initial shock, and he spoke confidently. "We never did anything like that, Pop, so don't worry about it. They're pissing up the wrong tree. But like you said, someone's trying to make trouble for us, and we'll look into it. Thanks for the information."

Dan O'Brien looked relieved. "You guys keep in touch with me. And come over and see your mom a little more often; for some reason she misses you," he added, in one of his rare attempts at humor. He got up and, without as much as a good-bye, left, stopping near the door long enough to light another cigarette.

Jimmy and Buddy remained at the table. "I think we can pin it down to a few people." Jimmy said,

"Who?"

"Sean, Sally—or Doreen," Jimmy answered.

"Forget Doreen," Buddy answered caustically, "she would never do me any harm. I'm sure of that."

"Okay, I don't think it's her either, but she *was* a member of our little group back then. That leaves Sean and Sally."

"I don't think it could be Sean," Buddy said. "There's no way he's going to implicate himself with the car accident. He's too smart for that."

"I agree, so that leaves my old girlfriend Sally," Jimmy concluded.

"And one other," Buddy said.

"Who?"

"Flossy!"

"Flossy? What in hell does she have to do with it?" Jimmy asked.

"She and Sean have been living together a long time," Buddy said, "and Sean's a pussy cat. She can be as tough a broad as you'd ever want to deal with; you know that. You remember how she lit into us in North Conway over that episode with the Jew couple. She was really teed off for a long time, and if it wasn't for Patti and Dory, she would have cut our dicks off."

"Yeah," Jim flinched involuntarily, "but Sean would have been stupid to tell her anything about the car business."

"True, but he's never really been as close to anybody as he is to her, and when people are that involved, they tell each other their little secrets."

Jimmy pondered briefly, and decided it was possible.

"What about Sally?" Buddy continued. "I never see her. Any reason she might have to cause us trouble?"

"As a matter of fact, there is," Jimmy answered, and related the event at length.

"Shit!" Buddy said when Jimmy finished his story, "she could always be a bitch when she wanted to, but to pull something like that; that's a little much."

"Yeah, but isn't there a saying about 'a woman scorned, be forewarned,' or something like that? I would have liked to have given her a bang, but there's no way I was going to chance an involvement. Things are going too good for me, and I'm not going to blow it."

"So it's Sally or Flossy; how do we find out which one?" Buddy asked.

"I'm going to have a talk with Sean. I think he'll tell me the truth, and if he doesn't, I'll know it."

"You want me there when you talk to him?" Buddy asked.

"No. I think he'll open up to me a lot more if I speak to him alone. No offense, Buddy."

"Buddy smiled. "You're probably right. He's always liked you better."

Jimmy ignored the comment. "I'll see if I can meet with him sometime today—without Flossy. I'll call you tonight."

Jimmy called the Club and canceled his massage appointment. He had more important things to do, and first on his agenda was to locate Sean. He called Flossy's apartment, and was disturbed when there was no answer. He drove home, arriving at 10:15. Patti was taking a tennis lesson from 10:00 to 11:00 and then playing in a doubles match. They had plans to meet for lunch at 1:30, but if he hadn't found Sean by then, he would cancel.

At 10:30 he tried Flossy's apartment again, and Sean answered.

"It's Jimmy. Something I need to talk to you about—alone. Any chance that we could get together this afternoon?"

"Anything wrong?" came the concerned reply.

"Yeah, Sean, there's something we've got to talk about right away. It's important."

"Well, yeah; okay. I'm meeting Flossy for lunch at 1 o'clock, and I don't know where to reach her now to cancel. She has a 3:00 p.m. meeting at the library, so I could leave her right after lunch and meet you somewhere at 3:00 or 3:30, if that's okay."

"Perfect," Jimmy replied, as he wouldn't have to change his own plans. "I'll meet you at Varley's in Lynn, between 3:00 and 3:30. Don't say anything to Flossy about our meeting; only you and I know about it."

Sean arrived 15 minutes late, cursing the Sumner Tunnel traffic. "No matter what time of day you get there, there's always a tie-up," he offered in apology.

"Yeah," Jimmy answered sympathetically. "That's what you get when you want to live in the big city. You want coffee or something else?"

Sean saw that Jimmy was drinking coffee, and ordered the same.

"What's so important, Jimmy?" he asked apprehensively.

Jimmy waited until Sean was served and, when the waitress had gone, leaned over the table and beckoned Sean to do the same.

"The cops received two anonymous letters saying that we were involved in the slayings of Robinson and Gordon."

Sean's expression changed from disbelief to fear. He let out a low gasp. "Jesus!" was all he could manage to utter. He set his coffee cup down as he felt a cold sweat spread across his brow and his hand tremble.

"Jesus," he repeated.

"Calm down," Jimmy ordered, not unkindly. "There's no possible way that anyone can link us to either event, so take it easy."

"Are you sure?" Sean asked nervously.

"You're damned right I'm sure. Think about it, and you'll know I'm right. I just want you to be aware of the situation in case anyone questions you about it. And if you react the same way you just did you're going to cause trouble for all of us. Do you understand what I'm saying? They have got nothing—not one shred of evidence—that ties us with either Gordon or Robinson. All they got is someone who's trying to throw suspicion on us, for whatever reason. It does becomes a problem, however, because we're probably the only suspects they've got. That means they'll be trying to trip us up. They might even try a bluff with some sort of trumped up story to see how we react, or to see if they can break one of us down. We've got to be careful and, most of all, we've got to keep calm."

Sean understood. Jimmy was right. If the cops had any proof, they would have been down on them already.

"Who do you think sent the letters, and how did you find out about them?" he asked.

"I'll answer your second question first," Jimmy responded. "We've got a family friend who's a cop. You know who it is. He took a big risk in letting my old man know, so we can never mention his name; you understand?"

Sean nodded. He knew who the cop was.

Jimmy continued. "Your first question is what I want to talk to you about. And don't get angry, but you gotta be truthful, for whatever the problem, we can work it out."

"Get angry about what?"

"Did you ever mention anything—and I mean anything at all—to Flossy about THE PACT or about Gordon or Robinson? Think carefully now; it's important."

Sean answered immediately. "Of course not, Jimmy. I'm not stupid. The Robinson thing is often on my mind, but it can't be undone, and I live with it. And I had nothing to do with Gordon…"

"None of us did," Jimmy cut in. "The Robinson business was an accident; none of us expected that he'd die. It was a bad break, but it happened. But I know Flossy's still teed-off over that time with the people in North Conway, and I thought maybe…"

"No, Jimmy—no way. I never told Flossy about the basketball game or anything about those two guys. I did tell her when we were kids we had our own clubhouse, and that we've been the best of friends all our lives, but I've never mentioned anything about THE PACT or what it stood for. It's true that she thinks we're all bigots, and doesn't like it, but I explained to her that's the way we were brought up. Believe me, Jimmy, she doesn't know anything."

"Okay. If you say so, I believe you. That leaves Doreen and Sally, and I've talked to Buddy and he said he knows it's not Doreen."

"Sally? Why would she do anything like that? She was your girlfriend…"

Sean stopped talking, and looked questioningly at his friend. "She angry with you for any reason?"

"Might be, Sean; might be."

"How are we going to find out?"

"I'll have a talk with her. I'll see what she has to say."

Sean's coffee was untouched and now cold. He called the waitress and ordered another cup.

"Something wrong with it?" she asked dourly.

"Yeah, there's a bug swimming around in it," Jimmy answered, winking at Sean.

The waitress grimaced, and returned minutes later with two mugs of steaming coffee. "If there are any bugs in these cups their asses will be burning," she said.

They sat several minutes longer sipping their coffee before Jimmy spoke.

"I guess that's about it for now, Sean. I'll call you after I speak with Sally and let you know what's going on. Remember, keep your head on your shoulders and be ready for anything. And don't mention any of this to Flossy. Buddy and I want to try to rebuild our relationship with her, so don't give her anything else to think about."

It was 5:15 in the afternoon when Jimmy arrived home. He could hear Patti walking about upstairs.

"I'm home, honey; what are you doing?" he called out.

"Trying on some clothes I bought today. You want to see?"

"Sure, but first I got to make a phone call. I'll be up in a few minutes."

Jimmy reached Buddy at home, and related in detail the conversation he had with Sean.

"Well, what do you think?" Buddy asked.

"I believe him. I watched him carefully as we talked, and although he was upset, he gave no signs that he wasn't telling the truth. You know how you and I could always tell when he was kidding or lying by his mannerisms—there was none of that. I'm sure he's telling the truth."

"Then it's Sally, Jimmy; it has to be."

"Yeah. I guess that bitch has gone off her rocker. But I want no part of her. She'd be trouble, and I don't need that kind of trouble."

"But now we got trouble anyway."

"True, Buddy, but I had no way of anticipating that she'd pull anything like this."

"Did you ever tell her anything about—well, anything?" Buddy asked.

"Hell, no! There was no reason for anyone to know about our business. How about Doreen, did she ever quiz you?"

"Only once—way back. Remember? We talked about that. She's never mentioned it again."

Jimmy remembered, and he now was certain Sally was the letter writer. The question was what to do about it.

"I'm going to the Country Club tomorrow," Jimmy said. "Sally's back in town and I heard that she and Alfie moved into a new home in Stanton. They'll very likely be at the Sunday brunch and I'll try to speak to her alone. If she's not there, I'll call her."

"It's not a home, Jimmy, it's an estate. They built it up high on the point, overlooking the harbor. Dory and I took a ride by a few weeks ago and were amazed at the size of it. Must be twelve or fifteen rooms in the damn place. Alfie must be rolling in money."

"Yeah, there's plenty of dough there. Patti heard rumors that he's been fooling around on his business trips. Supposedly Sally found out and this new place is to placate her."

Buddy laughed cynically. "Looks like they both got what they deserved. She's probably no angel either. What are you going to say to her?"

"Don't know exactly. But I'll say something to shock her and see if I can get her to open up. I'll talk to you later."

Jimmy hung up, poured himself a scotch, gulped it down, and headed upstairs to join Patti.

At the Country Club the next day Jimmy approached Sally as she exited a powder room. He had waited for the right moment; when she was alone and thinking of other things.

"Hello, Sally," he said as he moved close to her. "Have you written any more anonymous letters to the police lately?"

She froze momentarily, her face coloring, but to her credit, said nothing until she regained her composure.

"What do you mean?" she said hesitantly.

"You know what I mean. I didn't think you'd stoop so low as to pull a stunt like that, especially when it isn't true."

"I don't have the faintest idea of what you're talking about, nor am I interested in anything you've got to say," she said too loudly. "Excuse me; I have people waiting for me," and she hastily departed.

Jimmy had his answer. He saw it in her face, although she had covered up quickly.

He had frightened her with his accusation; he was certain of that. But would that be enough? Besides, what else could she do? She knew nothing and had no proof of her allegations. But the bitch had planted a seed, and they would be suspect because the police had no one else.

So what, he told himself, they've got absolutely nothing to go on. He and Buddy were outstanding community members, and though Buddy didn't get himself involved in local politics or attend Kiwanis or Rotary club meetings due to his work schedule, his wife was very active in community affairs and a work-horse for the Democratic party. He himself was involved in all the clubs and with the School Athletic Board, and knew he was well liked and respected.

They would be okay as long as nobody panicked and as long as they continued to live their exemplary lives.

Sally had looked frightened. He didn't think there would be any more letters from her. But the harm had been done.

He made a mental note to call Buddy and Sean to fill them in, and to schedule a meeting for the coming Saturday morning.

CHAPTER 56

SEPTEMBER 8, 1953

Sean was starting the fourth year of his 5 year course at Northeastern University and doing well both academically and in his work program. He had spent his entire work period with Filenes, and the last 2 years exclusively within the carpeting division. His boss, Earl Kaster, was a likable man in his early thirties; balding, good-looking, always smiling, and with a gift of gab that customers seemed to enjoy.

Earl could sell anyone by letting them sell themselves. Some customers were repeat customers moving to newer and larger homes. Others were first-timers who came to him on word-of-mouth recommendation, and within minutes were captivated and on a first-name basis.

As most of the buying decisions were made by females, Earl catered to them. He had style and Sean wanted to be like him; a super salesman.

At lunch one day, Sean asked Earl if he thought Filenes would hire him full-time after he graduated. Earl thought they would, but that he had something else in mind.

"Sean, this has to be between us and in the strictest confidence. I'm planning to leave Filenes and open up my own carpet and tile facility. I'm in the final stages of obtaining bank financing, and hope to have everything worked out over the next few months. I've got the site picked and an option on the land, and hopefully it will all be a go by the spring.

"I've got a big following of customers; relationships that I've built up over the last 10 years. Many of these people are moving from apartments and small homes to newer apartments and larger homes in Newton and Brookline, as well as in the North Shore towns of Swampscott, Marblehead, Stanton, and Pemberton. There's a building boom going on, Sean, and I think it will continue for many years to come.

"All these homes are going to need tile and carpeting. I want to be their supplier. Sean, I'd like you to come in with me after you graduate. I'll pay you a good salary and a fair commission, and down the road a few years I'll cut you in for a piece of the action."

Sean was interested; it sounded good to him. He decided he wouldn't tell anybody, including Flossy, until and if it happened.

Flossy wasn't home when he got there, but she had left him a note she'd be back by 7:00, and that Jimmy had called and wanted him to call him at home after 5:00 p.m.

"Hi, Jimmy. It's Sean. What's up?"

Jimmy related his confrontation with Sally and of his conclusion that Sally was the author of the two letters.

Sean felt a degree of relief. Flossy was no longer suspect, and Jimmy was positive there was no evidence of wrong-doing on their part.

"I talked to Buddy a little while ago," Jimmy continued, "and he's in agreement. It's got to be Sally. He also feels as long as we keep our mouths shut we're in the clear. As for Sally, we'll discuss her when we meet next Saturday."

Jimmy received one more phone call that evening, just after 9:00.

"You find out what's going on?" Dan O'Brien asked, getting right to the point.

"Yeah, Pop, my old high school girlfriend Sally Marsh and I had a disagreement over something, and this was her way of getting even. I think I've got it all squared away."

"Must have been a fucking serious disagreement. Any truth to it?" Dan asked bluntly.

"None at all, Pop—none at all. Be sure to tell Grady; and thank him."

"Yeah," Dan O'Brien answered, and hung up without saying good-bye.

The boys met Saturday morning as planned. "Before we go to breakfast, let's stop at the folks' house for a few minutes," Jimmy said. "Patti spoke to mom yesterday and she wasn't feeling well."

When they arrived at the house, they found Mary sitting at the kitchen table nibbling on a slice of dry toast and sipping a cup of weak tea. She told them that she hadn't felt well most of the week, but didn't want to bother them.

"I was a little dizzy and nauseous for a few days, but I'm feeling a far might better this morning," she explained. "And look at the three of you; grown men and looking like handsome devils, and me looking like the rag lady."

They each stooped to kiss her on the cheek.

Jimmy quipped, "You're a handsome woman yourself, Mrs. O'Brien," which she outwardly derided and inwardly enjoyed.

Dan O'Brien sauntered into the kitchen from his basement retreat, having heard voices and wondering who the hell would come visiting so early in the day without calling first. Upon seeing the trio, he nodded his head, and in a mocking tone asked if they were lost.

Jimmy ignored the sarcasm, directing a chilly look at his father.

Sean attempted to help the situation by breaking the sudden silence. "We have a breakfast meeting planned for this morning and thought that a little visit first would be okay. I'm sorry if we came too early."

"Nonsense," Mary interrupted, "I've been up for hours and feel like having some company; especially this company. I only apologize that I'm not quite up to making you a healthy breakfast, but I can offer you a cup of coffee and some toast."

The boys refused, but pulled up chairs and joined her at the table. They took their leave 30 minutes later, promising that they'd be back in a few days.

As they were leaving Dan led Jimmy aside, out of earshot of the others.

"You talk to that girl again to make sure?"

"No, but I know it was her. She played dumb, but I could read her face and she got the message. There won't be any more letters. We'll let things ride. Our noses are clean."

Dan O'Brien nodded and walked back into the house, miffed that they hadn't invited him to breakfast.

The boys took a corner booth in Stanley's Cafeteria, threw a couple of sets of keys on the table to show it was occupied, and got in line to order breakfast. They ate rapidly and, over second cups of coffee, discussed Sally Dillon.

"She tried to hide it, but she was scared," Jimmy asserted.

"I hope so," Sean replied. "She has to be insane to bring up a dead issue."

Buddy snickered at Sean's choice of words, and Sean reddened before adding, "you know what I mean."

Jimmy, uncharacteristically deadpan, said, "She's turned into a real snob and a real bitch, and I'm not sure how I want to play it with her. I don't think it would be wise to ignore her completely. I'll be sociable in deference to Alfie and see what happens."

"Maybe she should have an accident," Buddy suggested.

"Hell no!" Sean fired back. "She'd blame us and the cops would be all over us."

"I agree," Jimmy said. "They could be watching us, and it would be too risky. Like I said before, they've got nothing, and I want to keep it that way."

Buddy wouldn't give up. "We could hire somebody to do it and arrange it so we all had alibis and wouldn't be implicated. I could get it done for 500 bucks and no one would be the wiser."

"True," Jimmy said, "but the cops might think that we arranged it. The safest thing is to do nothing, and the cops will decide it was some disgruntled schoolmate trying to get even. It will all blow away. Sally knows if she were to send another letter we'd find out about it. I don't think she's stupid enough to risk it."

"I agree," Sean added eagerly.

"I don't," Buddy stated matter-of-factly. "I think she's going to be a continued source of trouble unless you hop in bed with her, and even then I wouldn't trust her. But I'll go along with the majority; if that's what you want."

"It's the wisest choice for us, Buddy," Jimmy said. "Later on, if circumstances change, we can reconsider."

"Definitely the wisest choice," Sean parroted.

"We'll see," Buddy said, with a far-a-way look on his face.

CHAPTER 57

SEPTEMBER 12, 1953
SATURDAY

The long-range weather forecast for the Labor Day weekend was for above normal temperatures, becoming warmer as the week progressed.

With such a promising prediction Sally decided to keep her pool open for another week before switching to the Club pool. She preferred the convenience of swimming at home.

Sally used her outdoor pool every morning, now changing her summer workout schedule by swimming at 11:00 rather than at 9:00. She wanted to allow the air temperature to warm up even though the pool temperature was maintained at a constant 78 degrees Fahrenheit.

Her target was 30 laps a day. She had trained herself to breathe every sixth stroke, which was nearly mid-way the length of the pool.

Her crawl was smooth as she knifed through the water using a rapid flutter kick, swimming close to one side of the pool.

She felt more comfortable when she could see wall all the time. Her one experience with a leg cramp had made her cautious, and she wanted that wall handy in case she needed something to hang on to.

She and Alfie often swam and frolicked in the nude on weekends, as the cleaning and gardening help were there only on weekdays. Sally wanted the weekends private so they could live some of her fantasies.

She had become more amorous after her debacle with Jimmy O'Brien, and Alfie benefited from her new mood; so much so that he was finding it worthwhile to stay around weekends instead of being away on as many business trips. Their marriage was improving, and they both realized it.

Alfie had left early that Saturday morning to play golf. He reminded her before he left not to swim alone, but she ignored his advice. As usual, she would do as she damn pleased.

Sally approached the end of the pool on her 30th lap, glided forward until her fingertips touched the wall, and lifted her head out of the water.

At the moment she used one hand to raise her goggles, and as her feet sought bottom, she glimpsed a figure kneeling directly in front of her. As she raised her head to see who it was, two gloved hands grabbed the back of her head and smashed her forehead into the concrete lip of the pool.

She was unconscious as the hands of the intruder, now lying flat on his stomach, held her head under water.

The intruder silently watched the flow of air bubbles until they ceased.

He waited a minute longer until he was satisfied there would be no more.

He rose and glanced in all directions, seeing no one, before walking back 10 feet to the paved path where he had left his small, black valise. He opened the bag and removed a hand towel, casually throwing the towel across his left shoulder before removing his wet cotton gloves and dropping them inside the bag, on top of the large, blunt-point butcher's knife.

The killer used the towel to dry his hands before making his way back to the pool. He studied Sally's lifeless form floating face downward in the water before bending to wipe up the excess water that had run from his bare arms and formed a small puddle on the edge of the pool deck.

He made a final check to see if anything had fallen from his pockets or came off his clothing as he lie at the pool's edge. He saw nothing.

He reasoned the sun would dry the remaining drippings and headed back to his valise, deposited the towel, re-zippered the bag and made his way down the paved path to the driveway. He continued down the driveway some 30 yards before leaving it for the wooded area by which he had entered the property.

Ten minutes later he was in his car and driving home, smiling at how easy it had been.

The knife that had served him so well was not needed, which was, at first, a disappointment.

Much better this way, he decided; it will look like an accident.

There won't be a need for alibis.

CHAPTER 58

THE SAME DAY

Jimmy, Buddy, and Sean eagerly awaited the 2:00 p.m. starting time of the first football game of the new season—Pemberton vs. Revere.

The girls had decided not to come to the game, and the boys were not unhappy. Now they could hoot, holler, drink beer and swear to their hearts' content without earning any dirty looks from their mates.

The boys made their way to a lunch stand and ordered two hot-dogs each and cokes. They planned to sneak the beer from their cooler later, when they were seated. They preferred this lunch to dining in a restaurant down town because it was part of the football scene they enjoyed as kids.

It was boys' day out and they looked forward to it.

High school football usually drew a large turnout in Pemberton and opening day, with perfect weather, would surely result in a sellout crowd.

Alfie Dillon and several of his friends were there, and Jimmy joined them briefly to exchange greetings.

Sam Coben was in the crowd, along with Barney Osham, who wanted to evaluate the Pemberton team prior to their playing Stanton. The two police officers walked by Jimmy, Buddy, and Sean, noting their presence but not exchanging words.

Pemberton won easily, 27 to 7, much to the entertainment of the home crowd. Jimmy, Buddy, and Sean headed to Violet's after the game to down a few beers with the ever-present arm-chair quarterbacks who reviewed every good and bad play as if they themselves were the coach. It was good-natured horseplay that made for a pleasant afternoon.

It wasn't going to be pleasant for everyone.

Alfie stopped at Moe's for his after-game respite before heading home. He stayed longer than he planned to.

He pulled into the entrance of his driveway at 4:35 p.m.

"Damn," he cursed out loud. He had told Sally he would be home no later than 4:00, as they were meeting friends in Boston at 6:30. He was relieved to see her car in the garage, which meant that she was probably getting ready, a chore which took forever. As for himself, he had ample time. He could be showered, shaved and dressed in 45 minutes.

Alfie called out as he entered the house. Sally didn't answer. He headed upstairs and was surprised to see that she was not in their bedroom or in her bathroom.

What the hell, he said to himself. If she had gone off with one of her friends, she should have been home by now.

He went down the stairs and headed first to the kitchen and then to the den, but she had not left a note.

Now he was angry. She would never be ready on time.

He picked up the phone and called Marilyn Shea.

"Marilyn? This is Alfie. My wife with you?"

"Hell, no, and I'm damned mad. I waited an hour for her and she never showed up and she never called me. I called your house and got no answer. She must have forgotten we had a luncheon date."

"Yes, I guess she did," Alfie answered, "I don't know where the hell she is. I'll have her call you tomorrow," he said, and hung up.

Something was wrong. Sally could be a bitch in many ways, but she was always considerate about keeping appointments. If she were going to be late, or if there were a change of plans, she would let you know.

Alfie went out of the house and headed to the garage. Nobody there. From the garage he headed down the path to the pool.

He broke into a cold sweat when he saw a figure, partially submerged, floating in the water. He ran to the pool, jumped in and brought Sally's limp form to the ladder and with difficulty pulled her out of the pool.

Sobbing and half out of his mind, he cradled her in his arms and yelled for help. He soon realized that nobody could hear him and laid her gently aside and ran to the pool phone. He dialed for an operator and shouted to her to get an ambulance to his house, giving his address between sobs.

He hung up and vomited.

Barney Osham called Sam Coben several hours later.

"I thought you'd want to know that Sally Dillon is dead."

"What?" came the shocked response. "What in the hell are you talking about?"

"Her husband found her floating in their swimming pool when he got home a few hours ago."

"Jesus Christ, Barney, fill me in," Sam cried.

"Alfred Dillon arrived home approximately 4:30 this afternoon. He had played golf in the morning with some male friends, had lunch, and went with them to the Pemberton/Revere football game."

"Yes, we saw him there," Sam reminded him.

"Correct. After the game he and his friends stopped at Moe's to down a few. They stayed there roughly an hour. Then Dillon left his friends and went home. His wife's car was in the garage, and he expected to find her upstairs getting ready for a dinner date in Boston. She wasn't there. He checked the house for a note from her as to her whereabouts, and found none. He called a girlfriend of his wife, with whom she had a luncheon date, and learned that his wife had never showed up or called to cancel. He rechecked the garage, found nothing, and then on a hunch headed for the pool area. He found her floating in the pool."

"Jesus," Sam shortened his response, "any sign of foul play?"

"No," Barney replied, "looks like an accident. She had a bad bruise on the left side of her forehead. The coroner thinks she was walking along the edge of the pool, near a corner, and slipped and struck her head on the adjacent edge with enough force to knock her out, fall into the pool, and drown. He'll be able to narrow down the approximate time of death once he checks the stomach contents. She had breakfast with her husband between 8:00 and 8:30, so we should get a pretty good idea of the time frame."

"Could someone have bashed her in the head and thrown her into the pool to drown?" Sam asked.

"There were traces of blood on the edge of the pool, Sam. The ME's theory is the bruise to her head resulted from the fall and was the cause of her drowning."

"What else, Barney? You sound unconvinced."

"You remember that she was Jimmy O'Brien's girlfriend in high school, don't you? She could have been the one who typed those letters and somehow he found out."

"That sounds a little far-fetched, Barney. The author of the letters was afraid of being identified, and wouldn't have told anyone."

"Leaks, Sam. There are always leaks. She could have accidentally tipped him off by something she did or said. O'Brien is not a fool. He hasn't climbed the ladder of success by being stupid."

"True, Barney, but it's also pure speculation. If the time of death was in the afternoon that will clear O'Brien. He was at the game and probably had lunch earlier with his friends, very much in public view. If the TOD was late morning, however, and a blow was administered by someone that caused her death, then anyone is suspect. It would be tough to prove who did it unless we find some evidence or a witness."

"You're damn right it would. There's a typewriter in the house, and I'm having it checked out for a match with the letters. I'll talk to you later."

Jimmy stopped at Raymonds Sunday morning for a cup of coffee, and the lunch counter conversation was about the drowning of Sally Dillon. He listened to the gossip, picked up a Sunday paper, and left for home without uttering a word.

Buddy called him around noon, relating that he heard the news, and mockingly offered his condolences.

Sean called an hour later, expressing his shock over the incident, but relieved that it had been an accident.

Jimmy's reply had been simplistic. "Yeah, too bad."

Barney contacted Sam the day after Sally Dillon's funeral and brought him up to date.

"The pathologist, based upon food digestion in the stomach and the pool temperature, placed the time of death between 11:00 a.m. and 1:00 p.m. He couldn't put it any closer. The blow on the head didn't kill her; she drowned. The blood on the pool edge was hers. There's no doubt in the coroner's mind that she slipped—struck her head and knocked herself out—and fell into the pool and drowned.

My Captain and the Chief both support the coroner's conclusion."

"You buy it, Barney?" Sam asked.

"I have to, Sam. I raised a couple of other possibilities with the Chief and he chewed my head off. Told me I've been reading too many dime-store novels. Incidentally, the letters were not written on the typewriter in the Dillon home, and I re-checked the pool area and the grounds and found nothing indicating foul play. There were no valuables missing from the house. I had to find that out discretely so the Chief wouldn't jump my ass. The case is closed, Sam."

"If it means anything, I side with you, Barney. It's just too convenient."

"Yeah, but I can't pursue the case on what I've got. Maybe another anonymous letter will come in, and point the way. We're due for a break."

"I wouldn't count on another letter, Barney," Sam Coben predicted.

"I wouldn't either," Barney concurred.

CHAPTER 59

20 MONTHS LATER
MAY, 1955

Sean graduated from Northeastern and went to work for Earl Kaster.

Flossy planned a graduation party for Sean, and invited Jimmy, Buddy, their parents, Sean's mother, Earl Kaster, and Jerry Robinow, her old stockbroker friend from San Francisco.

Jerry Robinow had arrived in Boston two months earlier. He had divorced his wife Cheryl—or rather, had agreed to a divorce—without remorse. She had been 10 years his junior when she married him. His good looks and healthy bank account had easily won her over.

As it turned out, they had little in common. Jerry was well read, highly intelligent, with a preference for the opera and the arts. Cheryl enjoyed the nightclub and country club atmosphere. It had taken her 8 years to find someone extremely wealthy and more to her liking and her way of thinking. Now in her early fifties, she was still beautiful, vivacious, clever and manipulating, and in the period of a few short months, convinced her new lover to leave his wife.

In a year her lover was a free man, and she approached Jerry and told him she wanted a divorce.

Jerry had no objections. He had tired of her as well.

The matter resolved, Jerry had called Flossy and told her he was coming to Boston.

He had come to Boston for 2 weeks and stayed for 3 months. Flossy and Jerry re-discovered in each other a warm understanding, and a mutual desire to share events they both enjoyed. They soon realized it was love.

Sean, surprisingly, had not been hurt by their apparent closeness and encouraged them to go their own way, joining them only on rare occasions. He liked Jerry, accepting Flossy's explanation that he was an old family friend, but in a short time realized their friendship transcended the usual relationship of a man near sixty and a woman in her twenties.

Actually, Sean was relieved. He was preoccupied with his work, and with his employer and mentor, Earl Kaster.

##

Flossy asked Sean to meet her for lunch one Sunday in early June, 1956, as she had something of importance to discuss with him. She got right to the point, and told him that she and Jerry were in love.

"I apologize, Sean, if I've hurt you. I didn't mean it to happen; it just did."

Sean was hurt, but not in the way of a rejected suitor. He loved Flossy not as a lover, but as a friend who shared common interests. Now he feared he would lose the close companionship that had brought him so much happiness.

"No need to apologize, Flossy. Jerry is a nice guy and I know he will take care of you. As long as we remain friends; that's all I care about."

"We'll always be the best of friends, Sean, and thank you for understanding."

"I hope it's okay if I stay a few weeks until I find an apartment. I'll be out as soon as I can," Sean added, realizing his predicament.

"Not a problem at all," Flossy replied. "Jerry's going back to California to sell some property and finalize his affairs there, and he'll be gone the better part of the month. You take all the time you need, and I'll be happy to help you find a place, if you want me to."

"Yeah, that would be great," he said with sincerity.

She leaned over and kissed him lightly on the lips. "Thank you for making it easy for me. I really like you so much, but it's a different feeling I have for Jerry."

The discussion had gone smoothly, and Flossy was elated. She hadn't been sure what to expect, but she wasn't completely surprised. She had always been the aggressor in their physical relationship, and often felt guilty, as if she had slept with a sibling rather than a lover.

He had been more a friend than a lover, and she was pleased that the friendship could continue.

The party was a success, although Dan O'Brien had too much to drink and talked too loudly. Sean told Jimmy and Buddy that he would be moving out, as Flossy and he had decided that although they were good friends, they weren't meant for each other.

The O'Brien boys weren't surprised. They felt she was too domineering for Sean.

Patti and Doreen were upset when Flossy told them, but understood when she explained that she and Sean were more like brother and sister than husband and wife, and it wasn't fair to her or Sean to continue their relationship the way it was.

Everyone approved of Jerry Robinow, for he was an affable man who told great stories. Even Dan O'Brien found him interesting before he became too drunk to listen or care.

Earl Kaster also met with approval, although Buddy thought him to be somewhat effeminate. But as long he was a friend of Sean's, and his boss as well, he was acceptable.

The party broke up at midnight, when Mary O'Brien had had enough of her spouse and his ribald attempt at humor. Slightly embarrassed, she announced that her husband hadn't gone on such a binge in years and hoped that he would have a good hangover in the morning to teach him not to do it again.

CHAPTER 60

Kaster Carpet and Tile Company's first year had proven to be a bigger success than Earl Kaster had envisioned. His prediction of a surge in home construction had come about, but he never expected the volume of business he was experiencing to occur so quickly.

Sean was in charge of the tile and linoleum section, and he saw to it when a sale was made that the installation was done expertly and when promised. Good service was their biggest selling point.

Kaster paid his help better then his competitors did, and was able to obtain and keep some of the best craftsmen in the Boston area. He reasoned correctly that if the company itself made a little less money the first few years by meeting or bettering competitors' prices, and they earned customer good-will by providing reliable service, repeat business and word-of-mouth recommendations would cause them to thrive. He was right. Their business was booming.

Flossy had found Sean an apartment on Atlantic Avenue and had helped him move in. He had quickly settled into the single-living scene, and now had nothing on his mind but work. He put in a 10 to 12 hour work day, 6 days a week, from June through November.

He arranged with Earl to leave noon time on Saturdays from January through March of 1957 to make the drive to North Conway to join his friends for dinner in the evening, and a day of skiing on Sunday.

Sean made the trip even when the others didn't, for it was the one activity that he could do well and enjoyed. The O'Briens usually came one or two weekends a month. Jerry and Flossy joined them one weekend each month, as Flossy, Doreen and Patti remained close.

Flossy had given up skiing, and she and Jerry did the shopping and sight-seeing bit, joining the others when they broke for lunch. They all loved dining and dancing Saturday evenings at the Inn, and Mrs. Graham and her staff catered to them as if they were royalty. No one ever mentioned the Berke episode.

They truly enjoyed the mountains; it was their escape from reality, conscience and memories.

The summer of 1957 proved to be one of Sean's best. Earl kept his promise and awarded him a 25% interest in the business, which he could pay for in a long-term, painless arrangement structured by the firm's accountants. In addition, his interest would increase 1% yearly until he attained a 45% holding, as long as he remained with the company.

Sean was ecstatic. He was doing work that he loved and making a lot of money. The week after his partnership had been signed, sealed and delivered, he made the biggest purchase of his life—a boat.

Earl had tried to talk him out of it. "Why buy a boat when I already have one. You can use it any time you want; you know that."

"Thank you, Earl, but your boat is too big for me. Now that I can afford one, I'd really like one of my own. Please understand, Earl, it's something I've always wanted and until now, could never have."

Earl understood, but insisted he buy nothing smaller than a 30 footer.

"You need a craft you can trust, Sean. The ocean can be treacherous and unforgiving, even in coastal waters."

Sean bought a 6-year-old, 28 foot Chris-Craft cabin cruiser from someone who was upgrading. It was in excellent condition, and Earl advised him to grab it. Earl also arranged the financing with his bank, and countersigned the note.

Sean registered the boat and, on a whim, renamed it "The Pact."

Sean had realized the life he wanted to live. He had his love for skiing in the winter, his involvement in boating in the summer and fall, and the enjoyment and satisfaction year round in his work.

Initially he never refused the fix-up dates thrust upon him by Patti and Doreen, but never followed up by calling for a second date, although he was often encouraged to. He kept telling Patti and Doreen that the girls were nice, and sometimes very nice, but there was "no chemistry," and he didn't want to lead anyone on.

After a while Patti and Doreen gave up, deciding that he was still in love with Flossy. They didn't want to embarrass themselves further with their friends or friends of friends. Sean inwardly smiled in relief. He didn't want to be fixed up.

CHAPTER 61

AUGUST, 1957

This month they were all to meet at the Continental, and Patti made the dinner reservation for eight people at 8 o'clock.

Jerry Robinow was a charmer and, although more than twice their age, fit in comfortably. He was a master story-teller who had visited many countries and seen much that was good and bad. He had a tale to tell about them all.

Sean stopped coming with a date and for the past several months showed up with Earl Kaster. No one questioned it. It was an evening to dine, drink, and have fun with old and new friends.

This night would be a different. They had been seated for some time, and had ordered their second round of drinks, when Patti attracted their attention by rapping on her wine glass several times.

"Attention, please; attention. I have an announcement to make."

When they quieted down, she continued. "Jimmy and I want you all to know we're having a baby."

The ladies squealed with delight and rose to kiss her, while the men were shaking hands with an equally animated Jimmy O'Brien.

After the group had regained their seats and the noise quieted down, Patti answered the main questions. "We're expecting in mid-February. If it's a boy, he'll be named James O'Brien II, and if it's a girl, she'll be named Kathleen."

Everyone made a toast, and when it was Buddy's turn he congratulated Patti and Jimmy, and with a glint in his ever-penetrating eyes, and the faint trace of a smile, added, "and to make this evening more of a celebration, Doreen would like to make her own announcement."

Doreen hadn't wanted to do any such thing. She would have preferred to let Patti have her evening and make her own disclosure the following month, when she could be the center of attention.

It was too late now. To an attentive audience, she forced herself to smile, and said, "Buddy and I are expecting the end of March."

The gathering at the table went into an uproar. There was a similar exchange of well-wishes, with everyone talking at once. Then came a series of off-color jokes at the expense of Jimmy and Buddy, with Jerry accusing the brothers of laying side-bets. Addressing the two, he asked if they had discussed parenthood at the bar and rushed home to see who could make it happen first.

Patti and Doreen lived through a sea of blushes, wishing that it hadn't turned out this way, but making the best of it. The ladies turned down the next round of drinks, saying they were famished and wanted to order dinner.

Sean had mixed feelings as he and Earl Kaster drove home that evening. He was happy for Jimmy and Buddy, but something bothered him.

CHAPTER 62

SEPTEMBER, 1957

Each time Barney Osham saw Jimmy O'Brien's picture in the paper as head of some committee or attending some social function, or saw either one of the O'Brien brothers on his frequent trips to Pemberton, his blood pressure rose.

Barney had nothing in the way of evidence, but his gut feeling told him the O'Briens were involved in some of the murders.

He had been ordered by the Chief to spend his working hours on other cases, and not to chase phantoms or hunches and speculations, and, as he was a disciplined cop, he did what he was told.

On his own time, however, Barney continued to search for a tie-in. The anonymous letters were obviously the work of an O'Brien enemy, but there could be some truth to them. *If* Jimmy O'Brien's old girlfriend had been the author, and was now conveniently dead by design rather than by accident, another lead had been covered up.

There had to be motives waiting to surface and he intended to find them.

Sean Boyle could be the answer. Barney learned from ex-classmates that Boyle and the O'Brien boys had always been a threesome, and that Boyle was the quiet one who was shielded by the others. He was told that nobody in grammar school or high school would dare cross Jimmy O'Brien, and his brother and friend were included.

Barney made his decision. He would focus on Sean Boyle.

He learned Boyle never married but had lived with a woman until they separated a year or so ago. The woman owned an Art Gallery in Boston. He felt a visit to Sean Boyle's ex-girlfriend was in order.

Hell, he thought, I have nothing to lose, and maybe—just maybe—I'll strike a nerve if I mention the anonymous letters.

On his next day off, he visited Flossy Sloan in her Art Gallery.

"Miss Sloan, I'm Inspector Barney Osham, with the Stanton Police," he explained, handing her his card and displaying his gold shield, "I would like just 10 minutes of your time."

Flossy looked at him for a moment before notifying one of her assistants she would be tied up with a customer, and she would be in her office if she was needed. She led Barney down a hallway whose walls displayed an assortment of oil paintings and watercolors, and into a lavishly furnished wood-paneled office.

"Please sit down, Inspector. Would you care for a cup of coffee?"

"No thank you," Barney said, smiling his refusal, "I've already had my quota for the day."

"What can I do for you?" she asked, outwardly displaying no discomfort by his appearance at her workplace.

"Miss Sloan, I understand you're a fair and honest person. I got that info by talking to some of your business neighbors before I walked in here. I didn't tell them I was a cop. I told them I represented an artist who may want to put some of his work up for sale, and needed all kinds of references. I'm sure they bought my explanation. I don't know you, and finding out what other people think gives me more to work with than my own first impression. You're well thought of, Miss Sloan."

"Thank you, Inspector, but I'm completely puzzled as to where this is leading."

"Let me tell you a few things, Miss Sloan, and you can decide if you can help me."

"Why don't you get to the point, Inspector and give me the chance to decide."

Barney detailed the Gordon murder and the Robinson death, filling in the specifics as he knew them. He then related the details of the murders of Coach Wilzinski, Larry Sandberg and the latest tragedy, the death of Sally Dillon.

He tied the events together for her. "Gordon, Robinson, and Sally Dillon (nee Marsh) were all schoolmates, in the same class at Pemberton High. Wilzinski was the Coach at the same school, and Jimmy O'Brien was one of his star players. Sandberg was Buddy

O'Brien's immediate supervisor, and was, incidentally, replaced by Buddy O'Brien shortly after his death."

Flossy was stunned. *How could this be? These people are friends!* She was speechless.

Barney continued. "I don't think it was one person acting alone, Miss Sloan. Jimmy O'Brien was in Korea when Coach Wilzinski was murdered, and as far as I can tell, he was the only one involved with the Coach. Yet the Coach was murdered in the same brutal way as Gordon and Sandberg."

He paused to give her time to mull over the information. He wasn't finished, but he wanted her to absorb the story.

It took Flossy a minute to respond. "What you've got is all circumstantial evidence, isn't it?"

Barney smiled. "Good question, Miss Sloan, and the answer, of course, is yes. But it's quite an interesting set of circumstances, isn't it?"

She involuntarily nodded her head. Then she asked the question she dreaded. "And you think Sean may be involved?"

"Yes I do, Miss Sloan; perhaps unwillingly. From what I've learned about Sean Boyle violence doesn't fit his character, but when you consider he has been close to the O'Briens all his life, I think he would have had to have known what was going on. He may have been swept up in the events, and had no other choice. I honestly don't know. But it's possible he's looking for a way out."

"What do you mean?" Flossy asked anxiously.

"We received information from an unidentified source naming the O'Brien brothers as being involved in the murders of Gordon and Robinson. Sean Boyle's name was not mentioned."

"You think it could be Sean who's the unidentified source?"

"A possibility, or it could have been Sally Dillon. We got the information prior to her death, and there hasn't been any word since. It also could be the reason she died."

"My God! That's horrible!"

"Murder is horrible, Miss Sloan, and multiple murders are abhorrent. I don't like living with the fact the responsible parties are still at large, and I want the murders ended. That's right, Miss Sloan; if we don't stop it, it could continue. There may be others at risk."

There was silence as she looked at him.

Then she spoke. "What is it you want, Inspector?"

"Your help, Miss Sloan. Did Sean ever discuss or even hint at any of the happenings that I've told you about?"

"No! Never! He talked about the O'Briens often during the first few months we met, and always in glowing terms. When I got to meet them, I could see that he idolized them; well, Jimmy anyway. He seemed less comfortable with Buddy, but there was no mistaking his loyalty and affection towards Jimmy."

"Did he ever discuss much about their life and doings in high school? Did he ever mention the names of any of the deceased, or the names of any other school friends?"

"He talked a little about Sally—I don't remember her maiden name."

"Marsh."

"Yes, Sally Marsh. He mentioned that she and Jimmy had been a hot number in school, but had broken up shortly after Jimmy had been hurt in a football game. Sean said she was a real bitch the way she dropped Jimmy and took up with Alfie Dillon when Jimmy was hurting so badly. She eventually married Alfie Dillon. I met her a few times; she's a beautiful woman."

"WAS a beautiful woman, Miss Sloan," Barney corrected. "Please continue."

"I meant 'was,'" Flossy answered, noting the Inspector was applying not-so-subtle pressure. "And call me Flossy; everyone else does."

"Thank you, Flossy. Were Sally and Jimmy enemies after that?"

"No, I don't think so. According to Sean, Jimmy could have had just about any girl he wanted, and I guess he just ignored her when he got back to school, and they each went their own way. Later on, after Jimmy and Patti got married, he and Alfie Dillon became friendly through business ties and their Country Club membership. Oh! Sean told me that Jimmy once mentioned Sally tried to come onto him at the Club."

That was interesting news to Barney. Might have been just enough to cause Sally Dillon to send off a couple of unsigned letters.

"Do you know when that took place?" he asked.

"Not exactly. Why, is that important?"

"Just curious," he answered, putting her off. "What do *you* think about the O'Briens?"

She hesitated. She hadn't decided how much she wanted to get involved, and needed time to think. After all, they were her friends—especially Patti and Doreen—and she didn't want to do anything that might cause them grief.

And she loved Sean like a brother. It was inconceivable that three people she loved could be linked with murders.

Maybe this cop has some kind of mental fixation because of the unsolved slayings and is out to nail anyone he can on the flimsiest of evidence. But he wouldn't make up the story about the letters accusing Jimmy and Buddy. Someone wrote the letters and sent them to the police. Someone knew something, or thought they did, and was afraid to openly discuss it.

Maybe it was Sally Marsh. Or maybe it was Sean! She needed to talk to Sean!

"There are few similarities between the O'Brien brothers," Flossie began. "Jimmy is forceful, smooth, good-looking, and has a winning personality. Buddy is sullen, quiet by comparison, often hard-to-take, and difficult to get to know and like. They both are well-spoken and have above-average intelligence. Jimmy married well, but I'm told he more than carries his own weight in her father's business. Buddy has done well on his own, and is now the Assistant Plant Manager where he works. Patti and Doreen are very much in love with their husbands, and as far as I can tell both men are in love with their wives. I have never seen any friction between either husband and wife, and I've spent quite a bit of time with them."

She paused, debating whether or not to add what else was on her mind, and decided to continue. "If it weren't for Sean, and later for Patti and Doreen, I wouldn't have continued the relationship."

"Oh?" said Barney, "Why not?"

"I have never been overly fond of either of the O'Brien brothers. Jimmy is too smooth, too charming, and too strong-willed for my liking. He calls the shots in the group, and generally gets his way. I've never heard Patti disagree with him on anything, and it has kinda bugged me.

"And Buddy is somewhat of a puzzle to me. There is something about him that is unsettling. I don't know how else to describe it, but he makes me uncomfortable and I don't like the feeling."

"Do you think either one, or both, are capable of brutally murdering someone?" Barney asked bluntly, his voice almost angry.

"Hell, I can't answer that. I don't know."

"Will you try to find out? If they are innocent, let's prove it. If they're not, then I want them!" he barked.

"How the hell am I going to do that?" she cried out. "Jesus, you're asking a hell of a lot."

"I know I am," he said, softening his voice, "but I'm trying to prevent more killings, and it could be that Doreen and Sean are in danger."

"What are you talking about!" she demanded. "Why would you think that?"

"Think about it, Flossy. Gordon, Robinson, Sally Marsh Dillon—all were classmates. *And so were Doreen and Sean!"*

The statement hit her hard. She rose and paced the floor, deep in thought. Barney watched her through narrowed eyes. He had said all he was going to say. Now it was up to her.

It took several minutes before she sat down, and when she did, he saw tears in her eyes. She spoke slowly and in a subdued voice. "I don't know what to do. I don't want to get involved—I truly don't. I don't want to believe any of this. But you think it's true, don't you?"

She was looking for a response, but he didn't give one. He knew she was struggling with her emotions and rationalizations.

"But there are too many connections to be chance events, aren't there? And yet, it doesn't necessarily mean that it has to be the O'Briens. There could be someone else in the class who had motives that never surfaced. Did you ever think of that?"

She had flung her last observation at him in desperation, and caught him by surprise. He had considered it and decided it was unlikely, but he knew he had to give a little.

"Anything is possible, Flossy, so let's try to find out. Whoever it is has got to be stopped."

"I will talk to Sean," she said, her decision made. "I doubt if he'll tell me outright if they are involved—in fact, I know he would never turn on his friends—but I can read his face. Then I will know, and I'll tell you if you're barking up the wrong tree."

"Fair enough; I couldn't ask for anything more." Barney pulled out his card, jotted down his home phone number, and told her that he could be reached day or night.

He stood, shook her hand and thanked her, and left Flossy Sloan bewildered and anxiety-ridden.

That night Flossy called Sean and told him Jerry had gone to the West Coast for a week.

"Sean, I want to meet you for dinner. What night can you make it?"

"Thursday night would be easiest for me," he replied. "I'll call and see if any of the others are available and want to join us."

“No, Sean; just you and me.”

“Is something wrong, Floss?”

“I don’t know, but we’ve got to talk. Just the two of us.”

“Okay. Where do you want to meet?”

“How about the Towne Lyne House at 7:30?”

“Fine. I’ll see you then.”

“Flossy, what-what the hell are-are you saying?” Sean Boyle stammered. They were seated at a table for two by a window, where they could watch the fast-fading light cloak the adjacent Suntaug Lake.

She had finished telling him of her conversation with Inspector Osham, and mentioned the accusatory letters.

Sean was upset. She couldn’t tell if he was disturbed by the Inspector’s notion of the O’Briens or by the fact the police had information from an unknown source and thought it could have been from Sally Dillon—or Sean Boyle.

Sean didn’t react the way she expected. She wished he would have either laughed at the story or been angry someone had accused them of perpetrating such hideous crimes.

His response shocked her. He was visibly shaken, and nervously attempting to deny any wrong-doing on his part or on the part of the O’Briens’.

He wasn’t convincing her, and she knew something was wrong. She told him so.

“Sean, I don’t think for one minute *you* would harm anybody. But I know how close you are with Jimmy and Buddy, and that you’d never do anything to hurt them. I only hope they didn't drag you into any situations you had no control over.

"Jesus, Flossy, I-I would never intentionally hurt anybody. It's-it's out of the question," he stated emotionally.

"I know you wouldn't, Sean," she said. "But what about them?"

"I-I can't believe they would do it either," he hedged. "They might beat someone up, or want to cause somebody some grief, but I'll never believe that Jimmy—or Buddy—is-is a cold-blooded killer. And-and you know the Coach was killed while Jimmy was in Korea, don't you?"

"Yes, Sean, the Inspector told me that. But Buddy wasn't in Korea."

"No, I know he wasn't," he replied meekly.

"Look, Sean, I've been thinking about this a lot. I'm certain before Inspector Osham came to see me he must have checked your whereabouts for the times the slayings took place, and come up with nothing. If he had anything more than suspicions he wouldn't have come to me. But somebody wrote letters accusing the O'Briens. He wanted to know if it was you."

Sean shook his head vigorously. "No, Flossy, honest. I never would have done that."

"I didn't think so, Sean, but I had to ask. It must have been Sally. Somehow word leaked out, and she was murdered to shut her up."

"She drowned, Flossy; it was an accident."

"Inspector Osham doesn't think so, Sean."

Sean said nothing. The fear on his face said it all.

A waitress refilled their coffee cups and took their dessert orders. When she left, Flossy looked at Sean with concern. She reached out with her hand, signifying that she wanted his. He obliged, and they looked at each other thoughtfully.

"I think you should break away from them before they get you in real trouble."

"I can't, Flossy. I could never do that."

"For God's sake, why not?" she cried out. "They don't own you."

"You don't understand," he said with emotion. "Way back, when we were kids, we had a club, and we all swore we would never let anything or anybody break up our pact."

"Your what?"

"Our pact—our agreement. We would always stick together."

"For Christ's sake, Sean, that's kid stuff. What did you agree to?"

Sean realized he had said too much. "Look, Flossy, it may sound like kid stuff to you, but it wasn't and isn't to me. I was never the strongest or bravest kid growing up, and they always protected me. If it wasn't for them, I don't think I would have managed to get through grammar school, and certainly would never have made it through high school. You don't know what it was like living in Pemberton back then. There were kids who would have torn me apart if I weren't with Jimmy and Buddy."

"You haven't answered my question. What was this 'pact' that you agreed to?"

"Forget I mentioned it! Please, Flossy, we don't talk about it except among ourselves. You'll have to take my word for it—it's nothing bad. I didn't do anything, and they didn't do anything, and that's all I want to say about it."

Flossy looked at him. She was hurt that he wouldn't confide in her. She knew something was wrong, but he wouldn't open up. His ties to the O'Briens were stronger than his relationship with her, and she should have realized it.

"All right, Sean. I'm just worried about you. You know how fond I am of you, and I don't want you dragged into their troubles."

She had tears in her eyes, and he softened when he saw how upset she was.

"I'm sorry, Floss; I-I didn't mean to raise my voice. I know you mean well, and I appreciate your telling me what the cop thinks. I'm not in any trouble, and-and please don't mention THE PACT to Jimmy or Buddy. Or to anyone. It may only have been kid stuff, but we took it seriously."

Flossy smiled weakly. "Just remember that I'm your friend, Sean, and that I care about you. I'll be there anytime you need my help."

"Thanks, Flossy; I love you."

"I love you too, Sean."

Sean was troubled as he drove back to Boston. Flossy's revelation that the cops didn't think Sally's death was accidental had surprised him. He thought the incident was clear-cut. Where was this cop coming from, and why was he trying to crucify them?

His biggest concern was what to tell Jimmy and Buddy. He didn't want to involve Flossy, but he had to warn them.

It would be late by the time he got home, but he needed to talk to Jimmy.

"Why did the cop approach Flossy, Sean?" Jimmy asked, anger creeping into his voice.

"I don't know. Maybe he figured we were no longer living together and split up on bad terms. Flossy and I couldn't think of any other reason."

"What did she tell him? I want to know every word."

"She told him he was crazy. She told him she knew all of us very well, and didn't believe any of it. He-he wanted to know if I wrote the letters."

"You? Why would he think you wrote the letters?"

"He told her all kinds of crazy things, Jimmy. I don't know why. I don't even know why he thinks that Sally's death wasn't an accident. Everybody said it was. The guy's gotta be nuts. What's he got against us?"

Jimmy could hear Sean's fear and bewilderment. He needed time to think, and he wanted Buddy's input. At the moment, however, he had to placate Sean.

"Look, Sean, there's absolutely nothing to worry about. Like I told you before, none of us are guilty of anything, and we can't let anything or anybody shake us or divide us. The hell with the damn cop! He's a sick-son-of-a-bitch who's looking for glory at our expense. Just keep your wits and don't let him rattle you; it's what he's trying to do. We stick together; just like always. You understand?"

"Yes, Jimmy; I just want it to stop."

"It will, Sean, I promise you. I'll take care of everything. I want to talk to Buddy so he'll know what's going on, and I'll get back to you tomorrow night. Where are you going to be?"

"I'll be home after 7:00."

"I'll call you then. Will you be okay Sean?"

"Yeah, I guess so. Thanks, Jimmy, I feel better. I'll-I'll talk to you tomorrow."

Jimmy reached Buddy at home, and told him about Sean's call.

"It's getting tacky, Jimmy," Buddy said. "Flossy can be a real bitch when she wants to be. She could hound Sean until he tells her about the car incident and who knows what else."

"I don't think so. We've been over it with him too many times. He understands he's as involved as we are, and he's not going to blow any whistle and chance losing everything he's got. I don't suppose it would do us any harm if we got together for breakfast on Sunday and gave him a little pep talk."

"Okay, Stanley's Cafeteria at 8:00 a.m. See you then."

It was Sunday, September 22, 1957 and Mother Nature was warning she might skip fall and bring on winter early. The outside temperature was in the low forties as Jimmy, Buddy, and Sean took their seats for breakfast.

Sean repeated in detail what Flossy told him in her conversation with Inspector Osham. Jimmy and Buddy listened, interrupting occasionally to ask a question.

When Sean finished, Buddy spoke. "Interesting about Sally. I wonder how the cop came up with that? All the papers called it an accident, and I never saw any hint of foul play mentioned."

"It's pure bull," Jimmy answered. "The cop made it up to get to her. He figured she didn't know any of the other victims, but she had met Sally, and talking about the death of someone you've met is a lot more meaningful than the names of a bunch of unknowns."

"Makes sense," Buddy agreed.

Jimmy continued. "Look, guys, it's the same as before. The cop is scooping up air. He's got nothing and is trying to create something by getting Flossie to work on you, Sean. Listen, I know the car incident with Robinson still bothers you; it does us too. *But it was an accident!* It happened, and it's over. Final! Nothing we can do about it! And we sure as hell don't want our lives spoiled by a freak event that happened a long time ago. Buddy and I have wives, and kids coming, Sean, and we're all doing well. And you're doing great too. We've got too much going for us to throw it all away. Do you understand, Sean?"

Buddy watched Sean nod his head in agreement, and then spoke.

"Sean, we've got to insulate ourselves against whatever anybody claims or theorizes. This cop is trying to make a name for himself. He's got a bunch of deaths that he can't solve and wants to stick them on us and make himself into a hero. Get that into your head and never forget it. And don't let Flossy's imagination get to you. The cop's done what he wanted; he's planted a seed. Knowing her, she'll keep after you. YOU MAKE SURE YOU TELL HER NOTHING, and we're home free. It's as simple as that. We've always stuck together—like we swore we would—and nobody breaks THE PACT. NOBODY!"

"That's the way it's got to be, Sean," Jimmy added vigorously. "There is no other way!"

"I know! I know! I promise!" Sean proclaimed, and then, as if embarrassed by his outburst, added, "You guys will never have to worry about me. I do have a lot going for me. I owe you guys, and we'll always stick together. I'll take care of Flossy—she'll get nothing out of me."

Jimmy and Buddy eyed each other and smiled. As always, THE PACT held up.

They ordered breakfast, ate heartily, and discussed other things. Then Sean excused himself, explaining that his boat was coming out of the water at 11:00 and he wanted to be there to supervise its removal.

When they were alone, Buddy said, "What do you think?"

Jimmy smiled. "I didn't know you were such a great orator. You got the message across, and I'm sure you convinced him that it's his ass on the block as well as ours."

"I was pretty good, wasn't I," Buddy acknowledged with a broad smile. "But seriously, what *do* you think? I don't like Flossy being involved."

"I don't think Flossy could get him to turn on us."

"I'm just worried about what he's told her in the past. Innocent as it may have been, it could get her thinking of things that were meaningless then, but significant now because of the cop's involvement. She puts up with us, Jimmy, because of our wives, but she could become a problem."

"Only if Sean talks, and he won't."

"I don't like Flossy, Jimmy."

"I think we can win her over. Let's try, okay?"

"Yeah, let's try," Buddy answered dubiously.

Inspector Osham phoned Flossy a week later. "I thought I would have heard from you by now, Miss Sloan."

"I have nothing to tell you, Inspector. I'm convinced Sean's not involved in anything you said. I spoke to him and I believe him. And frankly I don't think the O'Briens are involved either."

"You honestly believe that, Miss Sloan?" he asked, with a touch of sarcasm.

"Yes I do," she replied coldly, and hung up.

She had made up her mind to protect Sean at all cost, and if it meant protecting the O'Briens as well, so be it.

CHAPTER 63

Patti gave birth to Jimmy O'Brien Jr. in March of 1958.

A month later, Doreen had a boy, Buddy Jr. There were a string of parties thrown by parents, grandparents and close friends, and the next few months were happy ones.

Young Jimmy at birth tipped the scales at 9 lbs.11 ozs. He was light-complexioned like his father, with blond hair and blue eyes.

Buddy Jr. checked in at 6 lbs. 3 ozs., with dark skin and black hair.

After Patti had given birth, Buddy had secretly hoped that his child would also be a boy, and as big, if not bigger, than Jimmy Jr. He did get his boy, but not his wish for the big guy. He vowed that if his son couldn't be as big, he would be a hell-of-a-lot smarter. His kid would never play second fiddle to anyone.

In late May the two O'Brien families attended the annual Pemberton Art Festival and walked past a couple sitting on a park bench. The woman on the bench was talking, but her companion suddenly lost interest, and focused his attention on the two men who had just passed. He had seen the birth announcements in the paper and soon forgotten about them. But seeing the two men in person elicited a different emotion.

"Sam, are you listening to me?" the woman said.

"Oh, I'm sorry, Nancy. Something important came to mind, and I got lost in thought. Go ahead, I'm all ears."

She continued her conversation, and Sam Coben forced himself to pay attention, while making a mental note to call Barney Osham in the morning.

"Barney. It's Sam. I saw some friends of ours at the Art Festival yesterday, and I thought I'd check with you. What's the latest on the O'Briens?"

"Unfortunately, not a damn thing. I told you I tried to stir something up with the Sloan woman, but it didn't pan out. I could sense there was animosity between her and the O'Briens, but not enough to win her over. I've called her twice over the past 6 months, and she kissed me off both times."

"You know, Barney, nobody but you and I think that the Sally Marsh Dillon thing was anything but an accident."

"That's right, Sam; just our hunch," he repeated bitterly.

"You don't think the killings are over, do you Barney."

"No, I don't. I don't know who will be next, but I do know the O'Briens will be involved. The ties are there, but I can't unknot them. Keep your eyes and ears open, Sam, and keep in touch."

"I'll do that. I'll call you if I get anything."

CHAPTER 64

AUGUST, 1958

The fishing trip out of Boston harbor had been unsuccessful: They had boated only one blue the entire day. Jimmy had come close two other times, but had lost both fish and half his line.

Buddy and Sean never got a strike.

The men didn't really care. During the course of the day they had consumed two 6-packs of beer, two sandwiches each, several bags of potato chips and pretzels, and they had enjoyed an ideal day weather-wise.

It was after 4:00 p.m. when Sean berthed his boat upon their return to the marina, drawing loud cheers for his expertise in docking. The men secured the craft and cleaned up the remains of their picnic lunches before heading to the yacht club for a final drink.

As they entered the lounge, Sean was told he had messages in his box. One was for Buddy; the other for Jimmy. Both said the same thing.

"Call home immediately!"

Sean laughed as he handed his friends the notes. "I thought you guys said you had the day off. Masters of the house, huh," he teased. "I'm glad I'm still a bachelor."

He led them down a hall toward the phone booths and told them to meet him at the bar when they got through.

They rejoined him minutes later, displaying somber faces.

"What's the matter?" Sean asked, concerned.

"Flossy's dead, Sean," Jimmy said with trepidation.

Sean's legs turned to liquid, and he would have fallen if Buddy and Jimmy hadn't grabbed him. "What-what?" he managed to utter.

Jimmy and Buddy led him to a nearby couch and sat him down.

"It was Patti who called me, Sean." Jimmy said. Jerry called her when he returned to the apartment after playing golf. She could barely understand him, but that's what he told her."

"How-how-could that have happened?" Sean whispered.

"I don't know, Sean," Jimmy answered softly. "We'll go back to my home and try to find out."

Sean's brain was too muddled to do anything but comply.

It was 5:30 in the afternoon when the two cars pulled into Jimmy's driveway. Buddy, driving Sean's car, saw Doreen's car parked to one side.

Good, he thought, Doreen and the baby are here.

Inside the house, Patti, in tears, related what she could make out from Jerry's conversation. "Apparently the apartment was being burglarized when Flossy returned home and she was stabbed in the chest. She's dead, Jimmy. Jerry said he called the police and was waiting for them. That's all I know," she added, her voice breaking, leaving her unable to continue.

Jimmy picked up the phone and called Flossy's apartment. He talked to a voice who asked him to identify himself, and when he did, the voice explained that he was a police officer, and that Mr. Robinow was in rough shape and unable to talk.

"Is it okay if we come over?" Jimmy asked.

"No sir; I'm sorry," the officer said. "No one will be allowed to enter the crime scene until we finish up here."

"Please have Mr. Robinow call me at any hour when he's able. I'd like to assist in any way I can."

Jimmy left his phone number.

The Boston Globe carried the article the following morning, mentioning the murder and relating that a witness had been found. The witness gave the police a description of two male Caucasians fleeing the building approximately one hour prior to the body being discovered. The article concluded by saying that the police were pursuing several leads.

Flossy's funeral was held Wednesday at noon. After the funeral, the O'Briens, Sean, and Jerry returned to Flossy's apartment.

Jerry brought them up to date. "The police haven't located the suspects seen fleeing the building. The eye-witness proved to be unreliable. He changed his description of the two men each time he was questioned. He admitted he had a fair amount to drink that day, but he was sure there were two of them, and they were white."

Jerry added that Flossy's purse was missing, as was most of her jewelry and his Rolex watch. He said that it appeared to the police to be a burglary that turned into a homicide when Flossy unexpectedly returned home.

Barney Osham reached Sam Coben at the Pemberton Police Station that same afternoon.

"You heard about the Sloan woman, Sam?"

"Yeah, I saw it in the papers. Tough call," Sam replied.

"I talked to the detective in charge this morning. They have no description worth a damn on the two guys running from the building, other than that they were white, medium height, and of medium build. Joe Wilder's the Boston detective, and he said it looked like a simple break-in turned nasty. There were two knife wounds, one of which was fatal. No weapon was found at the scene, but Wilder said the coroner said it was a 5 or 6 inch knife; probably a switch-blade."

"So it wasn't a butcher's knife, Barney," Sam said, "and probably not connected to our home-town doings."

"I'm not so sure. I don't see why a change in weapons would necessarily mean a change in killers. Actually, it would be the smart thing to do. And the certainty is another member of the O'Brien group has been murdered!"

"Where were the O'Briens at the time of the murder? You run a check on them?" Sam asked.

"Oh yes," Barney replied in a disgusted tone. "They and their friend Mr. Boyle are all nicely alibied. They were all in a boat outside of Boston harbor, fishing and sunning. I took a trip over to the Boston Bay Yacht Club and made some inquiries. There were plenty of people who saw them depart mid-morning and return around 4:15 in the afternoon. One couple from the club recalled sailing by them out in the bay somewhere between noon and 1:00 p.m. They waved at the three people aboard the cabin cruiser because they recognized Sean Boyle and his boat. The woman on the sail boat didn't know the other two men, but one was "tall, well-built, and blond," and the other was about six feet and dark. Sloan's live-in boy friend told Detective Wilder that he had been invited to go fishing with them, but opted for golf instead."

"Damn it! I guess that leaves them free and clear," Sam replied, disappointment registering in his voice.

"Not necessarily, Sam. They've got money. They could have hired a couple of bimbos to do the job. They knew I visited her and asked a lot of questions about them. Maybe she was bugging them, or Boyle, and they didn't like it."

"It's possible, Barney, but we've got nothing unless the two suspects are found and cop pleas. Otherwise, there's no way in hell to link the O'Briens to this."

"Sad, but true, Sam; sad but true. I wouldn't be surprised if the bastards haven't gotten away with it again. I'll talk to you later, I've got another call."

Barney hung up, leaving a tired Sam Coben shaking his head in frustration.

CHAPTER 65

NOVEMBER, 1958

Dan O'Brien had not been feeling well for months but refused to see a doctor. Mary, frustrated by his constant refusal to go for a check-up, enlisted the help of her sons, but to no avail.

Dan, in no polite terms, told Jimmy and Buddy to mind their own damn business. "I got an ulcer and I know how to take care of it. I don't like doctors. Most of the time they don't know what the hell they're talking about. They just want to charge you a lot of money. I could tell you about any number of times a doctor screwed up, and the poor bastard of a patient suffered the consequences. So forget it..."

It was only after Dan saw traces of blood in his urine for a period of time that he took himself to the Pemberton Clinic.

He was 57 years old, still working full time, and as far as he was concerned, strong as a bull, and invincible. When he was diagnosed as having pancreatic cancer, and the cancer had metastasized, he didn't believe it, and would not accept it.

A week later two specialists confirmed what the doctor at the clinic had disclosed, and Dan had no choice but to believe them. The specialists told him in their opinion it was too late for surgery, but they could treat him with chemicals and delay the inevitable. He told them he would get back to them in a few days, after he had a chance to think, and walked away, a broken man.

That evening he told Mary, and they cried together for the first time in their married lives.

Dan made Mary promise not to tell anyone. He would do it himself when he wanted to. He didn't want anyone's pity or listen to anyone's patronizing conversation. He had always been strong in body and firm in his beliefs, and that's the way he wanted to live out the rest of his life. He didn't give a damn if people thought he was narrow-minded and bigoted. He knew what he knew—and how he wanted to live his life—and he never took crap from anybody.

Several weeks later Dan was obviously failing. He was pale, gaunt, and rapidly losing energy. He told Mary to invite Jimmy, Buddy, and their families over for Sunday brunch. "I got some personal business to discuss with them in private," he explained to Mary, "but I want them to bring their wives and kids so I can see everybody."

He also told Mary to invite Sean.

Buddy Jr. had a low-grade temperature on the day of the brunch, and Doreen canceled out. Buddy came alone.

Jimmy, Patti, and Jimmy Jr. came, and Sean had said he would change his plans and he would be there.

Mary O'Brien hadn't sounded her usually bubbly self when she had called him, and Sean sensed something was wrong.

When Sean arrived at the O'Brien home late Sunday morning, the others were already there. After the customary round of greetings, they seated themselves at the dining room table. Mary served scrambled eggs and ham steaks, home fries, toast and coffee.

Dan O'Brien was in his usual seat. He looked terrible. He was in his pajamas and bathrobe. He hadn't bothered to comb his hair and he was in need of a shave.

It was obvious to all of them he had lost considerable weight. Sean couldn't help but take furtive looks at him, and what he observed was no longer the man he had known and feared as a youth. This was the shell of the man.

He knew Dan O'Brien was seriously ill.

Sean said nothing, joining in on the conversation only when addressed. Mary's face remained somber throughout breakfast, and Jimmy and Buddy, although more subdued than usual, did most of the talking.

Dan said little, content to hold Jimmy Jr. and feed him mouthfuls of baby food, which the young O'Brien gleefully spit up.

At the end of the meal, Dan said he wanted to talk to Jimmy and Buddy alone. He also wanted to talk to Sean, and asked him to stay.

The three O'Brien men made their way into the parlor, leaving Mary and Patti to clean up and Sean to keep the baby amused.

"What's wrong, Mrs. O'Brien?" Sean asked, as he approached Mary and Patti at the kitchen sink, with the baby happily lodged on his shoulders.

Mary turned her head toward him just long enough for him to see the tears in her eyes.

"He'll tell you when he talks to you, Sean. It's the way he wants it."

Patti shrugged her shoulders as she looked at Sean, and turned away.

Sean walked away, redirecting his attention to the active baby.

A somber Jimmy and Buddy returned to the kitchen 10 minutes later, and headed for their mother and put their arms around her. She sobbed several times, but otherwise maintained control.

Sean watched in silence, knowing Dan O'Brien was dying.

Moments later Jimmy turned toward Sean and gestured to him to go in to see Dan.

Sean returned to the kitchen 15 minutes later, visibly shaken. He had to sit down.

"You want a cup of coffee, Sean?" Mary offered. "It will settle you."

"Please. Thank you. Where are Jimmy and Buddy?"

"They took Jimmy Jr. out to the garage. They're going to show him the clubhouse. Patti's out on the porch, waiting for them."

Sean climbed the ladder to the loft, and squeezed into the club room. Memories came flooding back, and they weren't all pleasant. He pulled over a chair and joined the group sitting around the small table.

"I'm sorry guys; that's terrible news," Sean said. He was completely unsettled; more so than Jimmy or Buddy. His conversation with Dan O'Brien had been the worst 15 minutes of his life.

"Yeah, it's a shocker," Buddy uttered, "he's really going down hill fast. Mom says he's got no more than 3 or 4 weeks. He's finally agreed to take some pain medicine."

Jimmy had said nothing, being fully occupied keeping his son amused and in check.

Finally he said "Let's get out of here; it's too cold here for the baby."

They joined Patti on the porch and returned to the kitchen. They told Mary they all would stop in a couple of times a week, and Jimmy and Buddy promised to call her every day.

Dan had gone back to bed, and Mary promised she would deliver their good-byes.

"Don't worry about me," she told them. "I'm all right and I can handle everything."

She refused their offer to send her help, saying "I've looked after him most of my life, and I can do it now."

Sean left, tears flooding his eyes, and drove to Boston, his mind in a turmoil.

Dan O'Brien died in Pemberton Hospital on Tuesday morning, January 13, 1959 and was buried in Pemberton Cemetery the following Friday.

There was a large turnout of family and friends at the wake and the funeral. At one point Buddy leaned over and whispered to Jimmy that all the bars in the city must be empty, and received a dirty look for his remark.

Mary held up fine; the heart of the family, as always.

CHAPTER 66

MAY, 1959

Sean Boyle was sitting alone in a booth at the Hilltop restaurant. It was a Thursday, and the one day a week he allowed himself to eat a large lunch and break the monotony of the tuna fish sandwich or garden salad that was his customary fare at the sandwich shop in the mall across from Kaster Carpet and Tile Co.

His thoughts were interrupted by a voice coming from above his head.

"Mind if I sit down, Mr. Boyle? I'd like to talk to you."

Sean looked up and into the unsmiling face of the last person in the world he wanted to talk to—Inspector Barney Osham.

"Sit if-if you must," he replied awkwardly.

Barney grinned and slid his lean frame into the opposite side of the booth.

"I'm Inspector Osham," he said, "you remember me?"

"Yes; I do," Sean said, with little enthusiasm.

"Great restaurant, isn't it. I come here a lot. I've seen you here before on a Thursday. Same day I usually come."

Sean nodded, all senses on alert.

"It's time we talked, Mr. Boyle, and I think we've got a lot to talk about."

"I don't think so," Sean replied bravely.

Barney smiled. "We'll see. I've got some things to tell you I don't think you're aware of, but should be."

"Such as?" Sean asked with guarded curiosity.

"Such as your friend Miss Sloan wasn't murdered because of a burglary. I think she was murdered for other reasons. The whole thing was a set-up because someone was afraid she had some information I would be interested in. Someone found out I talked to her and enlisted her aid, and he wanted her silenced."

Sean's head was spinning. *Could it be true?*

But he had picked up on something the detective said.

He said *"I think..."*

He knew the detective was obsessed with the Stanton-Pemberton murders and this could be a ploy.

Barney noted the struggle that seemed to be taking place on Sean Boyle's face before rushing on.

"Think for a minute, Mr. Boyle. An entire apartment house full of apartments. An entire street full of apartment houses and *the only apartment in that area to be hit by a burglary that day was Miss Sloan's.*

"Why Miss Sloan's? Because somebody wanted her dead! Perhaps someone with the money to hire a couple of punks who would kill their own mothers if the price was right. When we find these punks, I'll have the truth in minutes."

Barney had conjured up the story, considering it to be entirely possible. He knew if the two suspects seen fleeing the building were caught, they wouldn't know who paid them. The O'Briens would have worked out a method of payment agreeable to both sides that didn't involve direct contact.

Barney hypothesized his story was plausible and, in any event, it was meant to split and divide the O'Briens and Boyle.

Sean survived the initial shock. He wanted to think back months ago to see if he had triggered Flossy in any way when he discussed her and the cop's conversation with Jimmy and Buddy.

He prayed he hadn't, but he didn't remember. The first thing he had to do was get rid of the cop.

"I don't believe any of it, and I don't know why you're bothering me," Sean said firmly.

"To put it bluntly, Mr. Boyle," Barney barked, "I'm bothering you because I want the truth. I think the O'Briens are involved, and have dragged you, albeit unwillingly, into their conspiracy. I think they may be cold-blooded murderers."

Barney's face was grim, and had reddened during his outburst. He had lost control of himself momentarily and given in to his pent-up emotions.

Now he fell silent, and glared at Sean.

Sean withstood the gaze, and mustered his strength before speaking slowly and deliberately.

"You are wrong, Inspector. You have allowed yourself to become irrational and unprofessional. Jimmy, Buddy, and I have never been involved in any murders, regardless of what you think, and you should look elsewhere."

He said this with conviction, but Barney wasn't buying.

"You must think me stupid, or naive, Mr. Boyle," he snapped, "but I assure you I'm neither. I hope you come to your senses before it's too late, because I don't think the killing is over, and you could be a target."

Sean shook his head in disbelief. This cop was off his rocker.

"Thank you for your warning, Inspector. Now, if you'll excuse me, I'd like to finish the rest of my lunch."

Barney stared icily at him for several seconds.

"You know where to reach me if you change your mind," he said, and slid out of the booth and left.

Sean had dinner with Earl Kaster that evening, as he did most evenings. Tonight, especially, he needed someone to talk to, and Earl had become his confidant. They held both a close business and personal relationship.

"Wow, Sean, that's deep stuff," Earl said. "Where's this cop coming from? Is any of it possible?"

"No, Earl, it's not. He—he's obsessed."

"Can't you guys get a court order or something to stop him? It sounds like harassment to me. He shouldn't be allowed to hound you like that."

Sean smiled at Earl's suggestion. "I don't think so, Earl. It's not like he's hiding behind a bush every time we turn around. Besides, he'd deny he ever said it."

"Maybe libel then?" Earl offered.

"I don't think we want to bring that kind of attention to ourselves or our families, Earl. This cop will do his thing until he runs out of gas and goes on to something or somebody else. He's got nothing except his own stupid notions."

"What about what he said about Flossy?" Earl asked.

Sean paused. The thought had stuck in his mind also. *Why, with all the apartments on the street, had they picked Flossy's?*

It bothered him. Literally hundreds of apartment to choose from, and they had picked hers. He recalled most of what Flossy had told him about her visit with the cop, and later of his own conversation with Jimmy and Buddy, and there was nothing harmful in any of it.

"It has to be bull, Earl, pure bull, and I've got too much on my mind right now to think about it. Incidentally, I was proud of myself the way I handled the cop—I stayed pretty cool."

Earl didn't pursue the topic. "You're right, Sean; I bet it's all bull."

Sean visited Mary O'Brien the following Sunday, knowing that Jimmy and Buddy would be there. Buddy hadn't arrived yet, but as soon as he did, Sean pulled Jimmy aside and told him about his unwelcome luncheon visitor, and what he had implied.

Jimmy shook his head in disbelief. "That bastard. He followed you to the Hilltop?"

"No, I don't think he followed me. He said he eats there a lot, and happened to see me…"

"Bullshit, Sean; he followed you. You realize he's trying to stir things up, don't you?"

"I know, Jimmy."

"Flossy must have told him something to encourage him. He was never on top of us before he talked to her. You sure she didn't know anything about—you know—the old days? Something you might have let slip?"

Sean paled. He really didn't remember if he said anything to her he shouldn't have, other than he had mentioned THE PACT once, but he hadn't told her what it meant.

He was afraid to admit that to Jimmy. "Yeah, I'm pretty sure."

He felt himself begin to sweat. Damn it, he thought, I didn't mean to say that. I meant to say I was positive.

He was afraid to correct himself. He felt Jimmy's gaze on him, and he had to force himself to act normal under the scrutiny.

Jimmy stopped staring, and turned away to put his coffee cup down. As he did, he uttered, "It really doesn't matter, anyway. She's dead, and we don't have to worry about her anymore."

He said it with stark coldness. Sean felt as if he had been struck a blow to the face. His body began to tremble as he fought for control. Fortunately for him, Jimmy was still looking the other way.

Jimmy changed the subject, but Sean was only half listening.

Jimmy was saying something about staying in Pemberton for lunch. Sean told him he had plans in Boston and had to get back. He said good-bye, kissed Mary, and got away as quickly as he could.

"You Bastards!" he screamed, tears filling his eyes, as he sped back to Boston. The damn cop was right; they had her killed. Jimmy had said *"we don't have to worry about her anymore!"* They went fishing with me and all the time they knew Flossy was going to die. For what? She didn't know anything! Jesus! Jesus! Jesus!

He had to pull off the road and stop the car. He cried until there were no more tears.

Sean knew he was right. Jimmy and Buddy had planned Flossy's death. Who else could it have been? They knew he would never have agreed to it, regardless of the PACT, and decided to rid themselves of what they felt was a problem.

Sean knew he would become a target when things quieted down. They wouldn't dare come after him so soon after Flossy's death, but it was only a matter of time until they got around to him.

"I'm not going to let that happen," he muttered under his breath. "NO! I won't let that happen!"

CHAPTER 67

FRIDAY, JUNE 12, 1959

Buddy had come across the item in the Globe by sheer chance. It alluded to a testimonial dinner being held in New York for an Israeli philanthropist by the name of Harvey Cohen. The article went on to explain that Harvey Cohen was a former Chelsen resident and football team standout who graduated in 1949. There was no question in Buddy's mind this was the same guy that broke Jimmy's leg.

Buddy tried to reach Jimmy by phone, but had to settle for leaving a message. He phoned Sean with the news, and was surprised his usually placid and wary friend shared his excitement.

"Let me know what Jimmy wants to do," Sean said with enthusiasm.

When Jimmy returned his call that afternoon, Buddy gave him the news. There was a lengthy silence on Jimmy's part before he spoke.

"I've got a paper in the outer office. I'll read it and call you back later. Will you be home tonight?"

Buddy answered in the affirmative, and Jimmy hung up.

Jimmy read the article twice. Slowly, a smile spread across his face. At last, he thought, some unfinished business to take care of and a score to settle.

He phoned Buddy and Sean later in the evening and called for a meeting.

It would be the last such meeting, for he decided it was time to end THE PACT. It would be simple enough, for it required a two-thirds vote, and he knew Sean would vote his way. Buddy might be unhappy, but so what.

Jimmy believed it was too dangerous to do otherwise. As long as Osham and Coben were around, he, Buddy, and Sean would know no peace.

He didn't intend to give the cops any chance of pinning any of the murders on them. He, Buddy, and Sean never discussed among themselves who did what, and he wanted it left that way. *Closed out! Finished!*

Things had changed for all of them over the past few years. They had all achieved successes.

However, this one person—this Cohen character—would have to be taken care of, and Jimmy wanted to do it alone. He was the one who had suffered. Cohen had ended his dream of college football greatness, and Jimmy had to rectify that hurt. Buddy and Sean could alibi him, although he doubted he would need an alibi. He was sure no one would ever figure the connection. And then it could end.

They met Sunday morning for breakfast at Stanley's Cafeteria.

Buddy was in good spirits because it was *he* who had found Harvey Cohen, and was responsible for this meeting. In truth, he felt it was *he* who had always motivated the trio and it was *he* who had always been the true vanguard of THE PACT.

Sean's exuberance was elicited a short time later when Jimmy told them of his decision to end THE PACT. Buddy voiced his disapproval, but knew the count was against him and grudgingly conceded. A part of him thought perhaps it was for the best.

Jimmy explained in detail what his plans were for Harvey Cohen, and his determination to do it alone.

The testimonial, he explained, was to be held Sunday evening, July 26, at the Pine Towers Hotel in New York. He planned to book a room at the Quaker, a small, nondescript hotel nearby. He would take a plane to New York on Friday, July 24, sign in under an assumed name, James Brown, get settled, and visit the Pine Tower, where he would make himself familiar with the layout of the hotel and decide the best way to get at Cohen. If it looked difficult, he would abort and no one would be the wiser.

"Are you going to kill him?" Buddy asked, without a trace of emotion, "or just break him up?" He spoke with such indifference that Sean felt a shiver run through his body.

Jimmy replied without hesitation. "I'll decide that when the time comes."

Later that same day, in the posh apartment suite they shared overlooking the Charles River, Sean and Earl Kaster held a lengthy discussion. Sean related his entire lifetime story with the O'Briens and how they had manipulated him his whole life into doing their bidding. But the O'Briens had gone one step too far with Flossy, for she was "his family," and Sean, in tears, said he realized he had to break away.

"You have to do it, Sean," Earl stated unequivocally. "If you don't, you're a dead man, and I couldn't stand that."

Sean had an agenda in mind. He spent the rest of the day and evening discussing his plan with Earl, and Earl made a number of helpful suggestions. He assured Sean money was not a problem, and that he would help in any way Sean said.

"I'm with you all the way, Sean."

CHAPTER 68

SATURDAY, JUNE 20, 1959

Dennis McGuire, DMD, now in his late sixties, was a Pemberton fixture. He had been born and raised in Pemberton, and had lived his entire life in a large two-family home on Central street, only a "golf-ball" throw from Pemberton High School, as he liked to explain it.

Dennis had graduated from dental school in 1918, at the age of twenty-five. His club-foot deformity had kept him out of the war, and contributed enormously to his generally unpleasant disposition.

His parents owned the home they lived in and, upon his graduation, turned the first floor over to Dennis to be converted into his dental office. They no longer rented out the upstairs apartment, but lived there themselves, with Dennis.

Five years later, Dennis married Mary Conley, and his parents moved out, deeding the house to him.

He was a good dentist, and he was Irish, and therefore the choice of Dan O'Brien, as well as much of the Irish population of Pemberton.

Doc McGuire had kept to the same schedule as long as anybody could remember. He worked from 8:00 a.m. until 5:00 p.m. 5 days a week, and quit at noon on Saturdays. He worked alone, shuttling between two dental chairs situated in adjacent rooms. A waiting area, a reception room, and a small private office comprised the balance of the first-floor of his well-kept home.

His wife was his receptionist and his secretary and, in sharp contrast to her husband, was sweet and pleasant. From the first year of the marriage, friends and patients alike jokingly dubbed them "the unmatched match."

The McGuires had no children and spent much of their free time visiting museums and other cultural centers. It was common knowledge, come the good weather, Doc and Mary would be off to Boston on many a Saturday afternoon.

On this particular Saturday, their home was broken into. They had spent the afternoon and early evening in Boston, and arrived home shortly after 9:00 p.m. to discover a glass pane broken on their front door.

Dennis wouldn't enter the house, and he and Mary drove to the police station and reported the incident. Two officers were dispatched to inspect the house, with the McGuires in attendance. There was no sign of any other damage, and the preliminary examination indicated nothing had been stolen. The door-bolt of the door with the broken window was in the locked position.

A baseball was found under the settee in the hallway, and the police figured some careless youngster had been the culprit. They helped Doc McGuire board up the smashed pane area while Mary attended to the broken glass. Doc told the officers he and his wife would make a more thorough check in the morning.

They did, and found nothing missing, and the matter was considered closed.

They never discovered they had had an uninvited guest in their home, whose sole purpose was to locate the files and the dental records of Buddy O'Brien and Sean Boyle, and exchange one for the other.

CHAPTER 69

THURSDAY, JULY 23, 1959

"Hi, Buddy, what's up?" Sean asked cheerfully when Buddy answered the phone.

"Where the hell have you been?" Buddy barked in an annoyed tone. "I've been trying to reach you for two days. Something wrong with your telephone, asshole?"

Sean, unbothered, answered. "No. I've been tied up. You'll never believe it, but listen to this. I stopped Tuesday after work at the Mayfair bar and met a real live one. An older woman, but beautiful. We hit it off well, and I wound up staying with her the last couple of nights. Wait until you meet her; she's quite a dish. She's divorced, got a big home in Martha's Vineyard and spends her summers there. Got two young teen-age kids touring Europe somewhere, and she doesn't like being alone. We flew over to the Vineyard Wednesday, at her expense, and got out of bed only long enough to eat a couple of times and have a few drinks. I've never had a session like that in my entire life. Wild—completely wild!"

Buddy, accepting the interesting tale, lost his anger and laughed. “Coming from you, Sean, it must have been good. Got money and likes the sack: that’s a winning combination if I ever heard of one. I can’t wait to meet her.”

“Good, because I want you to meet her on Sunday. Doreen and little Buddy still going to be away?”

“Yeah, until Wednesday. She’ll have had enough of her mother by then.”

“Bingo,” Sean said, “that’s perfect. My girl has a girlfriend visiting her this weekend and wants me to fix her up. The girlfriend is married and doesn’t want any complications, but likes a good time. My friend told me, and I quote, ‘she’s beautiful, and she’s hornier than I am.’ With credentials like that, I thought you might want to join us. She showed me her picture, and believe me, she’s all woman.”

Buddy was interested. “Why not. I don’t think Jimmy will be back from New York until late Sunday, so I’m free and clear. What will we do?”

“Have a picnic at sea, and then go back to her place on the Vineyard. My lady friend owns a 40-foot Bertram and will meet us in Cape Cod Bay. We’ll wine and dine on her boat and then follow them back to Edgartown. Then it’s every man for himself.”

Buddy was all smiles. “Sounds great. Count me in.”

“I’ll confirm everything with you on Friday. If the weather forecast is good for Sunday, we’ll boat out and meet them as planned. If the weather is going to be bad, I’ll make other arrangements. If I don’t reach you by noon on Friday, call me at the store.”

"Okay," Buddy replied, "what do you want me to bring?"

"Just your ass, a gross of safes, and a bathing suit," Sean answered with a snort, and then got serious. "Just yourself, Buddy. I've got two cases of beer on board, and the ladies will take care of the food."

"Great!" Buddy replied enthusiastically. "I'll speak to you Friday, and let's hope the weather cooperates."

On Friday, Buddy called Sean at the store, and excitedly gave him the good news. "I called the weather bureau, Sean. Looks like picture-perfect weather over the weekend."

Sean smiled. *Hook, line, and sinker.*

"Yeah, Buddy, the marine forecast is good for the entire weekend. I was just going to call you. Meet me 9:00 a.m. Sunday at the yacht club. See you then."

Sean hung up and looked across his desk to a smiling Earl Kaster and gave him the thumbs-up sign.

CHAPTER 70

FRIDAY, JULY 24, 1959

Jimmy boarded the Eastern Airlines plane at Logan shortly after 11:00 a.m. and arrived at La Guardia at 12:47 p.m. He gathered his carry-on luggage, departed from the plane and, walking briskly, followed the exit signs until he gained the street. He was met with depressing heat and a swarming crowd. He located a line of cabs, entered the lead one, and gave the driver his destination. The cab shot off and entered the maze of traffic heading into New York City.

"It's gonna take a while—lots of traffic," his driver notified him unnecessarily.

"I'm in no hurry," Jimmy answered, and settled back in the well-worn rear seat, closed his eyes, and went over his plans in his mind—step by step.

He would knock Cohen senseless and break his legs, or maybe go the whole route.

He would have dinner that evening in a steak house and swipe a knife, hide it under his jacket, and no one would be the wiser. He would get to Cohen Saturday evening in Cohen's hotel room, or Sunday morning if he had to wait for a better opportunity. Then he'd catch a plane back to Boston before anyone was aware of what happened and...

The jerkiness of the ride caused him to open his eyes and take in the scene. The cab would accelerate rapidly, only to come to a screeching halt now and again. The driver weaved from one lane to another, jostling for an advantage that wasn't there. Jimmy could imagine the cursing that was taking place as other drivers fought for position. The ride reminded him of his youth and the Dodgem rides at Salem Willows.

Jimmy looked out the passenger side window and noticed the variety of buildings constructed primarily of wood or brick. They were old, drab, and seemingly built on top of each other. In the background were high-rise apartments of modern construction rising in obvious contrast.

An old area being re-vitalized, he mused. Life goes on.

Suddenly the cab veered sharply from the passing lane, crossed two inner lanes, and headed for an exit ramp. The driver explained that he would go into the city a back way. "It's a little longer route, but this time of day it will take less time," he promised.

Jimmy didn't bother to answer. Then he looked at the picture and name of the cab driver displayed on the rear of the driver's seat—Hyman Roddenberg—and lost some of his complacency.

"It had better not cost any more—your short cut," he said icily.

Other than a brief look in his rear-view mirror, the driver didn't respond.

Twenty minutes later the cab stopped in front of the Quaker Hotel. Buddy had suggested this hotel, as he had stayed there. "Clean, neat and nondescript," he had said, "and within easy walking distance of the Pine Towers."

Jimmy paid the driver, including a modest tip which the disgruntled driver did not appreciate. He was not about to complain, however, to his giant of a passenger with the menacing look.

Fucking Nazi, the driver mumbled to himself as he drove away.

Jimmy registered under the name Jim Brown and was escorted to a room on the seventh floor. He tipped the bellboy, locked the door, and proceeded to undress. He unpacked his carry-all and carefully put its contents away before shaving, showering and climbing into bed for a short nap. The nap didn't work out, for from his seventh floor location the cacophony of the street traffic was unbelievable. The ever-beeping horns, the noisy accelerating trucks, and the frequent sirens' incongruent blare were not conducive to an afternoon sleep.

He got out of bed. His watch showed 3:40 p.m.

The room was nothing to rave about. A six-drawer dresser fronted a malachite-green and white striped wallpaper. The other walls were painted a tinted beige. He had found the double bed comfortable, but the small reading lamps attached at each side were totally inadequate. There was a small round table with two drab fabric chairs placed in front of the window, and a huge imitation leather lounging chair off to one side. The lone window was nearly floor to ceiling, extended the width of the room, and was covered with transparent off-white curtains and nearly-opaque, russet-brown drapes controlled by traverse rods and draw strings. A small TV was positioned on one end of the bureau, and a desk and chair were situated around the corner from the entrance to the bathroom. A phone and a desk lamp with two bulbs that might have totaled 60 watts were strategically placed on the desk, as were a folder with hotel information and a Holy Bible.

Buddy's taste in hotels needs an upgrading, Jimmy thought.

He needed air, and decided to take a walk. The afternoon temperature was hotter than when he first arrived, and the humidity barely tolerable.

He was thankful that his stay would be of a short duration. He walked to Park Avenue, headed south 12 blocks to 51st street, and turned west for two blocks to Rockefeller Center. He stopped in a novelty shop to pick up a trinket for Patti, and wound up with a small teddy bear wearing an "I Love You" sweater. He moved on and sat on a bench, people watching. He enjoyed bantering with two young hookers who brazenly tried to pick him up, but he told them his mother and his wife were due to meet him in a few minutes and that he would have to pass. One insisted he take her phone number and call her next time he was in the city.

Jimmy began to think about Harvey Cohen, and his anger returned. He bolted from the bench, headed north to Central Park, made his way to 61st street, and continued on to Park Avenue and the Pine Towers Hotel. It was here—on Sunday evening—that Harvey Cohen was to be honored by the American-Jewish Philanthropic Society.

It was here he'd kill the bastard! Just hours away!

Jimmy entered the Pine Towers and located the events directory. The affair was scheduled for 7:00 p.m. Sunday in the Jefferson Room. He walked slowly through the lobby, acquainting himself with the location of the elevators and the stairways, and followed the signs to the Jefferson Room. He tried to gain entry, but the doors were locked.

It doesn't matter, he thought. It'll be done before he gets here.

He needed to find out who would be in the Cohen party. Was there a wife, a girlfriend, or someone else who might be staying with Cohen? Whatever the circumstance, he would find the solution, and only cop out as a last resort. It would be done tomorrow and hopefully in Cohen's room at a time when he would have several hours before anyone would be the wiser. Jimmy would be far away by then.

Abort was the last thing he wanted to do. He had waited too long for this opportunity. He would never forget that football game, and the humiliation and pain he suffered. It was his future as an athlete that had been destroyed by this man, and he would have his revenge.

Jimmy went into the bar, ordered a scotch and water, and sat contemplating. He believed he had covered all the possibilities, but wanted to review them.

He had told Patti he got a call from a couple of army buddies who were having a reunion in New York on Friday and Saturday before leaving for the West Coast on Sunday afternoon. She had told him to have a wonderful time, and to call her when he knew what time he would be coming home and she'd pick him up at the airport.

No problem there.

Sean and Buddy knew of his whereabouts. He told them he would call them when it was over.

Jimmy didn't feel he needed an alibi. No one could tie him to Cohen. They had met only once, and that was on the football field years before.

He could foresee no problems. He only had to isolate Cohen in his hotel room, and the rest would be easy.

That evening Jimmy washed and dressed, and went to Sandy's Steakhouse for dinner. He dropped his steak knife on the floor, guided it with his foot to a position under the table where he could casually bend over, pick it up, and slide it into his inside jacket pocket.

When his meal was served, he used the knife from another setting that had been left on the table. He ate quickly, passed on dessert, paid his bill and returned to his hotel.

Later that evening he called Patti, spoke to her for more than 40 minutes, then washed up and turned in.

Jimmy awoke early Saturday morning, refreshed and excited. He showered, shaved, and dressed in an expensive business suit. He went downstairs for breakfast and put away a big meal, marveling over the cost of a New York breakfast.

His plan was to spend a good part of the day in the Pine Towers, looking like one more business man attending one of the scheduled events on the day's agenda.

His priorities were to find out when Harvey Cohen was due to arrive and in what room he would be staying.

He would try to do this by phone so as not to be recognizable. If he had to, he would throw some money around and surreptitiously obtain the information he needed. One way or another, he would learn what he had to know.

It wasn't difficult. By 4:00 that afternoon he knew that Harvey Cohen was due in after sundown—after his Sabbath—about 9:00. He was traveling alone but had booked a suite.

Jimmy studied the newspaper photo of Cohen carefully, and knew he would be able to recognize him when he checked in. He intended to follow Cohen to his room, and once the bellhop departed, knock on his door and say he was from room-service and delivering a welcoming bottle of champagne. Once the door was unlocked, and before Cohen knew what was happening, he would knock him cold. Then he'd slowly kill the bastard and satisfy his need for revenge.

He would attack Harvey Cohen as soon as the door was opened, and *if* the hallway was clear. That was the intangible he would have to deal with, but he felt the odds were in his favor. He intended to make it look like a robbery, and when he left the room he would put the DO NOT DISTURB sign on the door, remove his gloves, take the stairs down two flights, and then board the elevator for the trip to the lobby. *I'll walk through the lobby, out the main entrance, and I'm home free.*

By 3:05 p.m. Saturday Jimmy had returned to his room at the Quaker Hotel. He intended to shower, shave, change his clothing and get back to the Pine Towers Hotel by 7:00 to begin his vigil.

He was out of the shower, bath towel wrapped about his waist, and shaving when he thought he heard a knock on the door. He shut off the tap and leaned out the bathroom door, this time clearly hearing the light rap on his door.

"Who is it?" he called out.

"It's me," a familiar voice answered.

"For Christ's sake, what are you doing here?" Jimmy exclaimed. He took three steps forward and opened the door.

"I thought I'd come down and see if you needed any help. Aren't you glad to see me?" his caller asked as he stepped into the room and closed the door.

"Of course I'm glad to see you but I told you I would take care of him myself."

Jimmy turned away and started to walk into the inner room. "You're here, so come on in."

Jimmy never saw the blow coming. He pitched forward and fell heavily to the floor, unconscious.

His assailant tossed the oak axe-handle on to the bed, set his black bag on the floor, and removed his jacket. He walked back to the door and threw the locking bolt. He returned to pick up his black bag, set it on the queen-sized bed, and removed a pair of cotton gloves and put them on.

He took out a 30-foot coil of nylon rope from the bag and placed it on the bed. Scanning the room, he took inventory of the furniture and decided the oversized lounging chair in the corner of the room would suit his purpose better than the bed. He approached the insensate Jimmy O'Brien, turned him onto his back and dragged him over to the lounge chair.

Straining his every muscle, he lifted the limp body high enough to drop Jimmy into the chair. Puffing considerably, he returned to the bed, unwound the coil of rope and, using the butcher knife he extracted from the bottom of the bag, cut 6 lengths of rope. He tied Jimmy to the legs and arms of the chair, and finished by wrapping the remainder of the rope around Jimmy's chest, waist, and back of the chair.

He double-checked to see that all the knots were secure before returning to his travel bag for a wide role of adhesive tape. He cut several strips and applied them securely over Jimmy's mouth. Satisfied, he headed for the bathroom and relieved himself. He inhaled deeply and slowly let the air rush out, trying to calm himself while waiting for his pounding heart to slow.

He removed his gloves to wash his hands and face, dried himself, took a glass tumbler from the shelf, filled it with water, and drank greedily. He returned to the unconscious Jimmy O'Brien to check his pulse, and listened to make sure he was breathing. Convinced that all was well, he again put on his gloves and walked about the room, wiping everything he had touched.

He went through Jimmy's things and found the steak knife and the ski mask and threw them in his bag. Satisfied, he took a seat on the edge of the bed and waited for Jimmy to awaken.

Ten minutes passed, and Jimmy remained unconscious.

His attacker began to feel panicky. Time was passing, and he wanted to stay within his timetable. He remembered he hadn't wiped down the bathroom and nervously did so before retrieving the water glass and filling it with cold water. He approached Jimmy and flung the water in his face.

Jimmy's head twitched and seconds later his eyes opened. Dazed, he attempted to speak, but his muffled sounds were unintelligible. His eyes widened, and expressed amazement as he tried to free himself. He could turn his head from side to side, and slightly forward, but all other movement was stifled. His thoughts changed from surprise to puzzlement; and then to fear.

From his seat on the edge of the bed, Sean Boyle watched. Then he spoke. "It's a long story, Jimmy, but I'm going to tell you everything. It's useless for you to struggle, so please don't—you'll only wear yourself out. I want you to hear what I have to say."

Jimmy refused to give up. He strained against the ropes until beads of sweat formed on his body.

To no avail.

His eyes opened wide, begging for an explanation.

Jimmy began to tremble, and goose bumps appeared on his body.

Sean rose, walked to the closet, and took a blanket from the shelf. He unfolded it, shook it open, and covered his victim, tucking the edges under parts of the rope so the blanket would stay in place. When he finished, he went to the nearest chair and, pulling it close to Jimmy, seated himself, and continued.

"You were always my best friend; always my best friend. I looked up to you from the time we were kids. In grammar school, and in high school, you were my protector. I admired you, and I guess I even worshipped you. I always tried to do everything you wanted me to, even when I was afraid, which was most of the time. Sometimes you really scared me when you became angry and threatened to do terrible things, but most of the time it just turned out to be a lot of talk. You could beat everyone up because you were bigger and stronger than the other kids our age, and I guess everybody was afraid of you when you got angry. I know I was. But you couldn't kill anybody back then. You were just a lot of talk. It wasn't until much later that you got the nerve to really hurt somebody, and you dragged Buddy and me along because you didn't have the guts to do it alone. Even now I don't think you intended to kill Robinson. Cripple him, YES! But kill him; NO! When he died, you made us think that was the way you wanted it, but I think you were afraid like I was. You see, at that time I didn't tie the Gordon murder to you or Buddy; it was too brutal to even think about.

"Buddy has a lot more guts than you ever had. But he's just evil: always was, and always will be. He was jealous and envious of you his whole life, and got his kicks from the many times he made you suffer without you ever knowing he was the instigator. Oh yes; he enjoyed stirring things up and making your life miserable every chance he got, and I couldn't tell you because I was afraid of what he might do to me. I didn't dare pick sides; I kept my mouth shut. He did everything he could to hurt you, and I did everything I could to help you."

Sean paused momentarily, choked with emotion.

"You were good to me, Jimmy, in many ways. I was a friend—a follower—who you could completely control, and maybe that's why you put up with me. But to me, Jimmy—to me—you were much more than a friend. I really loved you. You were my life. But I couldn't tell you that. I don't think I really knew myself for a long time. Do you get the picture, Jimmy? I'm—I'm queer. I don't like the word, Jimmy, but it's the one you know best and hate the most. I took out girls because I didn't want anyone to know how I felt. I DIDN'T WANT YOU TO KNOW! You would have made fun of me—ridiculed me—and Buddy would have tormented me. I couldn't let that happen, so I hid my true feelings all those years.

"You could never imagine how difficult it was for me to date, and I avoided it as much as possible. But I knew I had to, or someone would have recognized the situation. You know what would happen to me? I'd come home after a date and actually get sick to my stomach. I couldn't help it; it just happened."

He paused, his eyes glistening with moisture.

After several seconds, he continued. "All I ever wanted, Jimmy, was you, and I knew that was impossible. But I could dream. I did everything I could to please you, and I tried to get up the nerve to do more. I had even thought of ways to destroy Gordon, thinking you would be pleased, but somebody else beat me to it. I thought it had to be Buddy, and I was afraid. Then when Robinson died, and we were all involved, I knew I was trapped. THE PACT became more than a childish club with racist motives; it became a mode of survival. We either all stuck together or we all took the fall.

"When you got hurt in the Chelsen game, I was devastated. I knew how much football meant to you. And I cried at the hurt Sally caused you, and the raw deal the Coach gave you. I suffered with you. And when you ran off to the Army I thought my life would end. I prayed every night that you would come home safe. I wanted to hurt the Coach for you, Jimmy, but I couldn't. I was afraid! And when he *was* murdered, I figured it was Buddy who did it. Then you came home, and other things happened.

"Buddy's boss was murdered; just like Gordon and the Coach."

Sean paused, his face contorting into an ugly grimace.

"When you got married, I knew my dream was over. You ruined everything for me."

Sean rose from his chair, went into the bathroom, and returned with a hand towel. He wiped the sweat from Jimmy's brow.

"I'm talking too much, Jimmy, but there's so much ground to cover. It wasn't until your father got sick and called us in to talk to us—you and Buddy first, and then me alone—that I learned the truth. He told me things that I would never have believed.

"Yes, Jimmy, your father. HE killed Gordon and the Coach. He told me he was in the garage when we were in the clubhouse, and he overheard everything we said about getting even with Gordon and Robinson. He heard your anger, and he was afraid you would get in serious trouble.

"He told me a fascinating story—about HIS father and about HIMSELF. They both had killed before, Jimmy; your father and your grandfather. Your father said he witnessed his father slice up two men like they were animals. It happened when he lived in East Boston, long before he moved to Pemberton. He said your grandfather felt no guilt because he was protecting his family, and your father believed him.

"He—he didn't want *you* to become a murderer, Jimmy; he wanted it to end. He found out who Gordon and Robinson were and planned to take care of them before you did. He followed Gordon to Stanton and sat outside his cousin's house trying to decide what to do when he saw Gordon leave the house. He followed him and saw him go into the movie house. That was it for Gordon.

"He thought that would end it and decided to let Robinson go. When Robinson died, your father knew it was no accident and cursed himself for not taking care of the matter himself. He knew we had used his car that night—it wasn't parked as deep in the garage as he always put it. He knew we were the ones who stole the car from the K. C. parking lot and ran Robinson down.

"He killed the Coach when he learned you'd be coming home from Korea. He was afraid you'd do it once you got home.

"And Buddy had told him about the terrible time Sandberg was giving him, so he did him in to keep you and Buddy from getting involved. He killed the people you and Buddy hated most to keep you both from being tempted to kill.

"Then you told him you suspected Sally of sending the anonymous letters to the cops. Sally's death wasn't an accident, Jimmy; your father killed her and made it look like an accident. He didn't want any more heat on his family. He made sure he knew where we were and were alibied.

"He also told me where the murder weapon was hidden—in a black bag in his garage. He wanted me to get rid of it, but I didn't. It's right here."

Jimmy, hurt and uncomfortable, listened as if in a trance. He couldn't believe what he was hearing. He had thought all along it was Buddy.

"But your father didn't kill Flossy!" Sean continued, in a voice filled with venom. "I tried to convince myself that Flossy's death was what it appeared to be; a break-in that turned deadly when she unexpectedly came home. But the cop—Osham—didn't think so, and he got me thinking. And when you said 'she's dead and we don't have to worry about her any more,' I knew you and Buddy arranged to have her killed. You knew what she meant to me, and you didn't care. You acted the same way when you told me how you killed that Sergeant in Korea—cold blooded!

"You had Flossy killed—I know you did—just to make sure she wouldn't get any information out of me and give it to the cops."

Jimmy grunted, accompanied by a negative head shake, but Sean wasn't buying.

"Deny all you want," Sean said nastily, "I don't believe you. We always stuck together, but for different reasons. Buddy did because he felt he could egg you on with his constant lies and get you in trouble. Any girlfriend you had, he wanted, and he would find ways to stir things up. He did it with Sally.

"I stuck around and did your bidding because I hoped you would realize that women were untrustworthy. I hoped you would turn away from them and find me. It was a stupid, childish dream I lived, but I didn't know any better. Imagine! I hoped you would turn to me. But it never happened!

"Buddy and you always got what you wanted, and I never did. My life was pretty miserable until Flossy came along. We slept together a few times, but it was for her, not for me. She recognized almost immediately the way it was, and she didn't turn away from me. She helped me and she took care of me. She never liked you or Buddy, but because of me, she coexisted. She was the most wonderful person I ever knew.

"She knew about the dual life I was leading, and she knew about me and Earl Kaster. That's why I bought my boat. You and Buddy hated fishing and boating, so it gave me an excuse to be away from you and enjoy my own private life. I hated THE PACT, and wanted to break away from it and from you, but I was afraid what you and Buddy would do. I'm not afraid anymore. You took away one of the two most important people in my life, and I'm not going to chance your taking away the other."

Jimmy's face paled. He strained every muscle in his body in an attempt to free himself, but it wasn't to be.

Sean was through talking. He took a deep breath, picked up the butcher knife from the bed and in one, swift, calculated motion, plunged it into Jimmy's heart. He backed away, in tears, and turned around, not wanting to watch. "Good-bye, Jimmy," he murmured.

Sean did not look at the body or the knife again. The axe handle was already in the canvas bag—the same axe handle and bag that Dan O'Brien had used.

Sean would have a use for them one more time.

Sean called the front desk. "This is Mr. Brown in room 710. I'm not feeling well—a touch of the flu, I guess—and I'm going to bed. Please inform the chambermaid on duty this evening that I don't want to be disturbed, and leave word for the morning crew. When I want my room made up, I'll call. Will you do that for me?"

The reply came in polite English. "Yes, sir, I'll take care of that. Please put the DO NOT DISTURB sign on the door as a reminder, and I'll see that everyone understands. Do you think you require a doctor, sir?"

"No thank you. I have medication with me, and I'm sure I'll be fine with a good night's rest."

"Very well, sir. If you should need anything, please call. I'm on until 11:00."

Sean took one more look around the room, and remembering Jimmy's wallet, threw it into the bag and zippered the bag closed. He opened the door to the corridor, glanced in both directions, and seeing no one, hung the Do Not Disturb sign on the doorknob and closed the door.

He removed his gloves, stuffed them into a pocket, and made his way to the elevator. He paused, as it dawned on him that if someone was on the elevator, he could be identified.

Before the elevator arrived he was on his way to the exit stairway. He slowed his pace once he reached the stairs and walked down two flights without meeting anyone.

Sean entered the hotel corridor on the fifth floor, made his way to the elevator, and pushed the down button. He watched the dial above the door as the elevator descended from the seventh floor. He entered an empty car and relaxed for the first time when he reached the lobby.

He walked through the lobby at a normal pace, and when he gained the street, moved briskly to the first available cab.

"La Guardia," he said.

Sean had come to New York by train—he preferred not flying—carrying the butcher knife in his bag. The knife was now lodged in its final resting place, and no longer a consideration.

He had made a reservation on an Eastern Airlines flight to return from New York because of his time restrictions—*in the name of Buddy O'Brien.* He had charged the reservation to Buddy's American Express card, whose number he had purloined the week before when he feigned a forgotten wallet, and asked Buddy to charge a sport jacket to his account and he would pay him back. Sean had kept the charge slip so he would remember the amount, written down the account number when he got home, and given Buddy a pay back check the next day.

The airline flight home had been Earl's suggestion. It would put Buddy in New York the evening of his brother's murder, if anyone bothered to check the passenger list, and he was certain Inspector Osham would.

Sean boardered the flight back to Boston with trepidation, but looked forward to the next person on his timetable—*Buddy O'Brien.*

CHAPTER 71

SUNDAY, JULY 26, 1959

Sean arrived at the Boston Bay Yacht Club shortly before 6:00 a.m. He wanted the bulk of his work completed before the marina became crowded.

He pulled his station wagon close to his boat slip, parked, and unloaded three cinder blocks onto the dock. Each was covered with heavy wrapping paper. He transferred the cinder blocks one at a time onto the boat, unwrapped them, and concealed them in the bait-storage areas under the aft seat cushions.

He was sweating profusely. He paused for a few minutes to catch his breath, folded the wrappings, and dumped them into a trash receptacle before returning to his station wagon. He next unloaded two bags of ice cubes, two cases of beer, and a surplus army duffel bag.

It took three trips to get the ice and beer on board, one more trip for the duffel bag, and a final trip to drive his station wagon to the long-term parking area. He locked his wagon and, breathing heavily, headed for the locker room in the main building. He washed and cooled himself down before opening his locker to remove a bottle of sun tan oil and a pair of sun glasses. He spread the oil freely over his face, neck, arms, and legs and returned the oil to the locker. He locked up, donned his sunglasses, walked to a mirror to examine himself, and with a self-satisfying smile left the wash room. He made his way through the yacht club, stopping briefly to speak with a number of people. He wanted to be remembered as having been there, and in good spirits. Again, Earl's idea.

Sean returned to his boat, grinned as he read the name THE PACT, and climbed aboard. He opened the duffel bag and removed its contents. There was a coil of nylon rope, two 4-foot lengths of heavy chain, two large padlocks, a Swiss Army knife, and an axe handle; the same heavy oak handle that had performed so well the previous day. He concealed the axe handle in the cabinet where he kept his charts, and placed the chain, rope, knife, and duffel inside the cabin in a storage closet. He put the two cases of beer on the galley table and emptied the ice into a large cooler chest on deck before taking six cans of beer and forcing them into the forgiving mound of ice cubes.

Sean had again worked up a sweat. He took the time to towel himself and change into a Celtic's tee shirt and bathing trunks. He removed his socks and began to liberally coat the freshly exposed parts of his body with suntan lotion from a bottle housed in a cubby hole next to the helm. This done, he put his sneakers back on sockless feet, donned a baseball cap and dark glasses, and declared himself ready for the day's adventures.

Sean had filled the fuel tanks the prior weekend when he and Earl had returned from their day's fishing trip. He started the engine and listened for any sign of a problem. The engine performed flawlessly. He cut the power after several minutes, satisfied.

Everything was in order. It was 8:32 a.m.

Buddy showed up at 8:50. He was keyed up; the promise of the coming day's events excited him. He had never cheated on Doreen because the opportunity had never presented itself in as clear-cut a manner as today's offering, and Sean's description of what the day held in store was too good to pass up. He fantasized that this rich bitch would fall for him, but as far as he was concerned, it was a one-time fling.

Buddy parked his car where Sean had instructed and made his way through the increasing throng of men, women, and children arriving and preparing for their day of boating pleasure.

Sean watched grim-faced as Buddy made his way to the boat. Jimmy was done, somewhat reluctantly he admitted to himself, out of necessity. Buddy would not cause him one iota of regret. He had it coming for many reasons, but mainly for his part in Flossy's death.

Buddy stepped over the railing and onto the deck. He smiled when he saw the beer on the table.

"Looks like we're all set, Sean boy, and what a day for it. What are the plans?"

"I called my lady friend in Martha's Vineyard this morning and everything's a go. We chartered where we'd meet, and set the time. We should join up about 11:00. She told me she's got the steaks and the champagne, and added that her girlfriend said that she hopes my friend has plenty of stamina."

Buddy laughed. "We'll see who needs the stamina. Are we ready to go?"

"Yeah, in just a bit." Sean started the engine on the first try, and allowed it to idle.

"I thought I would have heard from Jimmy last night or early this morning," Buddy said. "I wonder what the hell is going on in New York."

"I don't know, Buddy; I didn't hear from him either. I'm sure we'll hear after we get back."

"I suppose," Buddy replied, and dropped the subject.

Moments later, Sean gave the word. "We're all set, Buddy. Cast off and we're on our way."

"Okay, Captain," Buddy responded, and proceeded to free-up the bow and stern lines.

Sean backed "THE PACT" slowly from its slip and made his way cautiously through a sea of manned and unmanned boats, waving occasionally to groups underway or preparing to start their own cruise day. Once clear of the harbor and its 5 miles per hour speed limit, he opened the throttle to a comfortable speed and headed out into Massachusetts Bay on his way to Cape Cod Bay.

Sean pointed to the ice chest. "Get us a beer. We might just as well start partying early."

"Good idea," said Buddy. "I thought you'd never ask. How long before we meet up?"

"About 2 or 2 1/2 hours," Sean said. "We'll get to the rendezvous and anchor. They've got further to travel.

They're coming by way of the canal, and that will slow them down. And knowing women, they'll be late. She said they'd leave early."

Sean feigned cheerfulness. He had no qualms that the day's events would be anything but perfectly executed, but his deed of the prior day coupled with what was soon to occur was a heavy burden, and he wasn't accustomed to so much pressure. He and Earl had gone over the details many times, but it didn't make it any easier.

Earl had insisted Sean sever all ties with the O'Briens. Only then would Sean be safe and free, and able to make a life for himself—for themselves—away from all the bad times and memories.

Several weeks before, when Sean poured out his heart to Earl, he had found the sympathy and understanding he craved. Earl had told him he had read of a family like the O'Briens. Their behavioral problems had been similar; one generation after another had someone who was mad; or evil; or both.

"Their old man must have been trying to protect Jimmy and Buddy, Sean. He did his sons' dirty work, hoping that they wouldn't get involved, but fearing his intervention was just a delaying tactic. It's a terrible story; and they dragged you in with them. You're in danger from them, Sean. You'll have to extricate yourself, and I'll help."

That next day, Earl had contacted a real estate agent on the island of Oahu, Hawaii, and leased a two bedroom, two bath condominium for a year. Papers were on the way, and Earl explained to the agent that his brother, Erwin

Kaster, would be arriving in a month or so, and he himself would be over at a later date.

"This is it," Sean announced to Buddy. "We're at 41degrees 52 minutes N. latitude and 70 degrees 15 minutes W. longitude. We're about 10 miles west of Billings Gate Shoals, if that means anything to you. We'll anchor here." He idled the engine and Buddy helped him free the anchor from its mount and toss it overboard. They drifted briefly until the anchor took hold.

Sean shut down the engine.

"How deep is it here?" Buddy asked.

"About 97 feet," Sean answered after checking his chart. "Do you want to take a swim?"

"Hell no; I wanna get laid," Buddy answered, and they both laughed.

"But for now, I'll settle for another beer," Buddy said and headed for the cooler to help himself.

Sean sat on the seat next to the chart cabinet and accepted a second can of chilled beer. He was relaxed as his eyes scanned the southwest horizon, looking for a particular boat.

A few sail boats passed in the distance, moving gracefully in the light breeze. Buddy talked about how well things were going for him at work, and Sean nodded politely, struggling to keep his attention on his guest. He removed a pair of ten-power binoculars from a rack on the wall and focused them at distant boats as he kept up his minor part in the conversation.

After several such searches, Sean sighted the craft he was looking for, and did a quick 360 degree scan to see what else was in the neighborhood. There was only one other boat nearby, and under power and moving away.

He would have to wait a few minutes; just a few more minutes. The timing was important.

"I see the girls' boat coming, Buddy," he proclaimed in a controlled voice to his sunbathing guest, and pointed toward a distant craft. Buddy opened his eyes and sat up, looking in the direction Sean was pointing. The 40-foot plus yacht was still at a considerable distance, but he could see it was a beauty.

Sean silently opened the chart cabinet, never taking his eyes from the back of Buddy's head. He rose from his seat, the axe handle clutched tightly in the hand behind his back. He glanced from side to side and, satisfied it was safe, crept up on Buddy from the rear.

He delivered a smashing blow to the back of Buddy's head, grabbing him by his bathing trunks with his free hand to guide his fall to the deck. He struck him once more, just to be sure, then moved quickly to the helm to idle his boat.

Gasping with excitement, he returned to Buddy and removed Buddy's wedding ring, watch, and the medallion from around his neck, and carried them into the cabin. He next retrieved his stashed duffel bag, threw Buddy's jewelry and the axe handle inside, and carried it to the deck. He returned to the cabin and gathered his Swiss Army knife, rope, chains and padlocks from their hiding place, and returned on deck and laid them alongside Buddy's unconscious form, according to plan.

Sean stood up to sneak a look in all directions, and no vessels but the one he was expecting were in close sight.

His luck was holding.

He cut several lengths of rope and tied Buddy's hands and ankles cuttingly tight. He took one of the lengths of chain and wrapped it tightly around Buddy's mid-section several times, securing it with one of the padlocks. He stood up, sweating profusely from his labor, and again noted the position of the fast-approaching boat.

Excellent, he thought; so far, so good. I need just a few more minutes.

He took the second length of chain and passed it through the one encompassing Buddy's waist. He moved to the bait-storage bays, shoved the cushions aside, and one-by-one removed the three cinder blocks. He passed the second length of chain through a cinder block and secured the ends with the second padlock.

Sean could now hear the steady drone of the approaching power boat, but didn't take the time to stand up and wave; he still had work to do. He attached the remaining two cinder blocks with lengths of nylon rope to the bound arms and ankles of the prostrate figure, double-knotting the ropes in each case.

"Done, almost done," he uttered out loud, and breathed deeply several times to calm himself down.

He placed the rest of the rope in the duffel, picked up the knife and purposely cut his thumb before closing the knife and throwing it in alongside the rope. He wanted to leave some blood—his blood—on the deck of the boat. This done, he wrapped his thumb with his handkerchief. He would bandage it later.

Sean's work for the moment was finished. He felt light-headed, and blamed it on the heat of the day, the physical exertion of the last 6 or 7 minutes, and perhaps the two cans of iced beer.

He smiled weakly as he held onto the railing and waved to Earl Kaster, who was easing the bumpered starboard side of his Bertram to Sean's boat. They secured the two boats, and Earl scampered onto Sean's Chris Craft.

"You okay, Sean?" Earl asked, his eyes fixed on the bound, motionless figure sprawled mummy-like on the wooden deck. "My God! You're bleeding; you cut yourself!"

"I'm fine, Earl; I cut myself intentionally. I want to leave a sample of my blood on the boat for them to find. Help me move him to the stern. We'll have to lift the end cinder blocks to the transom first, put him on top, and then put the block attached to the chain on top of him. Then we'll roll everything overboard together as best we can. Try not to let the blocks bang against the stern."

"Sean, he's not dead!"

"Don't think about it, Earl. Just do what I tell you to do."

The two men performed Sean's bidding, panting when they finished.

Sean scanned the surrounding water and there were no other craft close by. He picked up the cinder block chained to Buddy's midsection and carefully lowered it over the stern and into the water. He struggled under the weight, and began losing the struggle.

"NOW, EARL—NOW!" he shouted, as he let go of the chain and pushed Buddy over the stern. They simultaneously toppled the remaining two cinder blocks overboard and watched as Buddy O'Brien sank rapidly into the welcoming waters. Sean continued to watch until the air bubbles stopped rising to the surface.

IT'S DONE. IT'S OVER. I'M FREE!

Earl, voice quivering, broke the silence. "What do you want me to do now?"

"Haul in my anchor. My thumb's still bleeding and I don't want to drip any blood up there. I'll tidy up down here and load my gear onto your boat."

Five minutes later, aboard the Bertram, they freed the lines securing the two craft, and slowly powered away from THE PACT. The sea was calm and the breeze light, but Sean knew that his unmanned craft would drift with the current and travel a considerable distance from where they left Buddy O'Brien before it was discovered.

In Edgartown, at Earl's summer home, they buried the duffel bag and its contents in an isolated area of the compound. Sean showered and packed a minimum amount of clothing and toilet accessories, all purchased a week before, in a suitcase Earl provided.

He dressed casually and applied the expensive, authentic-appearing mustache to his face while studying himself in the mirror. Satisfied, he put on a pair of dark sunglasses. It would alter his appearance enough to make him unrecognizable as Sean Boyle when he boarded the 5:00 p.m. plane to Boston's Logan airport and his later connection at Logan to San Francisco. Then on to Honolulu.

His airline tickets were under his new name, Erwin Kaster, and his flights were confirmed. He would use Earl's American Express card only if necessary, and until his own recently ordered card arrived at Kaster Carpet Company and was forwarded to him. He had six thousand dollars in hundred-dollar bills in a money belt around his waist, and seven hundred dollars plus in his wallet. That should tide him over until he set up a checking account and line of credit in Honolulu.

Earl would take a vacation in a month or two, when things quieted down, and join him. Together they would shop for a permanent place to live when their lease ran out. Then Earl would return to Boston and within a year sell Kaster Carpet. It shouldn't be difficult; he had already been approached by the Jordan chain and tendered an offer. Then he could look into selling the Edgartown property and realize a tidy sum from the sale.

By then, Erwin Kaster would have arranged for a passport, a Social Security card, and a driver's license. Money could buy you anything in papers, and there *had* been an Erwin Kaster, although he had died in an automobile accident 16 years' earlier.

When all these things transpired and they had settled into living their new lives, they planned to spend time in Europe. Perhaps they would purchase or rent a place on the French or Italian Riviera, and enjoy life.

They had a great many plans on their agenda.

Together! And unafraid of the future.

CHAPTER 72

Word of Jimmy O'Brien's murder shocked Pemberton. The New York police had notified Patti shortly after 8:00 on Sunday evening. Patti, the baby, and Ted and Rita Baltas were already en route to New York.

It was after 10:00 that evening when Sam Coben reached Barney Osham and gave him the news.

"Jesus Christ, Sam—that's a shocker. I've been lake fishing all day and hadn't heard. Do you have any details?"

"Ted Baltas called me before he left for New York and gave me the name and phone number of the detective who called Patti. I couldn't reach him, but he called me back 20 minutes ago. Jimmy O'Brien was dead 24 to 30 hours before they found him in his hotel room Sunday evening. He was tied to a chair, with a knife stuck in his heart, and…"

"Jesus! A butcher's knife, Sam?" Barney interrupted.

"Yeah, Barney. The cop said 'a big bastard of a knife,' and when I pinned him down, he said it could be a butchers' knife, although he'd never seen one quite like it."

"That's because he was never in a tannery, Sam. What else?"

"The cop's a lieutenant by the name of Wolfe; Sheldon Wolfe. The investigation's ongoing, and he promised to fill me in no later than tomorrow. Incidentally, the room was reserved under an alias. The register was signed by James Brown, not Jimmy O'Brien."

"What the hell is that all about?" Barney asked, puzzled.

"Don't know yet. They found the Jimmy O'Brien name and address on the ID tag attached to his suitcase. They had assumed until then the name the hotel people had gaven them was who he was. There was no wallet in the room.

"I told the lieutenant the deceased may have had knowledge of several homicides we were investigating, and it interested him. I'll have more of the story tomorrow and I'll call you."

"Thanks, Sam. I'll be waiting."

That same day, another story was developing. The Coast Guard received a report shortly before sundown that a cabin cruiser, seemingly unmanned, was adrift in Cape Cod Bay. Upon locating and boarding the craft, the Coast Guard found it empty.

They discovered what appeared to be blood on the deck.

The boat was towed to shore and the local police were called. The craft was flying a Boston Bay Yacht Club pendant, and the Boston police were notified.

Further investigation indicated the boat was registered to a Sean Boyle. The yacht club was notified and the Boston authorities obtained a home address, a business address, and an "in case of emergency" name, address, and phone numbers for Earl Kaster.

There was no answer to the first dialing to the home address. The business address didn't answer, but the third call reached Earl Kaster in Edgartown on Martha's Vineyard.

Kaster was apprised of the situation, and he informed the police that Mr. Boyle and a friend had been scheduled to go on a fishing trip Sunday morning. He had attempted to reach Mr. Boyle several times between 6:00 and 7:00 that evening, without success.

The friend's name? Buddy O'Brien!

CHAPTER 73

SUNDAY, AUGUST 30, 1959

The two men sat hunched over a table in Stanley's Cafeteria.

It was after 10:00 a.m., and the early morning breakfast crowd had all but disappeared. The two were in no hurry, and lingered over their breakfasts.

They had all the information, but they didn't have Buddy O'Brien.

Barney Osham had checked all the airline passenger lists between Boston and New York for the Friday, Saturday, and Sunday of the weekend that Jimmy O'Brien was murdered, and came up with Buddy O'Brien's name on the Saturday evening flight.

Buddy had been to work on Friday, July 24 and was seen in Pemberton on Saturday morning, July 25.

There had not been a plane reservation in Buddy's name from Boston to New York on Saturday, but there had been a 9:00 p.m. reservation in Buddy's name on a flight from New York to Boston.

"How did he get to New York?" Barney wondered out loud.

"I don't know," Sam said, as he and Barney considered a number of options. They concluded that Buddy probably took the bus or train to New York, carrying the knife and whatever else in his carry-on bag for fear of losing it, and booked a reserved seat on the 9:05 p.m. from La Guardia to Logan to make sure he would be home in time to prepare for his fishing trip with Boyle on Sunday.

The knife wouldn't be going back with him—Buddy had planted it in his brother's heart!

Cain and Abel!

"I would have thought Boyle's body would have washed ashore by now," Sam said matter-of-factly.

"It could have been carried out to sea, Sam. The Coast Guard told me the currents are unpredictable, especially in bad weather, and it did rain and blow like hell the Tuesday and Wednesday after the disappearance."

"Unless he put an anchor around the body when he dropped him overboard," Sam offered.

"That's possible too. But where in hell do you start looking? The boat was adrift for who knows how many hours before it was spotted. Far too big an area to send divers down," Barney said. "And how did the bastard get off the boat after he did his dirty work? He sure as hell didn't swim to shore, and the boat wasn't towing a dinghy; I checked with the Yacht Club. Somebody had to have picked him up. He had to have had an accomplice!"

"Who the hell would that be?"

"I don't know!"

"You know, Sam; I just had a crazy thought. What if *two* bodies wash up, and one is a suicide!"

"Jesus Christ, Barney!"

EPILOGUE

NEARLY A YEAR LATER.

The 56 foot luxury yacht "RETRIBUTION," owned by Gerald Cote, a long-time summer resident of Nantucket, burned and sank in Cape Cod Bay in the summer of 1960.

There were eight guests aboard, all of them equally drunk.

They were cruising at a slow speed, with Dan Winshel at the helm.

Dan was a college student on break from his junior year at Harvard. He had spent the summers of 1958 and 1959 in Nantucket as a waiter and had the good fortune of serving the Cotes and ingratiating himself.

Dan was offered the job of taking charge of the yacht for the summer of 1960, and he accepted. The money he was offered was unbelievable.

He knew about boats, but it would be a challenge to handle something the size of the Retribution. Mr. Cote assured him there was nothing to it, and proceeded to train Dan over a period of weeks, until Dan could handle everything but the docking. Mr. Cote said he would continue to assist Dan until he mastered that feat.

It was Dan who saved the lives of the four couples.

Selma Cote knocked over a bottle of brandy on the counter in the galley next to where she was cooking steamers. In an instant there was a flash fire that spread in every direction.

Screaming, Selma fled to the deck.

By the time Gerald Cote reached the hysterical Mrs. Cote, smoke was pouring from the galley.

Dan, hearing the screams, turned in the direction of the galley and saw the smoke. He immediately cut the power, grabbed the nearest two fire extinguishers and ran toward the cabin.

He emptied the contents of the extinguishers, but it was too little, too late.

He threw the emptied extinguishers aside and, having the only clear head in the group of panicking partygoers, issued life jackets to everyone.

Smoke and flame were now billowing skyward, and attracting the attention of other vessels, but they were distant and at the rate the fire was spreading, Dan was afraid to wait.

He ordered everyone into the water. Yelling above the raucous, fearful group in order to be heard, he made them understand they were to swim clear of the boat as rapidly as possible, and that nearby boats were on the way to rescue them. He was afraid of an explosion, and wanted everybody as far away as possible.

The RETRIBUTION did explode some 10 minutes later, and sank shortly thereafter some 10 miles west of

Billings Gate Shoals in Cape Cod Bay. Other than some messed-up hairdos, wet clothes, and minor shock, everyone survived.

A week later divers, scavenging for loot, found more than they bargained for. They marked the area and notified the Coast Guard, who in turn notified the State Police.

Rumor spread quickly. The remains of a gangland killing had been found; a skeleton wrapped in chains and secured to a dozen cinder blocks.

##

There were more than forty people attending the retirement party for Barney Osham. They roasted and toasted Barney, and it was an evening to remember.

The party wore itself out shortly before midnight, and when the hall cleared, Barney and Sam sat down at the bar for a final nightcap.

"Quite a night, Barney. Can I give you a ride home?"

"No thanks, Sam. I've got my car, and I'm stone-sober. Well, nearly sober. I was hoping I'd get a chance to talk to you alone. Are you in a rush?"

"Hell, no. Tomorrow's Sunday, and I got the day off. I've got all night."

"Thanks, Sam, but I won't need all night. You know about the remains—really just the skeleton—they found last week?"

"Yeah, I heard about it. They got a name yet?"

"Yes, as of this morning. Dental records confirmed it. It was Sean Boyle down there, not some gang hit."

"It's what I expected," Sam said. "And I don't think there's another body out there. Buddy O'Brien is on the loose. It's just a matter of time 'till we get him."

"I sure as hell hope so," Barney said. "Boyle's mother knows and is in tough shape. I didn't want to talk to Buddy O'Brien's wife. What's the sense; the poor girl has had it bad enough. I doubt if he'd ever try to contact her, but we'll keep tabs on her whereabouts. I also called Jimmy O'Brien's wife and asked her if I could come by and talk to her. I know she was a close friend of Boyle, and I thought she should hear it from me."

"You talked to Patti O'Brien today?" Sam asked.

"Yeah. I know, I'm retired, but I'm too involved to let it go. I spent almost an hour with her this afternoon. A beautiful woman, Sam, and very much in control of her life. She's back in her father's business, and apparently working hard at it. Her kid was there, with a sitter or governess or whatever they call her, and he's quite a kid. Blond as can be, blue-eyed, and as handsome a kid as you would ever see. He's as smart as they come, too. She's proud of him, and I could see he was crazy about her.

"Anyway, I told her they found the remains of Sean Boyle, and she wasn't surprised. She thanked me for letting her know. I asked if Sean had anyone else besides his mother I should notify, but she didn't know.

"As far as she knew, his closest friend was his boss, the Kaster guy. She told me Kaster had broken down after he came to see her the day of Jimmy's funeral, fearing that Sean had to be dead too. She said they both had a good cry. I asked her for Kaster's address, but she told me he sold his business and moved away. He called her before he left and told her his heart just wasn't in it any more. He was going to move to Hawaii and live with his brother and start a new life."

"Hawaii," Sam said, "isn't that where you're retiring to?"

"Yes. We're leaving next week. The Mrs. has her only family, a sister with three kids, living there, and that's where she wants to settle."

"Nothing wrong with that, Barney. Supposed to be a beautiful place, and always has great weather. You can sit in the sun, go fishing, drink fruit drinks laden with booze, and look at all the swinging asses in grass skirts."

Barney laughed. "I hope it's as good as you make it sound; I don't want to be bored to death. If I do get tired of doing nothing, I'll just have to go and find me a job."

"What part of Hawaii, Barney?" Sam asked. "There's a bunch of islands out there."

"We'll be in Honolulu, Sam. Come to think of it, that's where the Kaster guy moved to. I think I'll look him up."

THE END

"For his mind had grown Suspicion's sanctuary."

Byron, *Childe Harold*

BIBLIOGRAPHY

Toland, John. *In Mortal Combat, Korea 1950-1953,* New York: William Morrow and Company, Inc. 1991

The New Encyclopedia Britannica, Inc. Volume 6. Chicago: 1998

Printed in the United States
15719LVS00001B/101